CRITICAL ACCLAIM FOR

DELIRIUM *of the* BRAVE

"An ambitious *roman à clef* . . . enough whispered scandal . . . to keep the reading lamps burning late."
—*Publishers Weekly*

"An entertaining novel that effectively evokes a Savannah of another time." —*Savannah Morning News*

"I'm not taking anything away from Mr. Berendt, but I personally believe that Dr. Harris's DELIRIUM OF THE BRAVE catches a lot more of the romance and intrigue that are the real heart of Savannah."
—Regina Odom, Regina's Books and Cards, Savannah

"Old-fashioned multigenerational saga of buried treasure, hidden sin, and the redemptive power of religion and family, set in balmy Savannah. [An] ultimately uplifting reaffirmation of Southern gentility, fair play, and blind faith."
—*Kirkus Reviews*

"Five years after the best-selling phenomenon, *MIDNIGHT IN THE GARDEN OF GOOD AND EVIL*, the Old South is rising again. This time, the title is *DELIRIUM OF THE BRAVE. DELIRIUM* . . . delivers in generous portions those things the South is known for and that Southerners love to see in themselves: the noble gesture, pride, honor, good manners, storied family histories, the romance of the Lost Cause . . . [and] offers a peek at ⸺⸺ gh the gauze of fiction. It's a sto⸺⸺ realness—and that well-⸺⸺ gy."
—⸺*Union-Tribune*

DELIRIUM
of the BRAVE

WILLIAM CHARLES
HARRIS, JR.

St. Martin's Paperbacks

Previously published by Frederic C. Beil, Publisher, Inc.

"September 1913," by W. B. Yeats, courtesy of Simon & Schuster Inc.

DELIRIUM OF THE BRAVE

Copyright © 1998 by William Charles Harris, Jr.

ISBN: 0-312-97713-1

Printed in the United States of America

St. Martin's Press hardcover edition / November 1999
St. Martin's Paperbacks edition / October 2001

St. Martin's Paperbacks are published by St. Martin's Press, 175 Fifth Avenue, New York, NY 10010.

10 9 8 7 6 5 4 3 2 1

FOR

MY FATHER, WHO SHOWED ME HOW
MY MOTHER, WHO TAUGHT ME WHY
AND
MY WIFE, WHO INSPIRED ME

September 1913

What need you, being come to sense,
But fumble in a greasy till
And add the halfpence to the pence
And prayer to shivering prayer, until
You have dried the marrow from the bone;
For men were born to pray and save:
Romantic Ireland's dead and gone,
It's with O'Leary in the grave.

Yet they were of a different kind,
The names that stilled your childish play,
They have gone about the world like wind,
But little time had they to pray
For whom the hangman's rope was spun,
And what, God help us, could they save?
Romantic Ireland's dead and gone,
It's with O'Leary in the grave.

Was it for this the wild geese spread
The grey wing upon every tide;
For this that all that blood was shed,
For this Edward Fitzgerald died,
And Robert Emmet and Wolfe Tone,
All that delirium of the brave?
Romantic Ireland's dead and gone,
It's with O'Leary in the grave.

Yet could we turn the years again,
And call those exiles as they were
In all their loneliness and pain,
You'd cry, 'Some woman's yellow hair
Has maddened every mother's son':
They weighed so lightly whay they gave.
But let them be, they're dead and gone,
They're with O'Leary in the grave.

—W. B. Yeats

CONTENTS

DELIRIUM
of the BRAVE

PROLOGUE

The Grand Dragon of the Invisible Empire watched from his hiding place among the palmettos as the *Admiral Graf Spee* rounded the last curve in the creek and inched up to the old earthen pier built by the Confederates in 1864. Two of his sons stood tensely by his side, watching the five men on the boat unload their supplies.

The Grand Dragon stood dead still; the early morning sun glistened off a paste of mucous draining from his nostrils, painting his upper lip. Occasionally his tongue darted up to lick some of the mucous before it stretched out in long silvery strings and splattered on the dried palmetto fronds at his feet. His bead-bright eyes watched every movement of the five men carrying their gear along the pier to the base of the big live oak at the island's edge. The Grand Dragon cocked his head slightly and snorted softly to himself, straining to pick up their words.

In the cover of the dense underbrush the Grand Dragon's breath frosted in the cold March air when he grunted the order to return to the hiding place deep within the dense twists of thick vines and thorny brush that darkened the northern two-thirds of Raccoon Island. As he left, he turned for one more look at the intruders, especially the big black one. Then in a primitive sign of ownership, he urinated where he stood, marking his property. His sons could smell the pungent odor as the vapor from the yellow pool burned the still morning air. The Grand Dragon was the master of all that he surveyed. These intruders from the mainland would tarry only briefly in his kingdom, or regret their invasion.

After camp was set up, the intruders gathered limbs fallen from the grand oak whose branches shadowed the entire campsite. Soon, busy flames whipped and curled around the wood and took the chill off the air. The men stood around the fire and warmed themselves as they talked of this last attempt to find the Driscoll treasure.

They were all in their fiftieth year. And all, except for Vinnie from South Philly, had been born and reared in Savannah. As young boys the four Savannahians had come to Raccoon Island regularly—three in search of the Driscoll treasure and one to tend the grave of his war-hero great-grandfather. It had been thirty-two years since they had been on Raccoon Island and seen the remains of the old fort called Battery Jasper.

"So, Lloyd," said Vinnie in his harsh South Philadel-phia accent, "John-Morgan tells me your great-grandfather and his great-grandfather were killed here during the Civil War and they took the secret of the Dris-coll treasure with them?"

Lloyd Bryan looked at John-Morgan Hartman and smiled. Then Lloyd looked into the fire. "Yeah, they died in each other's arms. There were about a dozen witnesses. My great-granddaddy Shadrack was a slave who belonged to Captain Patrick Driscoll, John-Morgan's great-granddaddy. Some say they buried everything the family owned to keep it from Sherman. As the story goes, they got killed together before they could get word back to the family where it was buried."

"You think it's true, John-Morgan?" asked Vinnie.

John-Morgan shrugged. "I used to. My mamma thinks it's true. I just don't know anymore. I've been thinking about it for a long time. Maybe we should call it the 'legend' of the Driscoll treasure. We dug this whole island up over the years, and all we could find were cannon balls and rusty nails. But we think we've got it narrowed down to a fairly small area. It's the only place we never looked when we were kids."

Bubba Silverman walked over to the picnic table and spread out the map that John-Morgan had made of Rac-coon Island back when they were boys. Though yellow and torn at the edges, it was very detailed. Every place they had searched for the treasure over the years was carefully marked.

"This is where we think it might be," said Bubba, pointing to an area on the map in which "Der Schwarzwald" was carefully printed in Gothic letters.

"Schwarzwald," said Vinnie. "Isn't that the German for Black Forest?"

"That's exactly what it means," said Mike Sullivan. Mike leaned over the map and smiled, recalling all the good times they had had on Raccoon Island looking for the Driscoll treasure.

"Why do you call it that?" asked Vinnie.

"Cause it's deep and dark and scary as hell," said Mike as he ran his hand caressingly over the map.

"What's so scary about some damn woods? You guys think there's spooks in there or something?" Vinnie was grinning, but nobody else shared in the joke.

"It's so scary that we never dared to go into it when we were kids," said John-Morgan. "There's something terrible in there. Something that could tear your ass up in a heartbeat."

"Aw, come on now, don't think ya gonna jerk around this dumb-shit Yankee from the big city. I been around too." Vinnie was still grinning.

"We're not kidding at all, Vinnie," said Lloyd. "That's what we got the guns for."

Finally the grin faded, for two very good reasons. First, Lloyd didn't act as if he were trying to yank Vinnie around. And second, Lloyd was a Catholic priest. Vinnie had never known a priest to lie.

Standing alone, a few feet away from the rest of the group, Vinnie was overcome with an odd, strangely exciting emotion. Maybe they weren't kidding him after all.

"So, ah, just wha'cha call this here, ah, 'thing' ya been talking about?" he asked after a moment.

As one, the four men looked up from the map. There was a moment of silence. Then Lloyd spoke for the group.

"We call him the Grand Dragon. He probably knows we're here already."

"The what?"

"We call him the Grand Dragon of Raccoon Island," repeated Lloyd without expression.

I

THE CONQUERED BANNER

Was it for this the wild geese spread
The grey wing upon every tide

Furl that banner, softly, slowly!
Treat it gently—it is holy—
For it droops above the dead.
Touch it not—unfold it never.
Let it droop there, furled forever,
For its people's hopes are dead!

—THE LAST VERSE OF "THE CONQUERED
    BANNER" BY FATHER ABRAM RYAN, POET
    LAUREATE OF THE CONFEDERATE STATES OF
    AMERICA

FATHERS AND SONS

SAVANNAH'S HEART BEAT cold in the autumn of 1864. Sherman had overwhelmed the defenses of Atlanta and burned it to the ground. His soldiers slashed and ravaged a path sixty miles wide down the center of the state to the coast. Like pestilent bacteria, scavenging packs of Yankee soldiers roamed the flanks and rear of the great Army of the Tennessee, spreading terror without remorse. Nothing was spared: homes and churches were levelled, crops destroyed, animals slaughtered. Women were defiled while young boys without weapons died defending earth and home. Sherman's march to the sea was the herald for a new type of warfare. Seventy-nine years later Joseph Goebbels would give it a name—Totaler Krieg, or "total war."

Sherman bragged that he would "make Georgia howl." He kept his word. Pitiful civilians began to enter Savannah in front of the advancing columns. Harried, broken Confederate soldiers filled the streets and smelly hospitals of the city. Most people had a sense that the war had been lost. But they also believed that duty, honor, family, even the soil itself, demanded that they fight on. They hoped that complete defeat could be avoided by continuing the struggle, that terms more favorable to the South could be gained if only they could slog on. There was no widespread panic, but Savannah became a chaotic comedy of preparation as the army instinctively strove to protect the city. Civilians went about planning to save all they could from the Yankee devil-thieves. They buried their valuables in their yards, swamps, and rosebeds, in deep wells and chicken coops, in places near and remote.

Savannah's defenses were both elaborate and extensive. To the west they consisted of a series of breastworks and earthen forts running from the Savannah River to the

Ogeechee River. To the east, almost a dozen earthworks and brick forts on the coastal islands defended the approach from the sea. The southernmost installation in this chain was Fort McAllister on the Ogeechee River, which protected Savannah (and the southwestern land approach to the city) from a seaborne invasion. The fort was not large, but it had excellent artillery—and a perfect location. As long as the Yankee warships could not pass Fort McAllister and her supporting battery, Savannah was safe from the south.

East of Fort McAllister is Raccoon Island, at the confluence of the Ogeechee River and the Florida Passage. A quarter of a mile long and three hundred yards deep, it was in excellent position to control whatever came up the Ogeechee toward the fort.

Raccoon Island lay behind the barrier island of Ossabaw in a huge expanse of salt marsh. Confederate artillerists had determined to build a battery there to mount a powerful large-bore cannon. In doing so, they hoped to spare Fort McAllister bombardment by Union ironclads. The fort should have been larger, but the hard-pressed Southern army could only provide one example of the type of artillery piece that could even hope to have a chance against the mighty Yankee ironclads roaming Ossabaw Sound and the Ogeechee River. Construction and manning of this fortification was assigned to a local volunteer militia group called the Savannah Coastal Artillery.

This group was comprised of Irish-Catholic boys and men from Savannah. Many of them were first-generation Americans, and fierce Confederates. Their loyalty was to the American South and her struggle with the colossus to the north. When Sherman lay siege to Atlanta in the summer of 1864, the Savannah Coastal Artillery, along with a hundred and twenty-five slaves, was sent to Raccoon Island to build a battery there. Among the builders was Patrick Driscoll, a third-generation Savannahian.

In 1864 Patrick Driscoll was a young man full of promise. His family had arrived in Savannah in 1780 from

Ireland with little but the will to build a better life for themselves in America. It was difficult at first, but Savannah proved to be a town of unexpected tolerance. In two generations his grandfather's blacksmith shop had evolved into a prosperous iron foundry. The Driscolls became quite comfortable.

The war with the Yankees brought even more work to the foundry, including gun carriages and fittings for the giant ironclads CSS *Atlanta* and *Savannah*. Now it was Captain Patrick Driscoll's unique assignment to install and then command the prodigious ten-inch, seven-and-a-half-ton Columbiad cannon at the newly completed battery on Raccoon Island. As was the custom in those days among wealthy officers, Captain Driscoll took one of his slaves with him to the island.

The Driscolls owned only five slaves; they were house servants and very close to the family despite being property. Two of them, Ezekiel and Mattie Bryan, had been purchased decades before the Civil War from a Pembroke family. The Driscolls never changed their last names.

Their son, Shadrack, was born on the kitchen table of the Driscoll mansion exactly a month before Patrick, so motherhood uniquely bonded Mattie and Patrick's mother, Kathleen Driscoll. These babies were the first for each woman, and they were reared together despite the unfortunate borders of slavery, which both challenged and defined their commonality and personal freedom. Kathleen and her husband, Patrick, Sr., were especially attentive to their servants and took a familial interest in Shad as he grew up. Thereby they earned the loyalty of Ezekiel and Mattie. Life for slaves at the Driscoll house was one that many poor whites could envy.

Shad became Patrick's manservant, a position that suited and pleased him. Pat, in turn, was a great deal like his father and treated Shad as a companion. The two boys grew up together, but lines were clearly drawn: slave and master, black and white. Nevertheless they shared memories of the good times hunting deer on Skidaway Island

or sailing with a full moon down the Wilmington River.
They explored Savannah's islands, and they fell asleep
together watching Venus and Orion under the sky of
Beach Hammock. Once, Shad was severely mauled while
saving Pat from a large dog that attacked him behind the
carriage house. Mr. Driscoll witnessed the event and later
credited young Shad with saving his son's life. For weeks
after the incident Driscoll feared that both his son and
Shad had been infected with rabies. To distinguish his
concern for each boy would not have been easy.

So it was that Patrick and Shadrack came to Raccoon
Island and began installation of the big gun. The earlier
crews had constructed an earthen causeway from the river
behind the island across a hundred feet of marsh to the
island proper. They built the fort out of island dirt. Bricks
and timbers were brought from the mainland. As a result
of the digging, an enormous borrow pit existed at the
western end of the island. It soon became a home for fat
aggressive water moccasins and long hungry alligators.

The fort had a typical inner bomb-proof room of bricks
and timbers covered with thousands of cubic yards of
earth—twenty feet high in most places, with walls thirty
feet thick or more. It was a crescent, the convex side facing the Ogeechee River and the potential adversary. On
top of the structure sat the cannon in a snug barbette.

Pat's father had designed and constructed an ingenious
method of raising the cannon to fire, and then lowering it
behind the walls for reloading. It functioned off a system
of jacks manned by slaves. Because Pat was the gun commander and therefore on top of the fort, there was no
doubt in Shad's mind that old man Driscoll had designed
the disappearing gun mechanism solely to protect his son.

The work was long and strenuous, but with white soldiers laboring alongside their black charges, the fort was
ready for action on November 2. Twenty-one members of
the Savannah Coastal Artillery were chosen to man the
fort along with twelve of the most loyal slaves in Savannah. The soldiers would load and fire the cannon while

slaves would pass the ammunition and work the lifting jacks. Pat was the commanding officer. Shad was in charge of the slaves.

Pat and Shad rowed throughout the Ogeechee marsh putting up range markers to gauge the gun's accuracy. For two weeks, after the fort was finished, soldiers practiced loading and firing the cannon. Slaves practiced raising and lowering it into place. On the day before Thanksgiving, Captain Driscoll pronounced the marksmanship of his command to be accurate and undoubtedly devastating to any ship that came within a mile of the fort. The next morning Shad and Patrick boarded the small steam packet *Tomochichi* and left for Savannah on a three-day furlough.

Patrick and Shad were met at the dock by Mr. Driscoll and his daughter-in-law Mary. Driscoll used the hour's trip home to discuss family matters with Pat and Mary: details of the ironworks business, her inheritance of it should Pat "not come back," the hiding of his cache of gold coins against the Yankee invasion.

"Patrick, I'm afraid that if we can't hold the Yankees up, they're going to come into our homes and strip them. I hear that's what Sherman's ordered. We've gotten some of your mother's things together, and we want you to take them back to the battery for safekeeping. Also, I want you to take the last of those gold pieces, the new Cavaliers made up in Dahlonega at the Confederate mint. It's all in a small strong box—small enough for you to slip back into the island with no one knowing that you've got a box on you. It's not a whole lot, but it's all we have. Most of what the family has is in the foundry and the house. Nothing much left but Confederate paper money. Most people refuse it now. Barter, tradin' in gold, Yankee greenbacks. We're coming on a rough time, son. We've got to be prepared."

Patrick looked at his father and then out down the road. He noticed the dirt still under his fingernails, the cuts and scratches on his arms. "I know, Daddy, I think about it

all the time. We've done our part out on that island. I'm
tellin' you, they're in for a time if they come up that river.
I'm just worried about what will happen when, I mean if,
the Yankees get into town. I'm worried what those marauders will do to Momma and Mary. Shad and I'll be
out on that damn island."

"Well, it's a tough bridge for sure. Now, I've moved
everything out to Isle of Hope. We'll stay there until
there's peace, no matter how it comes. I figure it's a lot
safer than back in town. God only knows what that scum
will do in a riot, white, black, and blue. For all I know,
maybe even gray if things get really out of hand. We've
got some members of the Coastals out there manning the
batteries at Parkersburg and along the bluff. They can provide a lot of protection. Hell, we'll burn the bridges to
the island if we have to. But I don't want you worrying
about us. We'll be fine. It's you we're worried about,
son." Then the elder Driscoll took his turn staring down.

Finally Mary Driscoll broke the silence, trying to
lighten the moment by saying in a cheery voice, "The
Coastals are having a party tomorrow night down at my
parents' house to name the new fort ya'll built. The wives
and girlfriends of the boys out on the island, we've made
ya'll a flag for the fort. A special one, out of cloth that
we got together from all our things. I sewed the stars on,
Pat, and all I thought about was you." Then, without
warning, and trying very hard not to, young Mary Driscoll, barely twenty and the mother of two, sobbed and
wept. Pat awkwardly put his arm around her and held her
close. His father didn't look their way; instead he turned
his head slightly aside so no one would notice his tears.
In the back of the buggy Shad's head drooped helplessly.
How were Carrie and the little boy Meshack going to
make it if he didn't come back?

THE BREASTPLATE OF ST. PATRICK

THE BLUFF AT Isle of Hope was different now that war had come. Easy views of the river and the marsh had been spoiled by the high walls of the earthworks fort along the river. Trees had been cut for better fields of fire, azaleas uprooted. Soldiers' tents and ramshackle huts lined the road at the top of the bluff, and cooking fires burned in front of them all. Lawns were ragged and downtrodden, shabbiness was everywhere, nothing looked so good to Patrick, when they made their final turn, as the sight of the home in which he had spent all of his summers.

Mr. Driscoll's great Irish wolfhound, sleeping near the front steps, suddenly rose and started barking. So alerted, others poured to the front of the house from every direction, to a grand chorus of the family dogs. Pat's mother came down the stairs to greet her son. Shad's mother and father properly came around the side of the house. Carrie was just behind Mrs. Driscoll with Patrick III and her own son, Meshack, in tow. Pat could hear his daughter's screams of delight as she ran down the great spiral staircase from her room. There, in front of the tall white columns of the Driscoll summer home, was a hearty commotion of embrace and welcome before the sun's autumn eye.

The Savannah Coastal Artillery consisted of two companies of men, sixty to a company. The commanding officer, John Francis Kelly, was a successful Savannah lawyer from Ireland with a degree from Trinity College, Dublin. He came from a family wealthy enough to give John Francis Kelly a moderately successful farm in Ireland or a degree from one of its universities. John knew he could not have both. After spending many a night on numbing knees with his Rosary, he chose a law degree, the potential of America over the farm. He never regretted his choice.

Because of his devotion to the Blessed Virgin, John had named his precious daughter Mary. She had married well, to Captain Patrick Driscoll, Jr., a loyal husband and caring father to his two grandchildren. Tonight John would host a gathering of his men and their families to name the new fortification on Raccoon Island. He knew what fate might befall his son-in-law and read hard terror on his daughter's face. But now they all must stand and be ready to sacrifice for their fragile republic.

The emotions of pride and horror tore at Major Kelly as he climbed to the top of the stairs of his home and stepped out on to the balcony. Behind him hung the colors of the Confederacy and of the Savannah Coastal Artillery. At his side stood Patrick, resplendent in his dress uniform of gray and white. The moon was sunflower yellow over the Skidaway River, its craters ominous and easily visible to all. The smell of burning hardwood drifted through the oaks along the river bank. Torches lighted the yard. Men circled around sipping liquor from their crisp silver SCA cups, where reflected fires burned again. Most were young; some were very young. The older, more experienced men had long since left for distant battles in the Army of Northern Virginia. Major Kelly was in Savannah only because he had been wounded so badly in battle that he was no longer fit for active duty at the front. Still, he served his country as commander of Savannah's coastal defense batteries. Now, at his signal, the drums rolled and the lawn full of laughing men and ladies was still. Major Kelly cleared his throat and spoke.

"We are here tonight to remember who we are and what we are fighting for. We gather in torchlight just as our ancient ancestors did on a hill called Tara in a faraway land. When they, too, were challenged by invaders who would destroy all that they held dear." John's voice trembled softly. His wife touched his sleeve and held her hand steadily to his arm. "Brave men, my boys, and you are their sons. Tonight we celebrate this place . . . Battery Jasper, to honor one of your kinsmen. Holding colors high, he fell. He gave his all in our first revolution against tyranny. Now we honor him in the second. Gentlemen, join me in a toast to the pious and immortal memory of that great Irish patriot, Sergeant William Jasper."

With that, the artillerists came to attention, raised their silver mugs and chanted: "To the pious and immortal memory of Sergeant William Jasper." Then down the gullets of a hundred and twenty young men passed the sweet fire of straight Kentucky bourbon. A great scream of spirit leapt from the men—bestial, triumphant, the Rebel Yell. Then a strange, bewildering silence. All eyes were transfixed on the major.

He turned dramatically to Patrick, addressing him and his men gathered below: "Your ladies have labored many hours and have gone to great personal sacrifice to make this flag that you shall fly proudly over the ramparts of Battery Jasper. Mrs. Patrick Driscoll will now present the colors to her husband, Captain Patrick Driscoll, battery commander."

Mary stepped forward and placed the flag in Patrick's hands. He thanked her with a kiss and moved to the railing to speak.

Letting the flag unfurl over the balcony so that all could see it, Patrick thanked the ladies. The crowd clapped in appreciation when the flag fell open. Quality cloth had been hard to come by since the blockade and the women who loved the men of the Coastals had sacrificed the silk of their finest gowns to make the flag. At that time in the war the Confederacy was using its second national flag design, having dropped the original stars and bars because it was confused in battle with the stars and stripes. The new 1863 flag was lovingly referred to as the Stainless Banner—all white except for the upper left quarter, which contained the famed Confederate battle flag. Hand-sewn on the white field was also the emerald green Irish harp, the same symbol blazoned on the Coastals'

uniform buttons and caps. The bright silk colors of the
flag seemed to whisper hope in the light breeze and watch-
ful moon.

The drums rolled. The crowd tightened to circle the
speaker's stand. Patrick thanked the ladies again, then
lifted his head to the night and continued.

"I will be brief. We have named our artillery piece. We
have asked God to make our aim true and our shot strong.
On the breech of our cannon there is a brass plaque that
reads 'The Breastplate of St. Patrick.' Now I should like
to close with the words of the prayer for which our gun
is named." Cups of bourbon were placed on tables, hats
were doffed. The ladies prayerfully held their hands together in front of them, heads bowed, some staring at
wedding bands.

Then Patrick made the sign of the cross and began to
recite the Lorica, or of Breastplate of Saint Patrick, an
ancient Gaelic prayer attributed to him. Patrick's words
rang our clearly in the cool night air as he chanted:

> *Christ protect me today*
> *Against poison, against burning,*
> *Against drowning, against wounding,*
> *That I may receive abundant*
> *   reward.*
> *Christ with me, Christ before me,*
> *Christ behind me, Christ within me.*

Captain Driscoll recited each strengthening verse from
memory, finishing with: "May Your Salvation, O Lord,
be with us forever."

A quiet but firm "Amen" was chorused by those gathered under the balcony. On this devout signal, jaunty
string music started again.

Patrick caught Shad's eye. As he turned to leave the
balcony, Shad smiled, nodding his head slightly. Patrick
returned the smile. A haunting hint of sadness. They both
turned away and moved out among friends to say their
good-byes.

HIDING THE DRISCOLL FORTUNE

PATRICK AND HIS FATHER talked that night as they sat by the fire in the study. The women were preparing for bed when the old man finally said: "This isn't one of those nights you spend with me into the wee hours by the fire here, Pat. You should be with your wife as long as you can. The morning will come scratchin' at you soon enough, and then you'd sell half of what you own for only one more hour. But Pat, we need to talk. I've asked Shad to join us." Then he turned to the door and called out: "Mattie? Tell Shad to come on in now."

A moment later, hat in hand, Shad stood before the great stone fireplace and said quietly: "You called for me, suh?"

Mr. Driscoll stood to address Shad, and so did Pat. The master wanted to speak to Shad as a man, because he had to have the actions of a man from him.

"Shad, I'm expectin' you to watch out for Patrick, you know that." Shad nodded his head, and the old man continued. "Captain Driscoll will be taking something with him back to Battery Jasper. It is very important to this entire family, to you and your family. Whether Mr. Lincoln is successful or not in getting freedom for you, the way I see it is that you will be as dependent on this family as you have been in the past. It's gonna be tough for everybody after this war ends, and we're all gonna be needin' help, colored and white. I've decided to trust you, Shad, and let you know what the captain will have out there with him. I ask that you guard it with your life as he will with his. It's your future you'll be lookin' after, just as much as it is ours, and I'm trustin' you with that. I've known you since the day you were born, Shad, and I truly think that you love this family and won't let us down. Is that true?"

Shadrack straightened his back and looked right into his master's eyes. Not many slaves would do such a thing, but he knew that it was what his master expected of him.

"You been good to me and you didn't have to. You ain't never mistreated none of us, suh, and there's many that do. I worked side by side with the captain and done drunk from the same cup as he done. I believe in God just like you taught me, and I don't go back on my word, no suh. And now I gives you my word that you can trust me, and that's a fact, suh."

Before dropping his gaze to the floor, Shad looked for a moment at Patrick. Then Patrick said to his father, "I can't think of another person that I'd trust more than Shad, Daddy. He won't let us down."

Patrick Driscoll, Sr., was a large man, and even now, in his seventy-third year, he still had good muscle mass. His shoulders were broad and his forearms well developed. His hair and beard had been completely black until he reached his late fifties. Now they were silver-gray, but he had only a very small bald spot in the back. He was, what some called the "Dark Irish," a physically imposing man. His son was made in his likeness. Their most striking features were their eyes: bright blue, the shade of blossoming heather that could change almost instantly from whimsical sadness to icy steel. Now the old man fixed that gaze upon Shad. After a few moments he said quietly: "All right then, I'll trust you."

The patriarch, haunted by the bedlam he sensed was sure to come, looked back into the fire and continued. "I have given Captain Driscoll a small strongbox to take back to that island and hide for safekeeping. If the Yankees get here, they will steal everything they can and burn the rest. What's in that box will be how we will get started after all this is over. Do you understand, Shad?"

Shad nodded his head and whispered: "Yes, suh."

"After a suitable hiding place has been found on the island, Captain Driscoll will write me a letter telling me where it is hidden and send it back by the weekly supply boat. You will also know where the box is because you're gonna help him hide it and keep it safe. This is in the event that something happens to the captain and the letter that he will write to me. I don't expect much will happen to you darkies. If the Yankees capture the battery, they will just let you go, but they'll take the captain off to a prison camp." Mr. Driscoll paused for a moment, then added: "We'll be countin' on you, Shadrack."

"Yes, suh."

"That's all, Shad. You can go now. Why don't you go spend some time with Carrie and your little boy. Ya'll have a long day ahead of you. It may be a while before you can see your families again."

Bowing slightly, Shad said: "Yes, suh. Good night, suh," and left the room.

Gazing in silence, Pat and his father studied the fire in communion. In a short while the old man turned to Pat and said, "You've got a wife and children too, you know, and you need to be with them now." He reached out and put his arms around his son. They hugged each other as they had done when Pat was a child. The old man yearned to bring that time back again. Without a word Patrick left the room and went to his wife, up the long curved staircase, lightly touching the bannister that he had played on as a child. He saw his reflection in its polished surface, shimmering and grotesque.

The old man poured himself a long drink, sat in his favorite fat cordovan leather chair, and stared into the fire until the early hours of the morning.

It was late in the afternoon as Pat surveyed the Ogeechee River with his field glasses. Nothing in sight except some smoke on the distant eastern horizon. It was just he and Shad and the Breastplate of St. Patrick up on top of Battery Jasper.

"Where do you suppose we ought to bury the box?" asked Pat.

"I reckon some place nobody'd be likely to look. Or would want to."

"Where would you say that might be, then?"

"I was thinkin' down at the borrow pit, where all them big gators and snakes likes to be lying about."

"Where nobody would want to look," said Pat as he boosted himself up on to the wall in front of the gun. Then he put the glasses to his eyes again and began to make a full turn around the fort from right to left. All of the trees and underbrush had been removed from the front and sides of the fort for a hundred yards or so in order to provide an unobstructed field of fire to the edge of the marsh. Behind the fort were the camps. Other than that, the entire island was primeval, wild, and heavily wooded. Just as Patrick was about to complete his turn he stopped and said again, "Where nobody would want to look. Come up here for second, Shad. I want to show you something."

Shad scrambled to the top of the wall and looked in the direction Driscoll was pointing. Out to the left and in front of the battery about a hundred yards away were the two latrines that served the battery's occupants—one for the soldiers and another, about twenty-five yards further out, for the slaves. Patrick turned to Shad with a twinkle in his eye and grinned. Then Shad broke into laughter and repeated the captain's words: "Where nobody would want to look."

In the days before running water and indoor plumbing, waste disposal presented two elemental problems—the smell that it created and the possibility of contaminating the well water. Both problems were solved by locating the latrine downwind and as far away from the well as possible. The prevailing southwest winds on Raccoon Island dictated that the latrines for Battery Jasper be in the northeast sector.

That night, after taps, Shad and the captain slipped away from camp with a shovel and the box full of jewels and gold. On the way they discussed into which latrine they should place the box. Shad finally settled the problem with a matter-of-fact observation: "Captain Pat, there's very few colored folk and no white people at all who would be much inclined to go pokin' through a pile of nigga shit alookin' for sumpthin." Pat laughed quietly and said: "Point well taken, Shad. The colored outhouse it is."

Together they slipped through the door of the rickety little building, and Shad watched as Pat dropped the box into the latrine. Shad quickly threw several shovels full of dirt into the hole to cover the box, and Pat lit a match. They both peered down into the hole to see if the box was visible.

"Don't 'xactly smell like da magnolia tree out back da big house, do it, suh?"

"I should say not, and that's just fine. Only problem now is how we gonna get it out when the time comes?"

"I 'spect we'll find a way, seein' what's down there. Gold can make just about anything smell sweet, can't it, suh?"

"Yeah, smells like lilac water already, don't it, Shad?" They both chuckled and then slipped away from the latrine as secretly as they had come.

Unlike the other slaves on the island, Shad stayed in the soldiers' camp along with his master. Captain Driscoll had a walled tent large enough for staff meetings and a cot for his manservant. It was the custom in many Catholic families to say the Rosary each evening after supper. Everyone would gather together, servants included, and the head of household would lead them in prayer. That night was no exception as Patrick and Shad knelt, side by side, at the map table and prayed the decades of the five sorrowful mysteries of the Rosary. When they had finished, Patrick sat on the side of his cot and motioned for Shad to sit next to him.

"We're not gonna win this war, Shad. The Yankees are too big and got too much of all the things that go into fighting a war and winning it. We had all hoped that the British would come in on our side and help us, but that ain't gonna happen now. Goddamn Brits, they took our

gold and made promises and . . ." Then he stopped and
shook his head. "Way I see it, and so does Daddy, is that
you're gonna be a free man by the end of next year, Shad.
All the darkies are, everywhere. Well, what I'm trying to
say is that we decided to set you free before Mr. Lincoln
does. You and Carrie and your momma and daddy, every
single one of you. Daddy's having the major draw up the
papers this week, and when you get back home from this
place, you'll be free. Ain't nothing gonna change around
the house, though. You can all stay and work for us, and
get paid for doing it. Except now, you can up and leave;
hell, you can go live in New York City if you want."

This was alien to Shad. Never in his life had he ever
believed that he would be anything other than what he
had always been—the property of another person. The
thought scared Shad. Freedom, no matter how wonderful
it sounded, was a frightening thing for a man who had
never known it, who had never thought that he would
truly be the master of his own fate, and who was totally
unprepared to accept it.

"I be scared, Captain Pat. What I do? Who take care
of my baby? What gonna happen to my momma and
daddy? They old now, suh. Dem Yankees is hateful people. You is all I ever knowed. I'se scared, suh, and I ain't
no coward of a man, and you know that, suh. But I be
scared of what gonna happen to us all, free or not."

"We're all scared, Shad. And I don't know what's
gonna happen when the Yankees come either, so don't
feel bad. Just remember what I said. Ya'll can stay on
with us if you want. You got a home and something to
eat. But one thing is for sure, there's gonna be a change.
That's why we put that box out there in that shit hole.
Now let's bed down and try to get some sleep. I saw some
heavy black smoke out towards the sound today. Couldn't
see any ships, but that kind of smoke doesn't mean anything other than the Yankee ironclads are moving around
out there and may come up the river to give us a little
visit."

A greatly troubled and befuddled Shadrack blew out the oil lamp and climbed into his cot. In the dark Shad whispered:

"Captain Pat?"

"Yes, Shad."

"Thank you, suh . . . and, and . . . I'll be praying to St. Patrick to protect you, suh."

"You're welcome, Shad. I'll be praying for you also. Good night, Shad."

"Good night, suh."

SCREAMS FROM BATTERY JASPER

MOVING WITH THE TIDE, the USS *Nahunt* made good time pressing its way up through Ossabaw Sound toward the Ogeechee River and an appointment with Battery Jasper. The men went to battle stations just as the flag over the fort came into view. The executive officer placed his spy glass to his eye for a moment and then blurted out: "Saints in heaven, Captain Grady, there's an Irish harp on that rebel flag. There're Irishmen in that fort, sir!"

"Let me see, Mr. Connor." The captain squinted carefully and then said: "I do believe you're right! We'll be shooting at our own."

"What'll we do, sir, when the crew finds out? Some may have relatives out there. Only yesterday the boys were talking about those that had kinfolk in Savannah."

"It makes the situation painful for us all, Mr. Connor, but the men will do their duty, harp on that flag or no. Now let's get below and prepare to say hello to our cousins in a big Boston Irish way."

The decks of the *Nahunt* were cleared as she slowed upon getting into gun range. The monitor class of warship presented very little in the way of a target for enemy guns. She drew only eleven feet and had no more than three feet of freeboard showing from the water along her 110-foot length. All the rest of the deck was flat except for the round gun turret in the center, which rose twelve feet in the air. This turret was covered in iron plates two inches thick, held together by bolts. In theory it could withstand anything the rebels could hurl at it.

It wasn't invincible; the battle for Charleston harbor back in the summer of '63 had proved that. But the crew of the *Nahunt*, being up against one lonely gun handled by the young boys and crippled men they assumed to be the conscripts on that island, felt certain they would maul the battery's defenders. In fact the Coastals who were stationed at Battery Jasper, though they were indeed young, were also proud volunteers who had trained hard and believed utterly in their cause. Yankee arrogance on the USS *Nahunt* was running higher than the tide she came in on.

It was four in the afternoon when, at a thousand yards, the fifteen-inch Rodman gun in the *Nahunt's* turret roared, then jerked back as its 420-pound ball began a long sweeping arch toward little Battery Jasper. Everyone in the fort could see the black dot on the horizon that zoomed ever closer, first going up in the blue cloudless sky, then starting to come back down, growing bigger all the time. The men ducked as the ball whizzed long over the parapet and fell with a thud among the tents behind the fort. The men inside the battery had hardly recovered from the excitement of the first shot when they saw smoke billow for a second time from the *Nahunt's* turret. This time the slightly smaller, eleven-inch Rodman had spoken. As before, Captain Driscoll and his men watched the cannon shot make straight for them until it neared the end of its arc. Then they huddled down behind the walls of the parapet, awaiting the shell's impact.

The shot fell short and hit twenty yards in front of the battery's sloping earth walls, cutting a two-foot furrow about ten yards long before the loosely packed earth brought it to a halt. Both projectiles had been solid shot designed for penetrating the armored hulls of warships or leveling the masonry of brick forts. It took about eight minutes for the *Nahunt* to reload a gun between shots.

Now it was Battery Jasper's turn to take a crack at the warship.

"Raise the gun, Mr. Graham, and make ready for firing."

"Yes, sir," came the reply from Lieutenant Joseph Graham, second in command. Then he turned to Shad and shouted: "OK, the captain wants you to lift the gun. On the count of three, put your backs into the jacks and heave to it." On the count Shad and five other slaves worked the jacking levers and, after six firm strokes, lifted the ten-thousand pound gun and carriage up above the parapet wall and into firing position.

Patrick Driscoll stood at the wall just to the right of the Breastplate of St. Patrick and dropped the field glasses from his face. Then he turned to Graham and shouted: "I make it nine hundred yards, Lieutenant. Set your elevation at eight degrees and shift your aim two points to the right, then prepare to fire on my order."

Patrick looked through his glasses again at the *Nahunt* and waited for her to draw exactly opposite the markers that he and Shad had placed in the marsh. When he thought that she was just about right, he yelled "Fire!" The Breastplate of St. Patrick let out a terrific roar and rolled backwards on its carriage to absorb the tremendous shock of recoil. The two hundred-pound solid-shot missile screamed out over the marsh and down the river straight for the revolving turret of the monitor. Because of the placement of the range markers, Battery Jasper's aim was true; the big cannon ball hit the side of the turret with a resounding bang that could be heard all the way back to the battery.

When the cannon ball hit the iron plate of the turret, the noise inside was deafening. More terrifying still to the sailors inside were the bolts that went flying when the ball hit. The gun captain of the fifteen-incher took a metal rivet in the side of the head and went down like a limp rag, falling into the rammer by his side. Sixteen-year-old Jimmy Bourke caught a rivet in his left shoulder that spun him around but didn't break any bones. Others in the turret screamed amid the smoke and confusion, but were drowned out by the clank of machinery as the turret was turned from the enemy's gun for safer reloading. Eventually the grizzled senior noncom in the turret was able to regain control of the loaders when he yelled: "I'll kill every last one of you myself if you don't snap to and get to your stations!"

There were screams on Battery Jasper too, but they were screams of jubilation as the men heard the crash made by their shot as it hit. Rejoicing soon faded, however, when Pat Driscoll told them that there appeared to be little damage. The Columbiad had already been lowered in the barbette and was in the process of reloading when another shot exploded from the *Nahunt*. This time the Yankees had the proper range—the shot hit higher up on the walls but did little more than plow the earth again. One after the other the shots came, but all they did was move the dirt around, and the men of Battery Jasper appeared safe. The system of raising and lowering the gun designed by Patrick's father worked flawlessly and afforded the defenders an extra margin of safety from the Yankee shells. Fire from the Breastplate of St. Patrick was exceptionally good, though its shot struck the turret of the *Nahunt* again and again to apparently little effect.

Although the ironsides of the *Nahunt* had not been freely breached, the impact of Battery Jasper's repeated hits was taking its toll on the gunner's mates. Heat inside the turret as well as deep within the ship was approaching 125 degrees. The smoke was so thick that breathing and seeing were virtually impossible. Two more men had been seriously injured by the flying rivets, and everyone inside the turret would suffer permanent hearing damage.

The sun had now set behind Battery Jasper, and Captain Grady could see the moon looming behind him over Ossabaw Sound. He had been shelling this insignificant dirt fort for almost three hours with little to show for it but the beating his own men had been taking.

"Mr. Connor, change to exploding shot and cut the fuses to blow right over their heads. Make it no more than fifty feet. We're gonna' make things hot now for these Irish rebs."

Captain Grady intended to silence Battery Jasper's cannon by taking out her gun crew rather than the gun itself. The projectiles he would hurl at his opponents would be set to explode right over the fort at a height of fifty feet and would shower the occupants with sharp pieces of steel coming down on them at more than four hundred miles an hour. If everything went according to plan, the men who fed and fired the Breastplate of St. Patrick would be shredded like birds hit with buckshot.

It was dark, but the Stainless Banner was still plainly visible flapping over Battery Jasper as Captain Grady passed the word to fire when ready. In the darkness the big Rodman spit out not only her shell, but a tongue of orange flame and sparks that reached out a hundred feet over the Ogeechee as the exploding shot left the muzzle. The burning fuse could be clearly seen as an orange glow trailing sparks as the shell reached its peak and then started to fall toward the little fort. About 150 feet in front of the fort, and perhaps seventy-five feet above the ground, there was a thunderous noise as the bomb exploded, raining pieces of hot metal in every direction. To some, it sounded like rain falling. To those who knew better, it sounded like death hitting the ground all around them.

It was only then that Captain Driscoll realized he had never been able to get the letter off to his father telling him where the strongbox was hidden. The supply boat had been scheduled to come to Raccoon Island that day, but had been kept away by the gunfire. "Good thing we thought of telling Shad about the box," thought Patrick as he directed fire against the *Nahunt*. "He may be the only one left who knows where it is." Pat was grimly aware that as soon as the Yankees figured out the proper fuse setting for their exploding bombs, the Coastals would all

have to go into the bombproof shelter or die on the outside
with their gun.

After repeated and rapid firing, the barrel of Battery
Jasper's cannon was almost too hot to touch. As happens
with metal when it is heated, the gun had expanded so
the diameter of its tube was smaller. The gun crew knew
this and packed the wadding behind the ball accordingly.
Now Patrick consulted with Lieutenant Graham about increasing the amount of powder being used in the cannon
in an attempt to penetrate the plating of the *Nahunt*.

"I think she'll take it, Pat," said Joe Graham, a childhood friend.

"Then load her up and let's have at it, Joe Boy, before
the Yankees get our range and run us all inside. They've
got two guns on that boat, so if they pin us inside they
can run up closer and then maybe breach the wall."

Graham gave a smart salute, looked into Pat's eyes,
and smiled. "We'll take 'em with this, Pat. She can stand
the load." Then he turned to the members of the Savannah
Coastal Artillery serving as loaders and shouted out the
orders to increase the powder load by ten pounds.

The *Nahunt* had just turned her turret to face Battery
Jasper and was lining up her first shot when Captain Driscoll looked over the parapet and noticed that the open gun
ports were exposed to his fire. He quickly but carefully
aimed his gun right for the open doors, hoping for a lucky
shot that would go through the open ports and into the
turret itself. He said a silent prayer to St. Jude, the patron
saint of miracles, made the sign of the cross, and stepped
back into the barbette behind the enormous cannon. He
looked directly into the eyes of Lieutenant Graham, who
was standing next to the gun with the firing lanyard in his
hand, and yelled, "Fire!" Graham, the only son of a widowed mother, yanked the lanyard.

The Breastplate of Saint Patrick roared as it had never
roared in its life. The iron ball in its throat was quickly
pressed down the muzzle, when the increased friction
from the expanded iron and the increased force of a larger

powder load simply proved too much for the cannon to bear. After the ball had traveled about halfway down the barrel, the iron began to split. Then it exploded, blowing off the distal third of the gun barrel. Young Joseph Graham disappeared in a bright orange flash as a piece of gun barrel the size of a horse's head caught him in the chest and carried what was left of him out over the side of the parapet and onto the sloping glacis of Battery Jasper. Captain Driscoll was swept up in the explosion also, being hit by barrel fragments in the right arm and leg, then blown back off the barbette and down into the ranks of the slaves working the jacking levers. All of the jacking crew had been stunned by the explosion, and several lay about unconscious.

Shad had been lucky; he was only slightly dazed. When he was able to see, he was horrified. Patrick Driscoll lay at his feet with a large portion of his right arm gone at the shoulder and an even larger portion of his right leg missing at the thigh. It looked to Shad as though some monstrous creature had bitten two huge chunks out of Patrick's body and then dropped him into the lower gun pit, covered in his own gore.

"Oh Jesus, Captain Pat, oh Jesus!" shouted Shad as he crawled to Pat and took him in his arms. Shad sat upright on the ground with Pat resting across his lap looking into Shad's face.

It was odd, but as severe as the arm and leg wounds were, the bleeding was not profuse. Shad's survey of his master's wounds brought him temporary hope—until he noticed the fist-size hole in Patrick's abdomen where he had taken another piece of metal. Despite his severe shock, Patrick had regained consciousness and was trying to speak.

"Shad . . . Shad."

"Don't try to talk, Captain Pat. It ain't no good for you. Just rest quiet and let ol' Shad try to fix you up here." Shad looked around desperately for some kind of help, anything at all.

With his left hand Patrick reached up and touched Shad's face. It was a caress, of the kind that a mother would give a child.

"Shad."

"Please, suh, save your strength. I'm gonna put you down and get some help from some of the boys. I gotta get you some help, Captain."

Pat's eyes opened wide, and he pulled Shad's head close to his face.

"Shad . . . you're . . . a . . . man . . . a free man now," gasped Patrick, his mouth only inches from Shad's face. "You gotta . . . take care . . . of the family now. You're the only one . . . who knows about . . . the box." Shad could see in Patrick's eyes that he was dying.

"No suh, Captain Pat. You gonna make it, suh, you gonna watch out for us all. You is gonna make it, Captain Pat!" he shouted in desperation.

"Pat . . ."

"What, suh? I can't understand ya, Captain Pat. Please don't try to talk, suh."

"I . . . I'm Pat. . . . Call me Pat, Shad, like . . . like all my other friends."

"Oh Jesus, suh! Please suh, let me get up so's I can help ya!"

With surprising strength, Patrick held on to Shad's neck and pulled himself even closer. His voice was weaker, but his eyes still had the gleam of purpose.

"You . . . you been my friend . . . all my life. . . . Now, say good-bye to me . . . like my friend."

Tears streamed down Shad's face and dropped on Patrick's. He had trouble getting the words out, but finally they came: "Good . . . Good-bye, . . . Pat. You is been a kind man to me, Pat, and I is your friend, Pat! I is your friend, Pat! I is your friend!" Shad was screaming as Captain Patrick Driscoll, Confederate States Army, relaxed in the arms of his former slave, looked directly into his eyes, and gave up the ghost.

* * *

Although the explosion of the gun had silenced it and its crew, the shot was still true. It screamed out over the moonlit marsh for the open gun doors of the USS *Nahunt*. St. Jude answered Patrick's prayers that night as the last cannon ball delivered from the Breastplate of St. Patrick crashed through the port-side gun door of the *Nahunt*, knocking the eleven-inch Rodman off its mount and down into the lower decks of the ship. The warship reeled from the blow as steam lines burst open, wood and iron splintered on the crew, and men cried out in agony. In the wheelhouse Captain Grady thought that the ship had suffered a mortal blow, so great was the impact.

In the turret several men who survived the hit struggled with the fifteen-inch Rodman that was still intact and properly on its mount. The gun was loaded with a round that had the fuse cut by the chief gunner's mate himself. Now that mate intended to fire it at the Rebs in that damn dirt fort. Vincent Mahan, native of County Limerick, checked the aim of his gun and pulled the firing lanyard. He watched with satisfaction as he followed the orange glow out over the river, then the marsh, and knew that he had found the range as he saw the shot explode low, directly over the fort. A piece of the shot cut the battery's flagpole in half, and Vincent cheered as he saw the Rebel flag fall into the smoking guts of Battery Jasper.

Shadrack Bryan was still down in the gun pit, near the jacking levers, still holding the dead body of his friend, when that last shell from the *Nahunt* exploded overhead. He was rocking slowly back and forth with Pat's cheek pressed to his as he quietly sang, "Swing low, sweet chariot, comin' for to carry me home. Swing low, sweet chariot, comin' for to carry me home."

Just as he started the second verse, the *Nahunt's* shell exploded not more than fifty feet above him. Shad neither heard the explosion nor felt the triangular piece of shell fragment that hit him squarely in the head. All he did was slump over on his side, carrying Pat's body with him as he, too, entered into the Kingdom.

II

THE FREE STATE OF CHATHAM

What need you, being come to sense,
But fumble in a greasy till

P. Introibo ad altare Dei.

S. Ad Deum qui laetificat
Juventuetem meam.

P. I will go in to the altar of God.

S. To God, the joy of my youth.

—THE BEGINNING PRAYER OF THE
LATIN MASS, PRE-VATICAN II

THE GRAVE, MOONSHINE,
AND THE BAGMAN

"YES SUH, dat do look fine even if I says so myself. You is just clear as a bell and is gonna fetch me a fine piece a' money back at Bo Peep's dis Saturday night, yes you is!"

Deep within the dense foliage of thick vines that now covered more than half of Raccoon Island, a pair of strong black hands tightened the tops of jars that, in a few days, many pairs of eager white hands would open. Another dozen mason jars were filled with the clear liquid and then carefully wrapped in rags and placed in an old croaker sack.

In the fading light of the setting sun Abednigo Bryan loaded his boat and prepared for the trip back to Coffee Bluff. He had been on Raccoon Island all day, arriving before dawn under the cover of darkness, and was now leaving with that same protection. The croaker sacks were placed close to the stern of his boat, where the ride would not be rough. A length of line, a casting net, and a pair of muddy rubber boots were thrown haphazardly over the top of the sacks, and his payload assumed the desired appearance of unimportance.

Later in the evening, after he was back at his house on Barnard Street, Abednigo would unpack the jars. With decided flair, he would paint the letter "A" on each jar in a shade of purple nail polish that one of his girlfriends had left there. The purple "A" on the side of a mason jar had become the symbol for the finest moonshine liquor to be found anywhere in Chatham County.

There was good moonshine and there was terrible moonshine, and then there was the "Purple A" brand. The good moonshine might make a person sick and the terrible moonshine might kill a man, but the Purple A was known for its clarity, smoothness, and punch, but most of all for its safety. When someone drank a lot of Abednigo Bryan's Purple A, he might wish he were dead the next day, but dying was one thing that would not result from the consumption of Purple A.

Abednigo's daddy, Meshack, had told him that if he worked hard and didn't get greedy, Prohibition could make him a rich man. Meshack had died before the prediction had come true, but not before he had taught Abednigo the secrets of making fine moonshine. Those skills were now paying off, because Abednigo (Abe to his customers) was quickly becoming one of the wealthiest blacks in Savannah.

Abe hadn't thrown away the money he made on moonshine like so many others had. He used it shrewdly to buy up little pieces of property at good prices as they became available during the hard times of the depression. As the end of Prohibition drew near with the inevitable repeal of the Eighteenth Amendment, and a decline in his revenue from illegal alcohol became a certainty, Abe was glad that he had wisely protected his income with his real estate purchases. For the time being, however, the moonshine business was still lucrative, and Abe continued his regular visits to Raccoon Island.

Abe had first visited the island as a young child with his parents and other members of his family. This was a sort of pilgrimage that the descendants of Shadrack Bryan had made each year following his death at Battery Jasper. It had continued on a regular basis until the Great Depression, when many members of the family were forced to move to cities in the North in search of work. After that, only a small handful of Shad's relatives, most of them elderly, would make the yearly voyage to Battery Jasper on the anniversary of Shad's death. Abe was the youngest of the Bryans who made the trip.

The now legendary death of Captain Patrick Driscoll in the arms of Shadrack Bryan, and Shad's subsequent death while trying to save the captain, had been witnessed by other soldiers and slaves in the fort. The Driscoll family offered to bury Shad on the family estate at Isle of Hope and even erect a monument to him for his bravery. Shad's wife wanted him to lie next to his beloved master, but she knew that whites and blacks were to be segregated even in death and that such an arrangement was out of the question. Carrie decided instead that if Shad couldn't be buried next to Patrick, then he would have the biggest tomb in the county, so she asked old Mr. Driscoll if it would be all right to bury Shad inside the fort where he had been killed. Mr. Driscoll agreed without hesitation and even thought about burying Patrick there too, but gentle Mary Driscoll had almost fainted when he mentioned the subject. He dropped the idea, then set about organizing the grandest funeral that any black man had ever had in Savannah.

After Mr. Driscoll got the bishop of Savannah to intercede with General Sherman himself, a small flotilla of boats was allowed back to Battery Jasper. Two weeks after Savannah had fallen to the Yankees, during a funeral mass in the gun pit where Shad and Pat had been killed, Shadrack Bryan was buried in the floor of the fort's bomb proof. The fallen remains of the Breastplate of St. Patrick were used as an altar. Mrs. Driscoll personally paid for the marble stone that was placed over the grave. It read:

SHADRACK BRYAN
1844–1864
FREE MAN
AND FRIEND OF
CAPT. PATRICK DRISCOLL, C.S.A.

Over the years Shad's descendants began planting azaleas on the fort's walls rather than bringing cut flowers that would soon die, and the entire fort was gradually covered in a pure white variety of the flower. At first it was Meshack who tended the plants on his father's grave, but when he became too sick to go out to Battery Jasper, Abe took over the responsibilities.

Battery Jasper and Raccoon Island became very special for Abe—his own private world, his secret place where he, a black man, could be king and absolute ruler. That soil, that earth, those trees were his; Battery Jasper became his Camelot, and he its King Arthur.

As a teenager, he would row for hours over to the island from Coffee Bluff and then stay for days, living off the deer and wild boar that roamed there. He knew every oak tree and every egret's nest, every blackberry bush and alligator trail on the island. He even knew how to get a boat up to the east end of the island by a small creek that nobody else knew about but his father. Meshack had named it "Runaway Negro Creek" and had used it to come in and out of Raccoon Island when he was making moonshine.

Just as the ruggedness and isolation of the Appalachian mountains had afforded moonshiners the secrecy needed to cook their mash, likewise did the great expanse and hundreds of islands of the Georgia coast granted similar opportunities to its inhabitants. The coastline that reaches from Tybee Island south to St. Simon's Island near Brunswick is the longest stretch of virtually uninhabited sea islands on the East Coast. Indeed, well into the 1960's the Georgia coast was, essentially, as wild as when Oglethorpe had first arrived in Savannah. The lure of easy money from the manufacture of illegal liquor, the sparse population of the coastline south of Savannah, the isolation and privacy of small islands, and the willingness of law enforcement to look the other way—all made the islands and marshes of Georgia a fertile ground for industrious moonshiners. Every island bigger than a city block had at least one still on it. Islands the size of Wassaw and Ossabaw, both more than twenty miles long, might have a dozen or more stills in operation at any one time.

The liquor would find its way all over coastal Georgia, Florida, and South Carolina. But most of all, it would be sold in Savannah, Georgia's state within a state, her penultimate zone of forbidden but tolerated pleasures, a beautiful and sassy child, where insouciant souls from upstate could seek a weekend's fleshy pleasures and libation in anonymity amid the decadent mystery of this defiant and seductive lady. In short, all of the rest of the state tolerated Chatham County's wide-open attitude toward illegal liquor, gambling, and the flaunting of a score of other state laws. Savannah, and most of all Tybee, was simply the place to go in Georgia and South Carolina to imbibe in these pleasures.

This indulgence did not come without a price, however, and the owners of the concessions and businesses that profited from Chatham County's independence did so by keeping the gears of government between Savannah and the capitol in Atlanta well lubricated with the lifeblood of politics. It was during this time that Chatham County became known to all Georgians as "The Free and Independent State of Chatham."

Meshack had explained to Abe how the system worked, and Abe followed the lesson well. When election time came around, Abe was always ready with discrete but generous donations made to both sides in any race. The bagman for the party in power was an Irishman by the name of Joseph James O'Boyle.

MONEY AND RESPECTABILITY

"JJ" O'BOYLE'S GRANDFATHER had come to Savannah from County Donegal, Ireland, in 1870, a seaman on a British merchant ship that transported cotton from Savannah to the great mills in England. A big and powerful man with a temper to match, Joseph found himself thrown off his ship at Savannah after nearly killing a shipmate in a fight. His three foes, all Englishmen, had tried to fleece him in a rigged card game. When he discovered the scheme, he attacked and beat all three men so severely

that one of them was in a coma for two days. Although
Joseph had been the victim of a scam, the ship was English, as were all of the crew except him, so he took the
blame. With no family back in Ireland except a brother,
he decided that Savannah was as good a place as any in
America to try to make a start. He took a job on the docks
loading cotton and naval stores with the black stevedores,
and over the years, through his hard work and keen mind,
he eventually became the foreman over hundreds of men
at the port.

Joseph O'Boyle was lucky enough to marry a beautiful
Irish girl named Rose McNevin, whose family had come
from County Galway to Savannah in the 1840's. Rose
gave Joseph two daughters, three sons, and a degree of
respectability in Savannah's Irish community. One of
those sons, James, followed in his father's footsteps and
went to work on the waterfront; he, too, married within
the Irish community and had two sons, Thomas Anthony
and Joseph James. Thomas became a captain with the Savannah Police Department; Joseph James, whom everyone
called JJ, worked with his father on the Savannah docks.

JJ O'Boyle had an outgoing personality and good
looks. He made friends easily and men naturally looked
to him for leadership. During World War I, he received a
battlefield commission. When he returned to Savannah after the war, everyone thought he would take over his father's old job at the docks.

JJ, however, had greater aspirations than spending his
life in the rough-and-tumble world of ships and the men
who worked on them. The war had taken him to France
and England and exposed him to the finer things in life;
and when he returned to Savannah and began work on
the river again, he realized an insatiable hunger for what
was out of his reach. Although he was what many Savannah Irish would consider "well off," it was not enough
for JJ. He wanted to find a way of making "real money,"
enough for him to leave the docks and never look back.
The ratification of the Eighteenth Amendment to the Con-

stitution in 1919 afforded him his opportunity.

No one in Savannah knew more about the river, the coast, the shipping traffic, and the people who worked the ships than JJ O'Boyle. As he watched the effects of Prohibition increase the people's desire for a way to quench their thirsts, JJ saw his opportunity to make the kind of money he had always wanted. Through his knowledge and connections, he organized a remarkable and profitable bootlegging business only months after "the Noble Experiment" began.

JJ's brother, Thomas, was quickly won over by the lavish amounts of money JJ offered to send his way for Thomas' (and the Police Department's) cooperation, and in no time at all a vast network of people, from the cop on the beat to the men who ran the whiskey past the three-mile limit, was making money out of JJ's bootlegging business. The Prohibition Amendment was heartily unpopular in Savannah, and within a few weeks the speakeasies that had bloomed silently all over town were JJ's best customers. Their best customers, in turn, were many of Savannah's "best," who were also quite happy with the arrangement.

When JJ first started running whiskey from ships off the Georgia coast, he would have his sleek and fast Chris Crafts sneak up the Ogeechee River to places like Kilkenny and Richmond Hill to unload. Then, when he realized there was little threat from the law, his boats would put in at private docks on Tybee, Wilmington Island, or Thunderbolt. Sometimes, in the dead of night, they would even pull up to a dock at Isle of Hope to unload their cases into the back of a waiting truck, paying the dock owner with a case of ten-year-old Glenlivet for his trouble.

By the beginning of the Roosevelt administration, JJ had become wealthy running whiskey into Savannah, but he, like the humbler Abe Bryan, had also been shrewd enough to invest his money into legitimate businesses. When the Twentieth Amendment was ratified and Prohibition repealed in 1934, JJ O'Boyle had fully divested himself of any connection to bootlegging and could truthfully say that all of his business interests were legitimate and aboveboard . . . almost. JJ owned an interest in several bars and a hotel at Tybee that served liquor on Sundays and had slot machines—both strictly against state law. But that was Tybee, and things were looked upon differently at Tybee. Besides, JJ had a fine home at the beach, and listed it as his official place of residence in Chatham County.

After JJ had amassed enough money to make himself feel comfortable, JJ set his sights on respectability. Knowing that he would never be able to completely shed his image as a bootlegger, he tried to become known as a philanthropist and community leader. Then, perhaps, his children could be accepted by Savannah's upper crust. To this end JJ involved himself in all manner of charitable and political campaigns, and soon became known as the man to see in Savannah when it came to raising money for political purposes.

In the beginning JJ was often the only one who had given anything at all to a campaign, but he told the person running that he had raised the money from a large group of people who wished to remain anonymous. Eventually this ruse garnered JJ a reputation as the political kingmaker in Chatham County politics; if a person wanted his political money to make the proper impact, he gave it to JJ O'Boyle—to be distributed as JJ saw fit.

JJ felt that he was finally reaching a certain level of respectability when his oldest child, Tony, graduated from the University of Georgia with honors in only three years and was quickly accepted to the school of law. Of JJ and Mae O'Boyle's nine children, Tony was the best, the brightest, and showed the most promise.

Mae Murtage and JJ O'Boyle had married before the United States became involved in World War I. By the time JJ had returned from France, he and Mae had a son and two daughters.

Mae was a simple and sweet woman who had never loved anyone but JJ. She was happy and content with his job on the river and the money he brought home, but she realized that he was a man who wanted and needed more and had done her best to help him along the way. She turned a blind eye to his bootlegging business, and the raising of so many children gave her neither the time nor the inclination to care. Mae became unusually depressed when she learned of her ninth pregnancy, and she began to drink quietly out of frustration and fear. At first she only drank late at night, but toward the end of the pregnancy she was drinking during the daytime as well. By the time Aloysius was born, Mae had become a full-blown alcoholic.

Aloysius Kevin O'Boyle was a problem from the day he was born. Premature and far too small, he almost died during his first few days and spent seven weeks in the hospital before the doctors at St. Joseph's finally allowed Mae to take him home. He was a slow learner in school and had difficulty getting along with other children. His temper was explosive at times; he was cruel to the family pets and went through long periods of withdrawal from social contact. Little Al didn't start talking until he was three, and was unable to ride a bicycle until he was nine. Everyone understood he was at least slightly retarded. Today Al would have been recognized as suffering from Fetal Alcohol Syndrome.

Little Al's condition was painful for the entire family, especially his proud and domineering father. But JJ did everything he could for Al and didn't try to hide the fact that something wasn't quite right with the boy. Over the years the devotion he displayed for the welfare of his son earned him the respect and admiration of everyone who knew him. Even those who didn't particularly care for JJ would admit that the attention Al received from his father was admirable.

Although Al was a disappointment, JJ's other children had all done well in school and seemed to be on their way to successful lives. The most successful of all, and JJ's personal favorite, was his son Tony. In Tony, JJ saw all that he could have achieved if he had been given the education that Tony was now receiving. He was determined that Tony would be as successful as he had been, but that this success would not come from breaking heads on the riverfront or running bootleg rum. Tony was going to give the O'Boyle name the respectability and social acceptance that JJ knew he would never be able to give it.

NEWSROOM FIGHT

JOHN MORGAN HARTMAN, born in the hills of east Tennessee, came to be in Savannah in much the same way that Joseph O'Boyle did. John's mother was of Northern Irish stock; his father was a stern Prussian. As a teenager he took a part-time job working as a copyboy for the hometown newspaper. In later years he would say it was the Irish in him that made him fall in love with words and turned the blood in his veins to printer's ink. He grew naturally into the newspaper business, and by the time he was twenty-one he had worked on the great dailies in Knoxville, Memphis, and New Orleans. A week before Franklin Roosevelt took the oath of office for his first term, John was forced to resign from his job at the *Chattanooga Times* because of a fistfight with his boss. Although he lost his job because of the fight, it made him a hero in the eyes of his fellow workers, a legend at the *Times*, and a much-anticipated arrival at the *Savannah Morning Gazette*.

It all began when a depressed, shell-shocked veteran of World War I, Zeke Scruggs, blew his brains out with a pistol in a Chattanooga whorehouse. A sallow, lanky hillbilly, Scruggs had fallen in love with one of the local bordello girls. Zeke, who hadn't been quite right since being wounded in the head at the battle of Belleau Woods, was prone to rash acts. When the girl Zeke loved gave him the heave-ho for another man with a larger bankroll, Zeke finally went over the edge. He pledged his eternal love for Miss Jenney Sweeps, placed to his head the Luger pistol he had brought back from France, and shot himself—in Jenny's room, in the naked presence of Jenny and her new boyfriend, interrupting their romantic exercises.

Zeke was a decorated war hero, but because of his injuries he had to live with his spinster sister and widowed mother. Their devotion to Zeke was their only comfort, and Zeke's death was a crushing blow.

John Hartman had the police beat that night, so he covered the story for the paper. It would have made great copy—but when Zeke's mother showed up at the hospital to see her dead son, John realized that her cherished memory of the war hero was her entire world. He wrote the story without any reference to the whorehouse or Miss Sweeps.

John's boss, the city editor, discovered the lurid details before the paper went to press and ordered him to rewrite the story, citing all the facts, no matter how painful to the family. They argued. John refused to hurt the dead man's mother any further. He was overruled, and the next day the story appeared in the paper with all the tabloid leering of yellow journalism: veteran hero, suicide, lady-of-the-night girlfriend. John's name appeared on the byline.

At his desk in the newsroom that evening, John received a call from Zeke's sister. She said her mother had read the story and had become ill with chest pains; she had to be taken to the hospital, where she died that afternoon. The horror of seeing the details of her son's suicide plastered across the headlines was beyond all bearing.

"How low can you be?" the sister asked.

All John could do was mumble an apology. "I'm not that kind of man."

"Cruel, hateful man. You'll answer to Jesus," she said, and hung up.

Anger and remorse boiled over inside him, and when the other reporters in the newsroom saw John drop the phone and head for the city editor's office, they sensed trouble. John confronted the man in front of the entire newsroom.

"I'm sorry about the old lady, but that lush should have thought about his mother before he took up with the floozy. Killing yourself over a whore. News is news, right!"

The editor's cavalier professionalism was unfortunate: John snatched him out of the chair by his lapels and threw him through the glass partition separating his office from the rest of the newsroom. Then he proceeded to beat the man all over the newsroom until he was stopped by the other reporters—who didn't mind seeing the editor getting thrashed, but who didn't want John to go to jail for killing him. As he delivered his last right cross to the city editor's jaw, John suddenly shouted.

"Is the full story of why I'm beating your ass going to be in the paper tomorrow, Mr. Hazelton? Is it, you rotten son of a bitch?"

The managing editor, Mr. Dicky Walters, got the whole story from the other reporters. Though he was inclined to side with John, he simply couldn't let the incident pass as if nothing happened.

"Damn it, John, you beat the living hell out of the city editor. What's gonna happen next?"

As a compromise, Walters offered to let John resign rather than fire him. To make things easier, he told John that he had a good friend at the *Savannah Morning Gazette* who needed somebody. A few minutes later, Walters was on the phone.

JOHN ARRIVED IN SAVANNAH on a Saturday after driving for the better part of two days in his used canary-yellow 1930 Ford coupe. With money borrowed from his parents, he had purchased the car for $367 just two weeks before the fight with his boss. His desire to pay back his parents on time was one of the reasons he had taken the Savannah job. The other was that he had never seen the town or the ocean before.

It was the first of March, a surprisingly warm day. As he drove his car around the squares looking for a place called the Hotel DeSoto, he noticed many trees sporting new leaves, and azaleas heavy with buds ready to pop open at any moment. John finally found the hotel on the corner of Liberty and Bull streets, and parked his Ford along the sidewalk next to the hotel.

The DeSoto was a grand Victorian villa of three floors constructed of red and yellow brick with a terra-cotta roof. Large rocking-chair verandas curved the length of the Bull and Liberty street sides of the hotel forming great rotundas on two of the hotel's corners. A bas-relief lion's head, which spat a constant stream of water into a pool flashing with plump goldfish, decorated the wall next to where John had parked his car. As John began to climb the stairs, a bellman greeted him. He asked his name as he took his bags.

"I'm John Hartman, just got in from Chattanooga."

"Oh, yes suh, Mr. Hartman, we been expectin' you since this mornin'. Mr. Wilkes at the paper done made a reservation for you last week, and we got you a fine room on the third floor that looks out over Madison Square. You is gonna be just as happy as a hog in a slop wallow with your accommodations at the Hotel DeSoto. How long you plannin' to stay with us Mr. Hartman?"

John glanced at the rocking chairs, the stiff palms, and the potted ferns moving gently to the rhythm of ceiling fans, and smiled. "For a while, I hope. At least until I get a more permanent place to stay. I've taken a job with the *Gazette* as their new political reporter."

"Well I is proud to hear that suh, I sho' is." The bellman walked John through the lobby and saw that he was properly registered.

The desk clerk had assigned him a corner room facing southwest, and as the bellman hung his clothes in the closet and filled the ice bucket, John stood at the windows and looked over the rooftops of his new home. He was immediately struck by the city's elegance and grace.

When the bellman had finished, he stood quietly at attention by the door until John noticed that he was ready to leave. Embarrassed, John reached into his pocket and pulled out a crisp new dollar bill. The bellman smiled broadly, bowed slightly, and said, "Thank you suh, thank you very much. My name is Thaddeus, Thaddeus Price. If you needs any help at all, suh, jes ask for Thaddeus."

"Well, I appreciate your kindness Thaddeus, and I'll keep that in mind," said John as he reached to close the door. Then he stopped and added, "Oh, there is one thing that you might be able to help me with."

"I'll do it if I can, suh."

John smiled, leaned forward, and in a low voice inquired, "Where can a fella get a drink around here?"

Thaddeus smiled also and answered in an equally low voice, "I knows jes what you means, Mr. Hartman. Course we got the Sapphire Room downstairs, but . . . I think you'll find what you wants at a place call Bo Peep's. It's over on the Congress Street lane, jes off Drayton. Lots of the newspaper crowd frequents that establishment in the evenin' time, suh. You can get somethin' to eat there too, if you desires it."

John smiled: Thaddeus had been right about Bo Peep's. It was the daytime place to eat and catch up on everything going on in Savannah, and the nighttime place to drink and relax and find out who was going to make things happen the next day.

Bo Peep's was typical Savannah of the 1930's—characteristically wide open, full throttle. The place was wet when wet was illegal; it had gambling when gambling was proscribed; and some say it even had girls upstairs. All of this took place just across the street from Christ Episcopal Church, where some of Savannah's finest sipped port on Communion Sunday.

During the day it was permissible for a lady to catch a bit of lunch in Peep's, but at night no decent Southern girl would be caught dead there. It was the watering hole and crossroads of the newsmakers and the social climbers, the wanna-bes and those who had already arrived and now enjoyed taking in the local color. Late at night, after the paper had been put to bed, the newspaper crowd showed up, and Bo Peep's took on their special form of cynical, bawdy, but cerebral humor. It was among the newspapermen, at this time and place, that what really was happening in Savannah would be discussed, dissected, digested, and cursed. There was nothing sheepish about Bo Peep's.

John hadn't been in Peep's for more than thirty minutes before somebody from the paper came in asking for him. It was a fellow named Frank Mullane, a reporter. He had been sent by Emory Wilkes, editor of the *Gazette* and friend of Dicky Walters, to meet with John and fill him in on the job. Frank pulled up a chair and introduced himself.

"Wilkes is a decent sort," said Frank, "he wants me to take you under my wing. Sort of show you the town. City Council's meeting Thursday, and the old man wants you to at least know where City Hall is."

Frank laughed, took a sip of his beer, and then continued. "We'll drive around a little tonight, hit some spots, and then tomorrow we'll drive down to the beach. Wilkes has a good friend down there, Colonel Emile Deitz. He knows a lot about Savannah politics. The old man has arranged for the colonel to have a chat with you."

Frank tilted his glass all the way back, drained the last of his beer, and then carefully wiped away the little line of foam that had formed like a slender mustache on his upper lip. "You're a lucky boy, John," said Frank playfully.

"Why's that?"

"Well, the colonel happens to have a very attractive daughter by the name of Beth, and she happens to be friends with the girl I'm dating. So you're gonna get to meet Beth tomorrow."

John smiled and put his napkin in his plate. Then Frank asked, "You finished with your supper?" The answer was obvious and without allowing John time to reply he added, "Come on, let's blow this place. I'll take you out to Remler's Corner. Nothing happens around here till after one."

TYBEE

JOHN AWOKE ON SUNDAY morning with a slight headache. He was surprised it wasn't worse. But then again, Frank had told him that the mason jar full of moonshine they had bought from a black man at Bo Peep's was the best in town and wouldn't give him much of a hangover the next day. "I'll have to remember that," John said to himself as he brushed his teeth. "The Purple A."

As John walked out of the Liberty Street entrance of the DeSoto he took a right, then looked up. Just as Frank had said, he could see the spires of the Cathedral of St. John the Baptist, where they were supposed to meet at noon and then ride to the beach. Frank had invited John to join him at the eleven fifteen Mass, but John had demurred, saying that he wasn't Catholic.

"How could you have an Irish mother and not be a Catholic?" Frank had asked teasingly.

"Her folks were from northern Ireland," John answered succinctly.

The cathedral was radiant in the morning sun, and the church's white façade reflected the sun's warmth back to John, who was standing on Abercorn Street, waiting for the Mass to end. He felt small when he looked up at the two towering spires spearing the cloudless sky. When the cathedral bells struck the noon hour, a rush of startled pigeons swept John off balance for a second. A few minutes later, the great doors to the church opened on to Lafayette Square. Organ music flowed out along with impatient children tugging at their mothers' arms. Elderly ladies wearing flowery hats still clutched their Rosary beads. John could see Frank's tall figure coming through the door behind several girls who looked to be no more than eighteen. He wondered if they attended the Catholic girls' school that he had been told was next to the church. Next to him was an attractive brunette who John assumed to be Agnes Flynn, whom he had heard so much about the night before. It was, and after a brief introduction they all climbed into Frank's Studebaker coupe and headed for Tybee, Savannah Beach.

It was a warm seventy-two degrees. The breeze felt good as it passed through the car's windows. They drove down Abercorn and around the squares, past a Methodist church, brick row houses, and grandiose stuccoed mansions. Live oaks dripped thick gray threads of Spanish moss above azalea bushes heavy with the bright green leaves of early spring, and flower buds everywhere strained to shout out their colors. They turned onto Victory Drive, where hundreds of orderly palmettos whooshed past in the median. Fat azalea bushes spanked the side of the Studebaker where they flowed out into the street between the palmettos.

The motorists glided through the town of Thunderbolt, where the palmettos that had stood at attention in the center plot of Victory Drive finally yielded their space. The four-lane road became two, bore left, then took a right over the marshland at the first of four bridges to be crossed on the road to Tybee. Out over a ribbon of road-way they cruised. Spring made the winter-brown marsh-grass aspire to its unique chartreuse. Islands were covered with oaks and pines so thick that the highway became a tunnel through a temperate-zone jungle. Tree limbs reached to the other side of the road to clasp hands with their partners. Clumps of low-hanging moss brushed the car's windshield.

Deeper into the woods they followed the tar road as it bounced and dipped on its soft underbelly of unstable sand. Then, when it seemed as though it would never end, the dense weald of hardwoods and vines all at once broke forth into a vista of open marsh that spread out before them for miles. They had arrived at the Bull River, where they rattled across its long, narrow bridge, and from there to another stretch of marsh road. John strained to see the end of the highway, but it seemed to stretch limitlessly into the distance, filled on both sides by lean palmettos and bushy oleanders.

Frank looked over at John and grinned broadly as he opened up the throttle. Agnes protested as wind whipped through her long brown hair, but the Studebaker continued to roar down the two-lane blacktop. John felt as if he were tearing through the water in a boat as scores of nameless creeks burst at their sides. Salt water twisted up to the road's edge and then curled out into the distance and over the horizon.

"There's Fort Pulaski," shouted Frank as he pointed to his left at a long, low, rectangular shape with scrub oak growing on its top. John stared at the fort for a moment: the name seemed to ring some distant bell. Then he sucked in a deep breath, filling his nose and lungs with the salty-sulphur sweetness of the marsh air, and stuck his arm out of the window, letting the wind flow over his hand. They rumbled across the Lazaretto Creek Bridge, drove through another mile or so of marsh, and finally arrived at Tybee Island.

* * *

Colonel Deitz enjoyed a large beach house on Tybee's South End, where the Back River meets the ocean. It had been built in 1905, when the only land route to the island was by a train. The house had large screen porches covering three sides of the first two stories.

On the third floor was Colonel Deitz's study, though it was actually more of an adult playroom where the colonel would entertain the many friends who came to visit him when he was staying at the beach. Large windows on all four sides of the room provided a spectacular view of the Atlantic Ocean, the beaches and marshlands, and of Tybee Island itself. The entire room was finished in pecan with exposed ceiling beams. A fireplace made of Stone Mountain granite took up part of the north wall, and an oil painting of the *Battle of Battery Jasper* hung over the mantel. A richly stocked bar filled one end of the room, and a pool table covered in red felt took up the other. A long leather sofa stood in front of the fireplace, complemented by roundly stuffed and inviting leather chairs. Access to the colonel's study was by a spiral staircase. Entry was by invitation from the colonel.

Colonel Deitz's only child, Beth, was sitting on the second-floor porch when Frank's car pulled up in the driveway. John was watching from the street below as she opened the screen door to greet them. A breeze from the ocean pressed the cotton dress against her body, revealing her well-known shapely figure. She had hazel eyes, flawless skin, softly rounded features. When the wind blew a second time, John watched with appreciation as delicate tendrils of dark brown hair blew from Beth's face and back on to her shoulders.

"Beth," said Frank, "I'd like you to meet John Hartman. He's the new political reporter at the paper."

Beth shook John's hand with a firm and confident grip, then gazed into his eyes with an unwavering glance. She smiled.

"Hello, John, I'm Beth. Won't you please come in,

Daddy's been waiting on you. He's up in his study."

The March wind whined through the screens and made them sing a high-pitched song of spring and the coming summer. Beth said she thought it was still a little too cool to be at the beach and pulled her sweater tightly around her. The four spoke briefly with each other, and on Frank's suggestion they decided to ride to the Brass Rail for lunch when the meeting was over. Then Beth showed Frank and John to the spiral staircase, and went back to the porch to visit with Agnes.

"Frank Mullane!" said Emile Deitz in a strong and un-flinching voice. "Damn good to see you again, son. And this must be the heavyweight champion of the world sent down here by the *Chattanooga Times*." The colonel chuckled as he vigorously shook John's hand, then looked over at Frank and winked. John's face turned slightly red, but both he and Frank laughed.

"I guess you heard about my little problem up in Chattanooga," said John.

"Hell yes I heard," bellowed Colonel Deitz in his thick Geechee accent. "Emory Wilkes told me all about it when I saw him at the Oglethorpe Club on Wednesday afternoon. When he asked me if I'd be kind enough to give you my slant on Savannah politics, I told old Emory that you sounded like my kind of guy. I just loved the story about how you beat the living daylights out of that cold-hearted bastard. Emory said the *Times* hated to lose you, but things were just a little too sticky up there after your little fracas. He told me Dicky Walters gave you a good recommendation. Hell, I know old Dicky too. We served together in France."

Colonel Deitz lightly put his arm around John's shoulder and walked him to the sofa in front of the fireplace, where the younger men sat down. The colonel chose to stand by the fireplace, where he rested his arm on the mantle and puffed furiously on a big Cuban cigar, which sent up voluminous clouds of blue smoke among the rafters. John and Frank listened in wonder as the colonel vividly described every prominent Savannah politician in delicious and colorful detail, down to the scent of his aftershave. With ease he carried them through the devilishly tangled maze of Savannah's political intrigues, punctuating his stories with hilarious anecdotes about some of the politicians.

After an hour the colonel stopped suddenly, walked over to the spiral staircase, and shouted for his daughter. While he was waiting, Frank leaned over to John and whispered, "Didn't I tell you this would be unbelievable? Is he a hoot or what?"

"He's fascinating," answered John. "He should write a book about all this stuff or go on stage maybe. The man's grasp of things is outstanding."

So was John's hearing. Even as he spoke he heard Beth's soft voice wafting up from below.

"Yes, Daddy?"

"Honey, I want you to take my car and go on down to the Brass Rail and bring us all some fried chicken dinners. These boys look hungry to me." Then the colonel looked over at John and Frank and asked, "Ya'll haven't had any lunch have you?"

The two shook there heads and simultaneously answered, "No, sir."

Beth looked pleadingly up at her father. "Daddy, we were all going to eat down there when ya'll finished talking."

"Beth, shugga', we got a lot of territory to cover up here, and I can tell that these two young men are gettin' hungry. Now run along and do like Daddy says. We'll all have time for visitin' when you get back with the chicken. I'm not gonna let Mr. Hartman leave here before he pays you proper attention, so don't worry none."

"Daddy, hush," said Beth through clenched teeth, and with a reddened face. A few moments later she left with Agnes for the Brass Rail.

The colonel chuckled, went over to the bar, and, without asking, poured two drinks of Chivas Regal and handed them to John and Frank. "You look like scotch drinkers to me," was all he said before he stood again at the fireplace and continued talking.

"Now, John, there's one thing that you need to remember about JJ O'Boyle." The colonel left his perch at the mantlepiece and settled into one of the armchairs. "Poor JJ has a severe inferiority complex. Most Irishmen do, especially him. He knows that his dockworkin', bootleggin' days will never allow him to be accepted by the bluebloods like some other Irishmen are. It eats at poor JJ 'cause it's the only thing he can't seem to buy. So he's put all his hopes on his oldest son, Tony, to bring some dignity to the O'Boyles. Tony's a smart boy, but he's bitten by the same bug of ambition. Nothing wrong with that, but I'd keep an eye on Tony. He'll be a rising star in politics after he finishes law school and comes back home."

"Tony's a bit full of himself," said Frank. The colonel nodded his head in agreement.

"Just remember that JJ O'Boyle calls the shots on most things around here, but there're folks who can tell him where to get off, too."

The sound of a car outside prompted the colonel to stand and say, "That must be my daughter with our lunch. Let's go on downstairs and spend some time with those lovely girls." He lightly patted Frank on the back as the three of them walked down the long spiral staircase, and all the way into the dining room John peppered the colonel with questions. It was obvious to Frank that Colonel Deitz had found an admirer in John Hartman, and John Hartman had found a confidant in Colonel Deitz.

The breeze from the ocean had fallen off by the time lunch was finished, and the afternoon sun now warmed the air. Beth turned to John. "Let's take a little stroll, OK? Maybe go up to the Tybrisa Pavilion for a snow cone. What do you say?" The tide was out, the beach wide and beautiful. It wasn't too far into their walk before John and

Beth lagged behind Frank and Agnes, giving them a chance to talk alone.

John was strongly attracted to Beth, but not only because she was pretty. Beth obviously had class. Her voice was gentle, her movements elegant, and she had all the virtues of good breeding without any selfish or haughty airs. John was cautious as he spoke.

Beth had forgotten that the summer season didn't start until May and the Tybrisa had not yet opened; and because there weren't many people at Tybee during March, the two couples had the beach entirely to themselves. John and Beth spoke about their families and tastes. John was surprised to find that Beth was attracted to the French Impressionists just as he was; and she was surprised to discover that John had a particular fondness for the works of Kipling, just as she did. They found further common ground in discussing Roosevelt, Prohibition, jazz, and the movies; but they differed when it came to beauty. She thought Katharine Hepburn was the most beautiful actress of the day; he inclined to Bette Davis. When they finally returned to the house, everyone was a bit sunburned, but Beth and John had learned a great deal about each other. John had even gained the confidence to ask Beth out for the next weekend. She accepted, and they made plans with Frank and Agnes to double-date.

Colonel Deitz came downstairs before John left and asked him if he had any plans for the seventeenth. John looked puzzled, but said that he didn't. Beth realized he didn't understand the significance of the date and explained.

"March the seventeenth is St. Patrick's Day. It's a big day in Savannah. We have a parade and parties the night before. It's really a lot of fun. It falls on a weekend this year. Will you be working?"

"I don't know. I guess."

"The reason I asked," said the colonel, "was that I wanted you to be my guest at the Hibernian Banquet that night. Do you own a tux?"

"No, sir."

"Well, if you want to go, make arrangements to get one. It's a black-tie affair."

"You'll have a great time," said Frank. "I'll get us all seated at the same table."

"I'd love to go, Colonel Deitz," said John. "Thank you very much."

The colonel took a puff of his cigar, exhaled the smoke, and replied, "You're a fine young man, John. It'll be a pleasure to have you as my guest. Well, good-bye." He started to go back to his study, but stopped halfway up the stairs. "Oh by the way, John, you're welcome to come down anytime. Most of the time we're at our home on Isle of Hope. Feel free to visit us there, too. Beth'll tell you how to get there. Oh, one other thing."

"Yes, sir?" said John as he looked up at the colonel through the railings on the stairs.

"You have my permission to come calling on my daughter."

John looked at Beth and smiled as he answered, "Thank you, Colonel. Thank you very much."

THE HIBERNIAN SOCIETY BANQUET

THE HIBERNIAN Society Banquet was traditionally held in the Grand Ballroom of the Hotel DeSoto on the evening of the seventeenth and was always the grand finale of St. Patrick's Day in Savannah. Everybody who was anybody was at the banquet, and invitations to it were highly sought after, particularly by the aspiring young politicians, both local and statewide. Every politician in the state, from the governor and United States senators on down to the commissioner of highways and the mayors of crossroads towns around the county, made an annual effort to attend. Presence at the Hibernian Society Banquet by a Protestant politician (and most were, in Georgia, at the time) meant that he cared about the Catholic vote.

Absence for anything other than a sick child or a national emergency was often construed as an insult—and vengeance would be taken in the voting booth.

It was at the Hibernian Society Banquet that John had his first meeting with JJ O'Boyle and his son Tony.

"JJ," said Colonel Deitz, "I'd like you to make the acquaintance of Mr. John Hartman. John is the new political writer for the *Gazette*."

JJ stuck his hand out and pumped John's arm vigorously, saying how pleased he was to meet him and that he had heard there was a new man at the paper. JJ's manners were charming and his personality engaging, and John instantly understood why he had been so successful in both politics and bootlegging. After telling John to "come on by sometime and we'll have a talk," JJ glanced around the room. When he spotted Tony, he motioned him over.

"Son, this is the new political man at the paper, Mr. John Hartman, formerly of Chattanooga. John, this is my oldest boy Tony, who'll be finishing up at Georgia soon."

The two shook hands and eyed each other curiously. John noted Tony's dark hair and eyes, his thin, well-formed nose, his strong chin and high cheek bones. His looks were almost patrician, and as John studied Tony's father again, searching for any resemblance, he decided the son must take after his mother.

John's work gave him the opportunity to rub shoulders with all sorts of people. He had known American aristocrats in three of the South's largest cities and could spot their subtlest mannerisms in an instant: the bored manner in which they looked away after meeting someone, the pursed lips and upturned eyebrows, the flippant remarks about money, the sumptuously tailored clothes. Tony had it all, and John was prompted to remember what Colonel Deitz had said about him down at the beach house.

For some the evening didn't end with the banquet. There were always several parties afterward to which a select few would be invited. At these gatherings political alliances were often formed and consummated, and an invitation could mean the opportunity to be a part of the influential inner circle of high rollers that dictated state and local affairs. For somebody like John Hartman, an invitation to such an affair would be an opportunity to see politics in the making.

The banquet usually ended around ten o'clock, and at about nine-thirty Colonel Deitz leaned over to John and whispered in his ear. "I'm having a few friends over to my place at Isle of Hope for some after-dinner drinks. I'd be pleased to have you and Frank Mullane join us, if you'd like."

John had heard about the gatherings at the colonel's house from Frank. "The governor always shows up. Wouldn't miss it for the world. He leaves with thousands in donations, all cash. A lot of big movers and shakers there."

"Thank you, Colonel. I'd be most pleased, and I'm sure Frank will too."

ROAD TO ISLE OF HOPE

THE ROAD TO Isle of Hope was part of the old Vanderbilt Cup racetrack of 1910 and 1911. LaRoche Avenue began at Skidaway Road, an intersection known locally as "Dead Man's Curve" because of the number of both legal and illegal racers who over the years had failed to negotiate the high-speed bend and thrown themselves and their machines into the broad trunks of the numerous oak trees lining the road.

A straightaway of almost two miles was flanked by large trees and dense woods. This gave way abruptly to circuitous twists and turns following the marsh until the road reached the creek separating the mainland from Isle of Hope. Another quick quarter of a mile across the marsh on a causeway and the deep forest of Isle of Hope had been penetrated. The road narrowed where bright lantanas and clovers, soft camellias and wild roses drifted randomly out of the woods. The ride through Isle of Hope was like a trip into the lavish canvas of a nineteenth-century Romantic water-colorist. The sweet smell of honeysuckle and the wisteria curling high into the pines made a mystery of moonlight shadows, speaking whispery things not quite of this world.

The slow moon came up on the silvering marsh side of La-Roche. A few minutes before reaching the colonel's house, John asked Frank about Beth Deitz's family.

"I heard Colonel Deitz's grandfather was some kind of a hero in the Civil War. Is that why he has that picture hanging over his fireplace at the beach?"

"Yep, he's related through his mother's side to a fellow named Patrick Driscoll, a captain in the Confederate Army who got killed in the battle of Battery Jasper. The colonel's mother was the daughter of Patrick Driscoll. Her mother was pregnant with her when the captain was killed. Colonel Deitz was the commander of that same unit over in France."

"No kidding."

"That's not all. On his father's side, his grandfather was part of the Confederate force that captured Fort Pulaski right after Georgia seceded from the Union."

"Are you putting me on?"

"Not at all," said Frank as he flicked his cigarette out the window and guided the Studebaker around the last curve before the bridge at Herb Creek. "Your friend Beth has quite a family tree. And there's more."

"There's more?"

"Yep. Beth went to the Catholic girls' school here, St. Vincent's Academy. It was founded before the Civil War by the Sisters of Mercy. When the South lost the war, Jefferson Davis was held as a prisoner out at Fort Pulaski for a while. His wife and two daughters came to Savannah to be near him, but they didn't have a thing to live on. St. Vincent's had a boarding school then, and the nuns took Jefferson Davis' daughters into the convent and took care of them. Taught them for nothing. Ol' President Davis and his whole family got to be real close to the sisters and never forgot them for what they did. Guess whose great aunt just happened to be the Mother Superior who was responsible for taking the Davis girls in?"

"No!"

"Oh, yes, and hold on to your seat!"

"Good Lord, there's more!" John was laughing by now.

"Much more. That family also has a buried treasure somewhere and a ghost that guards it."

"What do you mean?"

Frank snorted in jest. "Story is that Captain Driscoll buried a fortune in gold and jewelry out on that island where he died. Legend says he buried everything the Driscolls had on the island to keep the Yankees from stealing it when they captured Savannah. He and his colored servant, a slave named Shadrack, are supposed to be the only two who knew where the money was buried. Before they could get word back to the family in Savannah, they both got killed by Yankee cannon fire. After the war a few people dug holes all over that island, looking for it, but they never found a trace."

"That's absolutely fantastic!" said John excitedly. "Do you think there really is a treasure out on that island?"

"I don't know; probably not. People stopped looking over there years ago. Now the island's grown up like a jungle, and it's real hard to get to because of the tides. When we were kids they used to tell ghost stories about the Driscoll treasure. People said the ghosts of Captain Driscoll and his slave Shadrack protect the treasure, that's why it's never been found. Even now a hunter goes over there every once in a while and comes back swearing he's seen something spooky or strange. I got a cousin that went huntin' wild boar over on Raccoon Island and came back tellin' some story about hearin' strange noises coming out of the woods behind the fort during the night. He said he was so scared, he would'a got in his boat and left right then and there, but the tide was out and he had to stay."

"Do you think he's telling the truth?"

"I think he got the hell scared out of him all right. He's never been back to Raccoon Island again, that's for sure. But a ghost? I think it's more likely my cousin Jack got scared off Raccoon Island by some moonshiner protecting his still than by the ghost of Captain Driscoll protecting his money."

Frank and John laughed as they drew near Beth's house.

Driscoll House had changed little since its construction in 1852. It was still Bluff Drive's reigning queen, a delight of Southern Greek Revival in the finest tradition. It had managed to stay in the Driscoll family from the beginning, but Beth was the colonel's only heir. He had never said anything to her, but he was anxious for Beth to find a suitable young man to insure that Driscoll House would remain in the family after her generation.

Governor Russell, two United States congressmen, and Gene Talmadge were among the fifty or so men who stood about the formal parlor and dining rooms and spilled out on to the veranda. One of the congressmen drank some of Colonel Deitz's twelve-year-old scotch as he nibbled on the toasted pecans Beth brought by on a serving tray.

"Lovely home you have here, Colonel, simply lovely, and your daughter is truly a delight. I'll bet she has every young man within a hundred miles of Savannah knockin' on your front door." The congressman laughed and slapped the colonel on the back and then whispered into his ear, "I'm countin' on your support this time around, Emile. Is there somewhere we can talk privately?"

That same request would be made a dozen times that night, and Emile Deitz would always nod his head and say, "Yes, let's go into my private study; there shouldn't be anybody in there." The colonel would lead his suitors into a mahogany-panelled room that looked out over the

Skidaway River. By the fireplace, he and his guest would parley and deal as the colonel warméd his hands over the fire. An oil portrait of Captain Patrick Driscoll watched from above and held their secrets.

On John's arrival, Beth took his arm and introduced him to all the guests she knew. Her touch—the way she brushed her body against his while they chatted with the colonel's friends—excited John: he could barely concentrate on the conversations. John had been out with Beth three times since he had met her, and he was now infatuated. He knew that she liked him well enough, but he felt daunted by her wealth and his poverty. He had tried to control his feelings, but such a thing would be difficult for anyone, more difficult still for the young. That St. Patrick's Day evening, amid a swirl of Savannah's most powerful and monied, John Morgan Hartman started quietly to surrender, to slip sweetly and wonderfully away with Beth Deitz and her beauty, Beth Deitz and her charms, Beth Deitz and the dreams that she could weave for him.

EIGHT-MINUTE RACE

AFTER INTRODUCING John to two bishops—the bishop of Savannah and the bishop of Charleston—Beth said she thought they needed a breather. Slowly they worked their way out to the front porch.

It was slightly past midnight and guests were beginning to leave. Colonel Deitz, the governor, and several of the governor's aides were gathered under Patrick Driscoll's portrait discussing the upcoming election. A few men were on the front porch talking, smoking some of the colonel's excellent cigars. Seeking privacy, John and Beth found a quiet corner.

Over Beth's shoulder John could see Tony O'Boyle at the other end of the porch, speaking with a handsome, athletic young man about the same age. Both seemed to be feeling the effects of what was politely called "too much St. Patrick's Day," but John noticed that even with too much to drink, Tony and his friend maintained a certain air about them. They still looked resplendent in their sleek custom-tailored tuxedos, and not a hair was out of place on either man. Little Valentinos. Tony stood with one hand on the bannister; the other swept back his unbuttoned coat and was planted firmly on his silken cummerbund. It was a rakish pose, full of the confidence and arrogance that children of wealth can flaunt. Tony's friend was a painfully good-looking blond, blued-eyed heir to a fortune.

"Who's that with Tony O'Boyle?" asked John as he nodded in Tony's direction.

"Oh, that's Tony's best buddy, Thatcher Armstrong. He and Tony room together at Georgia."

"Is he studying law too?"

Beth rolled her eyes and said, "Good Lord no! Thatch doesn't do much but play at Georgia. He's been a senior for three years."

"A senior for three years? How can he afford it? His folks must have money or something."

"Goodness, they're almost Rockefellers." Beth lowered her voice, moved in closer to John, and continued. "Poor Thatch is a sweet boy, but it's lucky for him that he comes from money, because Thatch is lazy. All he wants to do is party and hunt birds off campus, and party and hunt coeds on campus. I don't see how he's managed to stay at Georgia. But overall, Thatch is harmless."

"What about Tony O'Boyle?" John watched as Tony made a certain gesture and Thatch broke out in laughter. "What kind of a guy is he?"

"Oh my Lord, just the opposite. Smart, ambitious, aggressive. The best thing that ever happened to Thatch Armstrong is rooming with Tony. He's the only reason Thatch has managed to pass a class at Georgia. Tony knows just about everybody up there and has arranged, shall we say, for Thatch to get the best coaching available before every test. Somehow, the people who coach Thatch just happen to always include in their lessons the material that pops up on his tests."

"Isn't that a resourceful friend to have?" said John sarcastically.

"I should say it is. Tony has helped Thatch a lot."

"But what about Tony, what does he get out of it? He doesn't strike me as someone who does favors like that for nothing."

"Well, I guess you have to know Tony O'Boyle and the kind of things he likes. Thatch comes from high-society folks, the kind of people Tony O'Boyle is not. Thatch is Tony's entrée into that world. He and Thatch are almost inseparable. When Thatch goes off to visit his rich aunt in New York or his rich uncle or whatever at Hyannisport, Tony is right there with him, rubbing elbows and trading stories with people who wouldn't give him the time of day otherwise."

"So it's mostly a symbiotic relationship."

"No, not really. I think maybe Tony uses Thatch a lot, but doesn't really and truly care about him. But Thatch absolutely worships Tony. Thatch looks on him like a big brother and just loves Tony to death. One time Tony got real sick up at school and had to be put in the hospital. People said Thatch was worried to death about Tony and paid a specialist a whole bunch of money to drive all the way from Atlanta to Athens just to look at Tony."

"Interesting," said John as he glanced over at the two young bloods one last time, then returned his full attention to Beth.

"You look like you might be getting a little cold, Beth. Would you like to go back inside?"

"Now that you mention it, I am a little chilly." Beth took John's arm and they walked back inside. Outside, another conversation continued.

"I think it can be done in under eight minutes."

"Bullshit, there's no way. Nothing under fifteen. Maybe ten at the absolute best."

"Ha! I've seen it done in eight minutes."

"Aw, come on. You know that's bullshit. Not in eight minutes."

"You wanna bet?"

"Yeah, I wanna bet. How's a hundred sound to you?"

"You're on."

Tony and Thatch shook on their bet and walked down the steps of Driscoll House toward the magnificent machine parked along the river road. The deep luster of its paint shined in the moonlight like the pelt of a black panther waiting for its prey. Its fenders rolled up over the wheels in muscular lines that gave the appearance of the legs and paws of a great cat drawn up and ready to spring. The front end was both elegant and powerful. The distinguished grill gave way to massive chromed exhaust headers that snaked through the sides of the engine cowling. Twelve large cylinders provided the horsepower to travel at frightening speeds in elegant and obscene luxury. Even the name of Mr. Packard's machine, the Dual Cowled Phaeton, suggested some awesome monster from Greek mythology. Phaëthon, indeed, was a son of the Greek god Helios, who drove his father's sun-chariot wildly through the sky until he lost control and was struck down by a thunderbolt from Zeus as punishment.

THE MAGNIFICENT
DUAL COWL PHAETON

THE BIG Packard was long and low, black and beautiful. It was a four-door convertible with wire wheels and a spare tire mounted in each front fender. The back seat had its own separate windscreen, with small vent windows on the sides to control the airflow. The car was one of the fastest and finest handling machines of the day. Because of these qualities, it had become a favorite among bootleggers, who depended on fast cars for their livelihood.

Thatch was his mother's beautiful baby boy, and she delighted in spoiling him at every opportunity. The Packard was a Christmas present from her.

Although the car belonged to Thatch, Tony had long ago learned that he could regard just about anything of Thatch's as his property too. This went from Thatch's high-society friends in Atlanta to his aristocratic relatives in Boston and New York; and certainly—most certainly—included Thatch's new Packard. But Thatch didn't mind, he didn't mind a bit. Tony was his best friend, and Tony would do anything for him, anything in the world. Why hell, Tony was the wildest, craziest, smartest, most fun guy that Thatch had ever known.

"I'll drive Thatch. Give me the keys."

"Good Lord no, O'Boyle, you're half drunk. You might wreck my momma's Christmas present, and she'd have a conniption fit."

"Half drunk? Well, you're *all* drunk. I'm only a little tight." With that, Thatch and Tony started laughing at their own jokes as only drunks can. Then Thatch reached into his pocket, pulled out the keys, and slapped them into Tony's hand.

"If you wreck my car, I'll kill you, you crazy Irish bastard." They both laughed uproariously again, then drained what remained of Colonel Deitz's best scotch whiskey. With great flair they flung the glasses into the marsh and climbed into the Packard.

"I threw my glass further than you did!" said Thatch with a childlike glee.

"You did not," shot back Tony. "I saw where it hit, and mine was a lot further out in the marsh than yours."

"Was not," insisted Thatch.

"Was too," replied Tony in a determined voice. Then he put the key into the ignition, pressed the starter, and brought the great V-12 to life with a satisfying rumble from the exhausts. Thatch let out a shout of delight as Tony sat in the driver's seat and gunned the motor. Its deep-throated roar caused Colonel Deitz to look out the window of his study.

Colonel Deitz and JJ O'Boyle were in the study discussing politics when they heard the caressing sound. JJ had decided that it would be advantageous to be the last person to speak with Colonel Deitz. That way he could pick the colonel's brain a little and perhaps find out where the governor stood on certain local issues. Colonel Deitz was well aware of JJ's intentions. Just for the fun of it he was about to lead JJ up a blind political alley with a bogus story, when Tony gunned the engine again and the colonel looked out the window to see what all the fuss was about.

"That sounds like Thatcher Armstrong in his Packard," said JJ. "He and Tony must be leaving for town."

"Looks like your boy might be the one kicking up all the racket out there."

"What do you mean, Emile?"

Just at that moment the car pulled away from the house and sped down Bluff Drive in the direction of LaRoche Avenue. The colonel returned to his place in front of the fire and shook his head.

"Oh, nothing, JJ. I thought I saw Tony driving, that's all. Hell, they're young. Folks are entitled to be a little loud when they're young, don't you think, JJ?"

"Loud as hell, Emile." They both chuckled a little and resumed their conversation, and the colonel spun a yarn that he knew would have JJ upset for a week. Thatcher Armstrong's parents lived in a large neoclassical mansion on Victory Drive, near Habersham Street, just about a five-mile ride from Driscoll House on the Isle of Hope. On a nice day with light traffic, and averaging about thirty miles an hour, the trip would usually take anywhere from ten to fifteen minutes.

Tony had bet Thatch that he could make it from Colonel Deitz's house to Thatch's house in under eight minutes, and he thought he had excellent reason. First of all, there was little if any traffic on those roads at that time of night. Second, most of the route was part of the old racetrack and lent itself to fast driving. Third, Thatch's Packard was one machine that Tony knew was up to the challenge.

As Tony tore away from Driscoll House, Thatch looked at the clock on the dashboard and shouted above the noise of the engine, "It's one-oh-three right now. You've got to be at my house by one-eleven sharp or you owe me a hundred dollars."

"Have your money ready, Thatch," Tony shouted back as he wheeled the Packard onto LaRoche and accelerated at ripping speed through all three gears. He was hitting eighty-five before he braked for the curve and the bridge at Herb River Creek. As if it didn't even exist, Tony shot over the bridge and pressed full throttle over the causeway linking the Isle of Hope with the mainland. He expertly braked for that first tight curve before Norwood Avenue, and rocks and oyster shells went flying in all directions.

Thatch hollered in delight as Tony cut the wheel sharply to the right and whipped the tail of the car around, and both boys were slammed back into their seats as Tony accelerated again through a brief section of straight road. The brakes were uncomplaining as Tony rode them hard through a torturous series of tight curves that made up all the rest of LaRoche Avenue until it got to Bonna Bella. There the road straightened again for more than two miles until Dead Man's Curve.

When they hit the straightaway, Thatch pointed at the clock and cackled. "No way, sonny boy! No way."

Tony desperately wanted to win the bet, but he had lost a lot of time working the car through so many twists and turns in the dark. The clock said one-oh-eight, and Tony quickly turned the numbers over in his head. The way he figured it, he'd have to run the Packard up past a hundred-and-ten to make up for lost time. In that car it would be easy, so he just laid into the gas pedal.

The Packard had two headlights shaped like large chrome top hats sitting on either side of the grill. Four more smaller lights were arranged along the front bumper.

All of these together lit up the entire road, cutting a path of light all the way down LaRoche, almost to Dead Man's Curve.

At a hundred the big car felt firm and steady in Tony's hands. Although the road was paved with oyster shells, it was smooth and in good shape, and the glaring lights of the Packard gave Tony even greater confidence. Without hesitation he pushed the car past a hundred. Thatch was huddled below the windshield, the jacket of his tux pulled up around his neck to ward off the cold. He leaned over and looked at the speedometer and screamed in delight, "A hundred and ten miles an hour, I don't believe this car!"

Tony was almost hypnotized by the thrill of the speed and roar of the engine. Trees zoomed by so fast they were just a blur of whooshing sounds as they tore in and out of view. Now, however, Tony realized that he needed to begin his deceleration, slowing for the bend to the right at Dead Man's Curve. He let his foot off the accelerator and watched the speed drop to ninety, then eighty. The clock read one-oh-eight. "Shit," he yelled, "I've only got three minutes left!" Thatch looked over and laughed triumphantly. Tony hunkered down behind the steering wheel, glared at the road ahead, and let his better judgment become a casualty of his pride.

Tony knew he could take the curve going sixty: he had done it plenty of times before, no sweat. He thought for sure that he could take it even faster in a car like this, but he had never tried. When he saw the needle on the speedometer hit seventy, he decided that the big Packard and his driving skills would be up to the challenge of Dead Man's Curve. Thatch barked out another taunt, so Tony held his foot steady on the gas and laid off the brake.

It seemed as if everything was fine through the first half of Dead Man's Curve. It always does. Tony let the car go into a mild slide and was able to keep the front wheels pointed in the right direction; but just as the *Titanic*'s fate had been sealed by the iceberg it was unable, with all its speed, to avoid hitting, so had Tony's fate been sealed by the laws of inertia at a point he now had passed. At about three hundred feet and nine-tenths of a second after that Titanic Packard reached its geometric iceberg, it began to take on the waters of lateral-force pressures and started a list to the left.

For a very brief moment. Tony thought he could correct the oversteer by cutting the wheel more sharply to the left. Then he felt the sickening pull of the car's rear end, and he knew instantly that they were in a serious spin. Tony heard his friend cry out, "We're gonna crash, oh Jesus save me!" and saw Thatch's petrified face, eyes gaping with horror, flash by somewhere in a blur. He even had a brief feeling of revulsion for Thatch as he heard him whimper like a baby. Then, as the car started to slow, Tony thought that they just might make it by spinning out and not hitting anything.

The car was spinning slowly now, going at about twenty miles an hour in a straight line when Tony began to feel confident that he could get out of this one without a scratch. Then, from out of nowhere, a thick stone of oak tree loomed directly in the Parkard's path. The timing of the spin was perfect for a front-end collision, and before Tony could say "Saint Patrick's Day," Thatcher Armstrong's magnificent Dual Cowl Phaeton ran headfirst into six tons of solid oak.

MOVING THE BODY

THE CAR WAS HEAVY and well constructed, so it wasn't seriously damaged. The bumper and all four head lamps were crushed into the chrome grill. Both of the fender head lamps were bent inward and made the car look like a cross-eyed child. The fenders were crumpled like paper in the front, and steam poured as if from a vision of hell.

Injuries were not so minor on the inside of the car. Tony had managed to hold on to the steering wheel and absorb some of the collision-force with his arms, but he had smashed his face against the steering wheel's hub. His nose was flattened, broken; his lips were deeply cut, and four of his front teeth were knocked out. Although he was severely dazed, Tony did not lose consciousness.

Thatch wasn't as fortunate. He had flown face-first into the dashboard, unable to raise up his arms or soften the blow. His right eye had been instantly gouged out by a sharp knob on the glove box, and other knobs had torn his face everywhere, in some places right to the bone.

When Thatch's head hit the dash, the abrupt force of the impact hyperextended his neck, pushing his head back as far as the bones in his neck could take and then a little more—just enough to break several cervical vertebrae and sever his spinal cord. Thatcher Ramsey Armstrong, IV, was dead before the dust from the crash had settled around his beautiful Packard Phaeton.

One o'clock on Sunday morning was a lonesome time in Savannah at Dead Man's Curve, which was really the edge of town back then and consisted partly of farmland. For Tony O'Boyle it was a stroke of luck in a very unlucky situation.

Tony found the white silk scarf that Thatch liked to wear with his tux and pressed it against his mouth and nose to stop the bleeding. When he had finally regained his senses sufficiently, he looked over at his friend, who lay crumpled on the floor with his head between his knees. When Tony pulled him back into the seat, he was horrified at the way Thatch's head flopped lifelessly to the side. Tony screamed at the patchwork of cuts and at the right eye protruding from the socket.

"Jesus Christ, I think he's dead!"

Tony hadn't moved out of the driver's seat, and he was still trying to hold Thatch upright and think when he saw the lights of a car coming up LaRoche Avenue.

"Shit! Oh holy shit!" Tony repeated again and again as the realization sank in that he had been driving drunk, and that someone had died. In Georgia that was a serious crime. Some people even called it murder. As the headlights from the approaching car grew brighter, Tony's mind raced and his nerves hardened. He opened the driver's-side door and tumbled out of the car. Then he reached across the front seat and began to pull Thatch's body behind the steering wheel.

The other car was getting closer now, and Tony struggled furiously with Thatch to get him into position. Blood was pouring out of Tony's nose and mouth and dripping steadily onto his tuxedo shirt; he even began to choke eventually as he wrestled with Thatch's body. Finally, he started coughing and as he did so he saw two of his teeth fly out of his mouth, hit against Thatch's left shoulder, and fall to the running board of the car. Grimly he continued, though the other car was almost there.

"Frank, I think that car up there has hit a tree!"

Frank Mullane peered closely through the windshield. "Son of a bitch, John. You're right!"

John could make out a man on the driver's side of the car pulling on something or somebody in the front seat. Soon they recognized both the Packard and Tony O'Boyle tugging at what looked like Thatch Armstrong. By the time Frank had finally braked, Tony had stopped struggling with Thatch's body. He had managed to position his friend's hips behind the steering wheel, but Thatch's upper body remained slumped against the passenger's side. Tony hoped that no one would notice.

"Oh Jesus, God! Ya'll help me get Thatch out. He's hurt bad."

Frank and John didn't ask any questions as they gently lifted Thatch out of his car and laid him on the grass. Tony started to cry as he crumpled up next to Thatch.

"I begged him to slow down," sobbed Tony. "I begged him, but he just wouldn't listen. Is he gonna be all right?"

The other two men merely stared at each other and said nothing.

* * *

Frank drove up the road to a house that had the porch light on. He made only one call.

"Colonel Deitz, this is Frank Mullane. I need to speak with JJ O'Boyle right away."

Frank told JJ what had happened, and after JJ had found out that Tony was not seriously injured, he asked about Thatch. Then he asked who was driving.

"Tony said Thatch was driving, but it didn't exactly look that way. We thought he was trying to put the body behind the wheel as we pulled up."

"You keep your goddamned mouth shut, Mullane. You didn't see anything like that at all. If I hear you saying stuff like that about my boy, I'll crush you like a goddamn mosquito. Do you understand me?"

"Yes, sir. I was only tellin' ya what I thought I saw. I could be wrong. Dead wrong, Mr. O'Boyle."

"Well, you *are* wrong. Now you go back down there and help my boy out. I've always been kind to folks that helped out the O'Boyles, you know that."

"Yes, sir."

"Good. Now then, Colonel Deitz and I are leavin' in a second. It isn't necessary for you to call the police. I'll handle all that myself. You go on and call the ambulance for the Armstrong boy, but it doesn't sound like he's gonna much be needin' it if I understand you correctly, son."

"No sir, Hartman and I looked at him real close and he wasn't breathin', JJ—I mean Mr. O'Boyle. I think his neck got broken."

"That's a terrible thing, son. Now you run on back down there and help Tony all you can. The colonel and I will be there in a few minutes."

"Yes, sir."

"Chatham County Police Barracks, Sergeant Conner speakin'."

"Jimmy, this is JJ O'Boyle here."

"Yes, sir, Mr. O'Boyle, anything wrong?"

"Unfortunately there is, son. There's been a terrible accident out at Dead Man's Curve. Thatch Armstrong has hit a tree and killed himself. My boy Tony was ridin' with him and he's been hurt, but he's gonna be alright. We need a car out there right away. Who's workin' this side tonight?"

"That'd be Myrick, Mr. O'Boyle."

"Good boy, I went to school with his daddy. Well, send him on out."

JJ and the colonel arrived at the wreck a little before the ambulance and went immediately to Tony. JJ was shaking as he pulled his son's hands down from his face. There were tears in his eyes as he wiped the blood from Tony's mouth and looked closely at his wounds. Then he hugged his son tightly for more than a minute as he kept softly repeating "My boy, my boy."

While JJ knelt on the ground with his son, Colonel Deitz called John and Frank aside.

"Who was driving, John?"

"Colonel, I swear it looked like Tony was trying to pull Thatch behind the steering wheel."

"You say the same thing, Frank?"

"Uh, Colonel, I uh . . ."

"This ain't goin' no damn further than me, son. Just tell me the truth."

"There's a good chance that what John says is true, but I'm not a hundred and ten percent sure, Colonel. Tony says he wasn't drivin', though."

"I'll take that as a definite yes."

A shrill siren keened in the distance. JJ got up and walked over to John and Frank. His tux front glistened with his son's blood in the glare of the head lights.

"What did you see, Mr. Hartman?"

"I saw your son pulling Thatcher Armstrong behind the wheel to make it look like he was driving."

"I think you're terribly mistaken, Mr. Hartman. Don't you, Frank?"

Frank looked at the ground and mumbled. "John, come on."

JJ, still looking directly at John, said, "I'll take that to mean that you think Thatch was driving, Frank." Frank said nothing and only continued to look at the ground. "Have you changed your mind Mr. Hartman?"

John stared right back at JJ and said, "No, I haven't changed my mind, Mr. O'Boyle. Not in the least."

JJ became very angry. "You couldn't see shit from where you were in your car. You're makin' all this up. You're a smart-ass little snot who can't see straight." Before O'Boyle could go any further, the colonel stepped in.

"Now wait a minute, JJ," he began, but then John raised both hands in front of his chest and interrupted.

"Mr. O'Boyle, let's get something straight right here and now. I know who you are and what's going on here. I also know that discretion must often be the better part of valor. But don't take me for a complete fool, Mr. O'Boyle. Tony was driving that car. All you have to do is look at the cuts on Thatch's face and the blood on the dash. His injuries match perfectly with those bloody knobs on the dash. Tony's match perfectly with the hub of the steering wheel. I have no intention of saying that Tony was driving the car, but I can assure you that I can and have seen *shit* from where I was tonight. I saw a lot of shit, a whole lot of shit."

The red flashing light of the ambulance emerged eerily down Skidaway Road, and the siren seemed too loud. Finally the colonel took command of the situation.

"Alright, alright now. Let's all calm down. You've got what you want here, JJ, there's not going to be any problem. Now go on back over there to your boy. I'll tend to these two fellas."

Before he turned away, JJ glared at John and said in a low, menacing voice, "Nobody fucks with JJ O'Boyle in the Free State of Chatham, mister." John just stood stone like, and watched as JJ returned to his son's side.

Colonel Deitz put his arm around John's shoulder and walked him toward his car. "JJ's all worked up about his son, John. He doesn't mean all that. Just let it go by."

John stopped before they got to his car. "Colonel, if you'll pardon my French, that was just plain shitty."

"I know, I know," the colonel said soothingly, "but don't let it get next to you. Play along with the pompous bastard. He can make a lot of trouble for you. Damn it, John, you haven't been here two weeks yet and you've gotten yourself into a crack. You're a nice boy, and Beth's taken a shine to you. Don't go gettin' all worked up and get in trouble."

"She has?"

"Oh, hell! I'm in trouble now. She hasn't said anything to me, but she might have mentioned your name a time or two at the dinner table that's all."

As the ambulance pulled up and its siren began to wind down through a series of low growls, the building pitch of the county police car's siren could be heard coming from LaRoche Avenue.

"Come on, boys," said Colonel Deitz, "let's go give'm a hand."

III

THE VICTORY DRIVE SLASHER

But little time had they to pray
For whom the hangman's rope was spun

MRS. BRYAN, MRS. HARTMAN,
AND MRS. O'BOYLE

WHILE THE DEPRESSION years gave way to the New Deal and America watched as the European pie was slowly nibbled away by a charismatic Austrian, Savannah danced a slow waltz with time. She inhaled and exhaled with the tide in a pace of life that was restful and restrained, comfortable and reassuring. Life in Savannah during the thirties did not hum; it sighed and moaned in the sultry voice of the beautiful seductress.

When Prohibition was repealed, most moonshiners were forced out of business. People didn't need them any longer to acquire liquor. One day the moonshiners simply walked away from their stills and never came back. This, however, was not the case with Abe Bryan. People liked the Purple A brand that Abe sold. Demand was high enough for him to continue making his shine. He was a sharp and cautious businessman who wisely invested his profits in real estate. He was also careful about his image in the community, so he did everything he could to enhance his reputation by giving generously to the city's most powerful black churches.

After the Civil War some of the descendants of Shad Bryan drifted away both from the city of their ancestors and from their religion. Consequently, Abe was not reared in the Catholic Church. His father hadn't been very religious, and his mother died before she had a chance to have Abe baptized. Although he didn't belong to any particular church and really didn't think much about God anyway, Abe still recognized the power that churches had among his people. So he saw to it that the preachers spoke well of him. Some even spoke well of the Purple A. It was through his friendship with one of these preachers that Abe met his bride to be, Miss Elaine Mae de Beaufort.

The Reverend Levi Ferguson, pastor of the Hope of Zion Holiness Church at Sandfly, was responsible for the introduction. Preacher Ferguson invited Abe to a picnic at his church. It was there that Abe became lost in Elaine's elegance and charm.

Elaine Mae was one of three beautiful girls whose father had grown wealthy in the funeral home business. Direct descendants of Henri Christophe, king and first ruler of a free Haiti in the early nineteenth century, the Beauforts were more than simply respectable people.

Elaine was beautiful and charming, Abe was handsome and genteel. Everyone said what a fine couple they made. At first, Elaine's father, the honorable Nathaniel Emmet de Beaufort, was against her involvement with Abe, but Abe eventually won him over. On Thanksgiving Day of 1938 Elaine and Abe were married.

Europe was trembling with war, and the changes this brought in the politics of America were naturally beneficial to the newspaper business. John Hartman was in the right career at the right time. Able to garner and focus his talents in Savannah as nowhere else before, John put them to good use at the *Morning Gazette*. His weekly column on local politics soon became the talk of the courthouse crowd in Wright Square, and people sought him out constantly for his opinions. He slowly evolved into the son that Colonel Deitz had never had and the sweetheart that Beth Deitz had always dreamed of.

One hot Saturday afternoon in July of 1939, John and Beth stood in front of the main altar at the Cathedral of St. John the Baptist and pledged their undying love. Colonel Deitz watched from the front row and JJ O'Boyle from two pews back, while the angels in their stained-glass perches witnessed, and the saints in their marbled bodies stood guard. Further back in the church, near the window of Saint Patrick, knelt Tony O'Boyle, admiring the shape in the next pew. Peggy O'Neal was her name, but it would change to O'Boyle three months after the Japanese bombed Pearl Harbor.

World War II shook Savannah from its slumber and made her cough up her sons to the machines of war. John Hartman volunteered for the Marine Corps and fought in the Pacific with the First Marine Division, while Abednigo Bryan was drafted into the Army and served with Patton in North Africa and Sicily. They both were wounded in battle and decorated for bravery. What Tony O'Boyle did for the war effort was a different story altogether.

When the war started, Tony was practicing law at his uncle's firm. He had inherited his father's knack for politics, and JJ was delighted to help his son follow in his footsteps. With a degree in law, Tony received a commission in the Army, and JJ's influence got him all the right assignments in Washington. Tony never saw combat, but he toured the European Theater as part of the military justice system. He was good at what he did and was able to impress all of the right people. By the time the war in Europe ended, Tony was a major eyeing one of the biggest postwar jobs in the Army—assistant prosecutor for the Nuremberg trials. It made him an instant Savannah celebrity.

When Tony returned to Savannah and his uncle's law firm, the success he had found in the Army followed him. The general law he had practiced before the war quickly evolved into a specialty in corporate law. Large industries in Savannah began to come to Tony not only for legal advice, but for help in solving the hundreds of political problems that interfere with the process of making money. Tony, with the help of his father, was able to make the proper things happen smoothly for all the proper people. Along the way, business opportunities presented themselves and Tony grew rich, while at the same time stuffing the pockets of some of his friends.

The Southern Union Paper Company had first taken

note of young Mr. O'Boyle when he solved certain zoning problems for them, and the association grew over the years. When the position of general counsel for Southern Union became open in 1950, Tony was the obvious choice. The job, which had previously been held by a member of one of Savannah's most socially prominent families, ushered Tony into the world that his father had always coveted. As the new decade began, Tony O'Boyle was making JJ proud.

Just as Tony O'Boyle had returned from the war a different man, so did John Hartman and Abe Bryan. Their changes, however, were more pervasive and lay deeper within them: silent during the day, but whispering evilly to them at night. John was able to take up where he had left off at the *Gazette* and tried to forget what he had seen. The gentleness and warmth of his wife's touch, the smile on his new son's face, gave him comfort.

But Abe—so close to death so many times—became obsessed with dying. Men had fallen as they stood next to him, and he had caught them in his arms, and watched their lives slowly drain away. He had danced with death and she had kissed his cheek lightly, caressed him and excited him; then on one exploding, trembling night she took his soul while leaving his body intact. For a while Abe was able to find solace in the loving arms and tender words of Elaine Mae. When his first and only child was born, the boy became the center of his world and Abe was able to forget once again . . . for a while.

The day Anthony O'Boyle, Jr., was born to Tony and Peggy was one of the happiest in JJ O'Boyle's life. It served as the elixir JJ needed to lift him out of the depression his youngest son, Al, put him in.

    Al O'Boyle was twenty when he barely got out of Benedictine Military School. If it hadn't been for JJ, the priests would have expelled Al a dozen times. As it was,

Father Steven had told JJ early on that Al wasn't college material. Because of the priest's kindness and JJ's generosity, Al was passed even though his grades didn't merit a promotion.

On more than one occasion JJ had been called to the school because of Al's violent and disruptive outbursts. It had become increasingly clear to him that Al might have problems the rest of his life, and JJ was afraid that, after he and his wife were gone, Al would never be able to hold down a job or take care of himself.

It was a great relief when Tony managed to get Al a job making bags at the Southern Union plant. It was additionally comforting for JJ to learn later from Tony that Al seemed to be happy with his work and was doing well in his job. "Heck, Daddy," said Tony over the phone, "the foreman says he's got a smile on his face all the time. Some of the single women who work the machines even flirt with him at lunch. He said Al doesn't seem interested though. He thinks Al's mind must be on more important things than girls."

AL MEETS ROBBIE

THE FOREMAN at the bag plant was correct: Al's mind was on more important things. It was on that feeling that he had grown to love. A feeling that he thought about all day long as he watched brown paper bags mount into stacks of twenty-five, and those stacks grow into bundles of fifty, and those bundles enlarge into walls of brown paper.

Al watched as those walls were moved around with forklifts driven by good-looking cracker boys from Effingham and Bulloch counties. He liked the way the muscles in their arms bulged when they turned the steering wheels on those little trucks, and he was fascinated by the way their blue jeans bulged "down there." He loved to go into the men's room and pretend to be using the urinal when Tommy Wasson from Clyo went in. He would take a secret peek and gasp with excitement when Tommy would flop out his big "thing" to relieve himself. Then he would almost laugh aloud with delight as Tommy shook it before placing it back into his britches.

The foreman had also been right about Al's smiling. Al smiled a lot, because he was thinking of other things. Things that he did at night, things that made him feel good all over.

"I'm leavin' now, Momma."

"OK, but I wish you wouldn't stay out so late, Al. Remember, tomorrow's Sunday and we've got to be at the ten-thirty Mass. Your new little nephew Tony is being baptized right after that and you have *got* to be there."

"Yes, mam."

"Good, now give your momma a kiss and tell me where you're going."

"Just around."

"Well, be careful in your new car. Daddy paid a lot of money for it and you must take care of it. It's got to last you for a while."

"Yes, mam."

Al's new Ford, a bright red convertible with a white top, was a high school graduation gift from his parents. JJ had wanted to get a six-cylinder engine, but Al loved the power of his brother's car and put up such a fuss over the engine that JJ relented and let him get the V-8 model. Al had no friends, none at all, and his nights away from his parent's house, where he had lived his entire life, were spent driving all over Chatham County in his new '51 Ford. Al learned every dirt road and back street for miles around Savannah. He knew a hundred secluded places and dozens of abandoned houses stuck off at the other end of nowhere. In six months Al had covered the entire county.

Al had never been on a date with a girl. He was interested in girls, but the girls he had gone to school with were afraid of him—none of their parents would have let them go out with Al in any case. He was, as one eighth-grade girl put it, "odd, different, and scary."

Al had a definite interest in the actual mechanics of sex—though he had learned most of what he knew about the subject from his brothers and the other boys at the Blessed Sacrament School. When he was younger, he would sometimes crawl out of his bedroom window at night, sneak around on the roof to his sister's bedroom window, and watch as she dressed for a date. Many times he had wanted to jump through the window and "do it" with her, but even Al knew that that wouldn't be a good idea.

In the bathroom at school Al had compared himself with the other boys, and much to his delight, they would exclaim, "Wow, look at O'Boyle, he's got a big one!" Then he would shake it like a snake and say, "Biggest dick in school! If you tell Sister I showed it to you, I'll beat your ass, swear to God." He knew all about mastur-bation, and had even been caught once in the act by his mother. She had pretended not to know what was going on, but later she told JJ about what she had seen and insisted he speak to Al about the sinfulness of such dis-gusting behavior. JJ could never bring himself to do it.

One evening before he started working at the paper mill, Al took his car out and wandered up Highway 21, on the way to Pooler. He got lost for a while, so it was late when he finally drove down Bay Street on his way back home. He had the top down when he pulled up to the intersection of Bay and Bull and looked over at the boy standing on the corner. The guy was about Al's age, with sandy blond hair and bright blue eyes. A cigarette dangled from his lips, which almost looked as if they were painted with lipstick. Al had no idea what was going on when the young man spoke to him.

"Nice car."

"Thanks."

"Is it fast?"

"Yeah, it's fast. It's got a V-8 in it."

"How fast?"

"Faster than anything you've ever been in."

"Oh, I don't believe you. It couldn't be faster than my daddy's Caddy."

"Oh yeah? Well, if you want, I'll give you a ride right this very minute that'll show you just how fast it really is."

The stranger stepped off the curb, took hold of the door handle, and said, "I'd love for you to take me for a fast ride."

As soon as his passenger had slammed the door, Al popped the clutch and hit the gas, not even looking to see if anything was coming up Drayton. The screeching wheels left black marks on Bay Street twenty feet long as Al tore away. The blond boy threw his head back and laughed out loud with delight, and by the time they had reached East Broad, the Ford was doing almost seventy; Al had to brake hard for the steep drop in the road near the gas company. The blond boy yelled out "Faster, faster, make this mother fucker fly" the whole way down Bay Street, and when they finally slowed down, he looked over at Al and said, "That was absolutely marvelous. It was wonderful, let's do it again."

Al was excited too and said that instead of going back down Bay, they could take the car out on President Street Extension. "There's not a bend in the road the whole way, and then I'll really show you what a Ford can do." So out President Street they ran, pushing Al's Ford to almost a hundred miles an hour as the wind whipped through the car and the blond boy yelled as if he were riding a bucking bronco in a Wild West show.

In those days President Street ended at the Wilmington River. There was no bridge there and the entire area was densely wooded, without a home in sight for miles around. The locale was called Causton's Bluff, and most of it was covered by a large, earthen Civil War fort—a remarkable piece of engineering almost obscured by trees and dense undergrowth. Fort Francis Bartow had never seen action during the war, and thus it had been abandoned fully intact. Its walls were thirty feet high in some places and formed many confusing angles in the undergrowth. Over the years a twisting trail big enough for a car had been cut throughout the fort. The road wound for perhaps half a mile without ever leaving the fort's walls. Al loved Fort Bartow. He had walked or driven every inch of it. The maze reminded him of the one he had seen in the Walt Disney animated classic *Alice in Wonderland.*

"Hey, what're we gonna' do now?" said the blond boy as Al brought his car to a stop at the end of President Street. Al looked over to his left and asked, "You wanna take a ride through the fort?"

"Oh yes, I'd love to. It's so spooky at night. Maybe we'll come up on some parkers," said the boy in undisguised glee.

Because of its remote location, Fort Bartow was a favorite for lovers who had only the back seat of a car in which to exercise their amorous intentions. At the stroke of midnight on any Saturday there were usually two or three cars deep within the confines of the fort, their occupants joyfully fogging up the windows.

"I haven't even told you my name," said the blond boy as Al eased the Ford through the narrow opening in the woods and down the dirt road to the fort. "I'm Robbie." He looked over at Al and smiled.

There was no moon that night and the woods were dark. The dirt road to the fort twisted and dipped in low spots washed out by the rains. Al had to watch what he was doing as he drove, but he managed a quick smile for Robbie and said, "Oh, uh, I'm Al. Al O'Boyle. Where're you from."

"Charleston. I haven't lived here very long and I don't know a lot of people."

They hadn't been riding through the fort for two minutes before they came upon the first parked car. When Al's headlights glared through the car's windows, a male head came up from the back seat and looked around. Then a girl's head appeared, and Robbie and Al could clearly see that she had nothing over her bare shoulders. They watched as she disappeared for a moment, and then popped up again, struggling to put on her blouse. They looked at each other, grinned, and drove on.

"I'll bet we caught them fucking," said Robbie.

"I'll bet we did, too," answered Al, noticing that he was beginning to have an erection.

"I'd love to watch them fuck, wouldn't you?" Robbie's manner was sly and probing.

"Shit yeah. I love fuckin'!"

As they drove deeper into Fort Bartow, they encountered two more cars and two more sets of similar reactions from their occupants. Al was completely aroused by this time, and all he could talk about with Robbie was "fucking." Robbie seemed to know a whole lot about the subject. When they got to the part of the road that skirted the Wilmington River, Robbie suggested to Al that they stop for a while and enjoy the view. Al pulled his car off the trail at a spot with a magnificent view of the entire river and turned off the engine.

"Oh, this is just gorgeous, it's perfect," said Robbie as he reached into his vest pocket and produced a pint bottle of Old Grandad. "I hope this is your brand." Robbie opened the bottle, took a swig, and passed it over to Al.

Al had tried some of his father's liquor back at the house, but he didn't like the way it tasted; and because he never went anywhere with the other boys at BC, he hadn't had much opportunity to overcome his aversion. Al was about as experienced with alcohol as he was with sex.

"Yeah, I like that kind," he said as he took the bottle, and with great bravado turned it upside down and sucked in a mouthful. Al coughed and wheezed, but he managed to keep down what he had swallowed, and even bravely took another pull.

As they passed the bottle back and forth for the next several minutes, Robbie talked about nothing but sex. His descriptions of intercourse were vivid and stimulating, and soon Al was aching with desire. Then Robbie turned the conversation to the subject of organ size, and in no time he had Al bragging about his penis.

"I don't believe it's that big," said Robbie in a taunting voice. "Prove it."

The liquor had taken its effect on Al, so much to Robbie's delight and glee, he proved how very big he was. Robbie was highly experienced in seducing young men, and a few seconds later he was fully engaged in demonstrating his "special techniques" to Al.

Al had never experienced anything like that before: he remained motionless until Robbie had finished. Maybe he wouldn't have let Robbie do anything like that to him if he hadn't been drinking, but in any case, when it was over, Al didn't know what to do or say. He was terribly confused, and therefore he grew very angry. What Robbie had done had felt good, wonderful even, but something was wrong. Something was terribly wrong, and Al felt dirty and nasty for the first time in his life. Then Robbie pulled out his penis.

"Now it's your turn to do me," he said.

Al went berserk; he jumped on Robbie and beat him severely. As Al was punching Robbie in the mouth and stomach over and over again, a wonderful feeling came over him. He felt he was ten feet tall, the king of the world, Superman! It was the most fantastic feeling that Al had ever had, even better than what he felt when he played with himself in the shower. Al couldn't stop beating Robbie; it just felt too good.

Robbie lost consciousness after Al's second blow to his temple, but Al didn't realize it or care. It just felt absolutely wonderful to beat the living shit out of Robbie. Al didn't stop until he simply didn't have the strength to hit Robbie anymore. Finally he fell back against the car door exhausted, his knuckles bleeding and perspiration running down the side of his head, but oh what a feeling he had now! Oh, what a wonderful, delicious feeling he had now!

Al lay against the driver's side door for ten minutes or more, enjoying the feeling, basking in the glow. Then he realized what he had done and started looking at Robbie. He got out of the car and went around to Robbie's side. When he opened the door, Robbie fell to the ground. In the light of the stars Al discovered he had beaten Robbie to death.

For a moment Al panicked. Then he saw Robbie's blood on the seat of his new car and went into a rage once more. He kicked Robbie in the head and screamed out, "You motherfucker, you messed up my car." Then he stopped, reached down, and shoved Robbie's body over the edge of the bluff and into the marsh below. "See you later, you piece of shit!" Al shouted as he climbed into his red convertible and drove home.

Robbie Fletcher's remains wouldn't be found for another six months. After the crabs had finished, only the bones remained. The people at the restaurant where he worked figured he had just left town and didn't bother to call the police when he never showed up for work again. All he had in Charleston was an alcoholic father who lived at the veterans' home and a brother he didn't speak to anymore. Nobody ever came around looking for Robbie in Savannah. He simply ceased to exist. The skeleton found at the fort was listed as John Doe, possible homicide, possible suicide. The case wasn't officially closed, but it might as well have been.

BOYS LIKE ROBBIE

THAT WAS THE FIRST TIME Al had gotten "my feelin'," as he recalled it to himself over and over again in the monotony of watching thousands and thousands of paper bags come streaming off the number four folding machine where he worked. There was little within Al to restrain him from repeating his act except the fear of getting caught, and soon he would overcome even that with his desire for "my feelin'."

It was a warm Friday afternoon in April when Al picked up an armful of the large grocery bags his mother had told him to get for her, then inserted his time card into the punch clock and walked to his car. Mrs. O'Boyle liked the bags and used them for the trash. Sometimes she cut them up for use as shelf liners. The bags were defectives left at the clock station for the employees to take if they liked—hundreds of bags in varying sizes. Nobody even gave Al a second look as he walked past the guard gate with his armload of paper bags, nobody at all.

That evening Al cruised the streets of downtown Savannah. Around eleven he met another boy like Robbie. Things were very similar to the last encounter, only Al knew so much more this second time around. There was fast driving again around long, lonely roads with the radio turned up and the top down. There was liquor and talk of sex and finally the suggestion from Al's new friend to "go somewhere quiet where we can just talk." Al had prepared for that and drove to an abandoned farmhouse he had found several weeks before. It was out in the county off Highway 17, almost to the Ogeechee River. Owned by Southern Union Paper, the old house was at the end of a dirt road that meandered over two miles through a large stand of slash pines.

The new boy's name was Rick. He was slender and had acne on his face and grease in his hair. Rick was twenty-one but looked only eighteen, and he wore his shirt unbuttoned so that his pale, hairless chest was exposed. A tattoo on his left arm was partially hidden by the neatly rolled-up edges of his short-sleeved shirt. The tattoo was a cartoon-character devil with a pot belly, little curved horns coming out of his head, and a pointed tail. In his right hand he held a pitchfork, and with his left hand he was shooting the bird to whomever cared enough to look closely. Under the devil were the words "Hell Raiser."

Rick had a pack of Camels in his shirt pocket and another cigarette tucked behind his right ear. After Al turned off the motor, the boy leaned back and rested against the car door. Rick was in charge of the conversation and every part of it was about sex, sex of all variations, sexual acts that Al had never even dreamed existed. Then, exactly as before, the conversation became focused on organ size. Al proved his manhood once again by exposing himself to Rick. It wasn't long before Rick had his head in Al's lap.

When Rick had finished and was wiping his mouth on his shirt tail, Al sprang into action. He grabbed Rick by the throat with both hands and began to choke him. Al was very strong and outweighed Rick by a good forty pounds. Rick fought for his life and even managed to scratch Al's face a little, but it was over in less than two minutes. Al derived intense pleasure from watching the look on Rick's face as he squeezed his life away.

Once Rick had stopped resisting and Al was certain he was dead, he lifted the body out of the car and carried it into the living room of the old house. There, by the light of Tony's old Boy Scout flashlight, Al carefully laid Rick on the floor and stripped his corpse. Then he removed all of his own clothes so they wouldn't get messed up and went back out to the car. Naked, under the light of a half moon, Al removed a dozen paper bags from the trunk. Then he reached under the driver's seat and pulled out a knife—a long, very sharp German SS dagger that Tony had gotten during the war and given to Al the Christmas of 1945. The scabbard was engraved with a swastika and the Nazi eagle. When Al removed the knife from its scabbard, the hardened nickel blade almost crackled in the moonlight. The long, double-edged blade was also engraved in German. Al remembered what Tony had told him the words meant in English. He spoke them out loud as he ran his thumb lightly along the knife's edge.

"My duty is my honor," Al whispered. Then again. "My duty is my honor."

Al went back inside the house, stood the flashlight with its beam pointed at Rick's midsection, and knelt down beside the body. Then he proceeded with his dissection.

He removed Rick's liver and one of his kidneys before deciding that internal dissection was much too difficult and time-consuming, no matter how much pleasure it brought him. Then, with surprising ease, Al started amputating Rick's arms at the shoulders and his legs at the knees. The dagger was sharp and Al was strong and accurate with the blade, having helped to gut and dress many a deer on hunting trips with his father. In twenty minutes two arms and two legs lay neatly side by side on the parlor floor next to Rick's severed head. When Al stood up to walk across the floor to get the paper bags, he noticed that he had an erection and laughed out loud with glee.

Al placed each of the individual body parts into a separate bag and then loaded them into the car, putting the heavy legs and head into the trunk and the lighter arms and internal organs on the floor of the back seat. He was careful to lay some empty bags underneath the remains to prevent blood from seeping out and ruining the carpets.

On the front porch he cleaned himself with water from an old hand pump. After that, he got dressed, cleaned his Nazi dagger with Rick's shirt, flicked off his Boy Scout flashlight, and drove away. Al left Rick's torso on the farmhouse floor.

VICTORY DRIVE

BACK UP HIGHWAY 17 Al turned off on the Ogeechee Road and followed it to the beginning of Victory Drive. It was now almost 1:30 A.M. without a car in sight. As Al started to slow for the red light at the intersection of Victory Drive and West Broad Street, he reached behind him and grabbed one of the paper bags. Just before he got to the light, and with the greatest of ease, Al tossed the bag into the center of one of the giant azaleas in the median on Victory Drive. He did this again just after he passed Abercorn Street. When he got to Daffin Park, he tossed the liver into more azaleas; a kidney went in front of the Victory Drive-In theater.

Al continued depositing body parts until he reached Thunder-bolt. There he stopped behind Nativity Catholic Church to retrieve the head and legs from the trunk. After that it was back up Victory Drive, where he tossed one of the legs into the Casey Canal, and then to Grayson Stadium, where he left the other one under the west-side bleachers. He had saved Rick's head for last because he had somewhere special in mind for that.

Although Al had always been attracted to girls, there was only one girl he had ever called on the phone in his entire life. She had been terribly nasty to him and had greatly hurt his feelings. He never got over it. Now it was payback time for Camilla Waters.

Camilla lived with her parents not far from where Al lived in Ardsley Park. When he reached the corner of Habersham and Forty-sixth, he turned down Forty-sixth, drove for another half a block, stopped his car on a darkened section of the block, and doused the headlights. Quietly, and with a feline quickness, Al moved along the shadows and slipped up to the front steps. He eased the bag under the steps and out of sight. Then he unzipped his pants and urinated on the steps. Revenge was sweet indeed.

It was past two in the morning when Al finally pulled up in front of his own house. The sky was clear, so he didn't bother to put the top up on his car. Before he got out, Al looked in the back seat, but in the darkness he didn't notice the bloodstains on the floor or the smeared blood on the seat.

When he reached the top of the stairs and turned down the hall to go to his room, his mother called out to him quietly from the open door of her room. "Is that you, Al?"

"Yes, mam."

"I'm so glad you're home. I was afraid something terrible had happened to you. I've been praying to St. Jude to protect you and keep you safe. St. Anthony too."

"I'm sorry, Momma. I've just been drivin' around in my car. I didn't get in any trouble, promise."

"Well, you go on to bed now. I'll see you in the morning."

"Night, Momma. I love you very much."

"Good night, son."

Al took his clothes off and carefully hung them over his clothes rack, just as his mother had showed him. Then he put on his pajamas, the ones with footballs all over them, and brushed his teeth. After he got into bed, he looked at the statue of the Blessed Mother on his dresser. He had won it in the third grade at Blessed Sacrament. It was first prize for being the fastest runner in his class on field day—the best memory of grammar school that he had. The statue glowed in the dark. Al would stare at it every night until he fell asleep. Sometimes, when he looked at the Blessed Mother long enough, she would float in the air in front of him; and sometimes, only sometimes, she would talk to him. Tonight she would talk to him.

Tony came by the next morning to drop off the christening pictures. As he walked past Al's car, he noticed something smeared on the back seat. He stopped, leaned over the side of the car, and looked more closely at the soiled area, about a foot long and two inches wide. It looked as if something wet had been dragged across a part of the seat. Tony reached down and touched the stain. It had dried by then and started to turn brown, but he could plainly tell that it was blood.

"I'll be damned," he said as he saw a second, larger stain on the carpet, a little under the driver's seat. This one was still damp. It, too, was blood.

Tony was sitting at the kitchen table, drinking coffee and going over the pictures with his parents, when Al came in. He didn't mention anything at the time, but as soon as he got Al alone he questioned him about it.

"What's that blood doing in the back of your car, Al?"

Al froze for a second and then said, "A dog. I hit a dog last night."

"Well just how in the hell did his blood get in the back seat of your car?"

"I picked him up and tried to save him. I put him in the back seat to take him to the hospital."

"Al, they don't take dogs at the hospital."

"I know. I mean I didn't know that then. So when I hit him, he was crying and everything and I felt sorry for him and I picked him up and put him in my car and wanted to help him, Tony." Al started to get excited, and Tony was afraid he was going to start weeping.

"OK, OK, Al, that's just fine. No harm done. I just wanted to know what happened. I saw the bloodstains when I came in this morning. You forgot to put the top back up. What happened to the dog?"

"He died, Tony. I killed him. I'm sorry, I didn't mean to do it, I promise I didn't. I won't do it ever again, I promise, on my Catholic honor!"

Tears started coming to Al's eyes and Tony put up his hands. "OK, enough already. Don't go getting all worked up. What did you do with the dog. He's not in the trunk of the car, is he?"

Al's eyes became real big as he answered, "Oh no, Tony. I didn't put him in the trunk. Oh no. I put him on the side of the road so the people he belonged to could find him and have a funeral for him. He was a nice dog."

"Alright, just go out and clean the seats off before Momma sees them."

"Please don't tell Momma and Daddy, please don't, Tony!"

"I'm not going to tell them, Al. Just be more careful from now on and watch out for dogs running in front of you, OK? One more thing—how did you get those scratches on your neck and cheek?"

"That's where the dog scratched at me when I tried to pick him up, Tony. He was hurt and didn't know I was trying to help him. I'm sorry, really I am."

"Alright, just tell Momma you got scratched getting your football out of the holly bush next to the house."

The weather can become quite warm in Savannah during the month of April, and this April was particularly so. It had been in the low eighties for three days straight when Rick's head began to putrefy and produce the most horrific odor. Camilla was the first to notice it on Monday afternoon as she was coming back from her English class at Armstrong Junior College. She assumed a squirrel had died under the house and called to her mother from the front porch.

Mrs. Waters had to hold a handkerchief to her nose as she peered at the grocery bag under the steps. All she could think of was that some crazy fool had stolen a ham or something from Smith Brothers' Market and hidden it under their steps for some reason. Mrs. Waters reached in and pulled at the bag, sliding it from under the porch. The top was folded over several times, but Mrs. Waters had no intention of looking into the bag. All she wanted to do was to get that thing as far away from her house as she could. She and Camilla fetched the garbage can from the lane and sat it on the steps next to the bag. When she reached down to put the bag into the garbage can, the blood-soaked bottom gave way and out tumbled Rick's head. Camilla immediately threw up. Mrs. Waters fainted dead away, straight into the Easter lilies she had planted the year before.

The other body parts were also discovered through olfactory detection within the next three days. The city began to buzz. The police came up with a complete blank. All they had were some brown paper bags made at Southern Union, which were in every grocery store in south

Georgia. They couldn't even get an ID on the remains until somebody was reported missing. That finally happened a week later when they got a call from Reidsville, about fifty miles away, up in Tattnall County.

Rick's parents had read about the arms and legs turning up all over Savannah. They got scared because they hadn't heard from their son in a long time. When they couldn't get an answer after three days straight, they broke down and called the Savannah Police Department. Rick was positively identified by his parents at Henderson Brothers' Funeral Home. They recognized his tattoo before they recognized his face.

THE VICTORY DRIVE SLASHER

IN EVERY NEIGHBORHOOD, across every racial and social strata, the actions of what the *Savannah Morning Gazette* had named "the Victory Drive Slasher" were the topic of conversation.

In Yamacraw Village nervous black mothers would shout across the yard to their neighbor, "Yo young'n be over here, ain't no harm gonna come to 'em long as I draws a breath a life in me." Back would come the reply: "I bees watchin' out this end here too. Ain't took my eye off a dem one second, no mam, no way!"

In Ardsley Park, mothers would look carefully around the front yard as they went for the morning paper. Clutching their pastel silk dressing gowns, they would patter quickly to where the paper had fallen and greet the nosy person in the window across the street with a grateful smile rather than last week's scorn.

While the people of Savannah thought about him a great deal and slept little, Al thought about the people of Savannah little and slept a great deal. His sleep was filled with dreams, and his dreams were filled with bright colors and loud sounds, horses running and water falling in great cascades. His mother was in his dreams sometimes, and sometimes his sister too. Occasionally he would soil his sheets during his dreams, and his mother would scold him for his evil thoughts. She would tell his father that he "played with himself every night," and every night she would extract a promise from his father to speak with Al. Every night JJ would break that promise. Painfully he would hide his shame for the boy and find sleep with a double shot of Jameson and a Seconal chaser.

Meanwhile Al was hooked. The feeling that he got when he carved up Rick surpassed the thrill of kicking Robbie into the marsh at Fort Bartow. His every waking thought was of how to do it again.

Although he knew that he was not supposed to be doing what he was, Al couldn't help himself: the only thing that kept him from telling the whole world about his pleasure was that he knew society would not tolerate his actions. There were no thoughts of guilt, no painful ruminations over the right or wrong, the decency or indecency, the good or evil of his actions. There was only the fear of being caught and the elation of getting away with murder.

"My feelin'," Al kept saying to himself as he cruised around Madison Square at Bull and Harris late one Saturday evening in June. It was two months to the day since he had carved up Rick and served him to the residents along Victory Drive. By now Savannahians still talked about the "slasher," but the sensation was beginning to fade. People weren't as vigilant as they had been in April. "My feelin'," whispered Al when a man who appeared to be in his fifties stepped away from the curb and into Al's path.

Al was circling the square, not going very fast, and was able to stop his car before hitting the man. The man looked startled at first, then embarrassed. He came over to Al and apologized profusely for his inattention; before too long they were chatting like old friends. In a few minutes the man was in the car, and they were on their way to Bloomingdale.

Terry LaSalle lived downtown in a magnificently re-stored home on Charlton Street. He was originally from New Orleans and came from a monied family with a fine name. During the war, however, he fell in love with some-one in Savannah, so he settled in the historic heart of downtown. Terry's heart was eventually broken, but not his pocketbook: he had been raised around dear antiques and *objets d'art*, so he was able to parlay his knowledge into a thriving business. Terry now owned antique shops in Savannah and Charleston, and an interior-decorating business in Atlanta. He had even become a celebrity of sorts in the city—one of its unofficial ambassadors—after having referred to Savannah as the "New Orleans of the Atlantic Seaboard" in an article about him in the *New York Times*.

Terry was wealthy, a playboy, but had sworn off long-term commitments because of his broken heart. "I'm not going to consider settling down until I'm at least sixty-five," he would tell his more tolerant friends. "Then maybe I'll be too old to care. But until that time, every cute young ass in Savannah is fair game as far as Terry LaSalle is concerned."

Terry was playing just as hard as he could and fighting the aging process even harder. He dyed what hair he had left an unconvincing black and wore an equally phony toupee. He dressed exquisitely, although his taste was a little more European than Savannah was ready for. Jew-elry was his real downfall, and his favorite piece was a ring he had found in New Orleans two Christmases ago, a fleur-de-lis of dark blue sapphires. The man who sold it told him that it had been made for a general in Napo-leon's army whose family had been forced into hard times. Terry didn't know whether to believe that or not, but he did have the ring appraised at several places in New Orleans. It was genuine—and frightfully expensive—but Terry bought it anyway. He loved to wear it whenever he went out at night, especially when he was feeling "just a little crazy," as he liked to put it. When he opened the door and slid into the convertible, his ring flashed and caught Al's eye. That night Terry wasn't the only one who was feeling "just a little crazy."

The downtown high school boys called Terry an "old fag." He was openly effeminate and assumed that everyone who knew him knew of his sexual orientation, and accepted him for what he was. Although Terry had lovers who were also gay, he was especially attracted to straight young men in their early twenties. He would pay well for these boys to prostitute themselves and was known about the downtown squares as someone who would "come across with the bread." Stepping in front of Al's car had not been an accident: Terry had done it on purpose after noticing Al driving around what he called "fellatio square" and was determined to meet him.

"Let's go to my house. I owe you a drink for almost causing an accident when I stepped in front of you back there."

"I want to drive some."

"Well, then, drive young man, drive to your heart's content. Make the wind rustle through my hair, make me wild with the speed. Make it heighten my pleasure."

Al had never met anyone like Terry before, and his words confused him. "Whatcha' talkin' about man?"

"I'm talking about passion, my young muscular friend. Raw passion."

Al just shook his head and drove over the viaduct on Bay Street and headed out Highway 80. Just before Bloomingdale, he pulled onto a dirt road and headed for another abandoned farmhouse he had found many months before. The scenario was the same, the slaughter just as complete. Only this time Al decided to take a souvenir and cut off Terry's finger to retrieve the blue sapphire ring. Surprisingly, the older man had put up more of a struggle than the others and had kicked the knobs off the radio. He had also scratched Al's right arm so badly that it bled. Other than that, however, it was another "good time Saturday night" for Al O'Boyle.

In the wee hours of Sunday morning, as Al dressed in his football pajamas, he admired the sparkle of sapphires in Terry's ring. After he had brushed his teeth and hung his pants neatly in the closet, he put the ring into the little box on top of his dresser that held his cuff links and tie clasps. Then he climbed into his bed and stared at the luminescent Blessed Virgin and waited for her to rise and talk with him. That night Al fell asleep before the Blessed Mother could float across the room, but he dreamed of waterfalls and whirlpools and his sister Kate undressing in front of him.

"What happened to your arm, Al?"

"Uh, uh, I hurt it at work."

"Did you report it to your boss?"

"No, Tony. I didn't know I was supposed to do that."

"Any time you get hurt at the plant, you gotta report it. Those are the rules. They told you that. I know they did. Now just do what you're told. Don't make me look bad out there."

"I'm sorry, Tony, I promise I am. I'm sorry, I won't do it again."

"OK, now tell me what happened to your car. Momma said the radio doesn't work in it now."

"I guess somebody broke my knobs off when it was parked at the plant."

"Well, keep the damn thing locked, OK?"

"OK, Tony. I'm sorry. Is Momma real mad at me? Tell her it was an accident for me, Tony. I don't want her mad at me."

"I'll handle it for you. Now come on and help me finish with the grass. Then we gotta' trim the walk. I'll swear, Daddy's gonna hav'ta hire a nigger to do this from now on in. I just don't have the time to take care of their yard and mine too."

"That's a bad word. You're not suppose to say nigger. It's a bad word and you'll get in trouble with Momma if you do."

"Oh, shut up, Al. Just shut up."

DECIDING AL'S FATE

TWO DAYS AFTER Al killed Terry LaSalle, the *Morning Gazette* carried a small story on the back page of the paper with the headline "LOCAL ANTIQUE DEALER REPORTED MISSING." Three days after the murder, another story appeared on the front page with the headline "BODY PARTS FOUND ALL OVER CITY—BELIEVED LINKED TO MISSING ANTIQUE DEALER." The headline on Thursday morning read: "LOCAL ANTIQUE DEALER VICTIM OF VICTORY DRIVE SLASHER." The story went on to say that the only clue the police had were the grocery bags in which the body parts had all been wrapped. The city was beyond panic at this stage, and retail businesses were beginning to be hurt, especially those open after dark.

It was purely by chance that Walter Geradeau happened to be in the detectives' office while one of the bags that had contained a part of Terry LaSalle was being examined. He was there to report the theft of his outboard motor the night before. All of the bags had been checked by forensics, and nothing of value had been found.

Detective Richard "Sweet Swing" Cubbage was in the squad room when Walter walked in. Sweet Swing had gotten his nickname from the guys he played softball with at Daffin Park because of his ability to hit home runs. As Sweet Swing held one of the bags up to the light, Walter noticed something peculiar about it and walked over to take a closer look.

"That one of them bags that the Slasher is using?" he asked.

"Yeah," replied Sweet Swing.

"Can I look at it for a second?"

"I guess so, but don't go pawing at it, it's all the evidence we got right now."

After studying the bag Walter said, "I can tell you exactly where this thing come from."

Two other detectives, reading newspapers at their desks, hadn't paid much attention to Walter at first. After he dropped this bombshell, however, they slammed their papers down. Sweet Swing almost choked on the chili dog he had been stuffing into his mouth, but managed to say, "You can?"

"Sure can. See this here fold on the bottom of the bag, right next to the company logo?" All three detectives gathered around Walter as he pointed to the place on the bag. "Well, this ain't supposed to be here. It's supposed to be another inch to the right. This bag is defective. Lemme see the rest of 'em."

Sweet Swing and his buddies quickly retrieved all the other bags from the evidence room.

"Uh huh, just like I thought. They're all defective."

"Well, what does that mean?" asked Sweet Swing.

"It means that these here bags was never sold. They was gived away at the clock station. When people come off their shift, they can pick up the rejects at the clock station. Everybody does it."

Sweet Swing was starting to suspect that if something sounded too good to be true, it probably was. "Walter," he asked with a little sarcasm in his voice, "just how do you know so much about paper bags, especially these?"

Walter, stepping back a foot or two from the detectives and holding the bag triumphantly in front of him, said with great indignation, "Hell, mister, I been making these bags at that plant for over twenty years. I oughta by God know a little somethin' about them."

Ten minutes later Sweet Swing was in the general manager's office at the Southern Union Paper Company. In addition to the general manager and his assistant, Tony O'Boyle, as general counsel to the company, had been called in to hear what Sweet Swing had to say.

"This is the first real break we've had in this case, Mr. Meade," said Sweet Swing. "It's a place for us to start.

There's a good possibility that the killer works for this company and goes through that clock station every day."

"Well, we'll certainly cooperate in every way we can," replied Ansel Meade. "Mr. O'Boyle is the head of our legal department and he'll work with you on this himself. I assume you want to keep this as quiet as possible?"

"Yes sir, Mr. Meade. Quiet, real quiet. We don't want to scare nobody away."

On Saturday morning the *Gazette* contained a story about how a fifteen-year-old who had been thumbing a ride to the beach along Victory Drive had found Terry LaSalle's left hand. The article stated that the ring finger had been cut off, probably to remove the expensive ring that Terry always wore. The article described the ring in great detail, stating that it had been valued at over twenty thousand dollars. Terry's friends had cautioned him about the dan-. gers of wearing it around town at night. The article further stated that AB-positive blood had been recovered from under the fingernails and that police believed it was the blood of Terry's murderer. Less than five percent of the population had that blood type.

When the weekend rolled around, Tony found himself over at his parents' house again. This time his father had become ill with what Mrs. O'Boyle thought might be pneumonia, and JJ was giving her a hard time about calling the doctor. Tony's mother thought he might have a little more influence and convince JJ to have Dr. Murphy drop by the house. That was Saturday morning, and Al was working at the mill.

After Tony had managed to talk his father into letting the doctor examine him, he started to go downstairs to tell his mother. When he walked past Al's door, he stopped and went in to use the bathroom. On the way out he paused momentarily for no particular reason and noticed the box of Al's jewelry, which Tony had made years ago as a Cub Scout. Al had always admired it, so one day Tony gave it to him. Out of sentiment and curiosity, Tony picked up the box and flipped it open. Right on top of a pile of broken cuff links, next to Al's Holy Name Society lapel pin, was Terry LaSalle's famous ring.

In the twinkling of an eye, with the force of a thunderclap, Tony knew exactly what the ring meant. He thought he was going to vomit and went into the bathroom, where he stood for several minutes with his head over the toilet. He gagged a few times but eventually regained his composure.

Tony cleaned his face with a wet towel, went back into the bedroom, and sat on the edge of Al's bed. He sat there thinking for a very long time. Everything fit into place—the ring, the defective bags, the scratches on Al's arm, the blood in the car two months ago, the broken radio knobs. Tony even remembered that Al had AB-positive blood from the time he had been hospitalized for his appendix. It was in Al's bedroom, sitting on Al's bed across from Al's statue of the Blessed Mother that glowed in the dark, that Tony decided Al's fate.

"Tony, are you still up there?"

"Yes, mam."

"Well come on down and tell me about your father."

Tony fought desperately to seem normal, knowing that when Al got caught—and he would most certainly be caught—his name and that of the entire family would be ruined for the next hundred years. Every plan of JJ's for Tony and Tony's for himself would be destroyed. His parents would spend the rest of their lives in agony, trying to live down the most terrible murders Savannah had ever seen. When people saw Tony, they would forever see not him but the brother of the Victory Drive Slasher. Tony could not let this happen to him or to his parents.

"You can call Dr. Murphy and ask him to stop by this evening and take a look at Daddy. I don't think it's as severe as you seem to believe, but it wouldn't hurt for the doc to check him out."

"I don't know about that. I don't like the way he looks

and I've seen a lot more than you have, young man. I'm just glad he'll let Jack see him. God in Heaven, JJ O'Boyle is the stubbornest man in Chatham County."

"Well, everything's going to he just fine, so don't get all worked up. By the way, do you know if Al is working tomorrow?"

"He said he was off unless they had him work overtime. Why?"

"Well, the weather's so nice I thought I'd take him fishing after church. We haven't been in a long time, and Al used to get such a kick out of it."

Mrs. O'Boyle smiled and hugged her son. "Tony, you're so thoughtful and kind. You've always looked after your little brother Al, no matter what. When he gets home, I'll have him call you. I know he'd love to go. He doesn't have a friend in the world, you know. It's so pitiful that it breaks my heart. I just knew something was wrong with him when I was carrying him." Tears came to her eyes as she looked down at the floor. "I guess I should be grateful that he can do as well as he does. It could be a lot worse."

"Yeah, a lot worse," said Tony in such a flat tone that his mother looked up at him in surprise.

After attending the ten-fifteen Mass at Blessed Sacrament together, Tony and Al drove out to Isle of Hope and put Tony's boat in the water at the marina. Tony told the man at the boat hoist that they were going out to Wassaw Sound to fish and wouldn't be back until just before dark.

Al loved to go fishing with his big brother. He was very excited and couldn't stop talking about how many fish he was going to catch and how big they would be. He sat in the front of the boat, chatting and gesturing as Tony pulled away from the dock and started out to the middle of the river. When they were well away from the marina, Tony turned south on the Skidaway River towards Ossabaw Sound rather than to the north and Wassaw

Sound. He quickly brought the boat up on a plane and was out of sight before anybody noticed.

Tony's boat was only fifteen feet long, all mahogany and quite beautiful. It was powered by a sixty-horsepower Evinrude and could make thirty knots. As Tony shot down the Skidaway and past Possum Point, Al sat in the bow of the boat, riding it through the swells like a horse, all the time shouting at the top of his lungs, "Faster, Tony, go as fast as you can!"

Tony had examined his charts the evening before and had selected the most isolated place around Savannah that he could find. He and Al sped across the Vernon River and found the shortcut through the marsh on the other side. Then they were in the Ogeechee heading for Raccoon Island.

Tony had been to Raccoon Island years before, hunting deer with his father. He had seen the fort and had even gone inside the bomb-proof shelter and cast a peek at Shad Bryan's grave. His father had bagged an eight-point buck on the island, and Tony had managed a good-sized doe. He hadn't been back there since then, but had always been impressed at how hard it was to get to and how far away and hidden in the marsh it had been. As they turned off the Florida Passage and started into the marsh, Al turned to his brother and asked where they were going.

"We're headed to a secret fish drop that I know about Al. It's deep in the marsh. The fish are huge there. You're really gonna like it."

"Hot dog, Tony, hot dog! I'm gonna like it. I'm gonna catch me the biggest fish in Chatham County, wait 'til Momma sees it!"

Tony guided the boat around the bends in the river until he was in the creek at the back of the island that led to the earth causeway the Confederates had built during the Civil War. He maneuvered his boat in closely and then dropped anchor. While Al chattered on about fish in the bow, Tony baited Al's hook and handed him the rod and reel. He pointed to a place about ten yards off the front of the boat and told Al to cast his line in that direction.

"OK, Tony, here goes." Al deftly flicked his wrist, making a perfect casting motion, and sent the bait exactly where Tony had pointed. He was a good fisherman and watched intently as he played out a little more line.

"Don't make any noise, Tony," Al whispered without looking back. "You might scare the fish."

"OK," whispered Tony in reply as he reached into the gym bag between his feet and pulled out a heavy object wrapped in a hand towel. He hesitated for a moment, and then decisively unwrapped the towel, all the while keeping a careful eye on his brother. His palm fit perfectly around the cool steel of the handle, and his finger slid with ease upon the trigger. Tony quietly slipped off the safety with his thumb and then took a ponderous, painful breath.

"I think I got one!" yelled Al as he started reeling in his line. Tony froze, then stowed the pistol behind his seat and watched Al pull in a fat, juicy whiting. The little brother exclaimed excitedly. "Boy, you were right Tony, this place does have big fish! You were right, I knew you would be! You're my brother and know all kinds of things!" Tony watched in silence as Al re-baited his hook and snapped it back to the same place in the river. Tears came to his eyes as he looked at the back of his brother's head. Then, with an effort that leached his soul, he forced himself to regain control.

I've got to get closer, thought Tony. I can't risk missing him. God, if I missed and he turned around and looked at me I don't know if I could finish the job. I've got to put the gun right next to his head.

"I'm coming up by you so I can watch," he whispered.

"OK," whispered Al in return. "Just don't rock the boat, and don't make any noise. I want another like the one I just caught."

Tony slipped into the seat behind Al after reclaiming his pistol, a nickel-plated Walther P.38 with mother-of-pearl handles he had picked up during the war. The Nazi emblem was plainly embossed on the sides. Tony had been told it was a ceremonial pistol belonging to Hermann Göring. He had bought it, along with the dagger he had given to his brother, for thirty-five dollars from one of the MP's responsible for guarding the field marshal at the Nuremberg prison. It was the only pistol he owned. His hand was shaking now as he raised it to the back of Al's head.

Tony had not slept at all the night before. All he had done was think about this moment and wonder if he would be able to pull the trigger. He knew that if he hesitated, he and his family would be lost: he would never be able to shoot. The barrel was only an inch away from Al's head when he looked out into the marsh, drew a deep breath, and closed his eyes.

Pow! came the report, and Tony opened his eyes in time to see the spent casing arcing through the air to plop with a little splash into the creek. Without a sound, Al fell backward as a stream of blood pumped from his head like a gusher, covering Tony in a baptism of red. For a few seconds he recoiled in panic and horror to the back of the boat, where he looked at his bloodsoaked arms and shirt and repeated over and over, "Oh Jesus, Oh Jesus, Oh Jesus!" But Tony was tough: he knew what he had to do, and in a few minutes he was in control of himself again.

CAIN AND ABEL

TRYING NOT TO LOOK at Al's body, Tony moved to the front of the boat and weighed anchor. Then he started the motor and slipped the boat over to the causeway, tying it off to a palmetto tree. From a duffel bag he pulled out an army trench shovel, which he tossed onto the bank. Then, with a strenuous effort, he moved Al's body to the land.

Al was stocky and well built. For a while Tony thought he might have to drag him into the woods, but he eventually managed to sling him over his shoulder and proceeded into the interior of Raccoon Island.

Soon tiring under the weight of his dead brother, Tony scanned the island for a well-concealed burial spot. When he noticed the dense undergrowth clogging either side of Battery Jasper, his eyes lighted up. At the edge of the jungle vegetation, Tony dropped his load. Al's body hit the ground with a thud that forced the air out of his lungs, and along with it a juicy suspiration of blood and air. Tony was startled; he jumped back from Al's body with a scream. Then he realized what had happened and looked at Al's face for the first time.

The sudden increase in intracranial pressure caused by the bullet had forced Al's eyes slightly out of their sockets, causing them to bulge. Blood still oozed from Al's nose, mouth, and ears, but it was starting to clot. His mouth hung open, and his tongue protruded like a thick pink grubworm. The death mask of Al O'Boyle was haunting. Tony was suffering greatly as he picked up the shovel and crawled into the undergrowth. About fifteen feet in, he stopped and started scratching out a shallow grave. The digging was slow and taxing because of the luxurious root systems snaking through the earth. After an hour's work, Tony had managed to dig out a two-foot deep grave for his brother's body.

Before he began to pile the dirt on top of the corpse, Tony quickly went through his pockets and removed Al's wallet. He didn't bother with the small change in his pocket. It only took a few minutes to cover Al in dirt and leaves.

Crawling through the underbrush, Tony stopped and looked around just to be sure that he was alone. He didn't hear a sound except the wind rolling through the tops of the pines.

Tony did not see him that day, but Abednigo Bryan had certainly seen Tony. Making moonshine when he heard the outboard, he crept to the edge of the island and watched as Al threw out his first line and smiled when Al pulled in his fish. He goggled in astonishment when he saw Tony point a pistol to the back of Al's head and pull the trigger. Aghast and unthinking, he was a witness as Tony carried Al's body to the island and buried him. After Tony pulled away from the causeway, Abednigo sat in the woods and thought.

"White man's business," he muttered to himself over and over again. "Ain't got no cause to go stickin' my nose in white man's business, no suh."

Abednigo was just about to go back to his still when he thought about something. He had recognized Tony O'Boyle; he knew who the murderer was. Maybe, he thought, just maybe what I knows about all dis here mess could come in handy to me one day. Abednigo went back to his still and got a shovel.

After uncovering Al's face, he whispered, "Lord have mercy, you sho is a mess, mista', you is one fine mess and that's a fact." Abednigo quickly went though Al's pockets but found nothing other than a few coins which he left. Then he noticed the belt buckle Al was wearing, in the form of a brass shamrock, and decided to remove it. This was a tenth-birthday present from the O'Boyles. On the back it said, "To our lucky boy Al, from Momma and Daddy." Abednigo rolled it up, placed it in his pocket and pulled Al out of the underbrush.

Abednigo had decided to bury Al in another place just in case Tony came back to move it. No one knew Raccoon Island better than Abednigo Bryan, and he determined to bury Al in the deepest part of the underbrush, in a trench he had found while crawling through the wild boar tunnels. Aloysius was a lot of trouble, but he was able to pull Al's body through about fifty yards of tunnels to a place with a trench around three feet deep and ten feet long. There, Abednigo laid out Aloysius O'Boyle and covered him with leaves. Filthy, exhausted, and still numbed by what he had seen, he went back to his still, where he let the strange day simmer him to sleep.

* * *

Tony had thrown his blood-soaked shirt into the creek and watched it sink to the bottom. Just before he reached the Florida Passage, he dropped the Walther and the trench shovel into the deepest part of the river. Then he took the bait bucket, filled it with river water, and washed the blood off the front of the boat. At full throttle Tony turned left into the Florida Passage and headed for Ossabaw Sound.

Even to this day the rivers and creeks around Ossabaw Island and its sounds have very little boat traffic. In the early fifties this area was virtually empty, except for the occasional shrimp boat or crabber. As Tony headed down the Ogeechee River for the sound, he searched for other boats and thankfully saw none.

The tide was running out strongly when Tony maneuvered his boat to within twenty-five yards of the beach at Bradley Point. Using the bait bucket, he filled the boat with water until it swamped and sank. Then he started swimming to the beach. The undercurrents were strong, and on several occasions he feared he would be swept out to sea and drown. Finally he was able to make it to the beach, where he collapsed, trembling with exhaustion and dread. The same currents that had almost killed Tony would carry his boat far out into the Atlantic, where it would never be found. The crime was complete, the mercy killing accomplished. As he lay prostrate on the beach, Tony heaved an enervating sigh: he had saved his family from disgrace, put a tormented animal out of its misery, and spared Savannah another brutal massacre.

When Tony and Al didn't return from their fishing trip by dark, JJ called the marina at Isle of Hope. The dock master told him that his two sons had gone to Wassaw Sound and weren't back yet. He also said he was a little worried because a storm was starting to blow up. In no time JJ had the Marine Rescue Squadron from Tybee out in Wassaw Sound looking for his sons. They searched throughout the night, but found nothing. In the morning the Coast Guard joined the futile search. At ten o'clock the following morning, a shrimp boat spotted Tony lying on the beach at Bradley Point.

The eyes were hollow. The voice was from the grave.

"We tried Wassaw first but didn't have any luck. Then we gave Ossabaw a try. We went through a little creek. Al caught a big fish and got all excited. It was a whiting, Daddy—biggest one I ever saw. Only he was so wrapped up he got a lot of water in the boat. You know how clumsy he was. . . ." Tony's voice trailed off for a moment. "We were ridin' low. Then a big ol' wave crashed in and sank us. Oh Daddy, we didn't have our life jackets on, but I tried to save him, I did Daddy, I tried!"

"Take it easy, son. We know you did all you could."

"Did I? I don't know. Al panicked. First he was there, then he took in a lot of water. Then he was just gone. And the sea took him out. He was just—he's gone, Daddy, he's gone!"

"Thank God you're not." JJ O'Boyle crushed his shivering son to his breast. "We're lucky we still have you."

For two days after Tony had been found, the Marine Rescue Squadron searched for Al's body. For two weeks after that, shrimpers and crabbers expected to find his bloated corpse washed up along a beach or mud flat somewhere. A month after Al's death, a memorial Mass was said for the repose of his immortal soul at Blessed Sacrament. The church was filled to capacity with JJ and Tony's friends. No friend of Al's was there to mourn him.

Sweet Swing and the other detectives continued their investigation of the Slasher murders, but they came up empty. After a few months, when all leads had been exhausted and no more murders occurred, the file was gradually ignored for more pressing cases and the Victory Drive Slasher was slowly forgotten.

JJ and Mae felt and looked a lot older after Al had

drowned. But they were at least grateful that he was one with the Lord. They no longer had to worry about what would happen to him after they were gone.

Tony kept his position at the Southern Union Paper Company. He continued to prosper and grow in importance and power.

TONY O'BOYLE'S DEAL

As WORLD WAR II changed the rest of the world, so it changed Savannah. The Cold War, television, and the Salk vaccine would blend the sounds and thoughts of the late 1940's into the realities, dreams, and fears of the 1950's. Savannah would see cars with tail fins, coonskin caps, and the birth of the civil rights movement. It would hear Elvis Presley, sonic booms, the beep of Sputnik, and feel the need for bomb shelters, double-sessions in schools, and mass transit. John Hartman would chronicle these dizzying changes from his position as assistant editor of the *Savannah Morning Gazette*.

John watched with curious detachment the ascent of Tony O'Boyle up the rungs of Savannah's political ladder. He noted how often Tony's name arose in conversation about Savannah's future and how many times he found himself writing stories that contained references to Tony and his accomplishments. It was, while researching one of these stories, that John stumbled upon something about Tony that could prove damaging.

Before the war Savannah had possessed an elaborate streetcar system. Tracks went in every direction and even extended all the way to Isle of Hope, where the line terminated in a beautiful park close to the river. A streetcar ride out to Isle of Hope on a Sunday afternoon for a picnic was a recreational institution for many families. During the war, however, a need for buses arose: shipyard workers and others involved in the war effort had to have easy access to manufacturing facilities farther from the city center. After the war, as the city began to expand even farther past its old boundaries, buses were seen as the logical way of providing public transportation to these areas. The streetcar system still functioned well, however, and provided passengers with more than adequate transportation. Unfortunately, for the streetcar and ultimately part of the character of Savannah, the streetcars' days were numbered because of a scheme devised by Chauncey Wellington Spencer, president and majority stockholder of the Coastal Empire Savings and Trust Company. He would be aided by an able young attorney and political officiant named Anthony Vincent O'Boyle.

Mr. Spencer and his family had become wealthy in the banking and real estate business after the Civil War and had prospered even more during the two world wars. Spencer's nickname, "Snooks," derived from the game of snooker, a variation of pool. Every day at lunchtime, Snooks would leave his office and go to Bo Peep's, where he would play snooker with the many pool sharks who roamed Eastern Seaboard cities. They occasionally would float through Bo Peep's seeking easy prey. Snooks was good at his game and took great delight in out-hustling the hustlers. He looked upon the accumulation of wealth in the same way. He didn't need any more money—he just liked the pleasure of making it.

Tony O'Boyle, Jr., also liked to go to Bo Peep's during lunch and play snooker. Over the years he became friendly with Snooks Spencer. After the war, when Tony's star began to rise, Snooks took a special interest in his political ascent. It was over a game of snooker that Snooks first approached him about his plans for the Savannah Bus Company.

"Tony, I'd like your help in trying to meet the needs of this city with an expanded bus service."

"I'll do what I can for you, Mr. Spencer."

"Snooks, son, just call me Snooks. Hell, you've fought in the greatest war the world has ever known while I sat

on my big fat ass behind a desk. That earns you the right
to call me by my nickname."

Tony was flattered, because the Spencers were at the
top of Savannah's social heap and possessed all the status
that JJ had always longed for and Tony now actively
sought.

"Well, thank you very much, sir. I'm greatly humbled.
Actually, you served in World War I, if I'm not mistaken,
and it could hardly be said that you sat around during the
second. You served on the president's War Production
Board, did you not?"

Snooks was flattered also, not realizing the extent of
Tony's talent for the blarney. "I guess I did my part."
Then he put his arm around Tony and walked him over
to a quiet corner.

"What I'd like to talk to you about son is getting the
City Council to vote some money so the Savannah Bus
Company can buy some more buses. This streetcar system
we have is just not able to do the job anymore. We need
to scrap it and move entirely to buses. It's the wave of
the future. The only problem is that we're one vote short
on the council, and that's just holding up the progress of
this whole town."

Snooks took a long pull off his cigar, looked at it quiz-
ically as if it might explode, and continued. "Now the
problem that we're having is comin' from one of our aldermen, named Danny McTully. Old Danny just can't be
made to see the wisdom of this idea. I understand that
you or your daddy—I've known ol' JJ for years—might
be able to reason with Danny and bring him around to
seein' things our way."

At this point Snooks stopped, took another puff off his
cigar, stood back a little from Tony, and studied him carefully, pointedly awaiting a reply.

"Well, Mr. Spencer . . ."

"Snooks, son, Snooks."

"Well, ah, Snooks, I'll give this my undivided attention. I think your plan to revamp Savannah's public trans-

portation system is certainly in the best interests of the city, and I can't understand why Danny would want to stand in the way of progress. I'll speak with Daddy about it tonight, first thing."

"Well, Tony, I'll greatly appreciate any help you can give us." Then Snooks glanced quickly around the room to see if anyone could hear him. In a low voice he added, "Of course Mr. McTully needs to understand that in return for his progressive way of thinkin', I'd be more than pleased to help him out with his campaign expenses come election time, which I believe is just six short little months away. We've got to get this city movin' forward into the last half of the twentieth century, and I'm prepared to support folks with vision if Mr. McTully cares to have any."

"How much vision are we talkin' about, Snooks?"

"Five thousand dollars worth, son."

"I'll see what I can do."

Tony didn't believe for a moment that Snooks cared about giving Savannah a modern transportation system. He figured the old reprobate was going to make money off the deal somehow, and he was right. Tony just didn't know how much.

Stock in the Coastal Empire Savings and Trust Company was not the only stock that Snooks Spencer owned. Before the war he had invested heavily in General Motors—and General Motors was a bus manufacturer. The bus division happened to have an executive officer who knew Snooks well and had approached him about trying to influence the city of Savannah to drop its streetcar lines and buy a fleet of buses from the company. Not only would it help Snooks's GM stock, but he would also receive a handsome under-the-table dividend. Even that, however, was small change compared to the big dollars that Snooks stood to make by having his bank finance the entire purchase of the buses for the city.

Snooks was happiest when he was wheeling and dealing and making money. After Tony left, he racked the balls and drove a solid shot straight into their center, dropping two balls into the pockets and scattering the rest all over the table like fawning cronies. As he chalked the end of his cue, he said to himself, "I'll have this deal wrapped up by St. Patrick's Day, thanks to that little billy goat."

And so it came to pass. Danny McTully saw the light about the value of General Motors buses, and Savannah's streetcars rattled off into the history books. Coastal Empire Savings and Trust made a gang of money handling the financing for the city. And Tony O'Boyle made another powerful friend who was now in his debt. Everything was going according to schedule. Or so it seemed.

POLITICS IN THE FREE
STATE OF CHATHAM

THE CITY OF SAVANNAH elected its mayor and aldermen every four years, and in 1958 it was election time again. Danny McTully was going around town building up his war chest, making the usual calls on the people he had done favors for in the past. His appointment today was with Snooks Spencer, at the top floor of the Coastal Empire Building, which housed Snooks's bank. This, one of the tallest buildings in the city, stood on Wright Square, a block from the river and City Hall. Snooks's office in the southeast corner boasted a splendid view of both the Savannah river and downtown, which was especially dramatic from the tinted, floor-length windows. Snooks, who took full advantage of the location to impress and cajole his business contacts, and to schmooze with and flatter his friends, greeted Danny warmly, fixed him a drink, and took him over to the windows, where they admired their beautiful city together over a Johnnie Walker Black. Then Snooks, ever the master of the game, cut to the chase as soon as the small talk dwindled.

"Well, Danny, what can old Snooks Spencer do for you today?"

"Well, Mr. Spencer I . . ."

"Snooks, son, Snooks. I thought we were on a first-name basis for years; now you go and get formal on me. I thought we were friends."

"Well, uh, OK, uh Snooks. You see, it's getting to be that time again and I'm planning on running for reelection and I was hopin' you would be able to help me with my campaign."

Snooks slapped Danny on the back and told him of course he would, then went over to his desk and immediately wrote a check. Danny, however, was clearly unimpressed with what Snooks considered a healthy contribution.

Snooks couldn't stand ingratitude, especially from a little snot-nosed billy-goat Irishman like Danny McTully. With more than a trace of irritation, and in a frigid voice, he inquired: "Is there something wrong with this contribution, McTully?"

Danny McTully was born in the Old Fort section of Savannah. He may not have had the social status of Snooks Spencer, but he could match Snooks's testosterone level any day of the week. He looked Snooks straight in the eye.

"Let's get one thing straight, *Snooks*," Danny emphasized the name with sarcastic familiarity. "Four years ago I cast a vote for you that made your fucking bank one shit pile of money, and all I got out of you then was a measly thousand dollars paid under the table by your bagman Tony O'Boyle. Now you can only come up with two hundred and fifty for the man who made it possible for your bank to finance the whole bus deal? This is a fucking insult, Mr. Spencer. I'm sorry, Snooks, son, Snooks."

Snooks's eyes opened wide; his face turned red and he was about to say, "A thousand? It was five thousand I gave that bastard O'Boyle" when years of training and experience came to his aid. He knew all about how the game was played; he also had a deep ingrained suspicion of politicians—and of hidden tape-recorders. Snooks regained his composure and smilingly returned Danny's glare.

"Why I'm sorry, Mr. McTully. I'm afraid I don't know what you're talking about. I know Mr. O'Boyle, but I can assure you that I never gave him one red cent to influence your vote in any way. I do recall makin' a modest donation to your campaign the last time around though. I think it was in the same neighborhood as this time. I'm sure my accountants can find the check to verify my recollection."

Danny just stood looking at Snooks and then shook his head slowly. With bravado he stuck out his chin.

"So that's it? That's all I get? OK, have it your way. I'll remember this the next time you need a favor on the City Council." Danny handed Snooks his empty glass, did an abrupt and silent about-face, and stormed out of his office.

Snooks stood in silence for several moments and then burst into laughter. Another man might have been angry with Tony O'Boyle for shorting Danny, but Snooks thought it was hilarious. He admired Tony's ability to buy a politician so cheaply as well as the cunning and balls it took to keep the rest of the money for himself. He even realized that he couldn't fault the ambitious mick: after all, Snooks gave Tony the five thousand to deliver Danny's vote. He just assumed that Danny would be getting the full five grand. Snooks got the vote, and in getting the vote he got his money's worth. Poor Danny McTully was just an easy lay, that's all, and the way Snooks looked at it, the only one to blame for that was Danny himself. But none of this could mask the fact that Snooks now had a problem with Danny, and he expected Tony to deal with it.

They met on the seventy-foot motor yacht *Encore*, on which the bank entertained its best customers. As cautious as Snooks was, he felt secure on the *Encore*, where he could talk openly and without restraint. It was an evening cruise and the wives were invited. After a dinner of fried shrimp and oysters prepared by the *Encore*'s French chef, whom Snooks had hired away from the Mayflower Hotel in Washington, he and Tony retired to the fantail, while the wives entertained one another in the ship's saloon. The yacht was passing Fort Pulaski on its starboard side, and the oceanside Tybee Light was coming into view when Snooks got down to business.

"I admire your enterprise, son, but it's created a problem with McTully."

"I'm sorry about that, Snooks. I didn't think it would ever be a problem. I didn't know he'd be comin' to you before he came to me. I could have taken care of him then with no stink at all."

"Well, that's water over the dam now, and he's small change. I'm afraid we're not gonna be able to deal with McTully anymore, so we need to come up with another candidate more amenable to seein' things our way. I'll be glad to finance the campaign. Only this time keep me informed about what you do with the money."

Tony was leaning against the railing and admiring the sunset over Cockspur Island when he thought for a moment and said, "I don't think that's in your best interest, Snooks. You want to be able to truthfully say that you don't know anything about who got what. Or really that anybody got any money at all. It all needs to be cash, passed to me not by you but by a third party in the form of what we'll call consulting fees. What we want, more specifically, what you want, is a term we use in the legal profession called 'plausible deniability.'"

Snooks, too, was leaning against the railing and watching the fire in the sky. He was more impressed with Tony now than he was after his meeting with McTully. He looked over at Tony and smiled. Then he reached out and patted him on the back. "Good, son, damn good."

Tony wasn't able to find an Irishman willing to run against Danny McTully, so he had to settle on a cracker in the dry-cleaning business named Chester Warren Quarrels. The name Chester just sounded too stuffy, so his friends out at the Forest City Gun Club started calling him "Shotgun" back when he was a teenager because he was so good at hitting the birds with his twelve-gauge. The name stuck, and everybody in town called Chester Quarrels by his nickname, except the blacks who lived around his dry-cleaning plant on East Broad Street. They were afraid of Shotgun, and gave him plenty of respect. He was Mister Chester to them.

The '58 election took place when the civil rights movement was just getting started in Savannah, and a lot of white people were eager to elect somebody they thought could "handle the coloreds." This usually meant somebody opposed to giving a single inch on segregation, and Shotgun was known to be a man who didn't take any static off "them uppity nigras."

In spite of all the money that Snooks pumped into Shotgun's campaign, it was going nowhere because Danny had been such a hard-working grassroots man during his tenure in office. His district included a lot of Catholics, and a sufficient number of blacks who could tolerate Danny McTully but couldn't stomach Shotgun Quarrels. A month before the election it was obvious to Tony that Shotgun wasn't going to make the cut unless something dramatic happened.

Tony of course knew that Danny was spending a lot of time at the Knights of Columbus Hall on Liberty and Bull, pressing the flesh and shoring up the Catholic vote. He also knew that Danny would get a little loose up there late on Saturday nights with a trio of old Benedictine friends. On the Saturday before the election, Tony arranged for a black prostitute to be waiting outside when Danny left for home.

Danny was alone as he walked to his car, which was parked on Bull Street before an exclusive women's clothing store named Lady Jane's. As he unlocked his car and then opened the door, he was approached by a light-skinned, black hooker who went by the name of Charity. Charity was very attractive, and many of her regular clients were white men who happened to appreciate what, for Savannah, was a walk on the wild side.

Danny was about half in the bag when Charity asked him for a cigarette. She needed a ride to the Union Station, where she said she was supposed to meet her mother, coming in on the train from New York. It wasn't far, Charity was attractive, and Danny was wound tighter than a three-dollar watch. Most of all he was a nice guy, so he told the girl to get in and that he would drive her to the station.

As soon as Danny started his car, Charity opened her blouse and hiked her skirt up, exposing herself. Danny's mouth fell open as she slid next to him and began to unzip his pants. The car swerved as he tried to push her aside, and that was when the police car that had been positioned for the encounter turned on its red light and pulled the motorists over to the curb.

Danny was charged with driving under the influence, reckless driving, and solicitation of prostitution. When the paddy wagon pulled up to the police barracks on Habersham Street with Danny and Charity inside, a photographer was there to take a picture as the politician, handcuffed to the hooker, climbed out the back. The Sunday morning paper carried the picture and the story under the headline "ALDERMAN MCTULLY ARRESTED WITH COLORED PROSTITUTE." Danny got creamed on election day.

Not only did Danny lose the election, he lost his job at the funeral home where he worked, and his wife only halfway believed his story. Danny knew he had been set up, and eventually he learned that Tony O'Boyle had been the man financing Shotgun Quarrels. He also learned from some friends in the black community that Charity was on Tony's payroll. Danny swore revenge.

He went to the FBI because some federal money had

been used to buy the buses, and at least part of his story leaked during the investigation. John Hartman got word of it and proceeded to investigate on his own. He uncovered even more dirt than the FBI because he had more contacts who were willing to talk, and he wrote a scathing story of political corruption involving both Tony O'Boyle and Snooks Spencer.

The only problem was that it never got printed. When the *Gazette*'s senior editor read the story, he contacted Snooks Spencer. Snooks's bank was a major advertiser with the paper, and Snooks was close friends with the paper's publisher.

John Hartman was furious at the quashing of what he considered to be an excellent—and truthful—story. He quieted down after a few weeks, but by then he had made sworn enemies of Tony and Snooks. Methodically they set about having him removed from his job . . . and not only did they want him off the paper, they wanted him discredited if not destroyed. A lot of people in town had heard about the story, and they tended to believe that Snooks and Tony were in bed together. This made the two men even more furious.

Finally they prevailed, with the assistance of a man at the *Gazette* in charge of expense-account information. John had kept honest but sloppy records of the expenses he charged to the paper, and it didn't take much for the accountant to make it look as if he had stolen money by padding his expenses. Under a cloud of public suspicion generated by the paper itself, John was forced to resign. He took a job teaching journalism at the local junior college.

Several weeks after everything had cooled down, Tony and Snooks were rehashing what had happened over a game of snooker at Bo Peep's. Snooks leaned over the table to put the three ball in a far corner pocket. Just before the shot he said to Tony, "I'm amazed at how well you can handle problems in Savannah. What's the trick?"

"There's no trick, Snooks. It's plain and simple. Nobody fucks with Tony O'Boyle in the Free State of Chatham."

IV

BC BOYS

Yet could we turn the years again,
And call those exiles as they were
In all their loneliness and pain,
You'd cry, 'Some woman's yellow hair
Has maddened every mother's son.'

Come fall in line you men of old BC,
For we will win another victory.
We're gonna' beat that High School team today,
We're gonna' beat them well and how we say, we say!

—THE OPENING STANZA OF THE FIGHT SONG OF
BENEDICTINE MILITARY SCHOOL

IN YEARS TO COME, John-Morgan Hartman would look back on the summer of 1963 as perhaps the best and most special of his life. He turned sixteen then and had his own car. Those sweet, broiling months seemed like an entire lifetime. He was at the stage when one looked upon time and youth as something that would never run out.

"John-Morgan, it's me. Listen, can you get your old man's car tonight? Ann Marie Kerry is spending the night with Katherine down at the beach and she doesn't have a date. Katherine says she'd probably like to go out with you, so we can double. Shit, man, she's tough. Beautiful ass. Think you can get the car?"

"I don't know. How do you know she said that?"

"I'm telling you, they're staying down at Tybee and I called Katherine to see what she was doing tonight and she told me about Ann Marie. I thought about you, and Katherine asked Ann Marie and she said yeah. Shit man, I'm telling you this is your chance. Remember when we saw her at the 'X' last week? Man, you were just dreamin' about her then. Get the car and let's go! I'm tellin' ya, I think she likes you!"

"OK, my father's not home yet, but when he gets here, I'll ask. What time do you want me come by?"

"About 7:30. There's supposed to be some kind of party down there. Katherine knows the girls, they go to Country Day."

John Hartman, Sr., was, at heart, a conservative man. He didn't like to take chances with the things that really mattered. But he was also a man who had what some people call a "flair for life." Because of this, he had purchased a bright red Chevrolet convertible. In the days before the foreign car invasion, an Impala Super Sport convertible was true to its name. The day he had purchased it, the salesman who sold it to him had joked on the showroom floor that this was a car for those who were young at heart, the ones who still liked to enjoy themselves. "Why heck, Mr. Hartman, my daddy always used to say, you don't have to play a sport to be a sport, and that's what this thing is for, sports." They laughed as his son John-Morgan fiddled with the radio and drooled over the car. John-Morgan had gotten his name because his father refused to have his son called Johnny or, even worse, Little John. So, to avoid confusion around the house, John-Morgan's mother set upon the idea of simply using her son's first and middle names around the house to distinguish him from his father. The idea had taken hold as he grew older and now "John-Morgan" was his name.

He won't do it. He'll probably buy that four-door Bel Air out on the lot, thought John-Morgan as his father continued to talk with the salesman about the car. That night, when John, Sr., pulled up in the drive way with the Super Sport, he couldn't believe his eyes.

"I'll let you drive it some, but you've got to promise me, no speeding. You get caught for anything and that's it."

"Yes, sir!" said John-Morgan with a grin from ear to ear as he stood next to the car, trying to take it all in. His eyes kept wandering back to the front fender, where the chrome emblem of two crossed racing flags was attached. Above the flags was the number "409"—the largest and most powerful V-8 that Chevrolet made.

As his father walked back to the house, he looked over his shoulder at John-Morgan and smiled. He liked the car, but he had really bought it because he knew that his son had wanted it so badly.

John-Morgan didn't really know Ann Marie Kerry. He knew who she was and he'd seen her around, but he had never spoken more than a few words to her. She had been at some BC dances with the boys generally considered to be the best looking and most popular, the "cool" ones who always seemed to make it with the girls. John-Morgan didn't think of himself as that type. He agreed to meet her at the beach, but if the truth were known, he was a little afraid of going out with Ann Marie. She was so pretty, and he so shy, that he had never even considered trying to talk to her, much less asking her for a date, and now he would be going out with her. His father's new car couldn't have come at a better time.

John-Morgan knew he would be able to borrow it. His father was, well, a sport! He was a good guy, and although he could occasionally be stern and hard, he would much rather be easygoing. John, Sr., hadn't forgotten what it was like to be his son's age, so when John-Morgan told him that he and Mike Sullivan were going to the beach, he got the usual admonitions about the dangers of the Tybee road and the Tybee police. But he also got the car.

"One other thing, mister. I better not be even suspecting anything about beer tonight. You got that?"

"Yes, sir. We got dates. No problem. You got it, Daddy."

Ann Marie Kerry had not known John-Morgan Hartman in grammar school because she had attended Sacred Heart, whereas he had gone to Blessed Sacrament. Now, however, she would be entering junior year at St. Vincent's Academy, the Catholic girls' high school in Savannah. John-Morgan was a student at Benedictine Military School, Savannah's Catholic high school for boys. It was there that he had first seen Ann Marie, at the commissioning dance during his freshman year. He had taken note of her then, as had the entire school, because she was so pretty, so graceful, and so very poised. He was certain that she had never noticed him, and with a sigh he had relegated her to that ever-growing batch of beautiful females who would never give him the time of day. He did not have a date for the dance.

In the ninth grade John-Morgan was small for his age and seemed to retain the little-boy look that most of the other guys were beginning to shake. Some even had whiskers, real whiskers, and needed to shave to pass inspection in the morning. John-Morgan wasn't much to look at in his freshman year, and in the heady days of ritual adolescent mating combat, he thought of himself as a lightweight.

Then nature started to assert herself, and after the hormones kicked in, John-Morgan began to grow and put on weight. From the beginning of his freshman year at BC to the end of his sophomore year, he grew six inches and put on thirty-five pounds. More than that, he had even begun to shave . . . a little. He had a mustache, sort of, and a bit of a beard on his chin. His arms and shoulders were beginning to fill out, and his many hours of swimming were starting to shape him like a man. With this came the necessary courage to approach that which enchanted him, and yet terrified him. He longed for the ease with which some of the boys could approach girls and speak with them. But what to say, and how to say it?

John-Morgan had dated some, and the girls were all cute. He thought he had even experienced that wonderful thing called love. Indeed it was surprising how fast people could fall in and out of love. He had French-kissed a girl. Simply stunning! He'd even copped a feel or two. More stunning still! But that was about the extent of it. As with his peers, most of his cognitive thoughts were about girls. It was hard to get past thinking about sheerly physical beauty and attributes, but he managed—sometimes. At that phase in his life, it was girls, cars, and boats. Occasionally it was girls, boats, and cars.

Ann Marie Kerry was the middle of three children, all girls, and had gained the early maturity that sometimes comes with middle children. She was a steady and good student, the kind the nuns always called upon to take care of the lower grades when one of them was out of the classroom. The children she had authority over liked her because she wasn't mean, which a lot of the other monitors were. When Ann Marie was in charge of a class, the boys didn't act up because she was so sweet and pretty, and the girls never misbehaved because they all wanted to be just like her.

Ann Marie had not been allowed to go out with a boy alone in a car until she was sixteen. Her favorite person was her father, and every boy she knew was, consciously or unconsciously, judged against him. Not many measured up. She was honest enough to recognize that she was attractive, but she never considered herself beautiful. In this she was almost alone. Ann Marie didn't have as many dates as people assumed she did because John-Morgan wasn't the only boy in town who was intimidated by her good looks. In fact, by her junior year of high school some of the girls and most of the boys thought she was stuck up. Actually, the word with the boys was that she was frigid. This was just another way of saying that Ann Marie had certain standards that weren't exactly popular in the back seat of a car.

One of her few friends was Katherine Dugan, also a student at St. Vincent's, whose parents had a large house on the beach side of Butler Avenue with a clear view of the ocean. She and Ann Marie were spending the first week of summer there together, where a person could stand on the second-floor screen porch and hear the waves breaking. A full moon was out over the water and the tide was all the way in. By the time John-Morgan and Mike had pulled up to the Dugan house, the moon was a large, buttery shade of yellow over the Atlantic.

"I love your car," said Ann Marie when John-Morgan opened the door for her.

"It's my father's. I've got an old '55 Chevy Bel Air. He let's me use this on dates."

Because of the bucket seats in front, Ann Marie couldn't slide over and sit next to her date, but she wouldn't have done so in any case. Her parents had forbidden her: they said it looked tacky, and she had to agree.

Katherine, on the other hand, was right next to Mike in the back seat, and he had his arm around her. But they'd been dating for several months, and Katherine said she was in love with Mike. Besides, sitting next to a guy in the back seat was a little different.

As they drove down Butler Avenue to Sixteenth Street, John-Morgan and Ann Marie talked. He was thrilled. She started the conversation and actually carried the ball. She asked all about him and even seemed interested in the Civil War. She had heard that he was a Civil War treasure hunter and found it fascinating. He was fascinated by *everything* about her.

The party was disappointing, so they left early. They hadn't known many people, and a lot of them were drinking. Ann Marie told John-Morgan that she hated it when guys got drunk, and he made a permanent mental note. They spent the rest of the evening on the screened porch at Katherine's house. John-Morgan and Ann Marie sat together on a big swing facing the ocean, and talked. Mike and Katherine were over on the sofa, mostly making out.

Somewhere toward the end of that first encounter, Ann Marie put her head back on the swing and turned toward John-Morgan. He, simultaneously and in all innocence, had done the same thing, and now they were face to face, no more than six inches apart. She simply looked at him, first his eyes and then his lips, and then his eyes again. John-Morgan didn't know what to do.

Ann Marie never kissed boys on the first date. She rarely kissed boys at all. But this night seemed different. Maybe it was because of the beach, maybe it was the excitement of the first weekend of summer vacation, and maybe it was simply him. Whatever it was, she didn't move and continued to hold his gaze.

John-Morgan had a soft look about him. He had tender eyes and full lips that smiled a good deal. His hair had turned a sandy blond from exposure to the sun, and his skin was deeply tanned. But most of all, there was a feeling about him. He was strong, but there was something sincerely gentle about the way he acted. As he started to move even closer to her, Ann Marie met him halfway, and they both let out a sigh as their lips touched.

It had none of the impatient prodding that some boys employed in their kissing. John-Morgan was easy, and for some reason Ann Marie drew herself into his arms. They held that first kiss for a blissfully long time. For the next hour John-Morgan felt as he had never felt before in his life. Every now and then he would pull back from Ann Marie just to look at her, perhaps making sure that she was really as pretty as he had remembered from the moment before. Years later, he would recall the smell of her hair, the touch of her lips, and the taste of her mouth. Sometimes it would sustain him. Other times it would be torture.

When the evening was over, and they stood on the steps to say good night, there was a certain feeling. Both of them sensed it. John-Morgan knew that this was the beginning of something unexpected and wonderful for him. They both knew, without speaking, that they would spend this summer together. More than anything else, although neither was aware of it then, that summer would be their time to enjoy the innocence and purity of young love—that comes only once.

BUBBA SILVERMAN AND

MIKE SULLIVAN

TYBEE ISLAND, also known as "the Beach" by just about everyone who went there, had been the playground of Savannahians since the railroad to the island was completed just before World War I. Tybee was wide open. You could get a beer, bet the dogs or horses, wager on ball games, even on Sundays. In the mid-1920's the Tybee Road was constructed, and even more young people were able to avail themselves of the island's charms, which were mostly sun, sand, and suds.

John-Morgan and Ann Marie, along with their friends, were at the beach at least three of the weekdays and every weekend that summer. Colonel and Mrs. Emile Deitz, John-Morgan's maternal grandparents, owned a spacious cottage at the south end in addition to their home at Isle of Hope. The Hartmans would spend each summer at the cottage, and John-Morgan became known as one of the "Beach Boys" long before the musical group ever became popular. The cottage was a magnet for him and for the two close friends with whom he spent most of his time, Mike Sullivan, and Neal Silverman, whom everyone called "Bubba."

Bubba lived next door to John-Morgan back in town; and even though he was Jewish, he also attended BC. To those uneducated in the social customs of Savannah, his attending a Catholic school would seem most unusual. Indeed, his relatives up north recoiled in horror when they learned about it. The shock deepened further when they also discovered that the Catholic school was a military academy, and reached its nadir of nefariousness when they found out that it was taught by the Benedictines, a strict order of German monks. An orthodox Jewish boy named "Bubba," who went to a Catholic military school taught by Krauts, and whose best friends were two Irish Catholics? This became the topic of many a discussion among Bubba's northern relatives. The conversations would usually end with the interjection that "at least he's not dating a gentile!" But Bubba only needed a little time.

Bubba's father, Bernard Silverman of Brooklyn, New York, wound up in Savannah the way hundreds of young men did: he came to the area during World War II, fell in love with either the city or a girl, and resolved to return when the war was over. Bernie first saw Savannah from a window on the East Coast Champion as it backed into the old Union Station on West Broad Street during the summer of 1942. He was in the city to become part of the new Eighth Air Force that was forming there. He didn't get much of a chance to see Savannah then, but after he had completed his training he spent a little time with a Savannah friend—John-Morgan's father.

John, who knew just about everybody in town, was able to fix Bernie up with pretty Lynn Fineman, a friend of Beth Deitz. On their first date Bernie and Lynn accompanied John and Beth to the Tybrisa Pavilion at the beach to hear the Dorsey Brothers play. The beach worked its charms on the new couple as it once had on the old. After the war Bernie returned to Savannah to marry Lynn and settle down into the banking business. It wasn't long before Lynn's father approached him about joining the family business, and soon he was running the finances for Fineman Motors, the Cadillac dealer.

Bernie quickly figured out that Savannah did not fit the picture of the South drawn for him by all those folks up in New York. On his first trip down, Bernie had visions of the Ku Klux Klan and burning crosses, hound dogs and barefooted rednecks, sloshing moonshine and spittoons full of Red Man chewing tobacco. He imagined Negroes shuffling along on their way to pick cotton as they sang spirituals, big burly white policemen with bag-of-meal stomachs bursting out of their shirt buttons, shotguns constantly blasting in the background. He remembered the Leo Frank case and how everybody in Brooklyn used to talk about how Leo had been kidnapped from his jail cell down in Milledgeville, Georgia, and lynched just because he was Jewish. Bernie was ready for God only-knew-what when he stepped off that train. He found something very different, and he used to chuckle when he thought about telling his aunts and uncles where his son went to school.

The Hartmans and the Silvermans lived in Savannah's first postwar subdivision. Fairway Oaks, on the city's southern boundary, had originally been a dairy farm. Then the pressure of the postwar housing boom pushed the cows off to make way for NashRamblers, Hudsons, and DeSotos, split-level and ranch-style houses, and lots of little girls and boys conceived in the passionate nights that followed the Japanese surrender—and, most of all, the return of all the young men caught up in the afterglow and pure energy of that victory.

Bubba's buddy, Mike Sullivan, had also arrived on this earth as an integer of that same collective passion known as the postwar baby boom. Although he had not migrated from the North, Vincent Sullivan, Mike's father, had earned his place in that fraternity of men by riding an aircraft carrier around the South Pacific as flaming Zeroes tried to land in a vertical fashion on its deck at five hundred miles an hour. He had been aboard the USS *Franklin* as it battled for its life off Okinawa. Mike's soul flew to earth the night his father returned to Savannah after a long stay in a Naval Hospital for injuries he received in one of those landings. That night Vincent and Carol knew that something special had happened. They were to know it six more times in the years that followed.

The war had changed Vincent for the better. He no longer lost his temper easily. He had seen enough fighting to last a lifetime. He had also moderated his drinking, and just about quit altogether. With the advent of this newly found self-control, Vincent Sullivan was able to make a go of it in the contracting business and had soon made Shamrock Builders into one of Savannah's largest.

RACCOON ISLAND

AS A YOUNG CHILD, John-Morgan had heard stories about his family, especially Captain Patrick Driscoll (his great, great grandfather) and the Battle of Battery Jasper. He knew about the box full of gold and jewels that was supposedly buried on Raccoon Island, although some members of his family now claimed that it was only a wild story. He had seen Captain Driscoll's sword and the uniform he had died in, and he had studied the ancient portrait of the blue-eyed Confederate artillery officer hanging over the fireplace in his grandfather's study.

More than once, his grandfather had spread maps of the area on the floor. Colonel Deitz would point to the locations of various Civil War forts around Savannah and then show John-Morgan Raccoon Island. Using Captain Driscoll's own sword as a pointer, he would demonstrate how the *Nahunt* had steamed up the Ogeechee and shelled little Battery Jasper relentlessly. With great animation the old man would describe how the shells had pounded the fort. Then, always with a radiant smile on his face, he would explain how the last shot from John-Morgan's dying great, great, grandfather had so terribly damaged the Yankee ironclad that she had to withdraw for fear of sinking. John-Morgan would sit wide-eyed as the colonel described Captain Driscoll and Shadrack, who had died in each other's arms.

John-Morgan loved sitting by the fireplace when the weather was cold, late at night, as his father and the colonel fought the battles of the Civil War all over again, and analyzed the Southern victories and defeats. During the evening, the colonel would occasionally pour John, Sr., some of the same mysterious brown liquid he had in his own glass as they continued their invisible journeys. His grandmother would refer to the liquid solemnly as "the colonel's medicine" and admonish little John-Morgan to leave it strictly alone. As the years went by, John-Morgan came to know "the colonel's medicine" as Jack Daniels Black Label. He even sneaked a taste, and found, much to his surprise, that it was awful. Because of that, he decided that it probably *was* medicine.

For his twelfth birthday John-Morgan's grandfather bought him a boat over the mild protests of his parents who mostly complained of the cost. It wasn't a large boat, only fifteen feet, but it was safe and it was fast. Colonel Deitz had insisted on purchasing a Boston Whaler, claiming that it was unsinkable. It was equipped with a seventy-horse Johnson so John-Morgan and his friends could water-ski. John-Morgan remembered the boat as the best present he ever received, because it opened a whole new world for him.

The boat was kept at the Deitz's Isle of Hope home, and John-Morgan, along with Bubba and Mike, used it to explore every creek and hammock from Little Tybee to Ossabaw Island. All three were in Scouts together and grew to love the freedom and self-reliance that camping gave them. The boat allowed them to expand their initial outdoor experiences from Camp Strachan into more extended trips to the surrounding islands.

During the summer of his thirteenth year, John-Morgan decided to go to Raccoon Island and have a look at Battery Jasper. Bubba and Mike went with him. With a boatload of hot dogs and Coca-Colas, and an army-surplus tent, the three set out to spend the weekend on Raccoon Island. That trip was the beginning of a fascination with the island and the fort that they would never lose.

Among the many surprises in store was the largest wild hog they had ever seen, along with his concubines and offspring. The enterprising Bubba Silverman quickly dubbed the great boar "the Grand Dragon" and the other boars the "Invisible Empire." The Grand Dragon was singularly ferocious; the boys carefully avoided his lair and afforded him the utmost respect. Nevertheless, their determination to find the Driscoll treasure outweighed their fear of the boar; and they did not know that the Grand Dragon feared the scent of human beings just as much. He usually retreated deep into the underbrush when they visited Raccoon Island.

During the next four years, the trio visited their place of wonder dozens of times. With the aid of a metal detector, they dug up all sorts of Civil War artifacts, from spoons to cannonballs; but despite all their labors and all of their pleas for luck or even divine intervention, they never found the fabled Driscoll treasure. They did find, however, one thing that confirmed part of the Driscoll legend—deep inside the fort's bombproof bunker lay the grave of Shadrack Bryan.

* * *

The island was very spooky to the boys, and in a way this made it even more alluring. They were particularly fascinated by the large azalea bushes that grew all over the fort itself. The bushes always seemed to be trimmed, and yet the threesome never saw signs that anyone had been there. When the boys told the colonel about the azaleas, he told them he had heard about them over the years from people who would occasionally hunt on the island. Some people thought the island was haunted by the ghosts of Captain Driscoll and Shadrack, he said, and these spirits had planted the azaleas and tended to them. The boys were petrified by this tale, although none of them would admit it, and their fear only enhanced the island's mystery.

Dire tales such as these discouraged the fainthearted from exploring. The ghosts, the bugs, and the difficulty of getting to the island had kept it almost as untouched as the day the last Confederate soldiers left. Except for the heavy growth of trees and bushes.

It was John-Morgan's idea to take a little jaunt out to Raccoon Island to see Battery Jasper on a triple date with Ann Marie, Bubba, Mike, and their girlfriends.

A good breeze from the south blew the gnats and mosquitoes into the undergrowth that day and also served to cool the couples as they climbed all over the fort. The bronze plaque reading "The Breastplate of St. Patrick" was still attached to the old cannon resting in the gun pit. Jagged pieces of the barrel's end attested to the power of the explosion that had shattered the great gun and taken the life of Captain Driscoll.

With the aid of a flashlight, they went deep into the bombproof shelter, still intact under the walls of the battery. Everybody was a little nervous about going into the tunnel, but Mike, eager to demonstrate his courage and manhood, went first and pronounced it clear of the snakes and alligators that loved to crawl into the coolness of the cave-like bunker. The inside was surprisingly free of the leaves and other debris that normally collected in such places. Shadrack's tombstone was eerily clean, and the white marble shone ghostly in the light of Mike's flashlight.

After the girls had satisfied their curiosity, they decided it was time to eat lunch and spread blankets under the shade of the oak tree where the boys always camped. The tree was so large, and its limbs so long and heavy, that they touched the ground under the stress of their own weight.

It was Ann Marie who first noticed movement out of the corner of her eye.

She took a bite from her sandwich and then looked upward with a start. At first she *hoped* she had been mistaken, but she could not believe it. Staring fixedly at the eastern end of the fort, she finally made up her mind. "I saw something move down there," she said to John-Morgan quietly, and with a measure of fear.

"Where? I don't see anything."

"Down there, just by that palmetto tree at the end of the fort. I saw something move, John-Morgan, I swear."

John-Morgan and the other boys looked carefully at the spot where Ann Marie was pointing.

"I still don't see anything. You probably saw one of the wild pigs that live here, or maybe a deer."

"No, John-Morgan, it was a person. I swear it was a person."

"But, it couldn't be. There wasn't any boat out on the point. If there were somebody here, there'd be a boat, unless somebody else just left 'em. Who'd do that? There's nothing here except the fort and some pigs. Naw, you saw a pig move."

Further protests from Ann Marie were unavailing, and everyone went back to lunch. Then Katherine, lying on one of the blankets, froze in her place and said quietly, "I see something moving out there too, and it looks like a colored person. There's a colored man out there."

The three boys jumped to their feet and moved closer to the place where the girls were pointing. When they were about twenty yards from the palmetto, a husky black boy stepped from behind it. Everybody jumped.

"Who are you, and what the hell are you doing on this island?" Mike called out in agitation.

The boy said nothing, so the three moved closer. The girls all bunched together and held on to one another for safety.

"Now look here nigger, I said who the hell are you and what the hell are you doing on our island." Mike was growing angrier by the second. "And what gives you the right to be spying on us, anyway?"

"I'm not spying on ya'll and this isn't your island. You can't keep me off it. And don't call me nigger if you don't want your tail whipped."

This startled everyone, especially Mike, who couldn't or wouldn't speak for several seconds. Finally John-Morgan said: "He's right. No need to call him names." Then he turned to the intruder. "Nobody's gonna do anything to you. You just scared us, that's all. We've been coming here for years and you're the first person we've ever seen out here. Come on over under the tree and sit down for a while. We were just having lunch. Would you like a Coke or something?"

Cautiously the young man followed. John-Morgan opened a Coke and handed it over. "My name's John-Morgan Hartman. This is Bubba Silverman and that's Mike Sullivan. These are our girlfriends: Ann Marie, Katherine, and Connie. We're out here to look at the fort. Sometimes we come here to camp. The guys, I mean. We like it here. We're all from Savannah. What's your name?"

The newcomer gazed at him steadily after a long swallow on the Coke. "Lloyd Bryan. I'm from Savannah too. I come out here to tend to those flowers and my great-granddaddy's grave." John Morgan's eyes bulged, but Lloyd Bryan coolly continued. "My family's been doing it since the Civil War. They planted the azaleas years ago, long before my father was born. We just try to keep them trimmed back. It's sort of a special place for us. A place nobody's supposed to know about. I guess that's finished now."

Bubba's face lit up. "The ghosts of Raccoon Island. Well I'll be! How about that? Where's he buried?"

"Inside the fort, down in the cave, at the end of the room to the right."

"No wonder the place is so neat and clean."

"Good Lord have mercy, your great-grandfather was Shadrack Bryan?" John-Morgan was still incredulous.

"Yeah."

"Well, my great-grandfather was Captain Patrick Driscoll, the Confederate soldier who died in Shadrack Bryan's arms. I'm pleased to meet you."

Lloyd Bryan was now as startled as John-Morgan had been. He sat back on the tree limb for a few moments before he spoke. Then he said in a matter-of-fact voice: "Then your relatives owned my relatives."

It was a fraught moment. John-Morgan drew a breath and shook his head and smiled. "Yeah, I guess so."

Lloyd smiled too, and the tension passed. One had called him a nigger, but that's just the way it was sometimes with white people. Black folks had learned long ago to roll with the punches.

"That's OK," he said, "I didn't mean anything by it. I'm just—*stunned* by the situation. What a way to meet somebody! Especially somebody like you. You could almost say that we're related!"

With that comment everyone broke into laughter. "Here, have a sandwich," said Mike. "They're good. Katherine made 'em."

"WHERE DO YOU GO to school?" asked Bubba.

"I have been going to St. Pius the Tenth." Lloyd stopped for a moment to take a swig of Coke, but mostly to prepare himself for what he was about to say. "But next year I'll be going to BC."

Everyone sat in stunned silence for a few moments. Finally Katherine managed a meek, "Are you sure?"

"Yep, I'm sure. As a matter of fact, I'm already registered. My momma already talked to Father Hector. I'll be starting along with the rest of the school the day after Labor Day."

This was a little too much for Mike, who began to move his feet around nervously. John-Morgan caught the action out of the corner of his eye at about the same time that Mike finally exploded.

"That's bullshit! BC is for white boys, and Pius is for coloreds. It's the law. They aren't gonna have no . . ." Mike stopped himself just short of saying "niggers," and lamely ended with "nobody but white boys at Benedictine. There'd be a riot. You know we carry guns at that school. Keep 'em with us all the time, right by our desks. The Cadet Corps wouldn't allow it."

John-Morgan shook his head in frustration and snapped: "Don't be stupid, Mike, he knows we don't carry rifles into the classroom. You know integration is gonna happen. The Supreme Court said so."

"Well, screw the Supreme Court. He can't go to our school. It just isn't right."

Lloyd had been told to prepare for such incidents, and his mother had spoken with him many times about how to act when it happened. Even the bishop had called him to his study one day and told him how he expected Lloyd to act when confronted with just such circumstances. "Just remember, it's a whole new thing for them, same as it is for you. Don't let your temper get in the way. If you start shouting and fighting back, then you've lost. You can't beat them on that level. You've got to maintain your cool. Show them what strength you have in your reserve. You're a strong young man deep down inside. That will show through, and they'll learn to respect you for that. If you gain their respect, you have won the battle."

The ten-second silence seemed to last ten minutes. Finally Lloyd looked at John-Morgan and said: "I'm Catholic, and the bishop says I can go to BC if I want to. Well, I want to. I don't want any trouble, though. I'll leave everybody alone. I don't expect to make any friends at BC. I'm not stupid. But I'll be there, this September the fourth, in my uniform, just like everybody else." Then he looked over at Mike and slowly added, "And I'll be carrying a rifle too."

"Oh yeah!" Mike blurted, before he was shouted down by Bubba.

"Shut up!" Bubba said, more an order than a request. "There's nothing we can do about it. BC'll still be BC. He's just one guy. Now calm down."

"This is bullshit! We're leaving. Come on Katherine, let's get the stuff in the boat."

Lloyd sat on the tree limb and looked down at the ground. Then he shrugged, stood up straight, and quietly looked at John-Morgan. "I guess I better get going now," he said as he began to walk back toward the fort.

John-Morgan and Bubba exchanged knowing glances for a moment and then John-Morgan called out to the descendant of his forbearers' slaves: "Hey Lloyd." Surprised, Lloyd turned to face the music. "See ya the day after Labor Day. . . . You know, at BC."

Lloyd stood for a second, then raised his hand and waved: "Yeah, the day after Labor Day."

"Just keep your cool and show them your inner strength," Lloyd repeated to himself as he returned to trimming the azaleas. "Inner strength," he repeated to himself again.

Football was the focus of sporting activities at Benedictine Military School. BC had basketball and baseball too, but nothing got the juices of the alumni and students going like the sport of the South. A winning football team really brought the spirit of the school to a burn; everything else seemed to get better when the football team was having a good year. Alumni donations followed right behind the score. The bigger the win, the bigger the donations from the "Old BC Boys."

In those days it was "Catholics versus Crackers," Irish against everybody else. It was butt-kicking elevated to an art form and then made legal. It was war, plain and simple, and nobody could do it better than the boys from the Catholic military school on Bull Street. Sometimes they lost, but the game was never easy. "Irish love to fight," the old alums at the Knights of Columbus were oft to say, "and football ain't nothing but fightin'."

In the fall the biggest day in Savannah was always Thanksgiving, but not because of the turkey. It was because of the "BC-High School" football game that took place that afternoon. In the early years Savannah had only two public high schools for white children, Commercial and Savannah High. Commercial High was for the students who did not plan to attend college and had courses weighted heavily toward jobs that didn't require a college degree. Savannah High School was the college preparatory school located in the center of what was then the city's most prestigious neighborhood, Ardsley Park.

In the days before forced busing caused a white flight to private schools, Savannah High was considered a fine place to send a child unless one were Catholic and wanted a religious education. Then it was Benedictine for the boys and Saint Vincent's Academy (which provided BC's cheerleaders) for the girls. But there was one peculiar exception to the rule. Because of BC's strict discipline and

high academic requirements, it had long been a tradition
for many Jewish families to send their sons to Benedictine. Therefore, on Thanksgiving Day, it became the "Irish
and the Jews" against the "Crackers."

The rivalry between Benedictine and Savannah High
was already more than fifty years old when Lloyd Bryan
tried out at running back for the Benedictine Cadets. On
Thanksgiving Day the year before, BC had been beaten.
Actually, it had been humiliated. The score was twenty-
eight to six. BC was lucky to get the six.

This year the Cadets had cruised through the season
leading up to the big game, but all their opponents had
been weak so far, so beating them hadn't been a real test.
Savannah High was also unbeaten, and the word around
town was that they would roll over the Cadets again. That
was intolerable, almost blasphemous to contemplate. The
Cadets were determined to win.

In the days before integration not much attention was
paid to the black schools and their athletes. The sports
page of the *Savannah Morning Gazette* didn't even write
about them. That was done in the *Herald*, a small paper
published for the blacks in Savannah. Segregation was so
strict that the *Gazette* didn't even carry wedding and death
announcements about black people. Those arrested or injured in automobile accidents were referred to as "colored." Because of this, no one in the white community
had ever heard of Lloyd Bryan and how well he could
run with the football. Because of segregation, no scouts
from white colleges ever went to football games at Pius
the Tenth.

When Lloyd walked on to the practice field in Forsyth
Park, about six blocks from Benedictine, Coach Dick
Myrick didn't even know if he would be able to practice
with the Cadets because the park was segregated. Until
that time, no "coloreds" had been allowed where Benedictine held its afternoon scrimmages. But Coach Myrick
realized almost instantly that Lloyd Bryan was going to
be one hell of an asset to his football team. Lloyd had

never worked out with weights in his life, but he was
muscular in a way that most boys would have to work at
for years. At seventeen he was already six feet tall and
205 pounds with a bullish neck that shouted out "damned
good athlete." He could run the hundred much faster than
anybody else on the team, and when it came to cutting in
and out of a field of defensive players, he did it as though
he were dancing. His running was fluid. He could think
on his feet. He could even catch the ball like a receiver.
Lloyd was the best that Myrick had seen since he had
been at BC, whether as a coach or a player.

For two reasons, however, both of them sound, the
coach held Lloyd back unless he really needed him. To
begin with, he didn't want to take a chance that Lloyd
would get injured and be lost to the team. In addition, he
didn't want to anger the alumni. They were upset enough
that Lloyd was even at the school; Myrick didn't want to
rub their noses in the fact that he was the star player over
all the Irish kids whose fathers and grandfathers had bled
for "Old BC." Only if it looked as if BC needed a key
play or a touchdown to win a game would the coach put
Lloyd in to pull it off. The idea worked, and Lloyd almost
never let him down. Over time, even though Lloyd was
"colored," the fans came to accept the fact that he could
and would score for BC. Slowly that became enough.

Benedictine was a relatively small school compared
with the public schools in the region. Because of that, any
student who had any size at all was expected to try out
for the team. Those who didn't make the cut were ordered
to turn out for the games and yell like hell. John-Morgan
wasn't an outstanding athlete, but with practice and determination he had surprised even himself and made the
first string as a tackle.

Mike Sullivan was a natural. He was big and mean and
could move quickly on the line. He knew how to block
and tackle in a way that *hurt* his opponents and made
them worry about the next play. He made first string without even trying.

Bubba Silverman was also a natural, but he didn't possess the size that would have made him a great running back. But his speed and finesse with the football, as well as his ability to "read the players," had placed him in a rivalry with Tony O'Boyle for quarterback. Tony was really better than Bubba, but Coach Myrick never wanted either one to know it. The rivalry worked well for the Cadets. It was nice to have two good quarterbacks when the going got rough . . . and it was about to get very rough.

The Thanksgiving Day game was held in Grayson Stadium, an old prewar structure on Victory Drive that doubled as the baseball park for Savannah's Sally League farm team. It was just across the street from the Triple X drive-in restaurant. The "X" was the hangout for teens from both Savannah High and Benedictine. In the days leading up to the big game, it would often become a battleground.

On the day before Thanksgiving each school would have a parade of cars decorated with either the blue-and-white crepe paper of the Savannah High Blue Jackets, or the maroon-and-white of the Benedictine Cadets. The students would ride through the otherwise peaceful and dignified streets of the city with kids hanging out of the windows, honking horns and sometimes yelling things like "B.C. sucks ass," or "High School eats shit." These were "bad boys" from good homes. But everybody looked in the same direction then as on Saint Patrick's Day—the other way.

The climax of the parade always took place on the corner of Bull and Broughton streets in downtown Savannah. That intersection was the ceremonial center of town in the days before suburban sprawl created the malls that now dot Savannah's southside. Savannahians always hoped that the two parades would not reach the intersection at the same time, because it was here that the "parading of the coffin" would take place.

It was a ritual for each school to build a "coffin," in

which the winning team would symbolically bury the losing team after the game. Each coffin, dressed in the colors of the opposing team, would magically materialize off the back of somebody's pick-up truck at the proper moment and be carried around Broughton Street to the singing of the school fight song. The football team and the cheerleaders were always in attendance, and they became the heroes and heroines of the hour. Sometimes the "corpse" would be burned. People would go hog wild. It was scarcely more organized than a riot—but it was a great time to be a football player and a wonderful way to get primed for the game. When the spectators had finally had enough, they would all go to the "X" for Cokes, or maybe even the trunk of a car for some cold Blue Ribbons, and enjoy an uneasy peace before the storm the following day.

This was how the people of Savannah felt when kick-off time rolled around on the last Thursday of November deep in the South, down between the moss and the oak trees, the turkey dinners and hammered silver pocket flasks of Jack Daniels. It was combat, Savannah style.

Lloyd had stayed away from all the pregame hell-raising. It just wasn't smart for a colored boy to be out there amidst all of that carrying-on by white people. His mother had told him to stay home, but she didn't need to. Lloyd had spent his time studying for a chemistry test in Father Al's class. It was a good decision, because Father Al was tough.

By game time Lloyd had his things packed in the new maroon tote bag the bishop himself had given him the Sunday before. On the side of the bag, in white letters, it said "Benedictine Cadets." When he handed him the bag in the sacristy after Mass, the bishop said, "Just remember, Lloyd, inner strength. Inner strength."

"I'm ready to go now, Momma," Lloyd called out as he went down the hall and peeked into his mother's room. She was on her knees before the little table on which she kept the statue of the Virgin Mary. On either side of the statue was a lighted candle, and in front of it was a single rose in a small glass of water. The glass came from his mother's best crystal, a survivor of her marriage of long ago. For several seconds she didn't move, didn't even look up. Then she slowly blessed herself and kissed the crucifix on the Rosary that she held in her hands. She looked at the statue of the Virgin for a final time, then rose, adjusted her dress, and walked over to Lloyd.

"OK son, we're ready now." Mrs. Bryan walked her son to the front door, and Lloyd leaned down for her to kiss him gently on the forehead. "You take care of yourself. Remember, it's just a silly game. It ain't worth you being hurt. Just remember that your momma feels every pain that you do. You do yourself proud, boy, but don't go doin' nothin' stupid."

"Yes, Momma."

When he opened the door, Lloyd was surprised to discover that Tattnall Street was full of people, mostly black—family, friends and neighbors, old schoolmates from Pius, even his former coach. In a corner near the back of the crowd was a small group of nuns, all of them white, who had taught him in grammar school. When he started down the steps they began to clap and wish him luck. Black Savannah knew that Lloyd Bryan could play football like nobody they'd ever seen. They also knew that white Savannah was about to find out how well Lloyd could play the game, and they were there to cheer him on.

The two teams played almost to a standstill for the first half of the game. Neither scored, and the Blue Jackets only had one first down—which was one more than BC. The defensive brawl was controlled by the big guards and tackles. Out of frustration, both teams tried to pass the ball on several occasions only to expose the quarterbacks to painful muggings. Mike Sullivan was having the time of his life as he easily muscled aside the Blue Jacket offensive linemen and leveled blow after blow at "Cracker" Smoaks, High School's quarterback. Once he hit Cracker

so hard he caused a fumble. Mike recovered it, only to
see the Cadets stopped again at High School's forty-yard
line.

There were numerous injuries on both sides, and in the
waning seconds of the half Tony O'Boyle took the snap
and fell back for a "Hail Mary" pass Coach Myrick desperately hoped would put some points on the board. Instead the quarterback got blind-sided just as he cocked his
right arm to hit Martin Purdy in the end zone. A meaty
kid named Barney Pearlman caught him in his unprotected
left rib cage, just under the armpit, and lifted him about
a foot off the ground. Tony hit the grass like a croaker-
sack full of potatoes and was out cold. The game was
stopped to remove him from the field, and the team doctor
feared he might have fractured a rib, or even worse. After
he came to, Tony insisted he would be fine. He even
wanted to continue the game after he had rested during
halftime.

Big Tony O'Boyle had seen the whole thing; he
winced as he saw his only son go flying through the air.
He ran to the field like a maniac, barking orders to Coach
Myrick as if he owned the team.

"You'd better take him out and keep him out or I'll
sue the living shit out of you, Father Hector, the fucking
Pope too, if anything happens to my boy."

Coach Myrick was shocked at the behavior; he stood
wide-eyed as Dr. Eagan hunched over Little Tony and
helped him catch his breath. Big Tony quickly realized
how he had acted to the coach in front of the team, and
he apologized over and over again for having lost his
temper.

"Yeah, Mr. O'Boyle, I understand," said the coach,
though he was still leery. "No problem, he ain't goin'
back in, no way. We'll play Bubba the rest of the game.
He ain't no Tony, but I think he can handle it."

"Uh, yeah, Dick. I'm sorry again that I lost my temper.
You're doing a good job."

Myrick knew all about Big Tony and the clout he

wielded around town. He had no desire to have him angry because his son had been hurt.

"Yes, sir, Mr. O'Boyle. We're gonna get it together. It'll be another team when we come back out. And hey, thanks for coming down, I know how worried you can get over your boy, it's natural." Nobody bucked with Tony O'Boyle in the Free State of Chatham.

The second half of the game wasn't very different from the first. Savannah High managed to drive to within two yards of BC's goal, only to be stopped by Mike's side of the line. Attempts by both teams to throw the ball resulted in negative yardage. It was late in the fourth quarter when the lid finally came off.

Cracker Smoaks came tearing up the right side after a fake handoff. There weren't any pictures to prove it, but those who saw the play swore that Cracker stepped up on the back of a High School blocker and jumped over the line. The quarterback seemed to fly over the guard and into the BC end zone. All Mike Sullivan could see was Cracker going over his head and six points going on to the scoreboard.

The High School side of the stadium went wild. The Blue Jacket mascot, a student in a wasp costume with blue stripes and a stinger on his tail, ran around to the BC side of the field and did flips in front of the stands. The Cadets, all wearing their dress uniforms, started to come out of the bleachers after him. The only thing that saved the boy from being dismembered was Benedictine's professor of military science: he rushed down to the field before the Cadets could, and ordered them to stop.

Up in the stands, all sorts of instructions were being shouted to the coach by parents and alumni on how to win the game. The clock was running down, and it looked as though BC was about to lose to High School for a second year in a row. The only good thing to happen was that Savannah High missed when they tried to kick the extra point.

Coach Myrick called Bubba over before the kickoff and told him to follow his instincts. "You gotta feel your way through this one, Bubba. Remember how I told you to try and think like they do and then make your plays. Now is the time. I'm gonna trust you, son. I'm not out there like you are. You got the feel for it, now call the right plays. It all counts this time, Bubba. Now go for it."

On the kickoff, BC was able to get decent field position, but they had to do something quickly. Lloyd had gained a lot of yardage during the game, but he had been stopped deep in enemy territory. "We gotta score right *now*, ya'll," Bubba implored, "or we're gonna lose again." Bubba did everything to read the High School line, to get the feel as Coach Myrick had told him, and then to give the play.

When the Cadets came out of their huddle, Lloyd looked up to the north-end bleachers—the colored section. They were close to where the line of scrimmage was, so he could make out the faces in the crowd. Normally, few blacks attended because both schools were white, but Lloyd's story had gotten around town, and those bleachers were full. Black Savannah was there to see Lloyd show the rest of the city that colored kids could play football too. So far, they had been disappointed.

Lloyd hadn't paid much attention to the crowd during the game. He never did. He just concentrated on the plays. But now, for some reason, he looked up to the colored section and saw his mother. She stood out as plain as day. It was almost as if nobody else was there except her. She was looking right at him—and then she smiled and nodded her head. Lloyd looked again a little closer; she had this brilliant smile on her face, and she nodded her head a second time. It was as if she were trying to tell him something. He saw her push aside some hair that had blown in her face, and he noticed that she had a Rosary in her hand. Then he heard Bubba Silverman yell out "Ready, down, hut one, hut two," and Lloyd was in motion. He took the ball from Bubba right in his gut and tucked it in. Mike had opened a hole in the line for just a second, and that was all Lloyd needed. He lowered a shoulder and slithered through without being touched. In a flash he was in the secondary, cutting, weaving, all of it so quickly that even he wasn't sure if his feet were on the ground. He was aware of nothing but his own breathing as he tore up the yardage to the goal. Then all he could hear was his teammates hollering and slapping him on his helmet. All he could feel was them lifting him into the air on their shoulders. He had to strain to look back to the north-end bleachers amid all of the back-slapping and rejoicing, but finally he caught his mother's eyes. They were shining, and tears were running down her face. She nodded to Lloyd again.

Even then he thought it was strange that he should be able to see his mother's face so clearly. In later games he would stand in the same place and look up to the same set of bleachers, but he could scarcely make out a face, let alone an expression. Yet he had seen everything with extraordinary clarity on that magical Thanksgiving Day.

Benedictine kicked the extra point and won the Big Game, and finished the season unbeaten. They then went to the state finals, where they fell to Valdosta in a close game that even Lloyd couldn't quite pull out. But it was Thanksgiving that had made the difference for him. After that, he was able to settle in to his studies and even make a few friends at BC. Some of the boys asked him over to their houses after school. To his surprise, Mike Sullivan was one of them. So was John-Morgan Hartman, though this was less surprising. Along with those two, of course, came Bubba Silverman.

THE FIGHT

BEFORE JOHN-MORGAN'S junior year began, he and John, Sr., had a long discussion. John-Morgan had been deeply hurt by the accusations against his father years ago, and whenever Tony O'Boyle's name was mentioned, John-

Morgan flinched in anger. It wasn't that he didn't understand why his father had lost his job; what he wouldn't
tolerate was that he could let it happen without a fight. It
was so unlike the man he had come to know. He knew
his father hadn't stolen any money, but the idea that other
people thought he had was unsupportable.

John Hartman had been told by his friends that if he
dropped the affair, nothing further would happen. If he
didn't, then Tony O'Boyle would make it impossible for
him to work in Savannah ever again. It was difficult for
John, but out of love for his family he swallowed his pride
and quietly pursued a teaching job at the local college.

Ignoring Tony O'Boyle was easy enough for John because he seldom saw him. Ignoring Tony O'Boyle, Jr.,
was difficult for John-Morgan because he saw him at
school everyday. Little Tony was spoiled and arrogant and
had assumed many of his father's worst traits; and what
he heard Big Tony say at home, he often repeated at
school. Soon he was making snide remarks behind John-
Morgan's back. John-Morgan was furious, and he had to
tell his father or burst.

"I know you don't understand now, son, but trying to
get back at somebody just doesn't work in the long run."

"But Daddy, how can you say that? How can you just
sit there and let them do that to you? Why don't you think
up a way to fix 'em? Look at what they did! Now Tony's
at BC acting smart and telling his friends that you stole
money from the paper. I gotta do something."

"I know how you feel, and I wish I *could* do something. I wish I could set it all straight right now, but I
can't. They got all the ink, and you don't get into fights
with people who buy ink by the barrel. Trust me, I didn't
do anything wrong, and it will eventually come out. I just
can't do anything about it now, and you've got to control
yourself at school. Don't let that little bastard get next to
you. Ignore him, it'll pass. Believe me."

"But Daddy, I can't. He says things about you. I know
he does. I want to punch him."

"Please don't get into any trouble, John-Morgan. Do this for me and your mother. It's hard enough on us right now. Just look the other way. Please."

But looking the other way wasn't easy.

John-Morgan and Ann Marie dated steadily throughout the entire school year. As summer approached, both assumed that the coming season would be as delightful as the last. In Savannah, summer comes early and the beaches start to fill up by the first weekend of April. On the last weekend of that month John-Morgan was supposed to take Ann Marie to Tybee, but something happened and she had to stay in town. She told John-Morgan to go to the beach with his friends, and she would see him that night. The tide was out, and numerous clumps of high school and college kids dotted the very deep strand. John-Morgan, Mike, and Bubba moved from one knot of people to the other, making small talk, occasionally taking sly sips from the cups that secretly held beer.

Over by the jetty, one of a group of girls from Savannah High waved to John-Morgan. She lived down the street from him and he walked over to say hello. He was introduced to her friends, one of whom was named Charlotte Drayton—a pretty, sandy blond who already had a good tan. She wore a single-piece bathing suit of the kind the girls wore in the Miss America pageant. It was black and made her tan look even better. John-Morgan sat down next to her.

"Do you go to High School too?" he asked.

"No, Country Day."

"Oh." John-Morgan was fascinated by her lips. Charlotte was wearing pale pink lipstick, the "in" color that year.

"Don't you have a red convertible?"

"Well, it's my father's. He lets me have it sometimes." John-Morgan tried desperately not to watch a bead of perspiration that rolled down her neck and disappeared between her breasts.

"I thought you looked familiar. I've seen you at the Triple X. You date a girl from St. Vincent's, don't you?"

"Yeah, Ann Marie Kerry."

Just as he was about to say more, Mike and Bubba walked up and John-Morgan introduced them. Standing behind the girl and out of sight, Mike and Bubba grinned and rolled their eyes at John-Morgan.

"Goodness, it's hot," Charlotte complained as she fanned herself with a magazine. "I think I'm gonna go in the water for a little bit, to cool off. Anybody wanna join me?" She looked directly at John-Morgan as she spoke, and then let the magazine drop to the ground.

In a voice audible only to Bubba, Mike let out a long "Sheeitt," and shook his head.

"Uh, yeah. I'll go in with you. Anybody else?"

"Naw, I don't want to get all sticky from the water," said one of the girls. The others agreed.

"We'll stay up here, too. Ya'll go on in by yourselves. We don't want to get sticky either," said Bubba.

John-Morgan cut a quick look at his two friends as he got up and started to walk down to the water with Charlotte. Bubba only grinned.

"Nine-and-a-half," said Mike as he watched Charlotte walk sexily toward the surf.

"A ten," was Bubba's reply.

Nobody could have said that John-Morgan had engineered his meeting with Charlotte Drayton, or that it was he who decided it was time to cool off with a swim in the ocean. It wasn't even his fault that the tide had started to come in and the waves were bigger and rougher. He simply wasn't thinking when he walked off with Charlotte in front of half the junior class of St. Vincent's Academy. He wasn't thinking because he couldn't think. He had been broadsided by her beauty.

Charlotte, unfazed by the surf, plunged in at once, diving headfirst into a large incoming wave. She quickly surfaced on the other side of the wave and called out to her escort to "come on in." Then she started swimming out further through the surf into the gently rolling swells. John-Morgan had always been a very strong swimmer and was quickly by her side, treading water, waiting for a big wave on which they could body surf. It was then that he realized he hadn't really noticed the color of her eyes because she was wearing sunglasses on the beach. They were green and stood out strikingly against her tanned skin and blond hair.

Susan Powers was the first girl from St. Vincent's to notice John-Morgan walking down to the water with Charlotte. She tapped Judy Lynch on the leg and said, "Get a load of this." Suddenly the occupants of four lounge chairs were carefully watching every move the two of them made. They constantly raised their eyebrows and exchanged "knowing" glances and then went back to staring at the couple. The girls watched as the two rode a big wave in and then picked themselves up laughing from the surf. They watched as the two stood in the surf waist deep and let the waves break into them. They heard Charlotte scream in delight as one of the waves knocked her off her feet. And they watched as John-Morgan avidly helped her up.

In order to avoid marks from the sun, Charlotte had untied the straps that helped hold up her bathing suit and tucked them into the front. She had forgotten to tie them back around her neck when she went into the water. When she bent down to dive into one of the waves, the force of the wave pulled her suit down to her waist. Charlotte was honestly unaware of it, but when she stood up and turned around to face John-Morgan, her breasts were bare.

It only took a second for her to read the look on John-Morgan's face and realize that something was wrong. Charlotte looked down, let out a little scream, and turned around quickly to pull up the top of her suit. She had trouble tying the strings, so John-Morgan, ever the gentleman, waded over and took them out of her hands.

"Here, let me do that for you. It's kind of hard to do it behind your back."

"Oh God, I'm so embarrassed." Charlotte squealed as another wave drove them back a foot or two. "Did you see anything? What a stupid question! You saw it all, didn't you?" Her face was a little red as she turned to John-Morgan, but then she began to laugh. "You saw it all, didn't you, you naughty boy. Everything I've got!" John-Morgan opened his mouth to speak but nothing came out. He just smiled rather stupidly. Then Charlotte put a hand impishly on her hip and stared very boldly at John-Morgan. "Well, did you like what you saw?"

John-Morgan nodded his head and finally managed a "Yeah, uh . . . yeah."

"I'll bet you did." At this point she was teasing, posing, almost daring John-Morgan. Then she turned to dive into another wave, looked over her shoulder, and said: "Come on, let's catch another one, a really big one. The big rough ones turn me on," and then she smiled in a way that made John-Morgan almost lose his balance in the surf.

"Oh my God in heaven," Judy gasped, "did you see what I saw?" The others nodded as if with stars in their eyes. "She pulled her top down and showed him her boobs, I can't believe it."

Susan was disgusted, but also fair.

"No she didn't, Judy. The wave knocked her top off. But the little bitch wasn't the least bit embarrassed. And John-Morgan just stood there loving every second of it. And now they're out there in deep water together, having a good ol' time."

"I feel so sorry for Ann Marie," hissed Sandy Owens from a chair on the left. "That bastard. She's wearing his BC ring and he's out screwing around with that little blond tramp. Can you believe that? This is just going to kill her, that poor thing."

Ann Marie thought about calling John-Morgan and telling him to forget everything then and there; she'd have somebody bring him his ring. Then she thought, No, I want to face him and look him right in the eye.

John-Morgan wasn't stupid; he was simply seventeen years old and still innocent in the ways of the heart. He didn't realize that the whole town, or at least his little part of it, would know about what had happened at the beach that day.

Before six o'clock Ann Marie received four different calls about the incident. Two were from eyewitnesses and two from others who had "heard about what happened and just thought she ought to know." Each tale was worse than the one before; the last one described how this blond bimbo and John-Morgan had kissed in the water and she had taken her top off. To make matters even more horrifying, somehow, her mother had heard about it and questioned Ann Marie.

When John-Morgan came to pick her up that night, she wouldn't let him in. She kept him on the front porch and told him that he had embarrassed her in front of all her friends. John-Morgan gave a true and full account of what had happened, but he couldn't understand why Ann Marie was taking it so seriously. That was his big mistake. He just kept smiling and shaking his head; even laughed when she told him that, according to one version, he had kissed the girl when her top was off. He believed he was completely innocent; he failed utterly to grasp that Ann Marie had been humiliated. "I didn't do anything wrong. All I was doing was swimming. I just met her and we went into the water to cool off when everything happened. What's the big deal?"

By that time everything was a big deal. Ann Marie was in tears, and John-Morgan was growing angry about the way she was acting.

"Why don't you just take your ring back if you think this whole thing is so funny? You acted like a complete jerk in front of my friends with that floozy."

"I told you what happened. You still act like I did something wrong. Maybe I *should* take my ring back."

"Take it!" Ann Marie reached up and ripped at the gold chain hanging from her neck. It broke with a pop, and she shoved the ring into John-Morgan's hand. "I don't want to speak to you ever again! For me, you don't exist anymore!" Ann Marie slammed the door, and left John-Morgan staring dumbly at the ring in his hand.

THE ASSAULT

THERE WASN'T MUCH about John-Morgan Hartman that Tony O'Boyle envied. Tony was bigger, stronger, a better athlete who even got better grades. Most of all, in his opinion, he came from a better family. Everybody in town knew about John Hartman and why he had to leave the paper. Little Tony had even heard his father say that Hartman should have gone to jail. There was one thing, however, that Little Tony did envy about John-Morgan—Ann Marie.

Something about her stirred Tony's attention and interest. She was pretty, though not as pretty as some of the girls he dated. She was nothing compared to Allison McCreary. But still, she had something. Maybe it was her sweet, virginal manner; Ann Marie sent out signals saying, Look but don't touch. Tony had tried to get her to go out with him in the past, but she had always turned him down because she was going with John-Morgan. When he heard about their break-up, he decided to give it another try.

Tony's parents were leaving town that next weekend, and he would have the house all to himself. He planned to have a party there with some of his friends and asked Ann Marie if she would be his date.

"Will your parents be there?"

"Nah, they'll be up in Highlands for the weekend. We'll have the whole place to ourselves. Just a few friends. I got a great record collection and a steer-eo player. It's got great sound. It'll be fun. You'll know most of the people."

Ann Marie accepted.

The following Saturday night Tony pulled his father's black Cadillac convertible on to Victory Drive and headed for the little town of Thunderbolt, with Ann Marie seated next to him. Savannah's early May evenings were cool and caressing, and Ann Marie reveled in the feel of the breeze coming into the car. She listened to the palm trees as they swooshed by in soldierly regularity, complementing the dead young soldier boys whom they immortalized.

Just after entering the Thunderbolt town limits, Tony turned into the parking lot of Bill Hilliard's "Famous Bar-B-Que Restaurant and Lounge." The restaurant was flanked by long curbside sheds on either side. Tony eased into the last slot in back of the building. In a few moments a skinny black man of about twenty, wearing a white coat with a name tag—Washington—loped over to the car.

"Washington, my man! How you doin?"

"All right, Mr. Tony. What's hapnin? Nice ride, man, nice ride. This here ain't yours, I know. Who dis here, yo daddy's?"

"Yeah, man, it's his. Hey, Washington, this is my lady, Ann Marie."

The waiter took off his baseball cap with great flair and then bowed slightly to Ann Marie.

"Washington Alfonso Cooper at your service, mam."

"Nice to meet you, Washington."

Washington put his cap back on and smiled. Then he turned to Tony. "Pretty lady man, very nice. Say, what can I get ya'll?"

"I need a fifth of Smirnoff hundred proof."

The drinking age in Georgia was twenty-one. Tony was only seventeen, and didn't look much older. Washington scanned the parking lot nervously and shuffled his feet a little. The vodka was $3.25 a bottle and Tony knew it. He had a ten-dollar bill tucked in his shirt pocket. He reached in and stylishly withdrew the bill, held it in front of the waiter, and said: "Keep the change."

"Yes, sir. Yes, sir. I'll only be a moment."

"What's that for?" asked Ann Marie.

"I'm having a party, remember? This is for refreshments."

Ann Marie wasn't stupid and she wasn't exactly a prude, but she was inexperienced. She had accepted teen-age drinking as a fact of life, especially among the crowd at BC, but, although John-Morgan and his friends would drink beer and sometimes liquor at parties, she had never done so. The girls she was closest to didn't drink—or if they did, it was only a "little" sip to make their dates happy. It just had not been a part of her life.

Not very far away, another couple was also out on a date that night.

Charlotte Drayton had felt bad about what had happened to John-Morgan and his girlfriend, but not *very* bad, and only very briefly. The fact was that she was attracted to John-Morgan, so she called him the following Friday under the pretext of apologizing for all the trouble.

This was the 1960's. Girls didn't call boys, and John-Morgan's mother made a face as she handed him the phone: "It's a girl and it's not Ann Marie," she whispered censoriously. He pushed the hall door shut with his foot as she looked around the corner from the kitchen.

"Hello."

"John-Morgan?"

"Yeah."

"This is Charlotte Drayton. You know, the girl who lost her top down at the beach?"

"How could I forget?"

"Well, I heard from Nann about all the trouble you had over the whole thing, and I called to apologize."

"Uh, that's OK. You didn't do anything wrong. Neither did I, for that matter. You don't need to apologize."

"Oh yes, I do too. And I insist that you let me do

something to make it up to you. This whole thing has just crushed me. I feel like an absolute witch."

"Don't feel that way. It's no big deal." Then for some reason John-Morgan lied to make her feel better. "We wanted to start dating other people anyway. We had already talked about it."

"Well I'm glad that you mentioned dating, because that's just what I'm calling you about. I insist that you let me take you out to dinner and try to make amends for this whole terrible mess. I simply will not take no for an answer."

"I couldn't do that. It wouldn't be right."

"Oh yes you can and yes it will, John-Morgan. Now, I haven't made any plans for tomorrow night. If you're free, then why don't you let me treat you to dinner at the Yacht Club?"

"Well, I'd like to go out and everything, but I'm not letting you pay."

"Don't be silly. Why don't you come by about seven tomorrow evening? Do you know where I live?"

"No."

"Burnside Island, number two Burnside Island Drive. It's on the water side. Oh, and I hope you'll have that lovely red convertible I saw you in."

"If my father will let me have it. Uh, well, I guess I'll see you tomorrow night."

"I look forward to it. Bye."

Two seconds more and Ann Marie would have missed it. Tony had pulled his car into the median on Victory Drive to make a left turn; as he was looking to his right to check for oncoming traffic, Ann Marie looked back over her shoulder to the restaurant. It was then that John-Morgan drove by with the top down in his father's Super Sport. Charlotte Drayton was sitting next to him.

The car in front of John-Morgan slowed to turn into Hilliard's; this caused him to come to an almost complete stop. He saw Ann Marie in the black Caddy convertible only a second or so after she saw him. It was the first time since "that day," and both of them stared in amazement. A moment later the car in front of John-Morgan had turned and it was time for him to go. He looked directly into her eyes and then over at Tony, who was leaning forward trying to see around the palm trees, and then back at her almost in panic. For a second Ann Marie felt like jumping out of Tony's car and running over to his. Then she saw Charlotte and her heart broke all over again. She turned around as the car behind John-Morgan blew its horn, and he drove away.

Ann Marie realized that she had been rash in her judgment of John-Morgan, and their break-up was too hasty. She had wanted him to call her so they could get back together. When he didn't, she decided to make the first move herself. She thought she was in love with John-Morgan, but when she saw him with Charlotte Drayton, her hopes were dashed. Ann Marie was hurt, and she could still feel the pain as Tony pulled down the lane and turned into the garage in back of his house. He hadn't seen what had happened, and she wasn't about to tell him. She wished that she could call one of her friends and talk.

"Hey, are you all right? You've been awfully quiet for a while."

"Oh, I'm fine. I was just enjoying the ride. Maybe I'm just a little tired tonight."

As they went through the back door to the kitchen, Tony sat the vodka on the table. "Maybe this will make you feel a little better. It's great with grapefruit juice and this stuff called grenadine. Makes it taste like fruit punch." The doorbell rang, so he started for the front door, saying his friends were a little early.

Ann Marie looked at the bottle and agreed. "Maybe this *will* make me feel a little better."

Tony and his guests sat in the den and sipped their drinks. Ann Marie had hardly consumed half a glass, but at Tony's urging she quickly downed the rest. It seemed so easy, she thought, and it did taste like Hawaiian Punch. Tony returned with another, and then started on his third. After a while the other couples drifted away to other parts of the house, leaving Tony and Ann Marie alone on the big sofa.

Ann Marie wasn't fully aware of it, but she could no longer feel her lips. Her arm tingled. She relaxed on Tony's shoulder and whispered into his ear, "I feel funny, but it's great." Tony sat up and began to kiss her—first her neck, and then her ear. They gently slid lower and lower, and Ann Marie blindly, intensely, returned his kisses. Then he was on top of her. Ever so softly he pressed his hips into hers.

John-Morgan had been the first boy Ann Marie had really kissed with passion and meaning, but alcohol and the pain of rejection now took the place of love. She started panting, and she could feel the physical pleasure in her breasts as Tony pressed himself even closer. Her mouth moved down to his neck; she tasted his skin and breathed in the smell of his hair. Her arms held him tightly, and she could feel the strength in his shoulders as he caressed her. Soon her blouse was wet with perspiration. Tony was beginning a descent from her neck when he cupped a hand over her breast.

Ann Marie tried to pull his hand away, but it was a half-hearted gesture—and Tony, from experience, could tell it. He continued, while at the same time pressing himself against her. She had been this far before but no further with John-Morgan, and it was a sensation not unlike falling. A drift, a leap into another level of consciousness, part pleasure, part terror—like sitting on a Ferris wheel as it suddenly drops. For maybe ten minutes perhaps they lay like this, as Tony carefully, patiently, expertly manipulated her passion. He was powerful, provocative, skillful at his work, and he sensed yet another conquest. This was what he lived for.

Ann Marie moaned softly. His tongue fought with hers, and then rhythmically, powerfully he thrust it deep into her mouth again and again. Each time she sighed; each time she relaxed with pleasure. Then, so silkily that she hardly noticed, Tony moved his hand inside her dress and over the top of her panties. He was at her navel when she first became aware; a moment later he was between her legs.

Ann Marie's eyes opened wide in surprise and alarm, and she jerked her head back. "No, stop, Tony." He pressed his body weight into her hard and she sank even further into the cushions. He was big and strong and had positioned himself for control. "No, dammit, I said stop!" Tony only responded by pressing his hand even further between her legs. Ann Marie was frightened by his strength. Her entire body became tense, and she began to fight.

"I said stop it!" she finally screamed, and in a fierce, instinctive movement she managed to ram one of her knees firmly into the softness of his scrotum. Tony yelled out in pain, and rolled off Ann Marie to the floor. He crashed against his mother's glass-topped coffee table, which held the original Frederic Remington sculpture of a cowboy riding a bucking bronco. The glass slid off and broke in half. The sculpture fell to the floor, bending the cowboy's arm.

In a nightmare consciousness, Ann Marie was on her feet. She was trying to to straighten her skirt when one of the other couples reached the arched doorway to the den. Danny Tyrone ran over to Tony, who was rolled up like a huge armadillo under attack.

"You OK, man? What happened?"

"Nothing."

It was hard for Tony to speak, but pride dictated it. He struggled to his knees and managed to crawl onto the sofa, where he hunched over, confused and almost afraid to hold himself where it hurt.

As soon as Ann Marie had arranged her clothing into a semblance of decency, she whirled around and snarled: "Take me home . . . now!" Tony started to stand, but Ann

Marie brutallly cut him off. "Not you, you creep. One of them!" Then she buttoned the top of her blouse. Danny Tyrone looked over at Terence Byrne, who had also entered the room. As Terence went for the keys in his pocket, Ann Marie shouted with defiance: "Not you, either. Give Shay the keys. I want her to drive me home."

The following Monday morning it was John-Morgan's turn to serve as an acolyte at Benedictine's 7 A.M. Mass. He didn't mind because Father Norbert was saying the Mass, and he would always take the altar boys to Gottlieb's bakery for doughnuts after the service.

John-Morgan couldn't get Charlotte Drayton off his mind during the Mass, and he even forgot to respond to Father Norbert's invocation of "Dominus vobiscum." The old priest stared at him and cleared his throat loudly before John-Morgan snapped out of it with a breathless "Et cum spiritu tuo." He was in the same sort of fog a short while later as he walked down Bull Street with a warm doughnut in his mouth—until Mike Sullivan approached him.

"Did you hear about Tony and Ann Marie?"

"No. What about them?"

"I heard that Tyrone and Courtnay caught them screwing in the den at O'Boyle's house Saturday night."

"Bullshit!"

"Naw, man, I'm serious. Swear to God. They were drunk on their asses and screwing on the sofa when Tyrone walked in. He saw them both. She didn't have anything on. She wore O'Boyle out, man. He was holding his dick it was so sore. She got pissed 'cause he couldn't do it anymore and made Shay take her home. Swear to God, man. You can ask Billy Fitzsimmons, he's the one that told me. Everybody knows."

With the speed of light, she was back. She was there again, her face, her smell, her movements, her promise. The soft place where his stomach started, right below his sternum, began to hurt. His mouth was so dry he couldn't chew. He could barely speak.

"I don't believe it. She wouldn't do a thing like that."

"Well believe it man, 'cause it happened. Ask around, you'll see."

He alternated between anguish and anger, between hatred of Ann Marie and loathing of Tony. How could she let him do it? Maybe she really was like that. Maybe she was laughing at him, too. This was the worst day of his life, worse than when he heard about his father's being fired from the paper. An O'Boyle had wounded him again. What am I going to do? John-Morgan thought.

He told Mike he would see him at formation; then he quickly ducked into the front door of the church and headed to the choir loft. The church was empty, and John-Morgan made directly for the loft closet where the hymnals were kept. He shut the door tightly behind him and sat on the floor—thinking, trying not to think, desperately trying to pretend he had never run into Mike. Then he pulled himself into a ball and cried.

He was in love with Ann Marie, but he hadn't really known it until this moment. Only now she was no longer the kind of person he had thought she was.

John-Morgan missed morning formation and his first two classes. Mike thought he knew why and told Bubba. Together they covered for him so he wasn't reported absent. When John-Morgan finally walked across the gym floor to the lunch line, Bubba approached him.

"Hey, John-Morgan, where've you been? You OK? Sullivan and I answered present for you in class."

John-Morgan just kept walking to the line.

"You OK, man?"

"I don't feel like talking."

That was all he could manage. It would be very uncool to let on how badly he had been hurt—even more uncool if anybody knew he had been crying. Tony O'Boyle would be thrilled to learn how John-Morgan had taken the news, so he tried to be casual, although his effort was a dismal failure. Fortunately he was with friends who understood what a heavy blow the betrayal had been. Mike joined them in the hamburger line.

John-Morgan first spotted Tony walking down the steps from the back of the gym to the indoor target range. He and Danny Tyrone were carrying their target rifles back to the arms room. At this point John-Morgan was functioning strictly on instinct.

"Shit," whispered Bubba.

"I see the bastard." John-Morgan's words were a guttural hiss. He didn't move a muscle; he simply locked his eyes on Tony as the traitorous O'Boyle walked across the gym floor.

Bubba glanced at John-Morgan and then quickly at Mike. Both of them knew that something was about to happen.

As he neared the basketball backboard, Tony looked up and caught John-Morgan's furious glare. He had been talking and laughing with Danny, but now his laughter turned into a sneer. In a flash John-Morgan was across the gym floor, but his friends halted him before he could start a fight. Tony handed his rifle to Tyrone.

"Come on you little piece of shit!" yelled Tony, "I'll kick your ass. Let him go, I'll enjoy this."

Mike and Bubba between them could scarcely hold John-Morgan back. Words were flying, and other Cadets were forming a circle around the two. "The fuckin' Park asshole!" John-Morgan screamed as his friends finally pulled him out of the gym. "The fuckin' Park!"

"I'll be there, asshole. You better call up Ann Marie to come get you afterwards 'cause you're gonna need all the nursing you can. She'll take care of you real good too—just like she did me! She was great, asshole. She was great!"

The gym hadn't stopped echoing from Tony's last taunt before the entire school was buzzing about the fight that would take place that afternoon. Some thought it would be the best fight of the term. Although the Cadets talked among themselves, no one said a word to any of the priests about what was going to happen. It was strictly forbidden by their code of honor.

Occasionally fights would break out on the school grounds, but that was rare. They were usually between freshmen who hadn't yet discovered that the punishment for fighting at school was worse than whatever had caused the fight. Because of this, most fights took place in "the Park."

"The Park" was Forsyth Park, whose southern boundary was where Bull Street ran into Park Avenue by a monument to the veterans of the Spanish-American War. The combatant Cadets would meet at the base of this statue, and a gray circle of Cadet spectators would form about the pugilists. If there was too much huffing and puffing and not enough body contact, the circle would tighten and the contenders would be forced into each other until fists truly started to fly. Such was the tradition of "diplomacy" at Benedictine Military School.

These affairs were usually brief but furious, and the shopkeepers whose stores bordered Forsyth Park knew that an assembly of Cadets at that time and place could mean only one thing. As the storm clouds gathered, the merchants would call the school to report the coming peril. By the time the priests arrived, the fights were usually over and the Park devoid of gray.

Five minutes after the last bell had rung, the entire battle group was at the base of the statue. This fight had received top billing all afternoon. The incident in the gym had assured that. O'Boyle, Tyrone, and Terence Courtnay were already waiting at the statue when John-Morgan arrived. Tony had made sure that everyone knew what the fight was about. It was his version of Saturday night that had circulated about the school courtesy of Courtnay and Tyrone.

Lloyd Bryan usually had much better sense than to

involve himself in such an affair. He knew not to go to
the Park, but something pulled him there regardless.
Maybe it was John-Morgan, his first friend at the school;
or maybe he was just like the rest of the boys and couldn't
resist the lure of excitement. If his mother found out, she
would be terribly upset; but he took his chances and stood
on the fringes of the crowd as John-Morgan, accompanied
by Bubba and Mike, walked up to the sneering O'Boyle.

Tony knew that John-Morgan had disappeared during
the morning "like a little pansy," and he spread this
around the Cadet Corps as well. As the two of them now
stood face-to-face and only about three feet apart, Tony
said in mocking baby talk, "Aw, is him gonna cry again?"
John-Morgan took off his overseas cap, handed it to
Bubba, turned, and walked onto the grass. With a smirk
on his face, Tony let out a slow "shee-it" and then followed John-Morgan as the Cadets began to form a circle.

Bubba's father, who taught boxing at the Jewish Educational Alliance, had often told John-Morgan and
Bubba that brains and training could always win, even in
a fight with a much bigger opponent. He had shown them
how to move in a fight, how to watch their opponents
eyes and feet to anticipate what they were going to do,
and how to thrust and parry. Bernie Silverman had been
the welterweight champion of the Eighth Air Force in
1944.

Savannah enjoyed a long tradition of successful ama-
teur boxers who came from the JEA, especially in the
lighter weights. John-Morgan, who lived next door to the
Silvermans, was often a guest there. The boxing was fast,
and the emphasis was on moving in, taking your shots
quickly, and then getting out.

Tony was taller and heavier than John-Morgan, with
greater reach. He also had that "look" about him that natural athletes have. He had started shaving in the eighth
grade, and by the time he was a junior at Benedictine, his
body had assumed the wide shoulders and narrow waist
of a grown man.

At seventeen John-Morgan hardly needed to shave, and he still had the remnants of a boy's physique. For all his shortcomings, however, he had no fear of Tony O'Boyle. He would stand up and take his licks, even if he were soundly beaten. He just prayed for a few good licks of his own, to put a few welts on that bastard that would let everybody know that John-Morgan Hartman had hurt him.

When he and Tony finally squared off, John-Morgan was glad he was wearing long pants—no one could see his knees shaking. Before he was ready, however, Tony danced into him and slapped him on the side of the face. "I'm gonna slap his sassy little face and see if he cries again."

The boys roared in approval as Tony backed off and then moved forward once again, dancing on his toes, ducking, weaving, slapping John-Morgan for a second time with his open hand.

"I promise I won't hurt the little fucker too bad," crowed Tony. "All I want to do is make him cry!" John-Morgan's cheeks stung badly, and they were red from both embarrassment and pain. Tony began to move in yet a third time when something finally clicked in John-Morgan.

All of a sudden there was no roar of the crowd; there was no crowd at all, only a blur. All John-Morgan could see was Tony's face as it came toward him and Tony's right foot, which suggested where he was about to attack. Without thinking, John-Morgan threw out his left arm to block Tony's right, just as it was about to hit him on the side of the face. At the same time, he stepped into the open space at Tony's chest, and with all his might he threw a right hand squarely at Tony's nose. There was a dull thunk and a smashing sound, and John-Morgan knew that his punch had done its damage.

The Cadet Corps gave out a tremendous moan, and then cheered. Tony staggered back in astonishment, cupping his nose as blood poured into his hands. It was then that John-Morgan should have moved in and pummeled him as often as he could, but instead he stepped back, perhaps as surprised as Tony was, and let his opponent recover. This he did very quickly.

Tony charged, fists flying like a windmill. John-Morgan landed a hard right into his gut before stepping out of the way. Tony buckled a little but recovered quickly; he wheeled about to face John-Morgan once more. This time, however, he tackled him, and John-Morgan was unable to swerve.

With his exceptional strength Tony lifted John-Morgan off his feet and slammed him to the ground. Then he started pounding his face with a series of savage blows. Somehow John-Morgan got a hand up in Tony's face; and somehow his index finger went up the left nostril of Tony's splendidly sculpted nose.

John-Morgan knew that he had to stop the blows to his head or he would be knocked unconscious. In desperation he pushed at Tony's face, forcing his finger further up that handsome nose and pushing his head back.

The blows stopped as Tony reached for that maddening hand. That was enough time for John-Morgan to lift himself up, exert all of his effort, and throw Tony off him. In that one powerful movement he tore open Tony's nose. Tony O'Boyle screamed.

The Cadets went wild as the two boys struggled to their feet. John-Morgan's right eye was nearly swollen shut, and blood trickled from the side of his mouth. His knees almost buckled, but he managed to remain standing as he put his fists up, squinting at Tony from his left eye.

Tony whipped out his shirt tail and pressed it to his mangled face. Blood spurted everywhere, and when he realized the extent of the damage he became enraged. He went at John-Morgan now like a maniac, but John-Morgan landed a solid shot under his left eye. Tony responded with a devastating roundhouse right that crunched John-Morgan in the temple and felled him like a tree.

In the excited movement of the crowd, Lloyd found

himself pushed to the front of the circle, less than two feet away from his unconscious friend. He watched in shock as Tony kicked John-Morgan in the stomach and drew back his right leg to kick him again. Without the slightest thought or hesitation, Lloyd scrambled over to John-Morgan and cocked his fist, ready to hit Tony if he tried another cowardly kick.

Bubba and Mike were at Lloyd's side in almost the same instant; they pushed O'Boyle backward, away from their fallen friend. Danny and Terence then leaped in front of *their* friend. The crowd was quiet now. Finally Danny Tyrone shouted: "OK ya'll, it's over. The fight's over. Let's get outta here." More than three hundred BC boys dispersed in an instant, just as a few women from the beauty parlor across the street came running up.

The ladies had been under drying lamps; they still had curlers in their hair and towels around their necks. One of them gave a towel to Tony as he was being walked to his car by Danny and Terence. The others fluttered around John-Morgan as Bubba and Mike pulled him into a sitting position.

"Did I hurt him, Bubba? Did I hurt him?"

"You hurt him, John-Morgan, you hurt him good. You were wonderful, man, you were just wonderful!"

"But he knocked me out. He beat me."

As Bubba pressed a towel against John-Morgan's mouth he snorted. "Nobody, and I mean *nobody*, will ever mess with you again."

"Shit," said Mike as he helped John-Morgan to his feet, "you ripped the fucker's nose half off. He's gonna have a scar on his face for the rest of his life!"

"For the rest of his life, no shit?" asked John-Morgan.

"No shit, for the rest of his life."

Even through his fat lip, John-Morgan managed a smile. "We got to get out of here before von Bock comes."

V

THE
FREE STATE OF
CHATHAM,
REVISITED

For men were born to pray and save

IRISH BOYS

THE DOOR TO FATHER HECTOR'S office flew open. In marched Tony O'Boyle, Sr., member of the bar, president of the alumni association, grand navigator of the Knights of Columbus, past president of the Hibernian Society, and member of the Benedictine class of 1931. Right behind him was a horrified Ethel McGrath, who panted: "Oh Father Hector, I'm so sorry, he wouldn't stop at the desk. He just pushed right by me and almost knocked me down. I didn't have a chance to let you know he was out here. I'm so sorry, Father."

"That's perfectly alright, Ethel. I can handle this. If you'll just shut the door, Mr. O'Boyle and I are going to have a little talk."

"Oh, Father Hector," said a trembling Mrs. McGrath, "do you want me to call Father Doerner?"

The priest was exceptionally calm as he looked straight at Tony O'Boyle and said quietly, "No, Ethel, everything will be just fine. Thank you for your help. You may leave now."

While he was speaking, Mrs. McGrath produced a knotted Kleenex from somewhere out of her dress and pressed it to her eyes. Then she let out a quiet "Yes, Father" and pulled the door to with a shaking hand. Before leaving, she cast one final peek at Big Tony, who continued to stand defiantly in front of Father Hector's desk. The priest returned his angry glare with unruffled calm.

"He's out of here right now, do you hear me, von Bock?"

Hector von Bock, OSB, said nothing, but continued to remain in his seat behind his large and imposing mahogany desk with a cold and fixed stare into the eyes of Tony O'Boyle.

Tony moved right to the edge of the desk and bent

over it to place himself about one foot from Father Hector's face. Then, in a low and menacing voice he repeated, "Do you hear me, von Bock?"

Hector von Bock tilted himself even closer to Tony's face and calmly but firmly said, "Sit down, Tony, and we'll talk, but I won't have you coming into my office and acting like this."

The angry man didn't move a muscle; he simply returned the stare. After a second or two, Father Hector lifted his eyebrows perhaps a quarter of an inch. His eyes also, suddenly, grew hot. Everyone at Benedictine knew what that meant.

"I said have a seat, O'Boyle. Do you hear me?"

Tony took a deep breath, puffed out his chest, and slowly, without taking his eyes off the priest, dropped into the chair in front of the desk. Then he pressed himself forward again.

"That Hartman kid is out of here. The son of a bitch will be lucky if he doesn't wind up in jail. His goddamned father is going to pay to fix my son's face. But, I want the bastard out of this school, now!"

The Benedictines were a German order noted for their discipline and high academic standards. In the rectory at night, over after-dinner drinks, they would sometimes joke among themselves about their "Irish boys" and how they handled them. They all agreed that the Irish were an emotional lot with good hearts, strong backs, but, for the most part, only average intelligence. Given the proper discipline and training, so the general consensus went, the Benedictines could produce sound young men of good academic and military performance who would be a credit to their school and their church. But one thing must never be forgotten when handling an angry Irishmen—one must never, ever show fear. An Irishman was like a animal; he could smell fear on a man.

Hector von Bock was not all German. His mother was Italian, and he had inherited her temper—which he had to fight to control. Usually he succeeded. Slowly he brought his hands up to his face and placed them under his chin, as in prayer. Then he leaned back in his chair, with his dark and piercing eyes boring into the blowhard's body, and calmly spoke.

"Now you listen to me, Mr. O'Boyle, and you listen carefully. I think it should be your son's tenure at this school that you should be concerned with and not Mr. Hartman's. My understanding of the circumstances of the fight is that your son is equally to blame. He probably provoked it, so I'm going to call that a push, if I may employ a gambling term. It is further my understanding that the fight was a tie of sorts, even though your son is much bigger than the Hartman boy, but I'm willing to call that a push also. I am much grieved, however, to inform you that your son acted in a most cowardly way during the fight when he kicked Mr. Hartman in the stomach while he lay unconscious on the ground. I haven't finished speaking," the priest coldly added as O'Boyle made an abortive effort to interrupt. "He would have kicked him again had he not been stopped by those around him. This is a fact that I suspect he neglected to tell you. Further-more—and I'm sure that this is also something young Tony failed to mention—the Hartman boy was defending the reputation of a young lady that your son had seen fit to besmirch before the entire student body. This young lady is one with whose family I am well acquainted, and I take deep and personal umbrage at his actions."

Father Hector moved forward ever so slightly in his chair, pursed his lips, and continued. "One more thing, Mr. O'Boyle, and perhaps this is the most important thing of all." Once more he smiled, and even Big Tony had to admire the chilling effect it produced. "If you ever again invade the privacy of my office as you have just done, or if you ever speak to me again in the manner and language that you most recently have employed, I will leap over this desk at you and knock your goddamned teeth down your throat. Is that perfectly clear, sir?"

Tony O'Boyle figured he had two choices at this point.

He could tell the arrogant Kraut bastard that if he thought he was going to get away with this shit he had another think coming. Or he could claim that concern for his son had caused him to lose his temper and that he was ever so sorry. If he chose the first option, he would have to call up the troops and wage a major war against a priest. It would be tough, but he could do it and have the prick fired. If he apologized, however, he could get him later, by intrigue, and perhaps *really* do him some damage. Tony preferred the latter option.

Tony let out a sigh and gazed at the floor. Then he glanced at Father Hector with sad and pitiful eyes.

"If you could see how bad my boy looks, Father, you'd understand. I'm terribly sorry for how I've acted; please forgive me. I didn't know all that had happened, and I understand now. I can't begin to tell you how badly I feel about this, but it was concern for my son that brought me to it. I hope you understand. I love the boy very much. He's all his mother and I have, and I guess I just flew into a rage about the fight. It sounds like you have the situation well in hand, and I'll abide by whatever you think is right, Father."

"What I think is right, Tony, is that the boys come back to school and finish the year. There're just two weeks left. I think they've pretty much taken care of the situation themselves, and if there are no more problems, I intend to leave well enough alone. Sometimes boys have a better way of solving their problems than we do. They'll be seniors next year, you know."

Father Hector stood up signaling the end of the confrontation. Tony rose to his feet and stretched his hand across the desk. The priest gripped it tightly.

"I'm sorry again for what happened. I hope I have your forgiveness."

"You do, Tony, completely. All is forgiven. Please remember me in your prayers."

"Oh yes, Father, I always remember the priests at Benedictine. They're so important to us all." With that, Tony turned and went out the door. He stopped at Mrs. Mc-Grath's desk and offered his his apologies with great aplomb.

Father Hector sat back down behind his desk and lit a cigarette. Exhaling a long stream of smoke in the direction of the door, he smiled. Hector von Bock had not been fooled in the least.

Tony did not return to classes for the rest of the week. His father flew him and his mother up to Emory University Hospital, where one of the two plastic surgeons in the state of Georgia repaired the torn nostril. The wound, in fact, wasn't as bad as the O'Boyles made out. It could easily have been repaired by one of the doctors in Savannah, but Tony wanted only the best for his son. He did not, however, pursue any action against John-Morgan or his father. What Father von Bock had told him put an instant damper on any such notions.

John-Morgan had a black eye for three weeks, but he wore it more as a medal than a humiliation. The night after the fight, when Mrs. Hartman had gone to Blessed Sacrament for her weekly novena to the Sacred Heart of Jesus, John, Sr., called him into the den.

"Now that your mother's gone, give me the straight dope on what happened. I want to hear about the fight from you. I've already heard about it all over town."

"It didn't last long, Daddy. I just did what Mr. Silverman taught me to do. I caught him a couple of good licks and maybe could have outboxed him, but when he tackled me I just had to get him off. That's when I tore his nose. I didn't mean to, honest. I was just trying to pull him off before he killed me. I wasn't trying to fight dirty or anything, it just happened." Though he assumed it would make his father even angrier, John-Morgan felt compelled to continue. "He'd been picking at me for a long time. I tried to ignore him like you said, but then it got to be just too much."

"I hear Ann Marie Kerry figured in this somehow. Is that true?"

John-Morgan put his head down and closed his eyes. His face turned red and his lips trembled. All he could do was shake his head.

John Hartman held his son tightly as the boy sobbed for the loss of Ann Marie. Then he gently stroked his hair and whispered, "I'm proud of you, son, awfully proud."

Ann Marie had heard several versions of what had happened and why. She was horrified to learn that her name figured prominently in the event. St. Vincent's had buzzed as loudly about that awful night on the couch as BC had, and she had had to force herself to come to class for several days thereafter. She wanted to call John-Morgan, but some of her friends had told her that he hated her now. Perhaps that was just rumor, but there was no questioning that he had been dating Charlotte Drayton. Now they were practically going together.

In spite of her poise, and because of her pride, Ann Marie could not bring herself to call John-Morgan. She tried several times, but whenever she picked up the phone, the words caught in her throat, and finally she gave up. She had been greatly injured by those horrible beach events, and she lost all interest in boys—except one. She was sadly adrift, and she knew it.

John-Morgan was still a little unsteady emotionally, and he wasn't sure what he felt about Ann Marie. Charlotte Drayton, however, was an unambiguous diversion and because of that he welcomed her more and more. When his family moved to the beach for the summer, she was almost a daily visitor. So was a variety of her friends.

For John-Morgan the summer of 1964 passed in days filled with gentle breezes drifting over the dunes from the ocean at night. In the mornings he was awakened by the sound of the breakers. He'd sit in a large rocker facing the ocean and watch the sun rise until Charlotte arrived.

They would walk the beach for hours, lie on the sand, and neck in the waves. The smell of suntan oil, the taste of Charlotte's lipstick, the feel of her cheek as they danced on the screened porch at night filled John-Morgan's thoughts.

There were boat trips to Little Tybee, where they would explore small hammocks and roam over deserted beaches. There was skiing all day in the Back River, drinking rum and coke late at night after his parents had gone to bed, watching as the wind picked up from the east, whistling through the bending sea oats, and cooling their sunburned bodies. They would take the convertible into town and go to the Victory Drive-In theater. Sometimes they would cross the river into South Carolina, where the drinking age was eighteen and the roads were long and dark, and go to a nightclub in Beaufort.

No promises were made, no senior ring given. "I love you's" were exchanged, but somehow John-Morgan knew that it was not truly love. So did Charlotte. They were immersed in the island heat and taken in by the smell of salt air and oleander, the sight of a hundred-thousand stars that filled the sky each night and touched the ocean from a billion miles away. John-Morgan and Charlotte lived for the moment only as their heads swirled in a gorgeous cacophony of beach music and meteorites streaking through the night. They cooled themselves in the sea. This was that last gentle, velvet summer, that endless summer of dreams that would never be over and never be again.

THE COMMISSION

THE LANGUID DAYS of August finally piled into September, and John-Morgan was forcefully wrested from summer's hypnotic grip by the coming of his senior year at Benedictine. Other than the football schedule, the highlight of the fall quarter was the commissioning dance. It was at this function that the seniors who had been chosen for command status would receive their commissions.

For the first six weeks of school all seniors would be rotated through a number of different ranks. Some would serve as Cadet colonel one week; the next week they might be privates. Throughout this period they would be evaluated for demeanor, poise, and command ability by the professor of military science and the priests. Classroom skills and drilling proficiency were also considered. All this, in conjunction with the impressions formed over the prior three years, would serve as the basis for choosing the officers.

One other, purely political, consideration also went into the selection process—the position and influence of a Cadet's parents. The final arbiter of rank was Father von Bock, who was fully possessed of the savvy required to make the proper political decisions in the best interests of Benedictine Military School.

On a warm Saturday night in the last days of October, the entire Cadet Corps marched into the school's armory in dress white uniforms to see who would command the battle group. On the stage sat the faculty and military staff. Laid out on tables before them were the symbols and insignia of rank: officers' swords, leather "Sam Brown" belts, maroon sashes, and "Pips and Diamonds," the insignia of officer rank in the ROTC.

Seated in the balcony and along the walls of the armory were the parents and dates of the Cadets. In those days it was a formal affair, and young ladies wore flowing gowns and elbow-length gloves. No one knew who would be receiving commissions except Father Hector and Colonel Robert E. Lee Flemming, United States Army, Retired, Professor of Military Science and Tactics.

At eight o'clock sharp, Colonel Flemming stood and walked to the front of the stage. He waited until he had achieved the proper theatrical effect, and then boomed: "Battle group, forward march!" The Cadets began to file through the arched doorway three abreast, their shoulders touching, their bodies moving in unison. As they marched at half-step, their cadence shook the entire building. The entire Cadet Corps marched into the building in perfect order, and soon the floor was filled with straight lines of motionless young men. Uniform brass twinkled, and shadows cast by hat bills made thirteen-year-old boys appear far older than their years.

Father Hector and Colonel Flemming each gave a short talk about Benedictine and the process of selecting the officers. Then commissions were announced, starting with the lowest rank first and finishing with the Cadet colonel. When a Cadet's name was called out, he would march to the stage and face the audience. His parents would also come on the stage, and his mother would pin her son's rank to his uniform's epaulets. His father would present him with his officer's sword.

As the names of lieutenants and captains were called out, Tony O'Boyle, Sr., sat calmly with his wife and his son's date in reserved seats near the front of the stage. Big Tony was sure that his son would be made a lieutenant colonel at very least, and probably better. Little Tony's friends had been calling him colonel all week, and it was the consensus at the school that he would achieve the highest rank. His grades had been excellent through the preceding three years; he had been an outstanding athlete, and Tony possessed what in military parlance was referred to as "command presence."

After the captaincies were given out, Tommy Logan and Jimmy Lyons received their major's decorations. Big Tony looked down at the floor, marking time until the final rank was announced.

When the next name, Anthony O'Boyle, Jr., was called out, it took Big Tony completely by surprise. His wife had to say "Honey, that's us, we're supposed to go up on stage now," before Tony realized what had happened. A gasp could be heard throughout the Cadet Corps as Tony was commissioned major. Big Tony didn't look at Father

Hector as he left the stage, but the priest could plainly tell that the politico was unhappy.

On the floor, standing at attention side by side, were John-Morgan and Bubba. As the applause for Tony died down, the former whispered to the latter, "Looks as if we finish up as privates."

Colonel Flemming, ramrod straight, blue eyes piercing the crowd, resplendent in his dress uniform, took the microphone and said: "The remaining commissions are for those of Cadet lieutenant colonel and Cadet colonel." He folded over a small piece of paper and said, "Cadet Neal Mark Silverman will come to the dais and receive his commission." Bubba looked at his friend in astonishment as John-Morgan eagerly grabbed his hand and shook it.

After Bubba had left the stage, Colonel Flemming again addressed the crowd. "The rank of Cadet colonel is a very high honor that entails great responsibility. The school is fortunate to have had several outstanding young men, any of whom could have held this command with distinction. However, there is only one commanding officer in this battle group. I want each and every one of you to know that this was a difficult decision for Father von Bock and myself to make, and one that takes into account not only academics, but leadership qualities, especially courage and determination."

Eyes cut back and forth throughout the room as Colonel Flemming paused for a another moment of deliberate theatricality. The girls in their fancy ball dresses stopped fanning themselves, the remaining uncommissioned cadets held their breaths, and Charlotte Drayton leaned forward, straining to see John-Morgan's face. Then the colonel boldly and forcefully spoke into the microphone: "Cadet John Morgan Hartman, Jr., will come to the dais to receive his commission."

"I'll be damned," said John, Sr., as he took his wife's arm and rose from his seat.

"Oh, I knew he'd do it!" squealed Charlotte.

"Goddamn Nazi son of a bitch von Bock!" hissed Big Tony through clenched teeth.

"Shit," said Little Tony under his breath, standing at attention and looking straight ahead as John-Morgan marched to the front of the battle group.

BLACK CADET AT THE DANCE

A SPOTLIGHT in the balcony cut a shaft of light through the darkness of the armory, illuminating John-Morgan and Charlotte as they stood at the front of the line of newly commissioned Cadet officers and their dates. Each couple was introduced to the assembly. Then they walked together through an archway formed of swords held by underclassmen. After all the introductions had been made, it was the privilege of the Cadet colonel and his date to lead the first dance.

Charlotte touched her cheek properly against John-Morgan's as they moved gracefully across the floor. She was easily the most noticeable girl there that night, in a strapless scarlet silk dress cut tightly in at the waist. Around her neck was a single strand of pearls given to her by her Grandmother Telfair, who in turn had received them from her grandmother.

Mike Sullivan and his date pushed their way through the crowded dance floor to congratulate John-Morgan. Mike had been made a second lieutenant and was surprised that he received a commission at all. When he reached the Cadet colonel, he came to attention and fired off a smart salute, which was returned with equal precision; then they shook hands and embraced. Soon Bubba Silverman was there, and all three were joking and slapping one another on the back. It became apparent to Charlotte that his friends were as happy about John-Morgan's rank as he himself was, and she was deeply impressed by the obvious admiration and affection they all shared. Indeed she felt a twinge of jealousy as she searched her memories for any friendship that had been so strong. Then she moved among the boys and put her arms around John-Morgan's waist. "Dance with me John-Morgan, I want you to hold me."

When they danced, she pulled in very close and gazed at him intently. Clearly she was suggesting that she was his and his alone. Hundreds of teenage eyes gazed upon the couple, and hundreds of teenage egos yearned to be in John-Morgan's place as he and the lovely Charlotte waltzed in a sea of brass buttons, medals, orchids, and lace.

In a corner of the room sat Lloyd Bryan and Miss Dee Ann Pelote, daughter of Chester and Doris Pelote, owners of the Pelote Funeral Home. Lloyd had not expected to receive a commission, and none had come. He had, however, been made a sergeant first class. It was a pleasant surprise. His mother would be happy. He was content for the moment with those thoughts until Dee Ann leaned over to him and said: "Let's leave now. I don't feel right here. Besides, not a soul has even spoken to us. I don't understand how you can take it at this place. Nothing has changed one little bit with white people. They hate us and they always will."

Lloyd turned and was about to speak when he caught sight of John-Morgan and Charlotte coming toward them. He looked at Dee Ann with a little smile and said, "Let's don't leave just yet, there's somebody I'd like you to meet. Congratulations, Colonel Hartman. I'd like you to meet my date, Miss Dee Ann Pelote."

John-Morgan came to attention and then bowed slightly from the waist. He took Dee Ann's hand and said, "I'm most pleased to meet you, Miss Pelote. I'd like to introduce you both to my date, Miss Charlotte Drayton." Responding to the cue, Lloyd took Charlotte's hand in a similar fashion, bowed, and replied, "I'm most pleased to make your acquaintance, Miss Drayton."

The conversation that followed concerned the remainder of BC's football schedule and whether they could continue their unbeaten season. The girls artfully sized each other up, and, when it became apparent that John-Morgan and Lloyd were ignoring them, they began to have a conversation of their own. Charlotte was skillful at small talk and soon had Dee Ann relaxed and comfortable.

As they were walking across the dance floor after the good-byes had been said, Charlotte whispered, "Did you see that dress she had on? It was gorgeous. It comes from Fine's and cost a small fortune. I know, I was looking at it." John-Morgan just smiled and said, "Great country, isn't it."

After the Cadet colonel and his date had gone, Lloyd turned to Dee Ann and told her that he'd call a cab so they could leave. Dee Ann took his arm and gently pulled him on to the dance floor. "Why don't you wait a little while longer, Lloyd? I think I'd like to dance some more."

THE GREAT CHRISTMAS TREE CAPER

THE BENEDICTINE CADETS ended their football season that year undefeated in regional play. They destroyed Savannah High School in the Thanksgiving Day game, in which both Lloyd Bryan and Tony O'Boyle performed brilliantly, and went all the way to the state finals, only to lose to a team from Atlanta.

Just as he had been told to expect, Lloyd spurred the interest of several colleges. When he told his mother about Notre Dame, which had always been his dream, she promised to say the Rosary daily. Lloyd took comfort in her prayers and knew that if anyone could be heard by God, it would be she. Slowly he began to allow himself to consider the impossible.

The Cadet Corps did well under John-Morgan's command. Even Tony seemed to be accepting his subordinate position without animus. There had been some grumbling about the fact that Bubba had been made lieutenant colonel over boys who a number of the alumni felt were "more deserving." What they really meant was a little different.

"This is our school," confided Eddie Murphy to his lifelong friends at the Knights of Columbus one Friday evening about three scotches past nine o'clock, "and no damn Jew should have a rank that high. Pretty soon they'll be running the school. You know how Jews are."

Charlie O'Hayer and Malcom McMillan both nodded their heads in agreement. "Probably made a big contribution to the school. Damned von Bock is a greedy bastard. Poor Irish kids get to be privates. Jews buy their way in." Charlie pushed his baseball cap back and scratched his forehead with fingers stained by long hours of work welding at the the paper mill—also known as "the Bag."

The bar at the Knights of Columbus was an unusual place that cut across various social lines. Though it was predominantly Catholic, working-class Irish, many wealthy Catholic businessmen and attorneys occasionally frequented the place to get a feel for the pulse of the community. From there they would travel to Pinkie Master's, only a block away, for more commentary, then to Johnnie Ganem's and then, perhaps, to the lounge at Johnny Harris Restaurant for a barbeque sandwich and a nightcap. It was Tony O'Boyle's political instincts that had brought him to the Knights that Friday as he carefully and discreetly listened to everything the group had to say. He would use it for later reference.

After the Thanksgiving Day game, the next big event on Benedictine's social calendar was the Christmas dance. This affair was the responsibility of the senior class, who always worked hard each year to make it something special.

The dance was held in the armory. Great care was taken with the decorations. For an entire week the senior class would work after school placing crisp greenery and twists of crepe paper about the room. They also made a backdrop for the pictures to be taken with their dates. The

girls from St. Vincent's, armed with holly sprigs and cedar boughs, rendered much-needed artistic assistance.

The focal point for each year's dance was a huge
Christmas tree in the center of the floor. The tree and other
decorations, along with the band and the refreshments,
were paid for out of the senior class dues. At the last
minute the band that had been booked to play the dance
cancelled, and the only replacement that could be found
on short notice was very expensive. This shortfall meant
that something had to be cut from the budget—their
Christmas tree. The boys were upset, and the girls were
heartbroken.

Somebody brought in an eight-foot tree that cost five
dollars, but when it was set up in the gym for the traditional decorating party two nights before the dance, it was
swallowed by the enormous room. The cavernous walls
and towering ceiling simply didn't have the same feeling
without the twenty-five-foot monster that dominated the
dance floor each Christmas. The lights on the big tree
would fill the room with an aurora borealis of reds, yel-
lows, blues, and greens, the only lights allowed during the
dance. Couples would circle slowly around and around,
making promises of love and devotion while admiring the
lights that climbed like stars to the ceiling.

"This is awful," said Charlotte as she and Katherine
hung ornaments. Mike, Bubba, and John-Morgan struggled vainly to find out why some of the lights wrapped
around their little tree wouldn't come on.

"It just doesn't seem the same without a great big tree,"
pouted Katherine. "There aren't enough lights on this one
to light up the whole room."

"It really isn't the same," agreed Mike as he stood back
and looked. Then he had an idea: How about old Kicklighter's tree?

Marvin Kicklighter was an upright man. He had worked
hard at his gas station on Bay Street since his return from
the war, and it was now the biggest Standard Oil station

in Savannah. Marvin was proud also of his family, and
he had provided them with a lovely home on Whitemarsh
Island. He owned five acres of waterfront property with a
large front yard on the Bull River. It was so big he had
to purchase a tractor just to cut the grass. Marvin enjoyed
riding around the trees and shrubs he had planted over
the years.

Just about anything grew in Savannah, and the Scotch
pine only three feet tall when he had planted it back in
1950 was over twenty-five feet now, a perfect tree. For
the last ten years or so, Marvin had decorated it for Christmas. Everybody on his street said that Marvin's was the
ideal Christmas tree. None like it anywhere, and Marvin
was a master at decoration. A member of the Baptist
Church and on the usher board, he took his religion seriously, so naturally he put a manger scene at the base of
the tree. The first year Marvin had only the figures of
Mary, Joseph, and the baby Jesus—lighted big plastic
models that glowed in eerie devotion. Each year he added
a little more: three wise men on colorful camels, shep-
herds with their staffs and sheep, even a chubby Santa
Claus bringing a gift to the infant Jesus. The year before,
the creeping commercialism of Christmas had gotten to
Marvin and he had erected a huge sign in front of the
manger: "Put Christ back in Christmas." A fellow Shriner
who owned a sign-painting company had charged him
only for the materials.

Marvin was especially looking forward to this year's
party on the coming weekend. A member of the clown
unit at the Alee Temple, he had invited all the boys in his
unit to come over on Saturday afternoon to help decorate
his Christmas tree and eat the barbecued pig he had been
hardwood-smoking since the night before. Although he
was a Mason and a Baptist, Marvin had long ago recon-
ciled those two organizations' stances against alcohol with
his appreciation for the fine qualities of branch-water
whiskey. No one wanted to miss Marvin's Christmas par-

ties. The clown unit was known to have a good time, and Marvin "pulled out the plug."

John-Morgan and his yuletide musketeers were also making their plans.

"I'm tellin' ya, we can do it," Mike urged. "Just listen to me, OK? We take my father's pickup and drive by the place about eleven o'clock tonight. If you're afraid to do the cuttin', I'll let you drive. You let me and Bubba out and then just drive up to Highway 80, turn around, and come back. By that time me and Bubba will have the thing down. You stop the truck right there in the street, we load it in the back, and we're gone. We'll use a saw; it won't make a sound. We can do it in five minutes. Then we drive over here to the school, slip it off by the front door, and tomorrow when everybody gets here, presto, Santa has left us a present. I'm tellin' ya, it'll work. Don't be a pussy, John-Morgan."

"I don't know, it sounds pretty risky. What about the man? He's gonna be pissed about his tree."

"John-Morgan, listen to me. That guy has a whole big yard full of trees. What's one more? He can grow another one. We need this thing to make the dance a success. You heard how upset the girls are. Who wants that midget piece of shit we got sittin' out there in the middle of the gym floor for the Christmas dance?"

"What do you think, Bubba?"

"I'm Jewish, John-Morgan, what do I know from Christmas trees?"

"Aw, come on, you know what I mean. You think we'll get caught?"

"It's only a tree. What can happen to you for stealing a tree? It's not like a car or a boat. It's a tree, for God's sake. Let's do it. The old fart's got a whole yard full of trees. He doesn't use 'em for anything. He won't give a shit. He probably won't even notice one lousy tree missing."

What came to be known in Benedictine folklore as "the

Great Christmas Tree Caper" took place that night without the slightest hitch. As the three participants pulled the tree off Mike's truck and stood it against the door to the armory, they pledged themselves to secrecy. Nobody would tell another living soul about how the tree got to Benedictine. It would be a miracle. Perhaps there really was a Santa Claus!

The Benedictine Military School Christmas dance of 1964 was the best one ever. All the participants said so as they danced around the magnificent tree that had mysteriously appeared at their door the day before. Charlotte cried with joy as she and John-Morgan danced in front of the tree to a passable, backwoodsy rendition of "Blue Christmas" by Buddy Livingston's band, the Versatones. Bubba's date was equally impressed. But Katherine was the most overwhelmed of all.

That night, after the dance, under the spell of a couple of bottles of Bull Dog malt liquor, Mike told Katherine the true story of the Christmas tree miracle. She accused him of not really caring for her, "keeping secrets and all."

"The hell I don't, Katherine. I chopped down that damn Christmas tree for you. Me and Bubba and John-Morgan lugged it all the way from Whitemarsh Island to the school in the middle of the night just so you could have a nice Christmas dance. I care a lot for you. I busted my ass because I knew you were so upset with that scrawny little piece of crap we woulda had if I hadn't gone and stole that big beauty. Now you tell me, does that sound like I don't care about you Katherine?"

Tears came to Katherine's eyes. She hugged Mike and kissed him with gusto, and told him how much she appreciated what he had done. "I guess I was really wrong about how you were acting," she whispered. "I'll never forget this Christmas dance as long as I live, really!"

Mike told her not to tell anyone. He even made her swear. "It's a big secret now. We're in a peepot of trouble if anyone finds out. You hear?"

Crossing her heart, Katherine pledged herself to silence. The next day, however, so proud of what Mike had done for her, she *had* to tell Judy Lynch; but only after Judy swore "on a stack of Bibles" that she wouldn't say a word to another living soul. Really.

Marvin Kicklighter and his wife, Crystal, had gotten all the decorations for their special tree out of the attic on the day of the party. Marvin tested the lights, and Crystal wiped a year's worth of dust off the baby Jesus' face, then the Three Wise Men, noting to Marvin (not for the first time) that one of them was a colored man.

Marvin had a few minutes to kill before people started arriving, so he thought he'd save a little time by taking the decorations up to the front. He hadn't been out of the back yard the night before because he was roasting the pig, and he hadn't been out of the house all day because Crystal had had him busting his hump doing things around the house. Marvin poured himself about three holiday fingers worth of Jim Beam into one of the glasses he gave away at the station, threw in a few cubes of ice, and filled the rest of the glass with Canada Dry. He got into his El Camino and started up to the front of his property to unload the decorations.

For a moment he thought he had driven past the tree. Then all he could say was, "What the hell, what the goddamn hell?" He raced back to the house and bellowed at his wife. "My tree, Crystal, my tree. Somebody's done stole my goddamn tree," he bellowed, sloshing whiskey all over as he ran to phone the Chatham County police and report the theft of his prized Scotch pine. "My tree!" he lamented, as if a family member had passed.

"I'm tellin' ya, somebody stole the best tree in this here city, and I want a car out here right away! I'm a by-God taxpayer and I want some action. I want that tree back dead or alive. I got a hundred-and-fifty people comin' out here in a hour to fix that thing up for goddamn Christmas

and I want ya'll to get it back and I mean business!" It
did no good. His tree-trimming, pig-eating, sour-mash-
sipping partygoers were forced to be philosophical about
the tree's disappearance and stick to the basics.

CONFESSION

ON CHRISTMAS EVE AFTERNOON Ann Marie went to the
cathedral for confession. Father Fitzwilliam was on duty
that afternoon. He was preparing to leave the confessional
when he heard the door open on his right and the sound
of someone kneeling down. The priest was tired and hungry, but he leaned back against the hardwood seat with a
mild sigh. Around his neck he once again placed the purple stole worn for the Sacrament of Penance.

Kevin Fitzwilliam, a native of County Wicklow, who
came directly from Ireland after his ordination, had been
in Savannah for only four years. He hadn't decided to
enter the priesthood until he was almost twenty-six, after
a failed love affair that left him lonely and spiritually desolate. As a result he was a little older than most new
priests. His mother thought Kevin had become a priest to
escape from Ireland and his broken heart, but he knew
better. The associate pastorship of the Cathedral of St.
John the Baptist was his first assignment.

Kevin's duties included teaching religion to the girls
at St. Vincent's Academy, which was adjacent to the cathedral. This was a godsend to the girls. The young priest
was a tall, muscular man with curly black hair, deep
brown eyes, a strong chin, and dimples in his cheeks when
he smiled. The students at St. Vincent's all thought that
it was "just awful" for such a good-looking man to be
wasted on the priesthood, but his beauty was not the only
reason he was so popular. Kevin was an excellent teacher
and an equally good listener, and many of the girls had
learned they could confide in Father "Fitz" about any kind
of problem. His advice was always sound. He had a way

of gently persuading rather than harshly ordering. He was the one who could always make a girl feel better when she was down, so he was the obvious choice for Ann Marie's confession. She knew he would understand.

After the opening prayers were completed, Ann Marie hesitantly began her story about what had happened with Tony O'Boyle. Telling Father Fitz about drinking and getting tipsy was the easy part. Telling anybody, especially a man, about what had happened next was hard. Ann Marie stumbled several times, but Kevin's gentle urging led her to tell the story in such vivid detail that the priest could almost *see* her experience.

He empathized with the great shame and guilt this young girl carried. To a degree, his own life was reflected in hers. When Ann Marie finished, she was in tears. Kevin wanted badly to leave the cramped cubicle, swing open the door of the confessional, and comfort Ann Marie face to face. Propriety gnawed at compassion, so the priest's voice hoarsely filtered through the opaque screen of the confessional.

In dark anonymity, Kevin Fitzwilliam proceeded to restore Ann Marie's self-respect and assuage her guilt. She had indeed sinned by drinking and putting herself in the occasion of sin; and although it was no sin to kiss a boy and to be held by him, it did place her in a position that could obviously lead to sorrow. As Father Fitzwilliam murmured the final words of the absolution prayer, Ann Marie felt herself grow light; memories of childhood and its innocent games rose and faded in pastel shades of dawn. She thought she heard pigeons in flight.

Kevin smiled to himself as he heard Ann Marie close the door and leave. He sat for a while, all by himself in the cryptic dark of the confessional booth, realizing the visceral joy that comes to a man when he feels the hand of God working through him.

Ann Marie had been relieved of the burden of sin, but she still carried the ragged pain of a broken heart, a pain intensified that evening at midnight Mass when she saw John-Morgan with Charlotte Drayton. She sat in the back of the cathedral, where she could not be seen. When the Mass ended, she stayed in the shadows of the vestibule and watched the two of them as they strolled into the cold night air. She watched their frosted breaths float from their mouths, intermingle, and rise as one into the desolate heavens above the cathedral spires.

At that moment she felt certain that John-Morgan no longer cared for her, and that her relationship with him was truly over. On Christmas Eve, Ann Marie pledged to herself that she would get over him no matter how difficult it proved, and begin to enjoy life once more.

The Cadets at Benedictine started drilling in earnest for the St. Patrick's Day parade after the Christmas holidays. Over and over, the band practiced the only two songs it could play, while the freshmen started the daily dread of carrying an eight-and-a-half pound rifle for six miles. BC was one of the most popular units in the parade, and it was a great honor for John-Morgan to march at the front of his school as its commanding officer. All of Savannah would be watching, and for John Hartman, Sr., the sight of his son leading Benedictine would install a feeling of supreme pride and satisfaction. For a short while John even entertained the idea of finding where Big Tony O'Boyle would be watching the parade and standing next to him, just to see the look on his face when John-Morgan passed in review at the head of the battle group. His son's success had enlivened John's spirit and allowed him, for this day, to enjoy life again.

Marvin Kicklighter and his wife liked to stop by Johnny Harris Restaurant every Friday evening on their way home. He craved deep, double-fried chicken and she adored the sherry-laced crab soup. They always took booth number one across from the barbecue pit in the kitchen. They were such regulars that the waiters knew exactly what to bring.

Making their own way down the line of wooden, upright booths, Crystal and Marvin talked and joked with folks. As soon as they took their seats, John Henry Gibbs—their waiter—would show up with a Wild Turkey and ginger ale for Marvin, and a vodka martini extra dry for Crystal. More often than not, members of the Shrine clown unit would wander by, and Marvin would insist that they sit and have a shooter or two. "Drinks on me boys. OK, Crystal?"

On the third Friday in January, Marvin and Crystal showed up at Harris' like clockwork. Jimmy Sikes and his wife, Gale, spotted Marvin and sat down with them. Jimmy was in the Shrine with Marvin and was a regular at his Christmas party. Just as the second round of drinks was brought out, Tony O'Boyle, Jr., and his date took a seat in the adjacent booth.

Soon the conversation turned to the Christmas party, and Marvin started reminiscing about his favorite tree. "What a crime it was that some son of bitch" had cut it down and "for Christsake" stolen it. As soon as Jimmy and Gale sat down, Marv had ordered his third Wild Turkey, so his voice rang clearly in booth number two. Tony soon realized that the tree Marvin Kicklighter was talking about was the one that had shown up so providently at the BC Christmas dance. Wheels began to turn in Tony's head. He excused himself and walked past booth number one toward the men's room.

Passing by Marvin's booth, he glanced in quickly and saw Marvin in the uniform shirt he wore at work. Just above the left pocket was a patch with the Standard Oil logo that read "Marvin Kicklighter's Bay Street Standard Station." Over the right pocket was the name "Marvin."

The phone rang at the station the next day, and the voice of an unknown teenager asked to speak to Mr. Kicklighter.

"You got him, buddy. What can I do for you?"

"Uh, well, you don't know me, Mr. Kicklighter, but I know what happened to your tree."

"Who is this?"

"I can't tell you my name, but I know what happened to the tree that got cut down in your yard last Christmas."

"What do you mean, son?"

"I mean I know where your tree went."

"Well, where did it go?"

"They used it for the BC Christmas dance."

"What do you mean? Who is this, anyway?"

"That's all I can say. I gotta go, but check it out. You'll see."

Now, Marvin was a Christian man who had received Jesus as his personal savior at the Black Creek Baptist Church when he was eleven years old. He didn't really and truly hate anybody, but he did have a lifelong, inbred distrust of Catholics. He didn't need much priming to call Father von Bock and tell him about the phone call he had just received.

Father Hector had often wondered about that tree and had even heard the rumor that John-Morgan and his friends had delivered it the night before the dance. He also knew that it was sometimes better to let a sleeping dog lie. He had not pursued an answer to the mystery of the tree.

When Marvin got him on the phone and told his story, however, Father von Bock felt certain that what he said was true. Marvin had indeed "sacrificed" his beautiful tree to the senior class of Benedictine, so von Bock told him that the school would reimburse him immediately. He sensed that the caller harbored a certain ill will towards Benedictine's catholicity, so when Marvin told him that the tree was worth at least a hundred and fifty dollars, Father Hector smoothly said that he had seen the tree and it was indeed magnificent. "I feel so badly about this, Mr. Kicklighter," purred the priest, "that I insist you accept two hundred dollars, and not a penny less."

"Well, Reverend Bock, that's all fine enough, but what about the little bastards that cut down my tree. What are you gonna do about that, Reverend, huh?"

Hector turned glacial and told Marvin that he had absolutely no idea who had cut down his tree and furthermore the payment of two hundred dollars should be enough to properly assuage Marvin's injuries. When Marvin began to press the issue, Hector cut him off by flatly saying that any further discussion should be taken up with Mr. McNamara, the school's attorney. That ended the conversation, as well as any further interest Marvin had in what had happened to his prized tree. But it was not over for von Bock.

"Mrs. McGrath?"

"Yes, Father?"

"Will you please have Cadet Colonel Hartman report to my office immediately?"

"Yes, Father. Right away."

"At ease, Colonel Hartman. Now suppose you tell me all you know about how that big tree we had at the last Christmas dance wound up at the door of our illustrious school."

John-Hartman wasn't surprised; people had been coming to him since the week after the dance, asking about the tree. Bubba and Mike swore they had said nothing. (Mike—in a defensive sophistry of conscience—didn't count Katherine as just "anybody.") Now, as he stood before Father Hector's desk and shifted his weight from foot to foot, John-Morgan was faced with a serious dilemma. Images of Theseus in Crete facing the Minotaur dramatically arose.

"Colonel Hartman, I believe we were talking about a Christmas tree, or at least I was. Let me rephrase my question to you, sir. Did you have anything to do with the procurement of said tree?"

John-Morgan stood in silence for a moment and then opened his mouth to speak. Hector raised his hand and added, "You do know how I so desperately detest liars, don't you, Colonel Hartman?"

"Yes, Father, I do."

"Well, then, Colonel, I suggest that you treat the truth with the utmost respect and consideration as you phrase your answer for me."

"Yes, Father, I will."

Father Hector reached into his desk drawer and produced a pack of Lucky Strikes, and then lit one with a silver Zippo inscribed with a bas-relief insignia of the Eighty-second Airborne Division—the same division he had jumped with in the Normandy invasion. He took a long pull off the Lucky, sat back in his chair, and blew the smoke at the ceiling.

"Well, Colonel, I'm waiting."

The priest could see the pressure that John-Morgan was under. He secretly pitied the young man. He was, however, the principal of a school that prided itself on discipline, and the discipline was hard. Then Hector leaned forward and placed his elbows on the great desk and stared his meanest, no-bullshit stare at John-Morgan and waited.

"I did it, Father. I cut down the tree and brought it to the school."

"Oh, I know you did it, Colonel. What I don't know is who else was with you, sir, and I intend to find out. Now then, who else was involved with you on this—ah, shall we refer to it as, ah perhaps, the Christmas tree caper?"

"Nobody else, Father. It was all me."

"Now, Colonel, surely you don't think I'm stupid enough to believe that you cut that huge tree down all by your little ol' self, do you? Before you answer, remember what we said about the truth. If you don't want to tell me, just say so, but don't insult my intelligence, Colonel. Do we understand each other?"

"Yes, Father, I think we do."

"Well then, Colonel, what is it?"

John-Morgan came to attention. Looking straight ahead and prepared for the worst, he fired off: "Sir, the Cadet colonel has no answer, sir."

Father Hector finished his cigarette and then lit another while John-Morgan remained at attention. He thoughtfully puffed on the Lucky and then said: "One more time, Colonel. Who was with you?"

"Sir, the Cadet colonel respectfully declines to answer the headmaster's question, sir."

"Very well, then. I'm sorry, but if you persist with this line, I can no longer allow you to serve as battle group commander. Is that clear, Colonel Hartman?"

"Sir, it is perfectly clear to the Cadet colonel, sir."

"In that case, in addition to your loss of rank, you will walk Jug every Saturday for the rest of the school year until you decide to come up with the names of your fellow conspirators. You've gotten off lightly—you could have been expelled. That's all, you are dismissed. . . . Oh, one more thing. On your way out, you may leave your Sam Brown belt and the diamonds off your shoulders at Mrs. McGrath's desk. Good day, *Cadet* Hartman." The emphasis on "Cadet" would ring in John-Morgan's brain for years.

John-Morgan crisply saluted and executed a perfect about-face. Then he walked smartly out of Father von Bock's office and stopped at Mrs. McGrath's desk. There he stripped off his Sam Brown belt and removed the three diamonds from each of his shoulders. The distraught secretary said, "Oh, John-Morgan, I'm so sorry, son. Is there anything I can do for you?" John-Morgan choked out a "No, mam" and left her office.

Von Bock sat at his desk and stared at the crucifix on the wall. Then he angrily crushed out his third cigarette while spitting out the words, "Shit, I hated to do that. I wonder who made the call to our dear Mr. Kicklighter?" After a few deep breaths, Hector pressed the intercom switch and calmly said: "Mrs. McGrath, will you please get Mr. John Hartman, Sr., on the phone for me? I need to speak with him."

WALKING THE JUG

FATHER VON BOCK was holding his lighter as he talked with John Hartman. At first he merely turned it over in his hand as a nervous habit, but then his eyes fell upon the divisional insignia. The Eighty-second's patch was two stylized capital A's standing together in a blue circle on a red shield. The A's stood for Army Airborne. Hector's thoughts often wandered to his days as a paratrooper, especially those early morning hours on June 6, when he and thousands of other young men had piled out of packed troop transports into the blackness above the Normandy coast.

Not many men knew the gamut of human experience and emotion quite as well as Hector von Bock. He had killed until killing all but ceased to have meaning for him. He had stared into the face of death and barely been missed by its bitter breath. He had loved to the extent that the axis his world turned on became love's white heat, and he had hated as he walked across the ruins of a Europe that made him a witness to human depravity. He had felt a pain literally unendurable when his faith had been choked to death by the sight of the gas chambers that had choked so many real lives and souls with their lethal fumes; and he had also tasted the sweetness of faith gradually reborn. He knew what it was like to hold bread and wine in his hands and feel all the power of the universe pass through his fingertips.

Hector sensed a father's pain that day as he spoke with John Hartman. Looking again at his lighter, he could think only of the courage it had taken for John-Morgan to sacrifice his rank and not betray his friends. Hector knew full well that in the courage he had just witnessed lay the seeds of greatness.

"John, I know how upset you are. I also want you to

know that you have a fine boy. I don't condone what he
has done, but I also don't consider it an indication that he
is a bad kid or possessed of a character flaw. It took a lot
of guts to take it on the chin for his friends the way he
did. Frankly I'm not the least bit surprised that John-
Morgan wouldn't talk. I think I would have been disappointed if he had. A few years from now this will be
looked upon as a boyish prank, as well it should be. Unfortunately I have been placed in a most difficult position
and I simply cannot allow this thing to pass by unpuni-
shed. Right now John-Morgan is a private. He may stay
that way until he graduates; I simply have not made up
my mind. He's got Saturday Jug too. Let's just give it a
little time. I may give him back his rank, I may not. It
remains to be seen. In any event, I wanted to speak to
you personally before you found out from any one else.
If John-Morgan had not been such an outstanding Cadet,
I probably would have expelled him."

"I've got just one last question, Father."

"Yes, John. What is that?"

"I'd like to know who the little chickenshit was that
called up this Kicklighter fellow. I don't want to hurt him
or anything, I'd just like to see what a coward that age
looks like."

"John, this has got to be just between you and me. I
don't want you to repeat what I'm going to tell you. OK?"

"You got it."

"We're on the same wavelength. Whoever told on
John-Morgan is indeed a coward and a rat to boot. I shudder to think that such a worm wears our Cadet gray, but
he does. Do you follow me?"

"Semper Fi, Father."

"Semper Fi, John."

The punishment detail at Benedictine was known as
"walking the Jug," or, more commonly, "the Jug." "Jug"
was an abbreviation of the phrase "Justice Under God"
and consisted of marching around the assembly ground

behind the school for a certain amount of time for each demerit received. Usually Jug time was walked off in the afternoons after school, but more serious offenses were assigned Saturday morning Jug. This was an additional burden in that it also required full dress uniforms. Jug started at 9:00 A.M. and ended at noon.

John-Morgan was the only person walking Jug that Saturday, so he had to find the janitor to get into the arms room for a rifle. He was not unobserved, though; Father Hector had been keeping an eye out for him as he sat in the rectory kitchen drinking his fourth cup of strong black coffee and reading the morning paper. When he saw the lad march by the kitchen window, he looked at his watch, smiled, and murmered, "Right on time."

It was a beautifully bright morning in the last part of January, and the sun hitting on John-Morgan's white pants, cross belts, and hat-cover made him stand out all the more against the empty parade ground. It was a hundred steps forward, about face, then a hundred steps back the other way. This was to go on for three hours. At about 9:30, Mike's '59 Ford convertible pulled up on the Thirty-second Street side of the school. Mike and Bubba got out. They were both in their dress whites, and fell in behind John-Morgan as he marched.

"What the hell are you two doing here?"

"We're not going to let you do this alone," said Bubba. "You're here 'cause you refused to squeal on us. We're gonna be marching with you every Saturday for as long as it takes."

"Ya'll are crazy. You don't have to do this. It's not going to change anything."

"Well," said Mike, "at least you won't get lonesome." Then he started to call out his favorite cadence as the other two joined in and all three marched in lock-step perfection:

"My shoes are shined and my belt is tight,
My balls are swinging from left to right.
Sound off!

Bee-Cee!
Say it again!
Kay-dets!
Say it again!
C-A-D-E-T-S,
Cadets!"

The noise in back of the rectory brought several more priests into the kitchen. Father Hector was standing at the sink watching as the other priests gathered around.

"Who is that out there and what are they doing?" asked the young Father Christian Otto.

"That's Hartman, Silverman, and Sullivan, and they're walking Jug, dumbass," quipped Father Braun. He was a few years older and prone to be a trifle hard on the younger priests.

"Aw, screw you, Joe," shot back Chris Otto, who was not one to take any guff. "I know what they're doing. What I want to know, Father Eva Braun," the name he used to get back at Joe, "is what Silverman and Sullivan are doing out there. They're not being punished," and then adding for emphasis, "dumbass."

"Now now, boys," said Father Hector without taking his eyes off the parade ground, "none of that, it's much too early." Then he smiled wryly and added, "What we have here, gentlemen, is the three perpetrators of our little Christmas tree caper."

"What are you going to do to them?" asked Chris.

"Nothing—nothing at all. What I'd like to do is pin a medal for bravery on all three of them. Just look at them, my boys. One refused to tell on the other two, and they in turn refuse to let him suffer alone. Loyalty, honor, duty. It's all out there this fine morning in our own backyard. Not only that, but they managed to cut down that huge tree in the middle of the night, right under our Mr. Kick-lighter's fine red nose, and bring it over here without being caught. During the war it was initiative and skill like this that made heroes and won battles. Now I have to punish them. Oh, well, they were wrong in stealing poor

Mr. Kicklighter's wonderful tree, but they are still magnificent in their spirit."

"Like young lion cubs learning to hunt, wouldn't you say, Father?"

"Why, Otto, I didn't know you were such a poet. I'm very proud of you."

As the next weekend neared, all the Cadets in the school had heard the story of why John-Morgan was walking Saturday Jug. They also knew about Bubba and Mike. John-Morgan had been a popular commanding officer, and his demotion for refusing to rat on his friends elevated his Saturday Jug to a level of almost divine suffering. A few more members of the senior class showed up in full dress that morning and joined in the punishment tour. By the third weekend more than half of the senior class was walking Jug with John-Morgan as a silent protest against his demotion. By the fourth weekend virtually the entire senior class was walking Saturday jug. The underclassmen showed up to watch. One of the band members provided drum music.

Father Hector sat in the rectory parlor, phone in one hand and a fresh doughnut from Gottlieb's in the other. "Well, John, have you heard about our little Saturday Jug parade?"

"Yes, Father. What do you think?"

"Between the two of us, I think it's spectacular. Too bad it's not football season—I've never seen school spirit so high. But I think they want to hang me."

"How much longer are you going to make John-Morgan walk, Father? I don't think he's going to say anything now, do you?"

"Oh, not at all. I never did in the first place, but I think we'll go on just a little longer. I'm interested in seeing how things turn out."

"What do you mean?"

"I have a theory about who our little rat may be."

"I'm listening."

"Well, I don't think there are any rats marching at Saturday Jug as yet. It would be my guess that he will either not show up at all or will be among the last ones who do. It will be the lazy and the mean who come then. What do you think?"

"I think I'll be having breakfast with you at the rectory next Saturday, Father von Bock."

"Delighted, my dear Mr. Hartman, delighted! I shall have our fine cook, the amazing Queen Ester Green, prepare her fabulous pancakes. Please, come hungry."

The following Saturday, John Hartman slipped unseen into the Sacred Heart rectory at eight o'clock, where he and Father Hector proceeded to stuff themselves on pancakes, poached eggs, sausage, grits, and biscuits.

"Queenie."

"Yes, Father?"

"Your cooking rivals your royal name. It was obscenely wonderful. Thank you."

The two men then took a discreet upstairs window and began their surveillance as members of the senior class arrived and fell into formation.

"Who's missing, Father?"

"Well, as I said, certainly the lazy ones. There're a few not here this week that were here last week. Some are sick. Ah, there comes a mean one, Tony O'Boyle. This is his first time, I believe. He's really the only first-timer I would not classify as lazy or uncaring. He certainly cares, but how does he care?"

"He sure has a motive."

"If you mean the fight, I agree."

"But why would he show up at all? Everybody knows that he and John-Morgan don't get along."

"Peer pressure from the class. This has really turned into a little exercise in tribalism. He doesn't want to be left out."

"So, do you think it could be O'Boyle, Father?"

"One can't be sure, but I've studied human nature a long time and have been around this school for years. My guess is that it's Mr. O'Boyle, but I can't prove it."

"Takes after his father."

"I've already had experience with him. These Irishmen can be magnificent or magnificently cruel. But their greatest flaw, Herr Hartman, is that they are insanely jealous, especially of one another. The Jews go across town to trade at another Jew's store. Most of these Irishmen wouldn't cross the street to trade with another. What a pity. They could be so much more."

Hartman and Father von Bock watched the senior class drill for about an hour before John took his leave. On the way to the door the priest told him that this would end his son's Saturday Jug. He also said he could not make him Cadet colonel again, but he had decided to promote Bubba to the rank and appoint John-Morgan lieutenant colonel as a punishment.

"One last thing, John. I wouldn't worry too much about Mr. O'Boyle. He has an application in to the Citadel, and it will be my say-so that gets him in or keeps him out. I have to think about it some, but I don't believe he is Citadel material. It's my alma mater, you know."

AT JOHNNIE GANEM'S

MANY PRIESTS LIVE lonely and solitary lives. It's true that celibacy for a Catholic priest is not voluntary, but still there are pressures and temptations. Some priests cannot resist them and eventually yield to the weaknesses of the flesh. Others fight the loneliness and the need for a woman's touch. Some pray, some drink, some seek relief in the ambience of a crowd.

An affable man, Hector von Bock had always made friends easily. In the evening he enjoyed dining out; and because there was a large Catholic population in Savannah, he was almost certain to see someone he knew. Johnnie Ganem's, on the corner of Habersham and Gaston streets, was one of his favorite places. Because it was downtown and owned by a Catholic, the friendly and exceedingly stout Lebanese Johnnie Ganem, it was a favorite hangout for the priests from Benedictine. The entire Ganem family worked in the restaurant, and they would all make a fuss over the priests whenever they came in. The food was always good. Ganem's was known around town for its choice cuts of meat as well as the late-night crowd that frequented the lounge and dined around midnight. At least half a dozen newspaper men were always in the lounge after putting the *Gazette* to bed.

Any number of Benedictines (moderate yet public drinkers all) could usually be found at Ganem's on a weekend night. Some parishioners frowned at even a single drink by a priest, but Father Hector did not. He felt comfortable at Ganem's among his fellow Benedictines, the newsmen, and other regulars. It was a place where he could greet fellow bon vivants and speak with women in the safety of a crowd, or enjoy the camaraderie of a group of old BC graduates. Hector was what some would describe as "hail fellow, well met," and he reveled in the friendship and popularity that soothed the wounds of loneliness.

Katie O'Begley was a similar soul but for different reasons. She had come to Savannah from Boston courtesy of the United States Air Force when her father was transferred to nearby Hunter Field. Because of her many moves as an Air Force brat, she had never had roots. After her graduation from St. Vincent's, she refused to move to California with her parents on another transfer, so instead she stayed in Savannah and enrolled at Armstrong College, attending classes during the day and waiting tables at Ganem's in the evenings.

Katie had had several boyfriends, but nothing had worked out. Now she lived alone in a downtown apartment not far from the restaurant. She belonged to Sacred Heart Parish and enjoyed Mass when Father von Bock was the celebrant. She also liked waiting on his table and looked forward to his entrance on Saturday nights. Katie wished that she could tell him what was on her mind this particular night. She hoped that her anxiety didn't show in the way she acted.

Father Hector had his usual dinner. Mr. Ganem sat and talked with the priest as he ate. Throughout the evening people stopped by to say hello or sit for a while and engage in low, guarded conversations. Father von Bock was a man whom many people trusted with their troubles. Toward the end of her shift Katie had made up her mind that she would speak with him tonight. To shore up her courage, she sneaked several strong drinks of Old Grandad. When the crowd finally thinned out around one in the morning, Katie was told that she could leave. Father Hector signaled to her for his check, and as she gave it to him she asked if she could speak to him outside.

Unnoticed by Father Hector, Tony O'Boyle, Sr., had entered the lounge from the Habersham Street side. As the priest walked with Katie past the rows of barstools and out the front door, Tony kept his head down; he was effectively blocked from view by the large man sitting next to him. To see a girl with Father Hector at this hour of the night piqued his curiosity, so Tony slipped off his stool to peek out the window. The priest and the waitress climbed into Hector's car. All of this was frustratingly innocent to O'Boyle. So far.

"If I weren't here to drive you home, how would you get there, Katie?"

"Usually there's somebody who'll give me a ride. Sometimes, though, I have to walk."

"That's quite a walk at this time of night. Aren't you scared?"

"Sometimes, but mostly people leave me alone. I'm a fast runner too."

Father Hector laughed. "Now, what is it that's been eating at you, Katie? You didn't seem to be yourself tonight."

She tried to get the words out but had trouble. Eventually Katie buried her face in her hands as she wept.

Hector removed a freshly pressed handkerchief from his breast pocket, and then patted her on the back as she cried.

Intently, from the corner of the bar, Tony O'Boyle had a clear view of everything happening twenty feet away from him in the front seat of the priest's car. He quickly checked the room and saw that there were still four people from the *Gazette* drinking at the bar. One of them was a photographer. Tony wasn't sure what he had, but he was willing to watch for as long as it took the scene to play out.

Katie finally composed herself and sat back in the seat, then looked out of the passenger's window. "I think I might be pregnant," and then started to cry again.

Hector reached out to touch her shoulder. "Oh my, this is serious, isn't it?" The two of them sat there in silence for several minutes until Hector placed his keys in the ignition and told her that they would talk about her problem on the way to her house.

Tony almost slammed the blinds shut as he turned away from the window, correctly interpreting the innocent scene for what it was. He cursed the fact that he had not witnessed some salacious impropriety.

"I'll have another, Dot, then I've got to get home." Two seconds later there came the sound of a crash.

"Jesus, there's been a car wreck!" somebody shouted. The remaining crowd pushed its way through the narrow front door and out to the parking lot. As Tony stood looking at the two cars piled up on Habersham Street, one of the hub caps from Father von Bock's Chevy rolled past his feet and into the grass. He smiled and murmured to himself, "Happy Birthday, Tony."

It was late at night, and Hector was tired as he backed his '59 Bel Air out into Habersham Street. Cars were parked along the side of the road, and he hadn't seen Ruth Boatright as she drove down Habersham after leaving the late shift at St. Joseph's Hospital. Nobody was hurt, but Mrs. Boatright was also tired. She was especially angry that her brand new Rambler Ambassador now had a re-arranged front end.

Father Hector was apologetic as he tried to explain why a Catholic priest would have a young girl with him in his car at this time of night while pulling away from a bar. The photographer from the paper was busy snapping pictures as the priest helped a sobbing Katie from the front seat. Police cars soon pulled up, their red lights cutting into the night and dancing off the sides of nearby buildings.

The following morning Henry "Hound Dog" Lassiter, the photographer at the scene, proudly displayed his best picture of the wreck to the assistant editor. It was the one of Father von Bock standing next to his wrecked car with his arm around Katie as she buried her tearful head in his chest.

It didn't take Tony O'Boyle long to reach Belmont Abbey and inform the abbot about the misdeeds of his priest. A copy of the incriminating photo took a little longer, but it arrived soon enough, along with a note from Tony. He told the abbot that he had managed to have the entire story quashed through his connections at the paper, but it had been difficult, and people were still talking. He insinuated that Father von Bock's actions had put Benedictine in a very bad light and that the alumni were outraged.

A week after Tony's phone call to the abbot, Hector von Bock was gone from Benedictine forever. Katie O'Begley attempted suicide and lost the baby as a result, later disappearing from Savannah. The new headmaster of Benedictine wrote Little Tony an outstanding letter of recommendation to the Citadel. He was accepted for the next fall term.

Nobody fucks with Tony O'Boyle in the Free State of Chatham.

VI

MORTAL SINS

Romantic Ireland's dead and gone,
It's with O'Leary in the grave.

Q. What is Mortal Sin?
A. A Mortal Sin is a grievous of-
fense against the law of God.

—The Baltimore Catechism, 1948

VIETNAM AND THE CLASS OF '65

THINGS EVENTUALLY settled down at Benedictine after Father von Bock left, and the members of the class of 1965 began to focus in earnest on what they were going to do after they left BC. Most of the boys had already selected a college. Tony O'Boyle was strutting around with his acceptance letter from the Citadel. Bubba Silverman had been accepted by several colleges, but had settled upon the University of Georgia. Lloyd Bryan, perhaps in answer to his mother's prayers, was accepted by Notre Dame on a full football scholarship.

This was about the biggest sports news in Savannah in years, and it made Lloyd an overnight celebrity. He handled it with quiet dignity, remembering the day the letter came in the mail. His mother read it calmly, then folded it, tucked it back into the envelope, and said: "I'm not one bit surprised, Lloyd. I told you the Blessed Mother was going to answer my prayers. Now go wash your hands for dinner."

John-Morgan was accepted by Georgia, Clemson, and the University of Tennessee. The last couple of years had been confusing for John-Morgan, and he was now at that stage in his life when he didn't exactly know what he wanted or even who exactly he was. He and Mike had talked about what they would do with their lives many times during their senior year, yet John-Morgan only seemed to be even more confused the closer he got to graduation.

Mike had never been a good student and secretly didn't believe he had the drive or persistence to succeed at college. He had always assumed he would work at his father's contracting business and eventually take over. In 1965, however, a major obstacle lay in the career paths of all healthy males of eighteen years—the military draft.

College-bound boys could get a deferment from military service for four years if they carried a full load and maintained a "C" average, but all others were subject to immediate call-up. At the time of graduation, eleven thousand miles away from the quiet tree-lined streets of Savannah, in a country that very few members of the Cadet Corps had ever heard of, eighteen-year-old boys were killing one another with manic abandon. This war would have a profound impact on the lives of the class of 1965, especially John-Morgan and Mike.

It was in late April when John-Morgan decided to tell his parents about his plans. The weather had been especially beautiful and the lemony fragrance of the big early blooming magnolia in the front yard filled the neighborhood with its cloying scent. Mrs. Hartman left the doors and windows open so the house stayed delightfully cool and pleasant and impregnated with the smell. Mr. Hartman hadn't turned off the TV in the den when he came into dinner. John-Morgan could hear Walter Cronkite's avuncular baritone describing a rocket attack on a place called Saigon.

"I've made up my mind where I'm going after I graduate."

"Why that's wonderful, son. Your father and I were wondering. It's getting to be that time, you know."

As his father filled John-Morgan's plate he said, "I was hoping you would pick Tennessee, but any of the schools you've been accepted to will be fine with me."

"I'm not going to college right away, Daddy. Mike and I have joined the Marine Corps. We leave for basic training on July the second."

There was a dead silence at the table.

"Did you sign anything?"

"Daddy, it's done. I've signed up. I'm eighteen, so I don't need your permission. I'll be having my preinduction physical in two weeks."

"Damn, you should have asked me! You should have talked to me. This is crazy. You should be going to college in the fall, not Parris Island. I'll get this thing erased, wiped clean."

"Daddy, you can't do a thing about it. It's done, I'm in, and I want to go."

His father dropped the serving spoon. "Don't you understand they're sending the Marines to that little halfass country over in Asia somewhere? Those monkeys are killing people; they're killing American boys. John-Morgan, I've never been so upset with you in my life. This is a stupid thing that you've done, and I'm going to get you out of it."

John-Morgan's mother sat at the table for several minutes in stunned silence; and then she put her hands to her face and cried. John-Morgan had been prepared for this, but his father's reaction surprised him. John, Sr., had served in the Pacific with the Marines during World War II, and he had always spoken of his service to his country with great pride. Because of this, John-Morgan had assumed he would be equally proud about his volunteering for the Marine Corps now. What he didn't realize was that his father had seen the frustration and futility of the Korean War and feared that the country was being sucked into the abyss of another land war in Asia.

All of his life John-Morgan had seen the pride of veterans as they spoke of their military service and observed the respect others showed for their courage. He had heard the tales of his gallant ancestors who had placed themselves in harm's way when their country needed them. John-Morgan had been raised on television episodes of "Victory at Sea" and "The Twentieth Century." He had listened intently as Edward R. Murrow reported from the beaches of Normandy on "You Are There." He had watched John Wayne kill Japs by the bushel on Iwo Jima at the Weis Theater on Friday nights, and Audie Murphy shoot his way across Germany at the Lucas Theater on Saturday mornings. He knew the Civil War from Fort

Sumter to the Appomattox Court House, and World War II from the invasion of Poland to the decks of the Mighty Mo in Tokyo Bay. He had attended a military school for the last four years and been the corps commander, and his entire life had been filled with uniforms, history, religion, obedience, military glory, and a sense of duty. All of them called to him now. He was ready for that great adventure, and he could not understand his father's anger.

"You don't know what you've done. All my life I've worked to protect you, to make you safe, and now you've placed yourself in the gravest danger. I'm so afraid for you that I can hardly speak."

"Daddy, I'll be drafted sooner or later. When I finish college, I'd still have to go. Now I'll put in my two years, come out, and go to college on the GI Bill. Besides, we've got to do something to stop the Communists or they'll take over all of Asia, and then they'll try for the whole world. Then we'll have World War III. I feel right about this and I'm glad I did it."

"I know you don't understand, John-Morgan, but this isn't World War II. The Vietnamese haven't bombed Tybee. The country isn't in any immediate danger. Something just isn't right about this whole thing. It smells like another Korea. In four years the war could be over, and you might have been protected by your deferment." He pushed himself decisively away from the dinner table. "Look, I'm sick about this whole thing. Let's just let it drop for now and let me see if I can get you out of it."

The entire next week John Hartman tried to move heaven and earth to have his son's enlistment declared invalid. He called on everybody he knew in Washington and brought all sorts of pressure to bear, but to no avail. Uncle Sam was having too much trouble drafting unwilling young men to let go of those who had volunteered. That meant that John-Morgan and Mike were headed for Parris Island during the summer. In a way this was fortunate, for it would serve to acclimate them to winter weather in Vietnam.

DOCTRINE AND DESIRE

THE LAG BETWEEN graduation from Benedictine and the start of boot camp at Parris Island was short. John-Morgan was determined to pack all of the living he could into that time.

The day after graduation he moved to the beach house and went to town only to pick up Charlotte, who told him how unhappy she was about his not going to college. She said that all proper people got a college education first, and *then* fulfilled their military obligations. "That way, they can become officers upon their enlistment, assuming a status befitting their social class." She was entering Emory in the fall and had already become swept up in the social stirrings that attended admission to such a school. She had made up her mind that she would surely find a new boyfriend at Emory, but until that time, cute little John-Morgan Hartman would serve her purposes well.

There was intensity and passion in the way John-Morgan lived his life in June of 1965. Rather than plunge himself into a rambunctious disregard for time, he was almost frantic as he counted the days that remained until boot camp. He tried to hold on to each and every hour, but they strangely slipped away. He knew that his life was going to change drastically.

At the southern end of Tybee Island, just across the Back River, lies a group of smaller islands collectively shown on the charts as Little Tybee Island. The whole area measures about five miles long by three miles deep and is bounded by the Atlantic Ocean on the east, Wassaw Sound to the south, and the Bull River in the west. Places had names like Buck Hammock and Beach Hammock, Myrtle Island and Jack Cut. They connected in turn with other places like Little Tybee Slough, House Creek, and the Wassaw Breaker. Many of the islands were no larger than a small house; others measured a mile or more in length. Their wide, pristine beaches were strewn with knurled driftwood and wind-brushed oaks.

Accessible only by boat, Little Tybee, even today, remains essentially void of human inhabitation except on summer weekends, when its extreme southern end becomes a port for a dozen or so day-sailors who come to enjoy the beaches. They are gone by dark. Thirty years ago, on a weekday, absolute privacy could be assured on the wide beaches of Little Tybee Island, and it became a favorite place for John-Morgan and Charlotte to go and spend the day, sometimes with others, sometimes alone.

They were alone on that last Wednesday before his departure for Parris Island as they rode across the Back River and into the Little Tybee archipelago. The eight o'clock sun pushed up from behind a cloud. Rays of light struck the sand, making it shine and sparkle. The ocean was calm, and its gentle swells carried their boat in a soft motion. As they cruised down the ocean side of the islands, John-Morgan pointed out osprey nests in the tops of dead pine trees. Charlotte squealed with joy when she saw two deer wander down a stretch of beach, then dart into the woods at their approach.

After a while John-Morgan turned his boat into a creek that divided the beach for a stretch and then ran to the ocean. Here the water was deep, and the beach had a steep slope running up to pristine white sand trailing off into woods of heavy-armed oaks. The area was wide and the water was protected like a lagoon, making it the perfect place for swimming and waterskiing. After John-Morgan tied the boat off and unloaded the cooler and chairs, the two of them started walking down the beach in complete seclusion. Charlotte was intrigued by the shells that washed up, and by the time they returned to the boat she was carrying an array of assorted beauties. As John-Morgan placed the shells in the boat, Charlotte came up behind him, wrapped her arms around his waist, and kissed him on his shoulders and back. Then she whispered into his ear. "What's wrong? You haven't kissed me all morning."

John-Morgan turned; he took her face in his hands and kissed her. Then he reached for her hips and pressed her closely to him. Charlotte returned all of his intensity and more as she felt for the muscles in his back that she had come to know. She tasted the salt on his skin as her lips moved across his cheek and down to his neck. They began to gently settle into the warm water without breaking their embrace. Small waves curled over their ankles as their emotion mounted. Then Charlotte pushed John-Morgan away and stood up.

She took him completely by surprise, and in one swift movement she removed her bathing suit. She reached out her hand and helped him up. Without a word she pulled his shorts down to his knees, and helped him to step out of them. Pressing herself tightly to John-Morgan once again, Charlotte pulled him slowly into deeper water. Soon they were floating through the lagoon wrapped in a hot embrace. Like dark fires, flesh and spirit alerted and transfixed him.

John-Morgan's parents had never lied to him, and he had never known a time when there was not love between them. When he had entered grammar school at Blessed Sacrament, the trust and admiration he had for his parents had successfully been transferred to the priests and nuns who taught him. He saw his parents devoutly pray at home and watched as they took Communion at Mass. He believed what his parents told him, and they said that the Catholic Church and its doctrines were the best path to salvation and eternal life.

John-Morgan had listened intently as the church's laws were explained. He believed in the essential goodness of its doctrines and dogmas. When he was told that sexual intercourse outside of marriage was a sin so grievous that it could cut him off from the gift of sanctifying grace, and thus sever him from the body of Christ and Christ's salvation, he had accepted it. He believed it with all of his heart.

By the time he had finished the eighth-grade, the Roman Catholic Church was so rooted in his psyche that he approached almost everything with a Catholic eye. By the time he had finished Benedictine, he was immersed in Roman theology. With John-Morgan, Holy Mother Church had done Her job well.

All of this, plus rage and the pull of natural passion and desire, swirled in John-Morgan's head as he held Charlotte and was swamped by all the forms and places of pleasure on her body. She pushed back from him and said, "Let's swim to the beach." Then she began moving toward the shoreline as John-Morgan watched the water glisten off her skin. She was waiting for him on the blanket and immediately pulled him on top of her.

"Do it, John-Morgan, do it!" she whispered as she thrust her hips toward his. Still he pulled back a little, though he began to kiss her breasts. Charlotte's voice was edged with frustration. "Why don't you do it, are you afraid or something? Why haven't we ever gone all the way? You always pull back just when I'm ready. I told you I'm taking the pill, there's nothing to worry about. I can't believe I'm lying here naked, begging you to make love to me. What's the matter? It ought to be the other way around. Is something wrong with you? Are you afraid you might hurt me?" John-Morgan looked at the ground and said nothing. Then her voice became angry.

"Well, don't! You won't be the first, buster, I can tell you that!"

By this time John-Morgan had rolled off Charlotte and pulled part of the blanket up over him.

"This is disgusting, it really is. It's that damned religion of yours. You people are so hung up on your religion that you can't think for yourselves. You're leaving next week for the Marine Corps and then to a war in that nasty little country that I can't even remember the name of and you might get killed or have your dick shot off and I beg you to make love to me and you refuse!" Charlotte stood directly in front of John-Morgan and suddenly said, in a much softer voice, "You're a virgin, aren't you, John-Morgan? And all along I thought you were just a gentleman and maybe I should be a lady and not have you think poorly of me."

John-Morgan still didn't say a word, so Charlotte grew mean. In a vulgar, taunting voice she sneered: "Come on, why don't you do it just this once? I won't tell if you won't tell. Take me, little man, any way you want."

John-Morgan reached up and roughly pushed her aside. Then he stood and looked her over coldly. "Yeah, I'm a virgin. That means that even after all the time I've spent with you I still have at least a little of my virtue and innocence left. And now, after today, I know that you have none of yours. I don't expect you to understand; I never did. Now get your clothes on, it's time to go."

"Bastard!" she shouted as she swung her arm to hit him in the face. He caught it and harmlessly held it there. "You son of a bitch!"

"I've never hit a girl before, Charlotte, but I'm getting awfully close." Now John-Morgan pushed her roughly away. "The party's over. Get your clothes on or I'll leave without you."

COMBAT, DRUGS, AND HORROR

THE MARINE CORPS kept its word to John-Morgan and Mike. They went through boot camp together and were both assigned to the same regiment in Vietnam. That, however, was as far as the corps' promise went. When they received their final assignments, John-Morgan and Mike were in two completely different units, though still in the same theater of operation.

The Third Marine Division arrived in Vietnam in May 1965 and was assigned to the area just below the demilitarized zone at the border of North and South Vietnam.

Part of that territory soon became known as Leatherneck Square. It was to this locale that the young Savannahians were assigned. Names like Cam Lo, Con Thien, and Gio Linh would echo in their minds for the rest of their lives.

Both John-Morgan and Mike had done very well at Parris Island. Their four years at Benedictine had placed them way ahead of everyone else in their platoon, and in short order they had been recognized as leaders not only by the other boots, but also by their drill instructors.

John-Morgan graduated at the head of the platoon, and according to boot camp tradition he was immediately promoted to private first class. His record would follow him wherever he went, assuring the attention and respect of his commanders. Once he arrived "in country," he was assigned to an infantry platoon that would be airlifted by helicopters to needed hot spots along the DMZ. His unit would then go on reconnaissance missions in search of enemy contacts. It wasn't long before John-Morgan had risen to squad leader, and then to assistant platoon leader.

Mike won an expert marksman award at Parris Island and was easily the best shot among the boots. Pressure was on him to become a Marine sniper, but after he had ridden in a Huey helicopter and fired the M-60 machine gun in flight, he was hooked on the thrill of hanging out the door, blazing away at targets below. Mike discovered a deep-seated affinity for weapons and the power they possessed. When he fired the M-60, he felt as if the gun were an extension of himself; he could point it as easily and as accurately as his index finger. His reflexes were quick, and he intuitively knew just the right amount of lead to give a moving target at any distance. Without thinking, Mike could spray bullets and cover large target areas with hundreds of rounds quickly and accurately. He soon became a legend among the gunship crews, who nicknamed him "Iron Mike." He was the guy to call upon when a particularly tough mission was planned.

*　*　*

It didn't take long for the war to exact its grinding toll on John-Morgan and Mike, and after a few nasty months in the DMZ they had assumed the posture and attitude of battle-hardened veterans. Their language was profane to the point of absurdity, and they both smoked two packs of cigarettes a day. Liberty, when it came, was often spent in seedy Saigon bars doing shooters of Russian vodka. When they were back at their base camps and relatively safe for a few days, the nights consisted of smoking Thai marijuana and listening to Jimi Hendrix or the Doors on expensive Japanese stereos purchased cheaply on the black market.

Although John-Morgan indulged in the liquor and soft drugs that were always available on liberty tours, he shunned the prostitutes in the bars and whorehouses that dotted the roads close to base camp. Like most other soldiers he accepted the habit of referring to the Vietnamese in derogatory terms like "dink" and "slopehead." He had little respect for the South Vietnamese army and even less for its government. John-Morgan viewed all locals with the utmost suspicion and came to hate the country; he even refused to recognize anything of beauty in the land. Nevertheless, when offered the flesh of a young woman on his first liberty, he was repulsed at the idea of buying another human being. He pitied the women and girls who worked the brothels, and his heart ached at the thought of a thirteen-year-old girl being taken for the first time by a drunken sailor for three dollars, American.

There was no love in this land for John-Morgan, and he viewed the sexual escapades between these desperate Vietnamese women and the horny men in his platoon as a perversion of all that he had been taught since childhood. As much as he detested the country, he still could not divorce himself from his core belief that these were human beings, and that what had been wrong in Savannah, Georgia, was wrong along the banks of the Cua Viet River or in Quang Tri.

Had he not been such an excellent soldier, the others

in John-Morgan's unit would have ridiculed him even more than they already did for his "restraint." For him, however, it wasn't restraint that tempered his behavior, it was revulsion. Still, he was referred to as "Father Hartman" or "the preacher," and sometimes even as "Miss Hartman." But the guys all knew that John-Morgan would never let them down in the field, where nothing counted except loyalty and firepower.

John-Morgan had been fortunate when he killed for the first time. It was on the run and at a distance of over a hundred yards. Still, there was no doubt in his mind that his shot had snuffed the life out of the little man he had held in his sights, because he had seen the red flash spew from the back of his target's head and watched as the man crumpled to the ground. After that incident, John-Morgan had been forced to move on quickly, and the other kills that day had also been at a distance. There were no recognizable faces, no eyes pleading for mercy, and no audible screams of the dying. He had none of those things to haunt him that night in his hooch as the Jack Daniels soothed his mind and the music massaged him into apathy. He sat on his rack in a half stupor, the others dancing around him in a kind of initiation ritual as if he had crossed the equator for the first time. Marines threw cigarettes at him and poured beer over his head. They even drew a target on his chest with lipstick that a whore had left the previous night. Before he passed out, John-Morgan kept yelling: "The fuckers were shooting at me too, goddamnit. The fuckin' dinks were shootin' at my ass. That's why I did it."

The next day on patrol, killing was at close quarters as John-Morgan's company entered a small village known to harbor Vietcong. As his squad approached one of the huts, they received fire from a shadowy figure in the front door.

Two men on his left were taken down by the distinctive pop of an AK-47, and John-Morgan would have gone down too had he not immediately yanked his rifle up and started pulling blindly on the trigger. He saw the burst from his M-16 hit his target in the gut and walk up its chest. He watched as the figure's straw hat flew off, revealing the face of a woman, and he was frozen in his tracks for the split second it took for a length of intestine and pieces of lung to blow out her back. Then, in a conditioned reflex, John-Morgan tore through the hut's door, spraying an entire thirty-round magazine into the filthy darkness smelling of pig feces. Only when he was forced to stop and reload did he see the two children into which he had slammed eight high-velocity rounds. Even then he had no time to mourn as the tree line came alive with little star-shaped flashes from the forest darkness. Hot 7.62 rounds skidded through shabby walls and broke clay pots sitting on nasty little cook fires.

There was no Jack Daniels that night, no hooch to party in. The survivors of the initial ambush at the Village of the Setting Moon were pinned down there all night long. Those who had poked fun at John-Morgan the day before now called out to "the preacher" in terror and begged him to pray for them.

It was on that night, in the Village of the Setting Moon, that John-Morgan first tasted fear so complete that his teeth chattered and he was unable to control his bowels. His mouth was scorching, but he could not quench his thirst because his canteen was empty and he had to hold his position. Enemy fire would have chopped him to pieces. The cries for help from his wounded comrades had almost cost him his life. He had tried desperately to reach them, but he was driven back by incoming fire.

John-Morgan kept the Vietcong away from his position until about three in the morning, when he ran dangerously low on ammunition. He was down to fifteen rounds as six VC crawled around the front of his perimeter. It was two hours to daylight when salvation came from the air. John-Morgan finally had time to think about his life. His thoughts were never clearer than on that night.

When John-Morgan finally returned to his base camp

from the Village of the Setting Moon, a transformation
had taken place. Through a perverse metamorphosis born
in intense combat, his mind was annealed, his soul gal-
vanized by a kind of deep spiritual bruise that forced him
consciously to center on only two things—keeping himself alive, and counting the days until his tour was finished.

For a while Mike shared these feelings, but his little hor-
rors were much worse than John-Morgan's. Iron Mike's
legend grew not only among those who flew on the choppers but also with the ankle-express grunts hauled into
and out of battle. Mike was barreling along on the adrenalin high that combat provides. There was no explaining
the feeling brought on by being shot at and missed, and
it was only topped by the feeling of shooting back and
hitting. Soon the high rush could only be achieved by
more and more dangerous missions. When those missions
were unavailable, the pilots who flew his chopper would
cut across areas known to be hot with Charlie in hopes
of drawing ground fire and a fight.

Others on the crew were as addicted to the rush as he
was, and his Huey had been named "the Stuka" after the famous World War II German dive-bomber. The bottle-cap
colonel who commanded their wing thought the crew was
"dinky dau" or crazy, and looked upon them as dangerous
but useful. The crew of the Stuka had made a Faustian bargain in which they dispensed destruction and mayhem in
exchange for the exhilaration of defying death again and
again. Eventually, however, through their naïveté they discovered that Mephistopheles drove a hard bargain. The
terms of that bargain finally became known to all.

These had been normal men before the war, but no
normal man could long endure the screaming he heard
when the fight was over and his saner thoughts crept in.
That screaming was from the conscience. At first Mike
handled the pain with alcohol and "dew," but once the

booze and marijuana could no longer adequately anesthetize him, he started smoking pot laced with heroin. That was sufficient to ease the pain and allow a deep and fascinating sleep to carry him away from the surrounding madness. The feeling was both physically and spiritually euphoric. Before long, Mike was an addict of a different kind.

John-Morgan and Mike only had a few days together on liberty, but it didn't take long for John-Morgan to recognize the change that had taken place in his friend. Not only did the drugs and the horror of war allow Mike to kill with mechanical ease and precision, they had also allowed him to partake of all the other grotesque things that defined this particular war. He had paid trifling sums for the favors of little girls twelve years old and had bet on the outcome of gun duels between opium addicts. Although John-Morgan had bent the rules of spiritual existence, he still believed in the God he had been raised to love. Mike, on the other hand, had long ago lost his faith. He was spiritually void, and if he prayed at all, he prayed to die so that the suffering might end. But there was no real conviction in that prayer. Mike still feared death because he wasn't quite sure what was on the other side. His world, however, was slowly bringing him to believe that there was nothing. And then, he hoped, he would fear death no more and could end his torment.

THE FIREFIGHT

JOHN-MORGAN AND MIKE were halfway through their tour when, by chance, they were involved in the same mission. John-Morgan had been assigned as a squad leader to a group known by in-country slang as "lurps."

Such men went on extended patrols looking for enemy activity. They were usually transported by helicopter to a remote section of jungle and dropped off to complete their patrols. Their duty was not to engage the enemy, but

rather to report on his movements and strengths. This was
the most intense day-to-day warfare that many infantry-
men ever engaged in during their time in Vietnam. The
lurps' war was one of running and hiding, of not being
able to count on anything more than what they carried on
their backs. Many times they were cut off completely
from all support and had to fight alone against superior
forces for hours that seemed like eternities. Sometimes
help wouldn't come at all, or would come too late, and
the members of the patrol would be wiped out—or, even
worse, be captured by the Cong.

Mike had been flying door-gunner missions in his skid
as it served to transport Marines to wherever they were
needed along the DMZ. His ship, along with another
Huey, had been selected to transport John-Morgan's patrol
into an area known as a stockpile and supply point for
VC activity. The job was deadly, gruesome, and delicate.
It required a stealthy insertion and extraction that stood a
good chance of turning "hot." Because of this, the Stuka
and its notorious crew and another wild-crew gunship
were chosen for the mission.

It was in May 1966, in the desolate beauty of a Vietnam sunset, that Mike and John-Morgan met again after
many grueling months. The change in Mike was wrenching. John-Morgan had already seen the ravages the last
time they were together, roving the rancid streets of Saigon, but now the transformation was infinitely worse.
When John-Morgan looked up at the glazed face of the
Huey's door-gunner, he recognized the *features* of his old
friend. At the same time he almost recoiled in horror when
he caught a glimpse of the dim, red light from the dead
spirit living behind the eyes. He saw a boy of nineteen,
his oldest friend, transformed into a hardened killer, a rap-
ist despoiling the land—and enjoying himself in some
hideous way. In John-Morgan's mind's eye, Mike lay like
a soft fleshy snail on a razor's edge, keeping his balance
only by living for the moment, about to be sliced in two.
A bubble of acid and sour food hit the back of John-

Morgan's throat. Then it burst, and he grimaced a smile as Mike leaned down to pull him into the Huey.

"John-Morgan, let me help your ruck-humpin' dinky-dau ass into this here hawg. I had no idea I'd be meetin' up with you on this run. I hear this is a deep-serious mission that requires we insert some crotch members into Bumfuck Booney. Make yourself comfortable next to me, we got a boo-coo blade time run to your LZ. Me and this here hog-60 will keep the slopes off of you. So whatcha been up to, Preacher?"

John-Morgan struggled to get himself and his gear situated as he kept an eye on his men while they climbed into the two helicopters. He let out a sigh when he was finally settled and said, "Same old same old. Countin' the days to my wakeup just like you. What do you hear from home?"

"Your little ex-girlfriend Ann Marie is in nursing school at St. Joseph's. Katherine says she's dating some swingin' dick that's an intern at Memorial. Otherwise the beaches are full at Tybee—Joe and Cathy college doin' their tans and thinkin' impure thoughts about each other. Ain't nothin' changed but us, I guess."

The rotors started to turn on the Hueys. Soon the power from the engines rumbled through the craft as the throttle was advanced and the ship prepared for liftoff. Mike handed John-Morgan a headset so they could communicate during the flight. This lent Mike's voice a distant quality that somehow fit the ghastly way he looked. When had the softness of his eyes been put out? John-Morgan wondered. Had it come as quickly to Mike as it had to him, or had it been slowly drained and spilled in small drops over the landscape of hot jungles that earned the collective name of "void vicious"?

"This supposed to be some important doings," said Mike over the intercom. "Cong are supposed to have boo-coo supplies hidden out there in the boonies. Buildin' 'em up for an attack. I guess it's your Irish ass that is supposed to lead this here pitiful clutch of cherries out there on a

snoop 'n' poop to find out where their dump is so's artie
can send them the mail."

John-Morgan came back over the headset to Mike and
said: "No cherries this mission, too important. I told the
CO it was NFW with cherries and tent pegs if they wanted
their bars polished by that bunch of Saigon cowboys they
suck up to. I told him it was eat the apple doo-mommie,
I wasn't going out there with nobody that was gonna' get
my young ass dusted."

John-Morgan could feel his weight increase as the
Huey lifted off the ground, imparting G-forces into his
body. The ship banked across the airfield and headed west
into a huge orange ball of sun. The landscape turned purple and pink as the sun's rays reached a rare golden moment, washing the tormented land in a gunflash joy of
spectacular color.

"One thing for sure," said Mike, "this is a field-grade
night. No problems with this kind of light in setting you
boonie rats right down on your designated LZ. We hear
you'll be down for a short-short. You're supposed to di
di mau out of there in three days and these two skids are
set to pull you up. That means I'll be coming back for
your Irish ass."

"Yeah, we expect to be on the ground no more than
seventy-two hours. Locate VC lines of supply and their
dump. Call in artie; stay for the show to see if it gets a
standing O, then di di back to the LZ. Glad to hear you'll
be on the extraction run."

"Wouldn't miss it for the world, Preacher. St. Patrick
and Iron Mike Sullivan will be looking after you, young
man. You got nothing to worry about."

In the darkness the two Hueys skimmed across the
Delta at tree-top level for an hour. Then they set down in
a clearing next to a deserted village. John-Morgan was the
last to exit the chopper, and as he jumped from the door,
Mike grabbed his arm and embraced him. Then he looked
into his eyes and yelled over the noise of the engines, "I

love you, man. I love your damn ass. I'll be back for you, you can count on it."

John-Morgan reached up and touched Mike's sweaty cheek and shouted back, "I love you too. I'll be waiting for you." He started to move away from the ship when Mike pulled him close again. "This place is killing me, man. I'm fucking dying inside. Sometimes I feel like eating my gun, only I ain't got the balls yet." Then the pilot advanced the throttle on the Huey and called to Mike over the intercom. "Cut the kissy face, Gunner. We gotta get this ship outta here." Mike yelled into John-Morgan's ear in a pleading voice, "Pray for me, John-Morgan. Pray for me," and then let go of his friend's jacket. As the ship lifted off, John-Morgan and Mike watched each other until the darkness and the distance erased their images.

The men crept like night-cats though the bush. As they tread, their eyes pierced the darkness for movement, ears probing the night for sound. Their faces and arms were camouflaged with stripes of green and black greasepaint. They were dark humanoid tigers in frightful guise.

For two hours they slipped through the jungle and across streams until they came to their checkpoint. There, half of them fanned out to sit and wait, to watch and listen. John-Morgan and the remainder of the unit marched for another two hours before they reached their designated area and spread out as the first group had done. Well hidden and silent, they waited through the dawn, catching catnaps throughout the day as the sun fired high and hot over the jungle. Steam rose from the soggy forest floor as the temperature boiled above a hundred degrees.

When the sun went down, the Cong came out. John-Morgan was the first to notice movement on the trail to his right as little slivers of moonlight sluiced through the tree cover. A line of slightly built men and women was slipping quietly through the jungle. Some carried weapons, others carried boxes balanced on their heads, and a few pushed bicycles heaped with baggage along the path.

John-Morgan counted each one as they passed is hidey-hole; he finally stopped at one hundred sixty-three. He waited a few minutes to make sure there were no stragglers, and then gave the signal for his men to assemble.

Examining a footprint on the trail by the light of a red filter, one of the men whispered, "Hanoi Florsheims." This was the footwear favored by many of the Vietcong and North Vietnamese soldiers; it was made from used automobile tires. "Looks like 'gomers' in this outfit." Gomer was slang word for soldiers of the North Vietnamese Army, a harbinger of further pressure being put on the shaky ARVN forces. It was a development that the brass in Saigon would want to know about.

On John-Morgan's signal the men began to move down the trail, following the line of VC and NVA to their supply drop. After several hours the supply caravan reached the drop point and began to unlimber. John-Morgan and his men watched in amazement as the supplies were stacked along with tons of others under well-camouflaged shelters invisible from the air. Carefully they plotted the location and then moved back as far as they could from the base and still have a good view. The radioman called in the coordinates to a firebase almost thirty miles away. After little more than a minute he looked up at the others and whispered, "They're away. Party time in one minute, fifteen seconds."

Eight-inch artillery shells don't whistle as they fly through the air; they rumble like a freight train at eight hundred miles an hour. The men in John-Morgan's squad heard the projectiles tear over their heads and saw them fly directly into the supply depot; then there was a stupendous explosion. Secondary explosions followed as the stored ammunition began to explode; the Marines could hear them thundering in their chests. "Tell artie to bring the max, tell 'em they got 'em boxed," ordered John-Morgan to the radioman.

The squad couldn't help admiring their handiwork. They rested until nightfall, when they started back to the pickup point. The march was nerve-wracking and exhausting, but uneventful; they met up with the first squad and started the last leg back to the deserted village.

The Vietcong knew that their supply dump was invisible from the air. Its location had to have been found by ground troops. Furthermore, they were well aware that observers must have been hiding in the woods during the artillery attack to call in any range corrections to the firebase. It didn't take them long to figure out where the best observation area was; a few minutes later they had picked up the trail. They alerted all of their units that enemy troops were in the area, and the search was on for the Marines.

Mr. Charlie had been hurt, and hurt badly and he wanted revenge. He wanted the imperialist dogs alive, if possible, but dead would do if it had to. Tracking at night was very difficult, but knowing the terrain as home ground made things easier. The VC had soon established the general direction in which the Americans were moving.

The Marines arrived at the village at two in the morning, and after checking it for VC, they settled down for dawn and the prearranged pickup. The village had a small walled-in Catholic church with a little graveyard. John-Morgan placed his men in defensive positions around the churchyard, some taking cover behind old gravestones and statues. Then he radioed his base camp that they were in place.

After assigning the guard-duty rotation, John-Morgan rummaged around the pockets of his BDU's until his fingers settled upon a familiar object. He crept to the low wall overlooking the approach to the church and settled down behind it with his rifle at the ready. John-Morgan took off his helmet with his left hand, and with his right he touched the crucifix of his Rosary to his forehead and made the sign of the cross. Then he whispered quietly "The Five Sorrowful Mysteries of the Rosary" and began to pray for Mike Sullivan while he watched and waited.

Behind that crumbling churchyard wall, in the pale light of a full moon, John-Morgan completed the Sorrowful Mysteries of the Rosary as well as the Joyful Mysteries and was into the third decade of the Glorious Mysteries when he noticed movement on the side of one of the village huts. There was a terrible welling of fear in his gut as he quietly alerted his little band of men. Two more figures appeared and moved quickly into the tumbled-down buildings, and John-Morgan was near to panic.

He eased the safety off his M-16 and instinctively felt for the extra magazines strapped to his body. Three more darkly clad men hurried past his perimeter and disappeared into the shadows on his right. John-Morgan held his breath. He motioned for the radioman to crawl over and whispered into his ear.

"Raise Bull Dog Base and tell them we're about to engage the enemy. Tell them that it's deep serious and they need to provide choppers most ricky tick with supporting gunships or our asses are history."

The Marine patrol was well concealed and positioned, and for a few minutes John-Morgan thought that they might remain undetected by the VC. Then two VC soldiers slipped into the graveyard and started poking around.

PFC Eddie "Boogaloo" Burns was as good as they came out in the boonies. He had chosen to take up position behind a broken statue of St. Joseph that afforded him an excellent field of fire for his M-60 machine gun. Eddie was a muscular two-hundred-and-thirty-pounder who had starred on his high school football team back in Dothan, Alabama. He wore a cammo jacket with the arms cut off, and his enormous biceps bulged when he held the M-60. His skin was so black that it shone when he sweated. In darkness, the eyes were the only visible part of Boogaloo Burns. Even though John-Morgan was a white boy, Eddie liked him more than anybody else in the squad because John-Morgan believed in Jesus, and Eddie's momma had told him to stick close to those who had been washed in the Blood of the Lamb.

Eddie could have quietly handled one of the VC by himself, snapping the little man's neck with his massive arms, without revealing the Marine presence in the village, but he could not quietly silence two. When the Cong wandered up to the statue of St. Joseph, Boogaloo Burns cut them in half with a burst from his M-60, and the battle was on.

At first it appeared the Marines would be able to handle the trouble; by the time the helicopters arrived, they might have killed enough VC to make a relatively safe escape. For a while the Cong refused to advance against the churchyard, instead choosing to fire from the houses. The rounds from their Russian-made rifles smacked madly against the old brick wall, but the wall was thick and it afforded good protection to John-Morgan and his men as long as only small arms challenged it.

The firing alerted the countryside, however, and soon other VC patrols in the area began to converge on the village. Two hours before dawn, the Marines in the churchyard were surrounded and grossly outnumbered, but if they could hold out until the Hueys arrived, the choppers would make quick work of the Cong, and most of the Marines would live to tell their grandchildren of the battle. If.

The Leathernecks were able to hold their own for a while, even against the larger numbers, but then the battle changed. VC arrived carrying a rocket-propelled granade known as an RPG-7; it looked like a bazooka and fired a projectile that easily penetrated brick walls. This decisively tipped the scales.

Because the Marines had been traveling light, the closest thing they had to such a weapon was an M-79 grenade launcher nicknamed the "Blooper" because of the way the weapon hurled its 40-mm grenade. Although an effective weapon, the Blooper had none of the concussive power of the RPG.

Three Marines were now dead and four more were

seriously injured from the small-arms fire alone. Ammunition was running low, and when John-Morgan saw the muzzle flash of the RPG, and saw it blow a four-foot hole in the wall, he knew they'd be lucky to last another thirty minutes. The radioman sent out a second desperate call to the two choppers scheduled to pick them up. The Stuka pilot radioed back that they were about twenty minutes away. He also said that two more gunships were only a few minutes behind them.

The VC were starting to tighten the circle around the church, and as they moved forward, Eddie took down the man carrying the RPG. This gave them a little breathing room, and John-Morgan signaled for his men to compress the perimeter by moving closer to the church. Eddie set up his weapon in the doorway, and John-Morgan took up a position to his left, behind a large palm tree. Then they had to try to hold on.

CREDIT TO THE CORPS

THE VIETCONG INTENSIFIED their fire into the churchyard, and soon only half a dozen able-bodied Marines remained. John-Morgan gave the order to strip the dead and wounded of their ammunition. After the extra rounds had been distributed, he took a quick poll of his men to discover their thoughts about surrendering. There was never any question about what they would do; no one wanted to fall into Charlie's hands, and they all voted to fight to the last man.

The VC suddenly charged with a blood-curdling scream that reminded John-Morgan of the Rebel Yell. Boogaloo Burns was magnificent with his M-60 and accounted for at least half the VC killed in the charge, but the enemy soldiers could not be held back. One made it right up to John-Morgan's position in a frenzied dash, and John-Morgan could see the rage in the man's eyes as he swung his M-16 around. He was less than fifteen feet away when he could feel the slight recoil that the M-16 had and hear the bolt slam back and forth in the rifle as it chambered one cartridge after another. He saw the man's chest cave in as a three-round burst hit him in mid-sternum. The Cong's chest caved in and splattered, but in his last, dying act he pitched an American-made fragmentation grenade. John-Morgan saw the grenade fly through the air and land just to his left. Then it exploded.

As John-Morgan dragged himself to cover, he could see blood pouring from the left side of his body. He managed to prop himself against the palm tree and somehow get off a few more shots at the retreating VC.

Although the Marines had been able to withstand the charge, their ammunition was almost gone, and three men had been seriously wounded. With the next charge, they would be either prisoners of war or dead. Then they heard the Hueys.

Mike Sullivan could see the smoke rising from the church as he stood in the door of the Stuka, machine gun at the ready. The two Hueys came in low and fast over the village to get an idea of what was going on. As they passed, the VC put up a withering barrage of fire from their AK-47's and both ships took hits. The other gunner in the Stuka was killed, and the pilots were only saved by the armor plating on their seats. Mike was hanging out the door looking for John-Morgan when they passed. He saw him sitting next to the palm tree, covered in blood. As the Hueys swung out for a second pass, he also realized that the VC were gathering for a second charge. It was clear that the little group would be overrun.

As the Hueys turned, the RPG fired. The other chopper was hit in the engine, bringing it down in flames with the loss of all aboard. When Stuka's pilot saw that, he jerked his ship up and back and started away from the village.

"Where the fuck are you going, Captain?" Mike yelled over the intercom.

"Out of here. It's too hot down there. We'll wait until the other support ships get here."

"No, sir. We're going back down there right now and get those guys out or they'll all be killed. Charlie's massing for another attack. I saw 'em."

"NFW, gunner. We linger out of range until we get support."

Mike knew that John-Morgan's situation was desperate. He knew that the men on the ground could last only a few minutes longer, and that if they weren't rescued soon, there would be nothing to go back to. He had reached a point in his life where he welcomed death as a merciful savior. Now, if he had to give that life trying to save his friend, it would be an honorable way to end a miserable existence. Perhaps, he thought, this was a last and forlorn gift from a God that he had long considered dead. Mike drew a .45 from his shoulder holster and placed it against the copilot's head.

"We go back now and get those guys or I blow his head off, Captain."

"You're out of your fucking mind, Sullivan! Get your ass back to your battle station, NOW. That's a goddamn direct order, mister. Do you copy me?"

"I said turn this ship around or I'll waste Patterson."

"You crazy bastard. Get back to your weapon now, and we'll chalk this up to combat fatigue. We go back down there, and we're all dead. Do it now, Sullivan."

Mike pulled the pistol away from the copilot's head, pointed it at his leg, and pulled the trigger. Blood spurted, and Patterson lunged forward. The pilot was frozen in his seat. Then Mike returned the pistol to the copilot's head. "Next time he's dead. Now get this ship back to that village and put it down right in front of that church. I'll cover them from the door as they evacuate."

He reached over and relieved the two men of their pistols, tossed them out the open door, climbed back to his battle station, and spoke over the intercom. "If you don't do exactly as I say, I'll turn this popper on you and blow both of you the fuck away. Now get moving."

John-Morgan could see his friend clearly as the Huey started to land in the street about fifty yards away. Mike raked the VC houses with precision as the remaining Marines began to scramble to the helicopter, dragging the wounded with them. They were about twenty-five yards away when the same VC soldier who had hit the other Huey with the RPG scored again on the Stuka.

The rocket entered the cockpit through the plexiglass on the front and killed both the pilot and copilot instantly. The Huey fell the last three feet to the ground, and Mike tumbled out of the door unhurt. He quickly grabbed his M-60 from its mount, snatched up two extra ammo belts, and started running to the church. There he shouted over the din of rifle fire and the cries of the wounded. "I told you I'd come back for you, John-Morgan! I wasn't gonna leave you for these bastards, no fuckin' way."

John-Morgan was too weak to speak. He bobbed his head in recognition before folding into an unconscious pile.

The VC, sensing victory, pressed forward en masse once more. Mike was in an absolute frenzy, and with ammo belts draped across his shoulders he went screaming toward the startled enemy, his hot M-60 blazing. When he reached the church wall he stopped running but continued calmly to pour out a steady stream of fire.

Then, from out of nowhere, a pair of Huey gunships roared over the village, their door guns raining down death and destruction on the attacking VC. As they swooped back for another pass, everyone inside saw Mike standing all alone like a vision of perdition, raking death on the enemy right and left. He scaled the wall and walked out into the street, firing the M-60 from his hip. VC soldiers tumbled and scattered as Mike continued to cut loose at them, until finally he went down with a sickening thunk. The men on the Huey winced.

* * *

"Bravest goddamned thing I ever saw in my whole goddamned life, Colonel. The fucking jarhead saved that
whole squad single-handed. It would have made you
proud to have seen it, sir. That boy is a credit to the whole
goddamn corps, sir. If the colonel approves, I think he
ought to be put in for a decoration. Both crews were an
eyewitness to everything. The grunts that survived on the
ground say they'd be dead right now if it hadn't been for
that Sullivan boy. Everybody around here is talking the
Blue Max for the kid, sir. I have to tell you, sir, I agree,
I think he'd make a hell of a candidate for the medal."

"Yes, well, from what I've heard, Gunnie, I must say
the Medal of Honor would seem a distinct possibility for
Lance Corporal Sullivan. You're not the first person to
approach me about this. It seems there might also be a
good PR angle for the corps. I understand that Sullivan
and the squad leader on the ground are best friends. Sort
of grew up together in Savannah. You know Savannah,
just across the river from PI? Well, they attended a Catholic military school there, enlisted together, even went
through boot camp together. Juicy stuff. The brass in DC
would just love to take it to the parade. I'll kick this on
up the line with my recommendation for something big.
Maybe even the Blue Max. Who knows?"

VII

INNOCENCE LOST
AND FOUND

For this that all that blood was shed,
For this Edward Fitzgerald died,
And Robert Emmet and Wolfe Tone,
All that delirium of the brave?

AT FIRST IT WAS a small speck of blue light in a large, dark room. Then there were unintelligible sounds, raw and disturbing.

The light grew a little a larger; it turned from blue to red, and words could also be heard, but not understood. There was a low buzzing sound that soon increased in intensity, and the red light grew very bright until it turned white. The buzzing became the voices of people, many people, and there was screaming and crying. Then John-Morgan opened his eyes, and he was conscious. John-Morgan's hip was on fire. Pain also seared in his groin. He reached to grab himself, but something was holding his arms down. When he struggled to focus his vision, he couldn't.

Then he felt his body being pulled and tugged; there was so much scalding pain somewhere around his waist that he screamed. But it was a muffled cry, as if someone were covering his mouth.

Then he was gagging and trying to spit something out. He could hear a woman's voice saying, "Take it easy, fella. They're finishing up now. I'm gonna' take this mask off your face and take out the airway. You'll feel better then. As soon as we get you to recovery, you'll get something for the pain. You did just fine."

This was John-Morgan's first lasting memory since the hand grenade. Although his wounds were not life-threatening, they were serious and extensive and would require months of recovery. His life had changed forever when that grenade riddled his body with inch-thick pieces of metal. His tour in Vietnam was over, and soon those immensely physical struggles of combat would pale in comparison to the spiritual trials he would face.

"Oh God, Jesus, please give me back my leg!" yelled

the boy on the stretcher next to John-Morgan. "Oh Sweet Jesus, don't do this to me!" The black kid across the room simply moaned with each breath. John-Morgan could tell he was black because a single hand was not bandaged.

Two cots down, another man-child fought with one hand to sit up as the stump of his left arm flailed against the air and the IV in his good arm was pulled loose. He cried out, "What am I gonna' do now? How am I gonna make it with one fucking arm, God? What am I gonna do now?"

In the days that followed there was more horror and agony, but John-Morgan soon learned that he could have little patches of time where nothing hurt and nothing mattered, where screams of the body and mind became stilled and he could breathe easily and sleep. This was the kind of deep and peaceful sleep that he had had as a child in his mother's arms, where dreams would come and carry him away. His savior, his friend, his only way out was referred to in his hospital chart by the initials "MS." It arrived riding in a gleaming nickel-plated carriage.

Morphine sulfate came from the end of a needle in an eighth of a grain dosage, or sometimes a quarter if the pain was really bad. It saw him through his trip from Vietnam to Japan and the States. It helped him as he was flown across the country to the Naval Hospital in Beaufort; and in Beaufort it helped him not to think about his injuries.

Injuries to nerves are divided into two classes. First, there is the cutting of nerve fibers, which results in loss of nerve function in the affected fibers; this is generally permanent. Second, there is crushing of the nerve fibers—neurotmesis—which results in varying degrees of nerve conduction loss; this can be either permanent or temporary. This damage is almost always the hardest to assess.

When the fragmentation grenade went off next to John-Morgan, a piece of metal penetrated to the hip joint. Another tore through the back side of his left thigh and kept going. It took a chunk of the hamstring with it, along with sizable pieces of skin, but he suffered no major blood vessel or nerve damage. These injuries were painful, and he would always have scars to remind him of the war, but the worst injury involved scarcely any pain at all. And that was the problem.

A piece of the grenade had hit him just above his penis on the left side, very near the dorsal nerve. Although it had not cut the nerve itself, the surrounding tissue had sustained damage from the concussion of the impact. Further damage had been caused by the surgeons at the field hospital when they removed the shrapnel. All of this had led to a crushing nerve injury that left John-Morgan's penis without feeling.

Another, smaller piece of shrapnel had also lacerated his penis along the shaft in a longitudinal manner. A skillful urological surgeon working for the Navy had been able to repair this wound in Beaufort and felt that no damage had been done to the organ's reproductive function, but he could give no reassurance to John-Morgan that the sensation would ever return. The doctor's words reverberated again and again. "Well, son, I don't know if you'll get the feeling back or not. Sometimes it returns in an injury like this, and sometimes it doesn't. Only time will tell." Time was telling now.

Mike Sullivan had been wearing his flak jacket when he got hit, so it had absorbed most of the energy from the round. But part of the bullet had made it through the jacket; Mike suffered a perforation injury to the abdominal wall and a small laceration of the bowel. He had recovered without incident in the same hospital as John-Morgan. He had also stopped using heroin, because none was available.

No one knew what had happened in the helicopter, and Mike had said nothing. He now was a celebrated and bona fide war hero with a third Purple Heart and a Medal of Honor on the way. It was the custom in the Marine Corps during the Vietnam War not to send people back into combat if they had three Purple Hearts. Because of this, Mike would finish his enlistment at Parris Island as a marksmanship instructor.

On the outside, Mike Sullivan had never looked better or stronger. People thought that Vietnam had matured him and given him a more serious and thoughtful approach to life. What they did not know was that he had become skillful at hiding the truth. On the inside, Mike was a tormented and debilitated old man with a gray-haired soul and a nitroglycerin heart. People believed him to be a lively Irishman who loved hanging out with other Marines at the NCO club, able to hold his liquor with the best of them. What they did not know was that Mike drank to make being around people easier.

Mike even grew tired of Katherine, and he broke her heart one night when he discarded her like last week's *TV Guide*. He was drunk when she told him that she had begun to feel he was a person she had never known.

"That's exactly right, you little bitch. You don't fuckin' know me. Nobody knows who or what I am." He looked at her with a wild and evil face and shouted at the top of his lungs, "Get the fuck out of my car! You remind me of some goddamn slope-headed dink."

Katherine recoiled from him as she struggled with the car door; when it popped open she almost fell to the ground. Mike squealed the tires as he tore away from her house, and he didn't call Katherine for months after that. When he finally did, she told him she was afraid of him and that she never wanted to see him again. She never did.

Mike frequently visited John-Morgan in the hospital. Although they discussed their many wounds, John-Morgan never told Mike about the damage he had suffered to his penis. It was too personal, too embarrassing, and too threatening to his manhood. He couldn't reveal it to anyone. His parents knew only because they had been told by the doctors. These doctors advised the Hartmans not to tell John-Morgan that they knew.

About a week before Mike was to be discharged from the hospital, he came to see John-Morgan in his five-bed ward. John-Morgan wasn't there. The bed next to his was occupied by a young black Marine who had also been injured in Vietnam. He liked John-Morgan a great deal. It was hard to keep secrets from anybody in a five-bed ward, so the other Marine had soon learned, not from John-Morgan but from the nursing staff, that his buddy had a serious injury involving his privates. He didn't know exactly what the injuries were, but he could see the bandages around John Morgan's groin and that his urine came out through a tube and emptied into a plastic bag.

Lester Simms was a sweet and gentle soul who had been raised mostly by his grandparents on their small farm outside of Statesboro. He was protective of John-Morgan and was always careful not to ask him any questions about his injuries. He had heard the nurses say that their patient couldn't feel anything "down there," so he innocently assumed that his penis had been blown off by the grenade.

"Hey man," said Mike, "you know where Hartman is?"

"Dey took him downstairs to work on him some."

"What do you mean?"

"I think dey tryin' to build him a new dick."

"A new dick? What's wrong with the old one?"

"Man, he got it blowed off in Nam. I thought you done knowed 'bout that."

"You shittin' me, Lester. There ain't nothing wrong with his dick."

"Yeah deah is. How come you think he got dat tube comin' out him? Dat's cause he ain't got no dick to pee with. Da nurses done told me he loss his dick in Nam. You his friend, man, I thought you already knowed."

"No, I didn't. I didn't know about that at all. Goddamn. Shit, that's awful."

"Hey man, don't go saying nuttin' 'bout dat to him.

He real shamed 'bout dat. He don't even be knowin' I
knows."

"Yeah. I won't. Hey, take it easy, Lester. Just tell John-
Morgan I came by. I'll see him in a few days. Is he in
any pain?"

"Naw, man, dude gets shots fo dat."

NEEDLEPOINT EXPRESS

FOR JOHN-MORGAN the physical pain began to fade slowly
as his psychological pain increased. Walking was uncomfortable but manageable, something that became a little
easier as the weeks dragged by. Thinking about the future,
however, had become a task, a job.

There was no dreaming of the idyllic life, filled with a
wife and children, a career and a home with a bed where
he would love and then sleep sweetly. Rather his days
were spent forcing smiles and conversations and counting
the hours until he could be relieved of his torment by the
deep intramuscular insertion of the twenty-gauge cold
steel tube that released warmth and security, nothingness
and apotheosis. Every three hours he could step on the
needlepoint express and ride its descending assent into a
nether world of chemical quiet. His nights were spent in
the darkness of his pillow with muted howls of rage at
the God who had made him and then tortured him, not
with pain but with anesthesia. He prayed not for grace,
but for the swiftness of time and the next morsel of poppy
resin that said a hundred sweet hellos and soft good-byes.
He had become addicted to the rose-red lips and full
bosom of morphine.

John-Morgan's addiction was different from Mike's in
that it was a controlled addiction, manipulated by the doctors and nurses who attended him. When the medical staff
felt that relief of his physical pain had been achieved, they
began the truly Herculean task of repairing his mauled
spirit. His ego was sympathetically spared any further

blows when his doctor told him that the amount of morphine he was being administered would be gradually decreased because he was making such good progress and obviously didn't need so much medication. John-Morgan put up a halfhearted protest, stating that he did indeed suffer greatly and needed the drug to endure his agony. In his mind, however, was a place that had not been affected by the opiates. That place in his mind, the eye of his soul, secretly and quietly told him that he had had enough.

The next day Navy Chaplain Norbert Wittmier, SJ, summoned John-Morgan to his office. Father Wittmier was a Jesuit who had been in the Navy since World War II. Nearing retirement, he had taken a particular interest in John-Morgan because of his injury. When John-Morgan entered his office, Father Wittmier closed the door, offered him a cigarette, and then motioned him into one of the large and comfortable chairs near the window overlooking the river. He lit John-Morgan's smoke first and then his own, finally taking a seat in the other chair.

"So, John-Morgan, the doctors tell me you're making a splendid recovery and should be able to return to your home in Savannah."

"I'm doing OK, Father."

"You hardly had a limp when you came in. Are you still having any pain?"

"Yes, Father, but I've been told that I shouldn't and they're taking away my pain shots. I don't think they believe that I'm really hurting."

"Of course they do. The doctors just want to see if you can make it on less pain medicine. You can't go on like that forever. Some day you've got to leave this hospital and make it on your own. The morphine won't allow that. She's a jealous bitch who won't stand for anybody else in your life. A beautiful and sensuous woman who knows how to make her man feel wonderful, but who demands everything you have in return. A nasty, spiteful, straight-razor toting bawd who can spend every last dime you have and then leave you for a richer man with a sneer on her face. You must start to look beyond today."

"I've tried, but how can I go through my life the way I am now?"

"Physical pleasures eventually leave us all. The pleasures of the soul stay forever and grow larger and more fulfilling than anything in the physical world."

"Easy for you to say, Father. But then again, what would you care?"

The priest laughed, took a long drag off his cigarette and blew the smoke out slowly as he looked at the marsh grass starting to turn brown for winter.

"Just because I'm a priest you think I have no sexual desires. On the contrary, I always have sexual desires. It has been a battle for me all of my life as it is for many men who choose the priesthood. I shudder to think how I might act if I had to face my life as you may have to face yours. I would always want to know that I have the option to use my body as I see fit. What you have been through is most frightening to me, to anyone. I want to see if I can help you come to grips with what has happened to you and perhaps understand what our Lord may have planned for you."

"That's just great, Father. I can't wait for us to figure out what our Lord has planned for me." John-Morgan grew increasingly distressed as his monologue continued. "Will you cut the bullshit with me, because I've heard it all. I'm beginning to think that there is no God. That this is all a crock of shit. That we are indeed descended from an amoeba, quite by the accident of evolution, and that out there in the darkness and stillness of outer space, there really is nothing more than meets the eye. No immortal soul, no supreme being that has known me since before I was born. I'm nineteen years old and I can't feel anything where I should feel everything. I'm not a man, I'm a eunuch who should be serving with the other eunuchs in the harem's tent because I'm harmless. You've got a choice with your body. I don't, and I'll be damned if there's anything you or anybody else can say to make it better. I want to know what it's like to make love to a woman, because I never have. I want to do it again and again and again if I so choose, but I can't. God or the VC, or maybe it was just the luck of the draw that took my pecker away, pardon my French. That's the most frightening part of all. Maybe I'm beginning to see God as a turn on a roulette wheel, holiness as nothing but the state of mathematical probability. That would make the real popes all mathematicians. Can you imagine that, the greatest pontiff of this century could actually be Pope Albert Einstein! If you really want to know, Father, I'm looking at a blank wall right now. I see nothing to live for and I'm pissed and I'm scared and I'm ashamed and I really don't feel like being alive!"

"May we cut to the chase here John-Morgan?"

"I wish we could, Father. I've got a lot of nothing to think about and I'd like to get started as soon as possible. It's damn hard work, believe me."

Father Wittmier clasped his hands together and leaned forward in his chair. John-Morgan noticed the nicotine stains on his fingers as he brought the cigarette up to his mouth. Through the power of a lifetime's practice, as he read John-Morgan's face, the priest was able to choose the perfect moment, to begin speaking. "Am I correct in assuming that if you could be made to truly believe in God, a loving God who made you and knows every hair on your head, you would then be able to look at what God has let happen to you in such a way that it would give meaning to your suffering, and in that, the ability to overcome it—to live a full life the way you are and not the way you want to be? Is that what you need, John-Morgan?"

"Yes, perhaps that would be a start. Yeah, I think that would make a definite difference. Any suggestions?"

"Yes, I have many, but I will only leave you with this one. I promise that you will begin to understand God's plan for you as early as tomorrow morning. But you must be willing do this one, low-cost, trouble-free, fully insured thing for me."

"Where do I sign up?"

"At the altar rail tomorrow morning, after the eight o'clock mass. I want you to promise me that you will join me in prayer and meditation for thirty minutes each day. You've got to be willing to formally pray, to get down on your knees and ask God to show you the way. If you confine your prayer life to only giving praise to God and never needing him, then maybe it *is* only the law of probability that governs your universe."

"Do I have to actually believe in this God? Is that a part of your little wager with me? 'Cause if it is, the craps are loaded against me, if you catch my drift."

"No, not at all, John-Morgan. As a matter of fact, I prefer that my little gamblers don't believe, if you really want to know, because when they do start believing, they're almost impossible to stop."

PRIVATE SORROWS

NORBERT WITTMIER was a native of Mobile. He had entered the Jesuit seminary at that city's Spring Hill College in the late 1920's, and it was there that he acquired his passion for German history and philosophy and received his undergraduate degree in the German language. From Spring Hill Father Wittmier traveled to Missouri and the University of St. Louis, another Jesuit institution. After eight years of study, he received his PhD in German history and philosophy. Twelve years later he was ordained a member of the Society of Jesus.

When World War II broke out, Father Wittmier was contacted by the War Department because of his expertise in German culture and language. He accepted a commission in the Navy. During the first part of the war, he served in Naval Intelligence, debriefing captured German U-boat sailors. When it became apparent that the ultimate defeat of Nazi Germany was only a year or so away, Father Wittmier applied for a transfer to the Pacific. He wanted out of Washington and where the action was, and was granted an assignment in the Pacific Theater as a combat chaplain aboard the USS *Benjamin Franklin*. This aircraft carrier became a major target of kamikaze planes during the Battle of Okinawa, and it was almost sent to the bottom. There were thousands of casualties, and Father Wittmier didn't sleep for three days. During this time he found his true calling in the priesthood, because he had a special way of connecting with dying and injured men. After the war he remained in the Navy, serving as a chaplain in hospitals that dealt with severe battle wounds.

Oftentimes he had to minister to men who had no faith at all. They were always the hardest to help. Father Wittmier possessed a remarkable gift; if he could find a spark of faith anywhere in a man, he could almost always fan that spark into a healthy fire. He had never encountered a man with faith who could not endure the unendurable. Although he had failed many times to pull certain men through the dark woods of disbelief, he believed that he could reach John-Morgan, for John-Morgan's "seed had fallen on fertile ground." With careful nurturing it could survive this drought and live to become strong and healthy. Father Wittmier was certain of that.

For three months John-Morgan and his priest-mentor continued their discussions. At breakfast a few days before John-Morgan's discharge, Father Wittmier posed the question to his pupil. "You'll be going home next week. Tell me what you have learned, what you think."

"I've learned that I am no better and no worse. My condition hasn't changed, I still have no feeling. As for what I think, I'm not really sure. I'm not as certain about a whole lot of things as I once was, Father. Maybe the prayer has worked some; I don't think about wanting to be dead all day long like I used to do. Maybe that's progress. I'm a little more willing to take things one day at a time, like you said. But I'm not on fire with faith. I'm still against this blank wall, trying to care, trying to think about what my life is going to be like."

"The prayer has worked, John-Morgan. You must believe me. You are not living on Eastern Standard Time or Daylight Savings Time, you are now living on God's time. That is the essence of Faith. You must be able to let God have the controls, to trust Him."

"Why does He hurt me so much? Is it punishment for the people I killed in Vietnam? I can accept that, I can live with that. It makes sense. Just tell me if that's what it is. But if it isn't, then why is this God filling my life with so much pain and sorrow? I didn't want a lot out of life, just the simple things, the normal pleasures. All I ever really prayed for was to pass tests in school. If there is such a loving God, then why all the pain? I can't understand."

"I don't understand either, John-Morgan. We can't because we are human beings without infinite minds. But I do know that with faith in God and His goodness you will be able to endure and one day understand some parts of what you have been through. Without it, your road will become very difficult and your thoughts will return to death. That's what free will is all about, John-Morgan. It's not choosing between good and evil. Free will is ultimately about the freedom to believe in a God, to believe in an existence for each one of us other than this earth and these bodies. If you choose to believe, all else will fall into place. People who truly believe that they will be held accountable for what they have done during their lives never have to choose between good and evil. They're too damn scared not to choose good."

"I don't know, Father, my whole life is different now. I just don't know."

"Do you have any plans for college?"

"I can always go to the one in town. I haven't really thought about it. I have no idea about what I want to do with my life."

"Let me make a suggestion. You know that I am a Spring Hill graduate. I'm sure that I can find a place for you there. It's one of the finest schools in the country."

"I'll think about it and talk it over with my parents. I've decided that I won't be making anymore major moves in my life without asking for their advice. If I'd talked to my father first, I would never have gone to Vietnam. And I'd have a whole and working body."

"Well, one thing is for sure."

"Oh really? What's that?"

"Praying has at least given you some common sense."

There was snow on the White House lawn the week before Christmas. Mike and John-Morgan arrived at the door of the White House in a Marine Corps staff car along with their parents. In their dress uniforms they stood at attention before President Lyndon B. Johnson and quietly marveled at the size of his ears. The leader of the free world smiled at John-Morgan and shook his hand after he finished pinning the Navy Cross and a Purple Heart on his chest. This was not the kind of medal that was usually awarded by the commander-in-chief himself, but John-Morgan and Mike were a package deal, a kind of two-for-one public relations bonanza sponsored by the Marine Corps and the President.

When the President reached the highlight of the award ceremony, he first read the commendation that accompanies each Medal of Honor, looking at Mike's parents over the top of his glasses and smiling every now and then. "Lance Corporal Michael F. Sullivan, with complete disregard for his own safety and well-being, returned to the scene of the battle aboard his helicopter. There, after the craft had been destroyed by enemy ground fire and the other crew members killed, Lance Corporal Sullivan secured his weapon and ammunition from the craft and engaged the enemy single-handedly and at great risk to his own bodily safety and personal welfare, thus saving the remaining members of the squad from certain capture or death."

That night, after their parents went to bed, Mike and John-Morgan tied one on in the hotel bar, and Mike almost told him about what had really happened. He wanted to confess that he was a phony; he wanted to bleed out all of his sorrow and guilt right on the bar's high-gloss finish, but Mike admired John-Morgan too much. He didn't want to risk losing his respect and friendship. Instead he decided to continue letting Father Jack Daniels hear his nightly confessions and fix his penance, to be paid in full each morning to the throb of distended cerebral vessels.

John-Morgan also had his private sorrows. It was almost one in the morning, and bolstered by booze and reminiscence, he decided to ask Mike if he had heard anything about Ann Marie Kerry. "Yeah," he said, "she's engaged to that doctor she was dating. They're supposed to get married when she graduates from nursing school. Sometime next year, I think."

John-Morgan had berated himself many times for turning down Charlotte that day at Little Tybee. How stupid could he have been? he told himself night after night as he lay in his hospital bed and touched around time and again, hoping to feel something. She was right. *I did get my dick shot off, and for what? I could have made love to a beautiful woman at least once in my life, but I refused because I was afraid I would be sinning. What is sin? Who decides?*

During those long and hideous nights, even while he thought most lustfully about Charlotte Drayton, John-Morgan's thoughts always seemed to return to Ann Marie and his memories of her. Over and over again he would wonder if she would understand him. Could they have a life together despite his disabilities? The doctors had told him that having children would be no problem; he was not impotent, he simply could not enjoy sex normally. The doctors had explained that millions of people experienced married life fully who had to engage in altered sexual practices because of some physical limitation.

Ann Marie had been the only girl he had ever really loved, his touchstone for the mystery of that emotion. It was with her that he wanted to make his first attempt to reenter that world. A thousand times he wondered if she ever thought of him, and finally he had decided that when he returned to Savannah, he was going to call her and ask her out. He was bitterly amused to note how much courage he had under fire and how little he had when holding a telephone.

Now Mike's words swept like a cold shroud over John-Morgan. He was glad he was drunk; otherwise they would have hurt even more. The memory of Ann Marie had become the only thing that teased him into believing that he could possibly have a relationship with anyone. He had told himself that she would listen, that she would remember the good times, all the special things said between them, and forget about the bad. He convinced himself that the joy they had shared without sex would be proof enough for her, and now they could take up where they had left off. Now John-Morgan's mind raced through the odds against him, and he came up painfully and pitifully short. What chance do I have against a guy who is a doctor? I don't even have a year of college or a nickel to my name. I'm scarred all over, I walk with a fuckin' limp, and I don't even have a dick that works. John-Morgan looked down at the medals hanging from his uniform and suddenly spoke aloud.

"I'd trade it all for an even chance with her."

Mike caught part of what he had mumbled, and said with a slur, "Trade who for what?"

John-Morgan just shook his head and called to the bartender. "Two more here."

SOMETHING AIN'T RIGHT, SON

EIGHT HUNDRED MILES and a culture away from Savannah, Lloyd Bryan was watching the evening news with the other jocks in his dorm at South Bend. He had a hot dog in his mouth when Walter Cronkite intoned, "At the White House today, President Johnson awarded the nation's highest honor to a twenty-year-old Marine corporal from Savannah, Georgia. Our chief White House correspondent Dan Rather has the story. Dan?" Lloyd almost choked on the hot dog when the pictures came up on the screen.

"I know those guys!" he managed to say as he forced down a mouthful of food. "They went to the same school I did! The guy on the right was the Cadet colonel. I can't believe this! I knew they'd been hurt, but I didn't know anything about a medal. I'd better call my mother more often."

Mrs. Bryan would have agreed. She had not been hearing from him as regularly as she had his first year, and she was worried. Lloyd seemed to have changed. The son she had placed on the plane to Notre Dame in August of 1966 didn't much resemble the one that returned in the summer of 1967.

Lloyd had done very well, both on the football field and in the classroom. He was riding high on his ego for the first time in his life and was as hooked on that feeling as John-Morgan had been on morphine. The Notre Dame alumni were the most rabid of football fanatics, and they had a tendency to fawn over any player they thought could propel the team to another national championship. The newspaper and television sportscasters had been quick to notice Lloyd and gave him big play in the Indiana papers and television stations, so he was no longer the only "colored boy" at an all-white high school in the deep South. He was the star running back for the biggest-name school in college football. At a place that should have known how terrible the sin of having false gods can be, he had been elevated to the status of demigod. To his throne came money, quietly given to Lloyd by the alumni to pay for all those little things that could make college life as much fun as everybody thought it was.

At the start of Lloyd's second year at Notre Dame, the bishop asked his mother how he was doing. In exasperation she answered, "Your Excellency, it's just like when he started the first grade. He was a sweet child, didn't have a bit of mouth at all. By the end of that year he had picked up every smart little comeback he had heard. Kids ain't never the same after they start the first grade. I guess it's the same way with college. All he wants to talk about is the house this one lives in or the car that one drives or how rich the other one's daddy is. I declare, Bishop Kelly, he's a different boy now. All he thinks about is how much money he can make. He even showed me a picture of a girl. Said that he'd been dating her. Didn't look like no kind of girl you'd ever catch kneeling at the altar rail on Sunday to take Holy Communion. No sir, not at all. Looked all made up and fast. That's what I'd call her. He used to write me every week and call me at least every two weeks just to say hello. Now I'm lucky if I hear from him once a month. I read about him in the sports section, though. Never was a bit interested in sports at all, but now I'm combing through the sports page every morning looking for my boy's name. I find it sometimes, too. The papers say he's a star, the TV says he a star, I just hope to God it don't go to his head."

"Is he still going to Mass the way he used to, Elaine? I remember he went almost every day. I used to hope that one day he might be one of my priests. He was always so devout when he served Mass with me. I've prayed for his vocation many times."

"Far as I know, Bishop Kelly. But that's not much. I pray for him every day too."

It was unclear whether those prayers were heard or not, but Lloyd did not make it home for the Christmas of 1967. Notre Dame was in a bowl game. Intense practices came immediately after the season ended. He couldn't even work in a short trip to Savannah.

Mrs. Bryan had known for a week that he wouldn't be with her for Christmas, and of course she was disappointed. One of her duties at the cathedral was to take care of the altar linens. Preparing them for Midnight Mass, she had an uneasy feeling about Lloyd. There was a different tone in his voice lately, she thought. The little private things she used to say to him didn't seem to reach him anymore.

Elaine had always been afraid of turning Lloyd into a "momma's boy," so she had taken great care to be sure that he wasn't. Still, he was her boy; she had raised him and he was hers. Now there was a distance between them other than the miles. Before he left for school, she had been his confidante in everything, and Elaine Mae de Beaufort Bryan had always given her son the best advice a mother could give. When he called now, he never asked her opinion about anything. It was always "I asked coach, and he said this," or "I called up coach and he said to do that." Lloyd had been gone for a year-and-a-half, and Elaine was afraid she had lost her wonderful, sweet, precious boy forever.

She talked with Bishop Kelly about her problems. He assured her that Lloyd was simply going through the natural process of growing up, of learning to think for himself. In this metamorphosis he was leaving his mother's nest. "Good Lord, Elaine, he's a young man now, and up until last year, all he had ever known was right here in little old Savannah. Now he's off at a big school up north where he's popular and having a lot of fun and meeting all kinds of new people. Those are things he's not used to, and he's naturally a little overwhelmed. Give him time, you raised a fine boy and you raised him right. I know, I watched you do it. Have faith in the virtues you taught him. Don't go getting yourself all upset because he's doing what all the other people his age are doing. He's beginning to live his own life now. I know it hurts you, but you must try to understand."

Elaine had tried to understand as Bishop Kelly suggested. She even reproached herself for having become an overbearing mother who was angry now that her child was beginning to assert a little independence. The bishop was probably right, she thought, "I guess maybe I was just getting too worked up over nothing. I should be ashamed of myself." It was three o'clock in the afternoon on Christmas Eve. A sudden crisp knock sounded at the door, and all of Elaine's fears came rushing back.

"Mrs. Bryan?"

"Yes."

"I have a package for you. Would you please sign here?"

Elaine quietly closed the door and walked to the dining room table with the package. She frowned at the return address—"Julio Rossini's Religious Gifts and Fine Arts, Fifth Avenue, New York, New York." With great care Elaine cut through the brown paper on the outside of the box, exposing the dark green Christmas wrapping underneath. She used one of her kitchen knives to remove the paper, which she was careful not to tear; Elaine liked to save such beautiful paper for the following Christmas. The box inside was a deep, handsome red. In the center, inscribed in gold letters, was the name "Rossini."

"Oh my goodness, what a lovely box." Elaine placed the papers to one side and gazed at the box for a moment under the glow of the lights from her Christmas candles. When she lifted the top, she found a fine tissue paper padding the interior. She gently pushed aside the tissues and uncovered a statue of the Blessed Mother.

Elaine cradled it in her hands and with great reverence,

lifted the statue from its box, and placed it on the dining room table. Then she knelt down at the table to get a better view of the statue. "Lord have mercy on my soul," she whispered, "this is the most beautiful statue I have ever seen."

It was just under twenty-four inches tall, carved from Egyptian ebony, and magnificently painted in textured, vibrant colors making the Virgin's precious face glow with such love she seemed to be alive. Her eyes were deep and sweet. On her head was a dark blue veil trimmed in gold. On top of that sat a crown of stars. Her flowing robe was a sky-blue cascading past her hips, cinched with a Rosary, ending at her bare feet. She stood on a globe of the world with her right foot placed on the head of a writhing serpent frozen in pain. Upon her left foot rested a single red rose. The base of the statue had an inscription: "Mary, Queen of the Universe, Pray for Us."

Elaine admired the statue for a few moments and then removed the wrapping from the box, looking for a card. She found one with "Mother" written on it in Lloyd's hand: "Dear Momma, I hope you like this statue. I'm sorry that I can't be with you on Christmas Day, but I'll be home for a few days after the game. Pray for me at Midnight Mass. Love and Merry Christmas, Lloyd."

There was no denying that the statue was extraordinary and that Elaine would have loved to have it in her home, where it could assume a place of honor, but it was precisely the statue's exceptional beauty that made her uncomfortable. Elaine was worldly enough to recognize quality, craftsmanship, and artistic excellence, and she knew that these things usually came with a price tag. The more she studied the statue, the more concerned she became about how Lloyd could afford such an expensive gift. The only way was if he was working a job outside of school. He wasn't supposed to be doing that. His life at Notre Dame was to consist of playing football and studying all he could to maintain his scholarship.

Occasionally she sent him a little spending money, but

she knew that that would not have been enough even if Lloyd had saved every penny. No, she thought, he's not doing what he's supposed to. He's out working somewhere and not studying like he said he would. Lord, I hope he doesn't fool around and lose that scholarship just so he could buy me this statue.

Elaine placed the statue back in its box and went into the kitchen to fix supper. As she stood at the stove, she began to think. After turning down the gas under the collard greens, she walked back and removed the statue again and took it into the living room, where she placed in on the mantel over her small fireplace. Elaine stood back and admired Mary, Queen of the Universe. Then she dropped to her knees in front of the statue and made the sign of the cross and began to pray.

"Blessed Mother, please watch out for my boy. He's never had much and this here is his big chance to be more than just a day worker like me. You know how his daddy is. And you know he wasn't never around to show him the way. I done the best that I know how, but I ain't no man, and sometimes a boy needs a man around to teach him about the kind of world that men live in that women don't know nothin' about. He's a good boy, Blessed Mother, you know that, but he don't know much about the world. Please watch over him and keep him safe for me."

A little after nine o'clock, the phone rang. It was Lloyd. He wished his mother a Merry Christmas and asked her if she had received the statue. Elaine had been thinking about what to tell her son all evening, but she still hadn't made up her mind when the phone rang. She had to say something about the cost of the statue, and ask where he had gotten the money. His reply gave her a chill.

He told her not to worry about how he had gotten the money. He said it in almost the same manner and tone of voice his father had used so many years before when she had inquired about the source of his income. The resemblance was frightening, and she was stricken by silence.

After a moment she managed to say, "I hope you're not gambling up there. Is that how you got the money?" Lloyd laughed.

"No—and I ain't stealing it, either. It's kind of like gifts from happy Notre Dame fans who want to show me some appreciation for my hard work. But don't say a word about it to anyone, Momma, you understand? Not to *anyone*."

"Why?"

"Cause some people might get jealous of me, that's why. Just keep quiet, OK?"

"If that's what you want. But I ain't comfortable knowing you taking money you can't talk about. Something ain't right, son. A mother's got a way of knowing, and I know." Elaine pensively hung up the phone.

Both sides of Bubba Silverman's family had their ancestral roots in Germany. His mother's family had been in Savannah since before the Civil War, and one of her distant cousins had gone there in the late thirties as he was fleeing the Nazis.

His paternal grandparents, who went to New York, had come later; they had fled the homeland during the difficult postwar years of the Weimar Republic, but before the Nazis came to power.

In the forties, as the crematoriums spit out their ashes in Nazi Germany, the ground in East Prussia became dusted with the remains of Bubba's father's kin. Distant relatives of his mother were also rounded up and killed in systematic fashion, their ashes dumped into a tributary of the River Vistula.

The history of Nazi Germany and what it did to the Jewish population of Europe had a profound effect on Jews born in the United States after the menace had ended. This generation grew up on stories of the concentration camps and the programmatic murder of millions, something that had not been visited upon their parents; and for the first time in history such horror was dutifully and carefully recorded on film—stark reality that no one could deny. As he grew older, Bubba heard the survivors of the camps tell their agonizing stories at the Jewish Educational Alliance; in the end they always assured one another, "Never again." These recollections were all the more frightening because they had just happened. Hitler had died only two years before Bubba was born.

In Jewish families whose close relatives died in the Holocaust, the horror was soul-shearing. Out of fear, desperation, and despair, many of these families were forced to turn inward and to cling even harder to their Jewish identity, history, customs, and religion. Some no longer trusted anyone who was not Jewish. This was the attitude of Bubba's grandparents in New York City. His mother's family felt the same, although to a lesser degree.

Bubba's parents were both Orthodox; indeed his mother's family were founding members of the Orthodox Congregation B'nai B'rith Jacob. Bubba had spent just about every Saturday of his life at the "BB," first at the old synagogue downtown on Montgomery Street, then, after 1965, at the new one on Abercorn. He grew up at the JEA and was the best pupil in Hebrew school. Although his parents knew that Bubba wasn't cut out for the rabbinate, they took great pride when the rabbi spoke of his hope for their son's spiritual calling.

The New York neighborhood in which Bernard Silverman had grown up was entirely Jewish. In Savannah the neighbors on both sides were gentiles. His son's best friend was a Catholic, and Savannah, overwhelmingly geared to Anglo-Saxon Protestant culture, except where it was run by the Irish, had far fewer Jews per capita than New York. Still, the Silvermans felt at ease in that city, where Judaism's religion and culture had flourished since the founding of the colony. They wanted their son to become a devout Jew who would raise their grandchildren the same same way they had raised him. Although Bubba had gone to a Catholic school and had many more gentile friends than Jewish ones, his links to the Jewish community were strong, and his parents had no reason to believe that Bubba would "betray" the Jewish experience. Alas, for an intelligent, handsome young man with money to spend and a car to drive, the University of Georgia in the mid-1960's could be heaven on earth. For Bubba, it was a time to spread his wings and play with angels.

Both of the large Jewish fraternities extended him bids, but he turned them down. During rush week he had been exposed to all of the fraternities, and he found the predominantly Christian ones to be the most attractive. To his surprise he had received a bid from one. Bubba immediately accepted. This launched him into a slow but steady move away from his family roots, and by the spring quarter of 1968 he was going with a Christian girl from Atlanta, and they were talking about marriage after he graduated. Her father owned the largest brokerage firm in Atlanta and was firmly ensconced in its social scene as well. Almost every weekend Bubba was in Atlanta staying at Gail Cleveland's house, taking in the social circuit at the Capitol City Club or the Atlanta Driving Club. Gail's father was a member of the Augusta National Golf Course, and he and Gail were her father's guests at that year's Masters.

Bubba was a gracious, personable young man with a gift for putting anyone at ease. He was exceptionally charming around older women, a talent he used with great effect on Gail's mother. Inevitably, his "Jewishness" had come up when Gail brought him home the first time. By the time her parents had realized their daughter was serious about him, however, they were also thoroughly smitten. Never did they mention Bubba's ethnicity again.

The Clevelands were an old-money Atlanta family whose forebears had fought for the Confederacy, some dying in the Battle of Atlanta. When Mr. Cleveland learned that Bubba, too, had relatives who had fought and died for the Southern cause, Bubba immediately earned a place of honor at Big Tom Cleveland's dinner table.

Back in Savannah, Bubba's mother was worried. She

was not terribly concerned that Bubba was dating a Christian girl. Silvia Silverman knew that most Jewish boys did so now and then. They would settle down, and start dating their own kind. What concerned both of his parents was that Bubba seemed to be cutting himself off from his family and heritage. He rarely came home anymore, and when he did, he never went to Shule or observed the Sabbath rules. "It's a phase he's going through," Bernie told Silvia. She "believed" him because she wanted to.

Rosh Hashanah and Yom Kippur are the highest holy days in all of Judaism. On Yom Kippur, the Day of Atonement, Jews go to synagogue for family prayer and fasting. Failure to observe the occasion insults the family and everything it holds dear. When Bubba's parents asked him about making plans to be with them for the event, he told them no, he would not be there this year. They assumed he would attend services in Atlanta, so they questioned him further. It was then that he told them: "All of that stuff is not important to me anymore. I don't believe in it. Furthermore, I've started attending church with Gail. As you know, she's Episcopalian. I might as well tell you something else—we're making plans to get married after I graduate. Her father has spoken with me about coming to work at his firm. I'm sorry to be so blunt about this whole thing, but perhaps it's best this way. I hope you'll understand."

Bubba's mother screamed at him in primal Yiddish. His broken-hearted father tried reason. Neither tactic worked. The rest of that evening Silvia wept as if for the dead. Bernie sat quietly in his Lazy-Boy recliner staring at the television, but not paying the least attention to anything he saw.

ABSCESS ON THE SOUL

"ANN MARIE KERRY of Savannah, daughter of Mr. and Mrs. Kevin M. Kerry and Dr. Stephen T. Farrington, Jr., of Atlanta, son of Dr. and Mrs. Stephen Farrington, were married at a solemn High Mass in Sacred Heart Church on Saturday evening, June 13th."

It happened, it really happened. The nausea was surprising. John-Morgan heaved a couple of deep breaths and then read on. A moment later he crushed the paper in a fit of rage. Then he flattened it out again on the kitchen table and smoothed it with sweaty, shaking hands. Tears moistened the new bride's face, making the print on the reverse side of the page show through. There was no way to stop, the rest had to be known.

"After a wedding trip to the British Isles, the couple will reside in Atlanta where Dr. Farrington will be completing a residency in plastic and reconstructive surgery at Emory University Hospital."

John-Morgan drove over to Beaufort that Sunday afternoon to see Father Wittmier. He told his mentor that he had decided to enroll at Spring Hill. In addition, he wanted not only to attend Spring Hill College, but to join the Jesuit seminary there as well. Father Wittmier studied him closely.

"Is being a priest the first choice you would make if you could have a normal sex life, John-Morgan, or is it a second choice, fostered upon you by what has happened?"

"I don't know, Father. I had thought about the priesthood while I was in high school, but I was too attracted to girls. I knew I couldn't live a celibate life, so I just forgot about it. Now it seems as though the decision has been made for me. I really don't know what I want to do, but I've got to start somewhere, and to be truthful, the seminary seemed almost a natural for me. The idea has a soothing quality about it. The Church has always been a huge part of my life, and the thought of being a priest has grown on me in the last few months."

"So you're not sure you really want to be a priest then?"

"No, I'm not."

"Well, very few men are sure when they step through the door of the seminary. That's why they're not ordained on the first day. Jesuit schools are tough, and Jesuit seminaries are even tougher."

"I think I know what tough is by now, Father."

Father Wittmier chuckled and nodded his head. Then he paused for a moment and frowned. "I was reading the Savannah paper this morning and saw a wedding announcement about the young lady you told me about when you were a patient here. As I recall, you were going to contact her and see if she would go out with you again. Obviously it didn't pan out, but I'm interested to know if you ever did speak with her."

John-Morgan had thought of nothing but Ann Marie all the way over to Beaufort, though his discussion with Father Wittmier had taken his mind off her for a few minutes. Now that twisted, sinking feeling hit him again with the shock of a sucker punch. He couldn't speak and dropped his head. Then he burst into uncontrollable tears.

A lifetime of talking with terribly injured sailors and Marines had honed the priest's instincts and skills. He did not want to hurt John-Morgan, but he knew that an abscess was present on the soul. It must be drained if this soul were to survive.

Father Wittmier got up from behind his desk and knelt beside his charge. John-Morgan remained bent over in his chair, face and hands now resting on his knees. His shoulders heaved as flows of anguish ripped through him. Tears splattered on the Navy's highly polished linoleum tile. The older man placed his hand on John-Morgan's back and let it rest there for a while. After a few minutes John-Morgan began to regain his composure.

"Feeling better now, son?"

"A little."

"When I was about your age, so very long ago now, a similar thing happened to me. I was jilted by a girl I thought I couldn't live without, and I was devastated. Her name was Claire Moultrie—the most beautiful girl at Mobile's cotillion that year. At the ball she pledged her love to me. Not too many weeks later, she abruptly dropped me for the son of man who was fabulously wealthy. It hurt me so badly I never dated again. That was really what set me on my course for the priesthood. Almost the same situation as yours. Strange, isn't it?"

Father Wittmier got up and handed John-Morgan a handkerchief from his pocket. He sat on a corner of his desk. "A few years after my ordination, I returned to Mobile. I ran into some old friends of Claire's and naturally inquired about her. What they told me was quite a shock. It seems that her husband's money wasn't enough to make her happy, so she took to drink. She literally drank herself to death. In the process she created a hell on earth for everyone. How I once had begged God that I could be that woman's husband! That night I got on my knees and thanked God for His mercy in sparing me from Claire Moultrie."

"Ann Marie's not like that, Father. She's different."

"I'm sure she's not, John-Morgan, you told me all about her. Perhaps my Claire more resembles your Miss Charlotte Drayton, the other young lady you told me about."

"Maybe she does."

"But that's not the point. The point is that you must not lose faith in God's mercy for you and His plan for your life. You must not lose your faith. Hang on to it with your fingernails if necessary, but never, never let go."

"I'm trying."

"I know you are."

The priest sat behind his desk and jotted down a note. "I'll call the school tomorrow, the seminary too. I'm reasonably sure they'll take you on my recommendation. Have you discussed this with your parents?"

"Yes, Father."

"They approve?"

"My mother is thrilled. My father said he just wants me to get a good education. He made me promise that I'd take courses I could use if I decided later against the priesthood. Can I do that? I mean I thought all the seminarians took was stuff about religion."

"Not at all. You'll have plenty of time to study for the priesthood. It takes twelve years to become a Jesuit priest. Your undergraduate degree from Spring Hill will have you well prepared to support yourself or go on to graduate school if you want. I assure you of that."

"Well, Father, I guess I've taken enough of your time. Thanks for everything."

"You've made me very proud. I'll call the school tomorrow and make arrangements for your entry in the fall quarter."

INNOCENCE LOST

THE LAST YEAR of the 1960's was fast approaching, and four members of the Benedictine class of 1965 had lost their innocence in those turbulent years that changed an entire nation. A fifth member of the class had not been affected at all. Perhaps he had no innocence to lose.

Tony O'Boyle was a leader at the Citadel, and a model Cadet. Many predicted that he would be the Corps commander in his senior year. He had a military obligation to fulfill upon his graduation and had decided to join the Army infantry.

Charleston was a Navy town, and during his free hours Tony spent time touring the warships at the naval base. Visiting in his Citadel uniform gave him easy entree into the wardrooms of these vessels, where the officers willingly and graciously showered him with attention, knowing that in only a year he, too, would be a member of the officer corps. Tony was greatly flattered, so trips to the warships became a regular diversion.

On a tour of the USS *Canberra*, a cruiser fresh from a Vietnam mission, Tony had a long conversation with a lieutenant temporarily stationed on that vessel. He was impressed by the man because of his confident air and rock-hard physique. From head to toe the lieutenant exuded power and authority; he was every inch a fighting machine. His uniform was immaculate; his stride was precise, yet it flowed like the movements of a great cat.

Over a cup of coffee in the officers' mess, the lieutenant told Tony about the Navy unit to which he belonged, a special unit formed in 1962 as the successor to the Navy's famed underwater demolition teams of World War II. This unit, the SEALS, underwent the toughest training in the entire world. He had just returned from Vietnam, where he had seen action for six months in the Mekong Delta. Next to sex, his *special* work in the Delta was the most exciting thing he had ever done in his whole life.

For two hours the lieutenant told Tony about his activities in Nam: hand-to-hand combat, firefights in chest-deep water, killing men with combat knives, midnight insertions via rubber boats into enemy territory, quiet assassinations of Vietcong leaders with a bullet to the head from the silenced muzzle of a Smith and Wesson auto loader. At the end of the conversation Tony was so impressed that he decided to take a commission in the Navy and become a SEAL.

Lloyd Bryan knew that he would face the draft upon graduation, and he resented it. By the end of his junior year, he was one of the most talked about running backs in the nation and easily Notre Dame's finest player. He had been approached by the pros; and the money they discussed was awesome. He could easily have turned professional at the end of his junior year and signed a contract worth millions, but he still had his two-year military obligation when he finished at Notre Dame, and this infuriated him. Lloyd had decided that Cassius Clay was right about the war—no Vietnamese had ever tried to invade America, so Americans had no right to be in another country trying to shove an unwanted government down people's throats. Besides, if it weren't for the draft, he could be making a fortune as soon as he graduated doing something he truly loved. It wasn't right and it wasn't fair.

"No, mam," he told his mother, "it's not right at all, no damn way."

"Shame on you for using that kind of language around your mother."

When John-Morgan entered the seminary, people said it was because he had lost his penis in Vietnam. The rumor started when Mike got more than a little tight one evening at the Knights of Columbus. People started pumping him again about what had happened in Vietnam. Although he had meant all of it as a compliment to his best friend, he blurted out to a bar full of wide-eyed Irishmen: "The guy that really deserves the medal I got is John-Morgan Hartman." Mike leaned on the bar and became very emotional. "Poor bastard, he got his fucking dick blown off trying to save his buddies, and I got the Medal of Honor." The rumor made the rounds that very night and Tony O'Boyle soon heard about it. After that he would snicker whenever John-Morgan's name came up. He referred to him as Father Dickless.

In the fall of 1969 John-Morgan started his third year in the seminary at Mobile. Mike was working for his father and trying to drink every bar in Savannah dry. Bubba had married Gail Cleveland, gone to work for her father's brokerage firm, and been sadly disowned by his parents. They had flatly refused to come to the wedding. Out at Camp Pendelton in California, Tony O'Boyle was getting his butt kicked by world-class professional butt kickers at the SEAL training depot and loving every minute of it. And in South Bend, Indiana, Lloyd Bryan was about to have his draft problems settled.

Notre Dame usually uses Purdue University as a football doormat. The 1969 season was no different. By the end of the third quarter, Purdue was down by twenty points and the coach had decided, after the next play, to pull Lloyd for the rest of the game. He had scored two of Notre Dame's touchdowns and was having an exceptional day. Lloyd knew that scouts from the pros were in the stands to watch him play, and he was determined to give them a show that they would never forget. So far he had done just that.

Notre Dame was on Purdue's twenty-five-yard line. Lloyd took the handoff from the quarterback and started toward the goal line untouched as he accelerated through a hole the right tackle had opened for him. At the fifteen-yard line, he shook off two tacklers by spinning in a complete three-sixty and raced for the end zone. At the five-yard line he was hit hard by one of Purdue's linebackers and almost taken to the ground, but he remained on his feet and fought for the end zone as two more men tried to pull him down. With superhuman strength Lloyd dragged all three men closer to the goal. He was about to score when he was hit on the right side by a two-hundred-and-fifty-three-pound farm boy from a small town outside of Des Moines. His knee took the brunt of the blow. It buckled inward as Lloyd fell across the goal line, scoring his third touchdown of the day and tearing his ligaments to shreds.

The school's orthopedic surgeon told Lloyd that it was a "Joe Namath knee." It could be repaired. He would certainly play college football again, but he was now medically ineligible for the draft.

"You mean the pro football draft or the military draft, Doc?"

"I mean you're 4-F now, cowboy. Your knee is more trouble to Uncle Sam than it's worth. This is a Namath knee if ever there was one."

"Will I still be able to play for the pros after it's fixed?"

"If Namath can, I guess you can too."

The sky was a clear and brilliant blue; there wasn't a soul on all of Little Tybee. A light breeze blew out of the southwest, enough to keep the sun from becoming unpleasantly hot. Charlotte and John-Morgan were together again, naked on the beach, and she pulled him on top of her. He could feel her hands press down across his buttocks, forcing him closer. "Now, John-Morgan, do it now. I want you." She was panting.

John-Morgan was wild with arousal, and his genitals tingled with desire. He closed his eyes, but when he opened them again, Charlotte's green eyes had turned to brown, her blond hair to black. She herself had now become Ann Marie, and he was so ecstatic he wanted to cry out "I love you!"—but he couldn't. His jaws were locked tight; and when he tried to kiss her, her lips were hard as stone.

John-Morgan screamed and sat up fully awake in bed. His T-shirt, hair, and pillow were soaked; he was breathing heavily and his pulse was rapid. He flopped back against the wet pillow and stared at the ceiling. Then he noticed a strange sensation, a tingling in his penis. He reached down and touched himself, and to his amazement, he had some slight but very definite feeling there. He was shocked, but he wasn't sure whether he was happy or sad. This brought amazement of another sort. John-Morgan was doing well in the seminary, and he felt as though he had finally found himself and his happiness. There were no distractions in his college life, and he had thrown himself into his studies. He looked forward to graduate school, to being ordained. He was sure that the priesthood was truly his calling. Now came this astonishing development. He didn't know what to do.

Over the next several weeks, all of the feeling he had lost in the hand grenade explosion returned. The crushed nerve had finally regenerated itself. Now John-Morgan wasn't sure that he wanted to continue in the seminary. He was torn between his desire for the priesthood and his desire for desire.

Finally, in the fall of his senior year, John-Morgan told his confessor that he had reached a decision. He said that he wanted to withdraw from the seminary to sort out his feelings. The vicar-general of the seminary was terribly disappointed. John-Morgan had planned to go to medical school and had already applied to several.

"Your grades are excellent, John-Morgan, and I will move mountains if I have to to get you into medical school. You would have made a wonderful priest, but I understand that you have heard the world calling to you and your heart must be in this work. You will be in my prayers."

By the time John-Morgan had completed his first year at the Medical College of Georgia, Lloyd had been playing with the Dallas Cowboys for three years. He made huge sums of money and bought an expensive house on the Wilmington River, where he stayed whenever he returned to Savannah. He was no longer the shy and humble boy who had left his city for Notre Dame in 1965. Now he was a member of the jet set, a national personality on the party circuit, and of course a football hero for "America's Team." By 1971 he was able to do things like show up at Madison Square Garden with a beautiful woman on each arm and take a front row seat to see Joe Frazier defeat Muhammad Ali.

Because it was part of both the professional sports scene and the party scene, Lloyd had even learned the thrills and spills of cocaine. He began to bet on games he was playing in, and even shaved points occasionally to cover or beat the spread. Elaine was not happy.

* * *

Mike got married. Then divorced. He was as estranged from his family as Bubba was from his. In 1973 Mike moved to Charleston and started his own general contracting business. The rift was now complete.

INNOCENCE REGAINED

IN HIS SECOND YEAR of medical school John-Morgan was sent to Memorial Hospital in Savannah for a three-month externship. On his first day there he was following one of the attending physicians as he made his rounds. They were at the nurses' station filling out charts when John-Morgan looked up and saw Ann Marie, staring at him across the chart rack. She smiled and said, "It's been a long time, John-Morgan. Are you still not speaking to me?"

John-Morgan was stunned. Ann Marie had started at the hospital only a month after her divorce, but news of her failed marriage had not reached John-Morgan's parents or any of his regular friends, even though gossip usually travels fast in the tightness of Savannah's Irish community. As a consequence he knew nothing of her divorce or her job at Memorial.

Two years ago, the news that John-Morgan had quit the seminary and entered medical school had been the juiciest bit of after-Mass gossip, even managing to filter up to Ann Marie in Atlanta. The seriousness and extent of his war wounds had saddened her fearfully, because over the years she had thought about John-Morgan as much as he had thought about her. When she got married, however, she dutifully placed him out of her thoughts— or tried to—and willingly devoted her mind and body to her new husband. But when she learned of her husband's infidelities, she resolved to be rid of him. She then reverted to memories of John-Morgan more and more. Ann Marie could only imagine how he must have felt about his injuries. Her fear had kept her from getting in touch with him.

John-Morgan stood up, a fantastic grin across his face. "Of course I'm speaking to you. How are you? I'll bet it's been almost ten years since I've seen you."

"I'm surviving. It's been eight years. Actually eight years and three months. You down here on an externship?"

"Yeah. What are you doing here? Last I heard you lived in Atlanta. Did your husband decide to come back here and practice?"

"I'm no longer married. I haven't lived with him for almost a year. My divorce was final last month, and I decided to come back home. I hated it in Atlanta. Too big, too many cars, no moss, and no Tybee. I took a job at Memorial and here I am."

"I'm sorry, I didn't know."

"Please don't be sorry. Be happy, because I sure am."

"Well, what I meant was that I'm sorry you've had problems—you know." He grinned more sheepishly and added, "Now that I think about it, I guess I'm happy too."

"Good, I'm glad you are." Ann Marie laughed and then took the plunge. "What are you doing tonight?"

That was the third major surprise of the last thirty seconds for John-Morgan, but he still managed to answer, "Ah, nothing, I think. Yeah, nothing."

"That's great, because you and I are going out together tonight, John-Morgan."

"Are we? I mean yeah, I'd like that, I'd like that a lot. What time do you want to go?"

"I'd like to leave right now, but I've got a zillion things to do. Let's go early though—we've got a lot of catching up to do. How about six-thirty?"

"That's fine. Uh, oh yeah, where do you live now?"

"You can pick me up at my parents' house. I'm staying there until I get settled. Do you still remember where they live?"

"Are you kidding? I've pictured the house in my mind a thousand times. What do you want to do?"

"Let's go to Tybee. I want to eat boiled crabs and drink

cold beer from a long-neck bottle in some little place where we can hear the waves breaking and then walk down the beach and let them splash on us. Then I want to go into one of those bars on Sixteenth Street. You know, the kind that our parents would have had a stroke over if they'd ever caught us in when we were growing up. I want to see what they look like on the inside and I want to drink a margarita. God, you don't know how much I've missed this place."

"Yes I do, cause I've missed it just as much."

Suddenly John-Morgan heard an irritated voice behind him saying, "Dr. Hartman. Anytime you're finished. I'm ready to make the rounds." It was the chief of surgery.

"Yes, sir, I'm sorry. Be right there." John-Morgan turned back to Ann Marie and said, "See you at six-thirty."

"Six-thirty. Bye."

"Bye, Ann Marie."

She winked as she trotted off, and the chief of surgery shook his head.

"You're something else, doctor. You haven't been here twenty-four hours and you've managed to get a date with the most beautiful girl in the whole damn hospital. I'm impressed." Then he stopped in front of a room and looked down at the chart he was carrying and then looked back up at John-Morgan. "You're good with the girls, now let's see how good you are with gall bladders."

Over the next two months, John-Morgan and Ann Marie saw each other in the hospital almost every day and dated almost every night. The attraction was as powerful as ever, but both of them moved with caution until another magical evening on Tybee.

Savannah has the most beautiful Indian summers. Late September and early October are golden days on Tybee Island. The noon sun is warming and pleasant, but not uncomfortable. The evenings are cool, with just a crisp hint of autumn in the air. The tourists are gone and the

beaches are all but deserted, save for those few who know
Tybee's secret and long to hold on to those last ambrosial
days.

Ann Marie and John-Morgan had always been Indian
summer people. They had long ago shared this feeling,
expressing the overripe taste of summer's passing in mu-
tual melancholy as they had watched September suns sink
into the marshes from his grandfather's beach house. They
distrusted winter and her demands; as teenagers in love,
they had openly spoken of their yearning for the warmth
and carefree satisfaction that summers at the beach gave
them. Now as they let the waves brush their feet and wash
the sand from between their toes, there was no more fear
of winter's coming, no more melancholy in their hearts.

They stood together in the surf and listened as the
waves broke and spread across the beach, fizzing away in
the thirsty sand. They watched the high clouds bounce out
over the ocean, reflecting the pinks and lavenders of the
setting sun and turning the sea oats gold. A warm South
wind rippled through their clothes and whispered through
Ann Marie's hair as she turned to John-Morgan and
smiled. Then she reached out and took his hand. "Come
on, John-Morgan, let's walk for a while."

John-Morgan had dreamed of Ann Marie's touch many
times, had tried to remember how it actually felt so many
terrible combat days and dark hospital nights ago. Now,
as their fingers interlaced, he could remember their first
embrace. "What'll we do next?" he asked. She didn't answer for a few seconds as they ambled in step toward the
South end. Then she turned with the smile that had first
captured John-Morgan's heart. "It's so nice just doing
this. But you know what I'd really like to do?"

"No, what?"

"I'd like to walk down to your grandfather's house. I
always loved that place. It's my favorite house down here.
Would that be OK?"

"I'd love to. It's been a while since I was there. The
keys are still hidden in the shower downstairs. And I'll

betcha a million dollars the liquor cabinet has the makings of a margarita in it. We can go up to the study, build a fire, watch the ocean turn black, and see if the stars come out."

Since the death of John-Morgan's grandparents, his mother and father had talked several times about selling the place. He had begged them not to. He promised to buy it from them when he started his practice, and they had agreed. To Ann Marie's delight, nothing much had changed in the old house. As they climbed the spiral staircase to the third floor, she almost giggled. "It still smells the same, I had forgotten about that. Mmm, leather, suntan oil, heart pine, and salt spray. God, I love it."

As John-Morgan lay the fire in the great stone fireplace, Ann Marie mixed the margaritas, and in no time a cut-glass pitcher stood on the bar. She even discovered the proper glasses, and dusted a snowy crust of salt on the rims. As she looked around the large and handsome room, she warmly smiled. "Your grandfather certainly had good taste. He knew how to live well. This room is so . . . so magnificent." She chuckled at her loss of better words.

They stood together in front of the fireplace and watched as the oak logs went up in a mild explosion of pale blue-yellow flame. For the first time in years Ann Marie and John-Morgan toasted each other, squinted together at the tart taste of the margaritas, and flopped down with a whoosh on the large leather sofa cushions in front of the fireplace. The sun was almost down. The room moved steadily into darkness. Soon, only flames painted the room in an orange dance.

The room grew smaller as the corners and the rafters darkened. Ann Marie drew closer to John-Morgan, and without a word she rested her head on his chest as they gazed into the fire. His hand rose and touched her back, the softness of her hair, the smoothness of her shoulder and cheek. She looked up at him, and in that moment an utterly ephemeral, effervescent timeflash caught them.

Without fear, without hesitation, Ann Marie spoke quietly to John-Morgan.

"I love you John-Morgan. I've loved you all my life. There was a time when I wasn't with you, when I didn't think about you, but you were there, inside of me, part of me. I love you with all of my heart. I never want to be without you again."

The darkened room suddenly became his universe, the fire his sun. Stars seemed to pulsate among the rafters, and his world lay on his chest. Without wondering what to say, John-Morgan answered softly.

"I love you, too. I wish we had never been apart. Some things happen for the best. Now, I don't question them anymore. When I learned that you had gotten married, it tore me apart. I could hardly stand the thought that you loved someone else and that you were gone forever. Every girl I knew, I compared to you. I've never loved anyone else in my life."

She put her arms around his neck and pulled him to her. They kissed. There were no searching, no wandering movements. Each knew the other's desires as though they had always been together. Ann Marie slid slowly back on the sofa, drawing John-Morgan on top or her. She had thought about his war wounds at dinner, and for a while on the beach, but somehow she had forgotten about them since they had been in Colonel Dietz's study. Her love for him was so great that if he still loved her, if he still would have her, the rest would make no difference. She had known physical love, and it could not compare to what she felt for John-Morgan. Having his love was infinitely more important than anything else, but then suddenly, in the passion and closeness of their embrace, Ann Marie realized the rumors about his impotence were untrue. She had worried about how John-Morgan would feel, exposing the secret to her that she thought he had, and then, with more joy for him than for her, she knew that pain would never come.

"Let's get more comfortable," Ann Marie whispered into his ear.

A large polar-bear rug filled the floor in front of the fireplace. She stood up and took John-Morgan's hand, and as they stood in the deep white fur before the fireplace, Ann Marie undressed John-Morgan and then herself. They embraced, let themselves softly crumble into the rug, and made love.

A river wind thrashed the great oaks and pulled a sweeping rain across the marsh, bringing the smell of salty spring grass and new earth. Horizon thunder echoed where lightning glowed, shimmered again, and passed on. They cuddled for a while. Keatsian lovers now making soft moan. Ann Marie finally spoke to John-Morgan.

"This was your first time, wasn't it?"

With absolutely no shame, John-Morgan replied, "Yes. You're the only girl I have ever loved. This is my first time."

"I believe you, John-Morgan. I wish it were my first time too. I wish I could have given you that. But I can tell you that what I felt tonight, I have never felt before. You are the love of my life." She squeezed his hands in hers, then kissed them.

"You know how we were raised, Ann Marie. I had a chance before I left for Nam, but I was afraid. There's something you don't know about, though. I got hurt badly there. I was told I might never be able to have sex at all, ever. A nerve had been damaged and I had no feeling. I probably went into the seminary because of that. Then when the feeling came back, that's probably the reason I left. It's only been two years since I got the feeling back, and I just was not ready, still not really able. There was so much in my mind I had to sort out, and there was no one like you. The war, the killing, the nightmares, my injuries. I guess during those two years I just never cared because for so long I wasn't able to care."

He sat up and looked at the fire. A log fell into the coals, sending flowers of sparks up the chimney. He watched them fade away, then turned to Ann Marie and asked: "Will you marry me? I know it's sudden and your divorce has only been final for a little while, and I've still got years before I finish school and my residency program and . . ."

Ann Marie put her hand up to John-Morgan's mouth. "Of course I'll marry you, silly. The sooner the better. We can do it tonight if you want. You're everything, all I'll ever want, and I can't stand the thought of being away from you for even a second."

People talked about their short courtship, and the fact that Ann Marie would have to get an annulment before they could be married by a priest. Nevertheless, that following Christmas, John-Morgan Hartman and Ann Marie Kerry were married on the lawn of his grandparents' old house at Isle of Hope. It was the same lawn that Captain Patrick Driscoll had stood on when he toasted his men and young wife before marching away to die for the Confederacy. It was also the same lawn on which John-Morgan had stood as a child and looked southward down the river, wondering where the river flowed and what life had in store for him.

VIII

THE RESURRECTION

Yet they were of a different kind,
The names that stilled your childish play

Because this my son was dead, and has come to life again; he was lost, and is found.

—Luke 15:24

ST. PATRICK'S DAY, BUBBA, AND MIKE

A FRESH YOUNG VOICE called from the foot of the stairs, "Telephone, Daddy." A few seconds later the voice greatly increased in intensity: "Telephone, Daddy!" A slightly irritated fortyish female voice wafted from the kitchen. "You don't have to shout, Brendan, I'm sure your father can hear you. Just give him a chance to answer you."

"Yes, mam."

From upstairs John-Morgan's voice answered. "Who is it, son? I'm in the bathroom."

"It's Mr. Silverman. He says he's calling from Atlanta. Says it's about St. Patrick's Day."

"Tell him I'll be right with him."

Wrapped in a towel and with shaving cream on his face, John-Morgan picked up the phone next to his bed. "Bubba, how ya doin'? Can ya make it?"

"I'll tell you the truth, it's been a long time since I've been home and I've had my doubts about comin' back, but yeah, I'm comin' down. You can count me in."

"That's fantastic, man. Mike's coming over from Charleston, and Lloyd Bryan's going with us too. You and Mike are going to have the guest house all to yourselves. I can't wait to get out to the island again. We're going to have a great time!"

There was a long pause on the Atlanta side of the connection before Bubba finally asked, "John-Morgan, have you seen my parents at all?"

"Your father hasn't been in the office for about a year. He's due for a checkup, but he's healthy as an ox. David Berman said he sees them both at the synagogue all the time and they look just fine. Have you ever talked to them?"

"Haven't laid eyes on them in over twenty-five years.

Or spoken. Hell, I haven't been back to Savannah either. When your family declares you dead, I guess you're just plain dead and that's that."

"Yeah, I know. It's been hard on everybody. But, changing the subject, Ann Marie and I want to thank you and Gail again for such a wonderful time in Atlanta. Your new house is spectacular."

"Thanks. We're real happy with it and were glad ya'll could make it. Speaking of houses, I can't wait to see the old place again. That house was always the most beautiful one on Isle of Hope. There's only one Driscoll house and they're not making them anymore. You are one lucky dog to have inherited a place like that, and even luckier to have the wife and children you do. I hope you realize that."

"I'm well aware, believe me. You driving or flying?"

"Driving, I want to have my car."

"I'm sorry Gail won't be coming with you."

"Well, she's a little apprehensive about the whole thing. So much has happened. If things work out OK, maybe next time."

"I hope so. Anyway, I look forward to seeing you next Sunday."

Ann Marie had a small TV on in the kitchen and was listening to Bryant Gumbel interview a senator from New England about his deficit reduction plan as she fixed John-Morgan's breakfast. John-Morgan came into the kitchen and kissed her, then playfully patted her on the backside. "Still the cutest tail end in the whole city of Savannah." He went around the counter and took his place at the breakfast table. Ann Marie rolled her eyes and shook her head. "Is Bubba coming down?"

"Yep, sure is. He gets in Sunday afternoon. Gail isn't coming with him though. She doesn't feel comfortable about his parents. I've got a feeling he may try to see them, so Gail's being here too may not be the best thing right now. I hope something good happens. Not talking to your parents for twenty-five years has got to be hard.

Anyway, he's coming. So is Mike, and we're gonna have a great time. Lloyd's going with us out to the island. He hasn't been there either since the BC days."

Ann Marie finished John-Morgan's eggs, placed them on a plate next to the grits and bacon, and sat them on the table. "Your favorite."

"Thanks. Oh, by the way, I almost forgot to tell you. Vinnie DiNapoli is going with us too."

"That's great. I like Vinnie. He's a lot of fun. Ya'll should get a kick out of having him along. I'll bet he's never been to a place like Battery Jasper."

Around St. Patrick's Day in Savannah, the temperature usually hovers in the mid-seventies during the day and the fifties at night. Spring flowers are rarely at their peak, but a warm spell around the seventeenth can easily send them into full bloom, causing the entire town to explode with color. This particular March had been cooler than normal and the buds were holding back, although nothing but clear skies had been predicted for the entire week.

As Bubba drove his car down the lane next to John-Morgan's house, his nose sought out the familiar smell of magnolia, but didn't find it. The great tree in the backyard had not yet put forth its May-time blooms. Bubba tapped on his horn as he pulled to a stop in front of the old servants' quarters behind the main house, which had been turned into a guest cottage. Mike and John-Morgan came running from the cottage at the sound. All three embraced and began to sing the Benedictine fight song as they stood rocking rhythmically with their arms around one another. For a brief golden moment the old days had returned.

At the end of the song they let out a loud cheer as the kitchen door to the main house opened and Ann Marie came down the steps. She hugged Bubba.

"Glad to have ya'll here," she said. "Come on inside, and we'll fix ya'll a drink."

"We'll be on in after a while. I want to show the boys something."

"That's fine. Dinner will be ready around seven. Stay out of trouble now, you hear."

John-Morgan led his old friends back to the antique garage at the end of the property, which had been built in the early twenties, when cars were smaller and narrower. The building was in remarkable shape. It stood under a hefty sweet gum tree, where a rope dangled with a car tire on the end of it.

"Lord have Mercy," said Bubba when he saw the swing. "This old thing is still here. I remember falling off of it one time and cutting my lip. Do you remember that, John-Morgan?"

"Yeah, I also remember falling off it when I was ten and breaking my arm."

John-Morgan slipped a key into the ancient padlock on the door. It popped open without complaint. Then they pushed back the doors. "Well, I'll be damned," said Mike in a gruff whisper of reminiscence.

Inside the garage sat the Boston Whaler that John-Morgan's grandfather had given him over thirty-five years before. The boat and motor were in immaculate condition. Mike ran his hand over the gunnels and smiled. "Man, did we have some fun in this thing. This is a beautiful restoration job."

"Looks great, doesn't it," said John-Morgan, "but that's not the real reason I brought ya'll back here." He reached up and turned on the lights, which revealed work benches and shelves against either wall filled with hundreds of artifacts the boys had found on Raccoon Island over the years: old musket balls in paint cans, crusty cannon balls, parts of Confederate and Yankee shovels and pick axes hanging from hooks on the walls, rusted carpenter's tools, even a set of leg irons resting on the work bench. Dozens of bottles of every color and shape lined the middle shelves; parts of old rifles and half of a broken sword filled the upper ones. The garage was a neatly ordered, museum-like jumble of odds and ends that Confederate soldiers and slaves had lost or abandoned on the island.

"Man," said Bubba, "this really brings back the memories. Look at all this stuff! I had completely forgotten about it."

The back of the garage stored all their old camping equipment, including the old Army surplus mine detector they had used to find most of the metal objects.

"This is unbelievable," said Mike as he sorted through the collection. "We really had a great time finding this stuff." Then with surprising earnestness he added, "It was probably the best time of my whole fucked-up life."

John-Morgan chose to ignore the remark; he looked at Bubba and shrugged. "Hey, the good stuff's inside. Come on in the house and we'll discuss the trip."

Inside Colonel Deitz's old study, the three lifelong friends sat on the floor and went over the plans for their journey to Battery Jasper. John-Morgan had even saved the old map they had made of the island back in the early sixties when they still went there to dig for the Driscoll treasure. When he spread it on the floor, Mike and Bubba let out a simultaneous "Damn." Then Bubba added, "I remember making this thing, John-Morgan. I can't believe you still have it."

"I always left everything here. My grandfather didn't throw a thing out. When we got interested in girls and stopped going out to the fort, he collected it all and either put it in the garage or in a trunk. After he died and I moved in here, I found the trunk in the attic. This map and all of the really good stuff you saw on the shelves was in there. It was as though he knew I'd want to go back to the island one day and look for the treasure again and that we'd need this map. He thought it was great that we were so interested in Battery Jasper. He wanted to go out there with us, but he was too old then. Anyway, he was always interested in the stuff we hauled out of there over the years. After we stopped going and I was away at school, that 'bugga' cleaned every single piece we found and even made a catalog of it. You know my old boat? I didn't restore it. The colonel had it done, just a few months before he died. He was quite a guy."

John-Morgan then turned his attention back to the map and pointed to an area marked Der Schwarzwald.

"As ya'll know, the one place we never explored was the Schwarzwald. I think back then we were too scared to go into the place. I know I was. Anyway, that's where we need to look. Over the years I've learned a little more about looking for artifacts. It seems that the one place where things are almost always found is in the old latrines. People used to throw all sorts of things down in them."

John-Morgan took a sip of Jack Daniels and continued. "I know we aren't going to find any real treasure. That's a family legend. I wish it were true, but now I'm afraid it isn't. What I'd like to do is to find those latrines and see what's in them. We never found them because I think they're in the Schwarzwald. The way I figure it, the latrines are to the northwest of the fort, because the wind blows out of the southeast. We know where their old campsite was by the stuff we've already found. See, it's marked right here."

Mike took out his glasses as he and Bubba leaned forward to study the map. Pointing to the area where he thought the latrines would be located, John-Morgan continued.

"It can't be more than fifty yards or so from where they slept. So on this trip, gentlemen, we invade the great and terrible Schwarzwald, home of the Grand Dragon of the Invisible Empire."

THE ISLAND

OF THE FOUR HIGH school friends going on the camping trip to Battery Jasper, Lloyd Bryan had changed the most dramatically. Indeed his entire life had changed course. In the middle of his career, at the peak of his athletic development, Lloyd had experienced what he later came to call his "spiritual epiphany." He witnessed a tragic event—the murder of a woman as her child looked on—that affected him so profoundly he quit his football career and went into the seminary. After he was ordained, he returned to Savannah and was stationed in the city's poorest parish. He had accumulated millions while playing professional ball and used his personal fortune to help Savannah's inner-city youth. Because of his fame as a football star, and the fact that he had given it all up to become a priest, Lloyd had become a legend in the city. In many ways his time was not his own, and he let himself become overworked. The strain began to tell on him. And the sudden and brutal murder of his father disturbed him more than he ever imagined it could.

After their return to Savannah, John-Morgan and Lloyd became very close. Lloyd was John-Morgan's father-confessor, dispensing not only his deepest friendship, but also the formal act of forgiveness through the Sacrament of Penance. John-Morgan in turn became a safety valve, of sorts, a way of releasing the pressures that a priest must endure. Lloyd could relax and be himself when he was with his friend; he was not treated as a celebrity or a curiosity, and he trusted John-Morgan with his feelings. Because of this, he welcomed the invitation to revisit Raccoon Island.

Lloyd parked his car in front of John-Morgan's house along the bluff and unloaded his camping gear. He was the last to arrive, and all of the others were already at the dock. Lloyd almost trotted down the long walkway, afraid that he had delayed the trip. An unexpected cold front had moved into the area the night before, so the air was deliciously cool on his face. Lloyd was glad, because the chill would keep down the gnats and mosquitoes that lived by the billions on Raccoon Island.

"So this is the new boat I've heard so much about."

Lloyd was genuinely impressed. "Wow, Grady White, twenty-six feet, twin Mercury Two Hundreds. This is one fine rig, John-Morgan. It looks like the Queen Mary."

"Thanks, Lloyd." John-Morgan smiled proudly as he helped the priest load his equipment onto the boat.

Although Vinnie DiNapoli had heard about Father Bryan, he had never met him, and he was unquestionably fascinated. The priest looked even bigger in person than he did on TV, and Vinnie gawked when Lloyd picked up one of the sixty-four-quart ice chests, fully loaded with its cargo, and shifted it around with effortless grace. His massive shoulders and chest, his eighteen-and-a-half-inch neck might have belonged to one of the Greek gods he had read about in high school.

Vinnie, an orthodontist who took care of John-Morgan's children, had first visited Savannah when he was serving in the Army at Fort Stewart. To this sharp-eyed little man, born and raised in the heavily Italian neighborhoods of South Philadelphia, the South in general and Savannah in particular was a whole new world: he fell in love with it. Vinnie returned and established a practice after he got out of the Army, and he met John-Morgan at the hospital. He was now amazed by John-Morgan's friends.

Loading done, it was time for John-Morgan's first rush of the day. When he hit the ignition switch, four hundred horses roared to life on the stern of his boat. It sounded like a well-oiled army as he brought the throttle up to fifteen-hundred rpms to warm the engines. Ann Marie was standing on the dock holding the lines. When her husband gave her the signal, she tossed them to Bubba and pushed the bow away from the dock. "Ya'll have a good time now. Lloyd, you make John-Morgan be careful."

"OK, Ann Marie, I'll watch out for your boy." He gave her a hearty wave.

John-Morgan piloted the boat at idle speed through the no-wake zone, then quickly brought it onto a plane as they moved past the marina. As they tooled by Green Island, he slowed the boat and pulled it to within twenty yards or so of the island's easternmost point. Vinnie had never been out on the water around Savannah, so John-Morgan motioned for him to come and stand by the wheel. He pointed at a rise on the tip of the island and said, "There, see those bluffs? They're eroded, but you can see how high they are compared to the rest of the island. That's part of an old Confederate earthworks fort, very much like the one we're going to."

Vinnie studied the ramparts and noted the massive, moss-covered oaks that thrived on parts of the old fort's walls. They seemed primordial; some of their gigantic branches reached thirty feet or more across the river. A few had fallen into the water, collapsing under their own weight. Vinnie also noticed how the smell of the air had changed.

Up at Burnside Island, the smell was almost sweet, like the aroma of sourdough bread, but still different from anything Vinnie had known. "What *is* that smell?" he asked.

The others laughed. "It's just the marsh." A moment later, Vinnie encountered a scent he *could* place, one very familiar from his youth at Atlantic City.

"Hey, I smell the ocean real strong," he said excitedly to John-Morgan as they studied the old fort.

"Yeah, it's only about three miles from here. The wind is picking up from the east and blowing it our way." John-Morgan pointed to his left. "That's Wassaw Island over there. To the right here is Ossabaw Island. Between them is Ossabaw Sound, and then the Atlantic Ocean." He turned the boat south. "Now we're heading for Hell Gate. Once we're through that, we'll be in the Ogeechee River. You'll be able to see Raccoon Island in a little bit."

Ten minutes later, John-Morgan handed Vinnie the binoculars and pointed to a clump of trees in the distant marsh. "There, that's the island we're going to. We gotta go up this river a little more and then make a turn down the Florida passage. No creeks from the island on this side. It drains from the south into a series of creeks on the island's back side. Back during the Civil War, the marsh in front of the island wasn't this big. When the Corps of Engineers dug the channel through Hell Gate and cut Egg Island and Raccoon Key in half, it changed the way the river flowed. The periodic dredging by the corps to keep the Intracoastal Waterway with twelve feet at low tide has caused some problems too. All this has made the creeks that drain the area behind the island a lot shallower than they were during the Civil War. It's made Battery Jasper real hard to get to unless you know just what you're doing and are determined to do it."

With a hard turn to starboard, John-Morgan headed the boat into a river about a third the size of the one they were on. The others grabbed the railing when they saw he was about to make another hard right turn where the river narrowed again. The boat moved deeper and deeper into the marsh. John-Morgan never eased up on the throttle as he maneuvered the big Grady White, sliding around turns that seemed to loop in upon themselves. Soon, however, he cut back on the engines as the creek severely narrowed a third time. They were approaching their landing point on Raccoon Island.

The tide was at its zenith as John-Morgan let the boat creep up to the peninsula on the back side of the island. On most tides they would not have been able to approach with a boat that drafted like the Grady White. But this was a spring tide, and it gave the boat just enough extra water under the keel to nudge it against the causeway the Confederates had built to the island. Even at that, however, they would not have been able to make it if they had arrived an hour later. In less time than that, the boat would be mudbound.

Camp was set up at their old site—that very site where years ago, under the same oak tree, Lloyd had first met John-Morgan, Mike, and Bubba. Nothing much had changed, except the azaleas that grew on the fort. No one had been to the island to tend to them since Lloyd's last visit thirty years ago, and now they had grown wild and unruly, though also spectacularly beautiful. The enormous bushes were covered with thousands of white buds about to explode into action—but they would wait just a little longer; the temperature was expected to drop into the forties that night.

As they walked along the edge of the dense undergrowth they called the Schwarzwald, John-Morgan came to the spot where, as twelve-year-olds, they had decided the Civil War camp must be. He pointed into the thick foliage, telling Vinnie that he thought the latrines were located about fifty yards in. "As boys, we never went into the Schwarzwald. We were afraid of it. It was so dark inside there. Gutteral sounds came from behind that wall of growth. That scared the crap out of us."

They all sat on a downed log. Bubba picked up the story where John-Morgan had left off. "You can't walk upright in it at all. Trying to cut your way through with a machete is real slow. Even then it's almost impossible. It's not worth the effort. If you want to explore the Schwarzwald, you've got to do it on your knees, and you still have to cut your way though. At ground level the branches aren't quite as dense, but it's still real slow going and you can't see more than a few feet in front of you."

"Then how do you expect to find those latrines? We don't have a whole week."

Bubba smiled mischievously. "We've decided to use the tunnels. We're going to explore them first and see what we find. We may stumble onto something."

Vinnie was obviously puzzled. "What tunnels? You mean they had underground crappers out here?"

"Naw, these tunnels are above ground. They're paths cut through the undergrowth by the wild boars that live on the island. They're tunnels through the bushes. You'll see."

Mike, after finishing his beer, crushed the can in his hand and added to the discussion. "These boars were brought over by the British before the Revolution. Imported from Germany. They're extremely tough and grow very large. The British liked to hunt them for sport because of the fight they put up. Many a good hound dog has been chewed up by a boar half his size. An unarmed man doesn't stand a chance against a big one, especially in a place like the Schwarzwald."

"No shit. How big do they get?"

Mike looked at John-Morgan and Bubba and then back at Vinnie. "Average size male is about a hundred pounds. Depends on how good the diet is and how long they live. The alligators keep them pretty well thinned out in places like this. But the dominant male can easily reach between three and four hundred pounds, the big females maybe a hundred and fifty. I saw snout prints by a palmetto over there. The boar had been eating the roots. They absolutely love them. One print was over eight inches wide. Let me tell you, mister, that's one hell of a big hog."

"How tall are they?"

John-Morgan reached down to tie his boot lace. "You can tell how tall they are by how big the tunnel is. Last time we were out here, I think I saw one about two-and-a-half feet high and maybe two feet wide."

"No shit," said Vinnie.

"Absolutely no shit," replied Bubba.

John-Morgan stood. "Come on, let's go back to camp, have lunch, and then get cracking. We need to explore those tunnels. Vinnie, did you bring your pistol, the way I told you?"

"Got it in my pack."

"Great, 'cause I think it's a good idea if we all carry one while we're crawling around in there. We probably scared the boar back to the end of the island. They'll be too afraid to come out. Probably. But you never know."

Vinnie's mind was working fast. "What about you, Lloyd? I don't care how big and strong you are, those hogs could really hurt you."

Lloyd smiled and reached into the knapsack at his feet. Out came a nickel-plated Smith and Wesson .357 magnum.

"You carry a gun?" Vinnie was stunned.

"I carry a gun when I have to. My parish is in the roughest part of Savannah and I've made a lot of enemies—some of the most vicious people you can imagine. I've had two attempts on my life in the last three years. Both of them drive-by shootings. One of my little third-graders had to pay the price for it. Took one in the gut and almost died. Sometimes I wear a bullet-proof vest. I don't mind dying for Jesus, but I do mind dying over a couple of ounces of crack."

"Amen, Father," said Vinnie softly. "Amen."

There are no natural rocks on any of the barrier islands, or anywhere around Savannah. Anything that looks like one was brought there by man. In addition, the ground on the barrier islands is essentially flat. It may have a gentle incline out to the marsh or some other drainage plane, but these are mild slopes. The islands contain few naturally occurring gullies or sinkholes. Any abrupt change in the forest floor, therefore—a sharp drop or a high mound of earth—must be made by either man or large animals. These were the signs that the searchers were looking for as they laboriously crawled through the Schwarzwald.

When it came time to search for the latrine, the five men spaced themselves about twenty feet apart along the edge of the underbrush, then dropped to their knees and entered the thicket crawling. Progress was very slow, but Vinnie managed to move ahead of the others after they had penetrated about twenty-five yards. John-Morgan was perhaps fifty feet or so behind when he heard Vinnie cry out.

"Yo, John-Morgan, I think I found something! Can you hear me? It's me, Vinnie. I think I found something!"

"Yeah, I hear you. I'm coming as fast as I can." John-Morgan began furiously cutting his way toward the sound of Vinnie's voice.

"John-Morgan. I really think I found it. It looks like a ditch or something."

About twenty feet away from Vinnie, John-Morgan poked into a boar tunnel. The tunnel ran east-west, perpendicular to the explorers' line of advance. "Jesus, Mary, and Joseph," John-Morgan muttered as he crawled into the tunnel. "This son of a bitch is big." The ceiling of thorns and dry vines was at least two-and-a-half feet high, and the tunnel was over two feet wide. John-Morgan noticed tracks on the well-worn path—some no bigger around than a quarter, others the size of a half dollar. The freshest ones, however, were at least three inches across.

The tunnel seemed to lead in the general direction of where John-Morgan judged Vinnie to be, so he started crawling along it, hoping he wouldn't run into any hogs. After about ten yards, the ground abruptly rose about a foot or so, and then, just as quickly went down. After descending, John-Morgan suddenly found himself face to face with Vinnie. He called out directions to the others.

It took about an hour for the men to clear away the growth from the depression, along with the dirt that had been heaped up on the sides. When they finished, they had a trench about twelve feet long, four feet wide, and two feet deep at the southern end. It was shallower at the northern end. The trench seemed to run for another ten feet into the woods, but at that point it was ill-defined and scarcely more than a slight depression in the earth. The boar tunnel crossed the trench obliquely at midpoint, then continued on into the woods on the other side.

"You did great, Vinnie," said John-Morgan as he surveyed their achievement. "Now we have to see if we've hit paydirt."

SAVANNAH'S FIRST BLACK PRIEST

THIS HAD TO BE THE LATRINE. After it was cleared, John-Morgan and Bubba swept the entire area with the metal detector, marking metal strikes with a peg. Then, with a six-foot metal rod, they probed for objects below the level the metal detector could reach, gently forcing the rod into the ground, testing for any obstructions. At the southern end of the latrine, the probe hit something two feet down.

As John-Morgan and Bubba started digging, Lloyd, using the metal detector in another sector, found a fist-sized piece of rusted iron. "Shrapnel from an exploded shell," said Mike the minute he saw it. "We've found hundreds of those out here." Bubba and John-Morgan nodded in agreement. Vinnie turned up a similar piece, and Mike found yet another. When John-Morgan and Bubba finally got to what they had been digging for, Bubba shined a flashlight into the hole.

"Looks like an eleven-inch piece of solid shot," he said as he sat back on his knees. John-Morgan took the light and examined the round metal ball.

"I agree. With one exception."

"What's that?"

"I don't think it's solid shot. I think it's exploding shot. Look here." John-Morgan played the light on the exposed side of the cannon ball. "That looks like a fuse hole and setting to me. Must have been a dud."

Bubba stuck his hand into the hole and felt the side of the old cannon ball. "I think you're right. Let's just leave this alone. It's still a live shell. Anyway, the thing must weigh over two hundred pounds. Nothing special. Besides, we're looking for gold this trip, aren't we?"

The digging was slow work, but by supper time the entire area had been examined with the metal detector and the probing rod and all of the additional strikes had been marked. The next day they would reenter the Schwarzwald and start to dig in earnest for whatever lay hidden in the old latrine.

Mike as always was the chef. His fare was simple: steak, baked potatoes, and corn on the cob—cooked to perfection with the fresh-woods smoky flavor an open fire gives to food. Bellies full, the five men relaxed around the campfire. Mike placed large cedar logs over the hickory coals, and fire soon lashed around the wood, rolling ribbons of flame up into the cold, clear, star-heavy sky.

Sitting around on open fire is man's oldest social custom. Language and conversation must certainly have been born while ancient man hunched around his campfires, reflecting upon his day, and grunting wonder about his tomorrow. Little has changed since then—nor is modern man significantly less superstitious. Darkness transforms a forest into something almost supernatural, and in evening shadows, the familiar daytime shape of a rotted tree trunk becomes the menacing outline of a predator. Night sounds of the deep woods take on ominous and malevolent connotations as darkness robs vision, and only ears can be used to interpret what lies behind the veil of night. Thus John-Morgan and his friends pulled their seats in a little closer, instinctively seeking safety and warmth, kinship and conversation, as their fire on that tiny Georgia island turned the tree trunks amber and shaded their faces an apricot tint.

Even Vinnie had heard about Father Lloyd Bryan. He knew that Lloyd had quit professional sports and joined the priesthood, but he didn't know the details. He was greatly intrigued by the man and asked him if he would mind telling the story again.

Lloyd leaned forward, resting his elbows on his knees. Then he took a sip of his drink and made a little face. "You make 'em strong, Mike." Mike only smiled, and Lloyd started to talk.

"Maybe it's the way I was raised. By my momma mostly. The nuns, too. I guess you might say they made me care, first about myself and then about others. Then they switched it around on me when I was about thirteen. After they figured I could take care of myself well enough, they started teaching me to think about others first. When I started playing pro ball, I bought myself a brand new Mercedes sports car. I used to drive it home at night after the games. I had to drive through some rough parts of town to get where I was going, and when

I stopped for a light I used to look at the people. It was the children that got to me the most, their little faces— snot running down, dirt plastered around their mouths. Just little kids out on the streets late at night, no more than eight or nine." Lloyd breathed deeply, sipped his drink, and smiled.

"Finally, after almost three years of trying to force this kind of stuff out of my mind, I began to have trouble sleeping at night. I guess it all came to a head the night we beat the Redskins in a tight game. I was really on top of the world that night. My girlfriend and I had done a little coke in the parking lot. We decided to go back to my place, where we could really have a big time. You know, it's funny, I can see that girl's face now, but I can't remember her name. Anyway, we were passing through this rough neighborhood when we came to a stop sign just a second or two before this guy shot his girl over some dope. She had a kid with her; it might have been his, I don't know. Anyway, I watched this guy shoot this girl and then reach down and grab her purse and run. The kid was just sitting there on the sidewalk next to his dying mother, screaming. It was like no sound I had ever heard in my whole life. It entered my body. His pain took over. When I got back to my apartment and looked around at all the things I had, and then thought about that child, I knew my life had changed forever. Just like that. I sent my date home and went into my bedroom. And I wept— for—I don't know how long. Hours maybe."

Lloyd kicked one of the logs with his boot and sent a cockscomb of sparks reaching up into the night sky. He watched them for a moment and then continued.

"I was on my knees by the bed. Praying like I hadn't done since I was at BC. The phone rang. It was my momma. 'Are you all right, Lloyd?' she asked. 'I was saying my Rosary and this feeling came over me and I knew I had to call you and see if you were all right.' 'Momma,' I said, 'I'm quittin' the Cowboys and I'm givin' all this stuff up. I think I wanna be a priest. I can't

stand their little faces no more. Football don't need me,
Momma, like these babies do. I don't need football like I
need to get this empty feeling out of me I've had for years
now.' Just before my mother called me I had this very
strange feeling. I was happy and peaceful when I
shouldn't have been. When she called and I said those
words about going into the priesthood, I had never
thought about it before that moment. It just came out of
my mouth. After it was all over and I had time to sit and
think about what I had said, it seemed like the most natural and logical thing to want to do. After that, things just
fell right in place for me, and I enrolled in the seminary.
The rest is just history now, I guess."

There was a long silence. Only the rush of the fire with
its pops and cracks could be heard in the still night. Finally Vinnie spoke.

"I've never heard anything quite like that from a man
like you. I've heard a lot of hokey television preachers
come up with some pretty wild stuff, but nothing like
this."

"It's a true story, Vinnie. Every word of it."

"I believe you, Lloyd." Then Vinnie asked his last
question. "What about your old man? Is he still alive?"

John-Morgan cut his eyes to Lloyd's, but they were
intent upon the fire. For a few seconds, Lloyd didn't answer.

"He's gone now. He's with Jesus, as some might say.
Didn't have much to do with him when I was comin' up.
A few months ago, he surprised me and joined the
Church. Even insisted on me hearing his first confession."
There was another pause as Lloyd sipped his whiskey.
Moisture was in his eyes. "Not quite two weeks ago, he
got beaten to death. They just crushed his skull with their
bare hands. I got to bury my daddy, too. Confession, com-
munion, and a funeral." Lloyd looked down into the cup
he was holding, swirled it around, and took another sip.

"Do you know who did it?" asked Vinnie.

"I got an idea. A good one, but it's only an idea."

THE SKELETON

FIRST LIGHT ON Raccoon Island comes from over the tree line on Ossabaw Island four miles to the east. On clear days the first noticeable color is a pale gray that rises to a light purple, quickly followed by magenta transforming to hot orange as the sun peeps up over the Ossabaw tree tops. Thin arms of light poke between the palmettos and cast sword-shaped shadows across the ground.

In the creek behind Battery Jasper the morning dawned like mountain air as rays of sunlight skipped through the condensation vapors hovering over the warm water. Save for the sounds of sleeping men, the island was quiet and still. The wild animals were awake, but not yet stirring; and the turkey buzzards in the top of a dead oak tree would not move for several hours. They would sit in the branches and catch the infrared rays of the sun with their flat black feathers; when they were warm enough, they would open their mighty wings and fly high into the sky on the thermal updrafts caused by the warming air. There they would soar, searching for their meals.

John-Morgan was the first to open his eyes on that new Wednesday morning. The synchronous snoring of Mike and Bubba had awakened him, and he knew from experience that he would not be able to get back to sleep. He didn't mind, though, because the best mornings he had ever spent had been right here, on Battery Jasper, roaming around with his friends. Quickly and quietly he started a fire, and soon he had his old fifteen-cup coffee pot perking away. Then he set to work at the mess table making pancake batter and pressing patties of Jimmy Dean sausage. A smiling Aunt Jemima watched from the syrup bottle as he laid out the plates and tableware. When he had finished, he poured himself a cup of coffee and settled into

one of the lawn chairs to watch the sun climb higher over
Ossabaw Island. He smiled back at Aunt Jemima.

Down at the east end of Raccoon Island, other residents
were also stirring. They too were hungry, and most of all
they were thirsty. They had not had any water since the
day before, when the humans invaded and the Grand
Dragon had moved his Invisible Empire into safekeeping.
The Grand Dragon and his subjects had eaten well enough
from the palmetto roots down by the old moonshine still,
but they needed water to soothe their throats and aid in
their digestion.

The Grand Dragon listened closely; his ears were eight
inches high, and he could move them around like radar
dishes searching for signals. He also sniffed the cold air;
his nose, as well, was eight inches across. As he caught
the smell of sausage cooking and heard the sound of human voices, the hair on his back stood on end. Now he
looked even bigger than his three hundred and ninety-two
pounds. That was part of his defensive weapons' system.
His offensive weapons were the large tusks that protruded
from either side of his massive snout, an ample mouth
with powerful jaws, his massive size, and most of all, his
cunning and absolute devotion to the battle once it had
been enjoined.

The Grand Dragon had become the master of his universe by knowing that he could not defeat the humans.
He would simply retreat into his fortress of thickets along
with his wives, children, grandchildren, and great grandchildren and wait. The humans never stayed very long. A
few came only to look at the old fort. Some came to kill
his subjects. But very few ever tried to enter his fortress,
where he and his imperial subjects had always been safe.
Some of his children and wives had been killed and taken
away, but those were the ones who had been stupid
enough to let themselves be seen. When this happened,
the humans would always make the thunder come and the
stupid one would fall like a tall pine hit by lightning. The

Grand Dragon did not really care if the stupid ones got killed. He was glad they could not live to produce more stupid wild hogs and pollute the gene pool he had worked so hard to protect.

As the morning passed, the Invisible Empire began to stir and complain of thirst. It was clear that the master would have to go and see if the humans were still in the fortress home and then return and lead them to the old borrow pit that was their watering hole. The Grand Dragon moved quietly and quickly through the high grass, over the carpet of pine straw, and into the eastern end of the Schwarzwald. He passed through yards of tunnels that twisted and turned and intersected with other tunnels deep within his fortress, stopping often to listen and smell as thick saliva dripped from his mouth and rolled down the coarse hair on his broad chest. Then, about halfway through the thickets, he stopped. The smell of the humans was too strong. If they were in his fortress and saw him, they surely would make it thunder. The Grand Dragon was not ready to abdicate his throne, not yet.

He returned to his subjects and told them in a series of low grunts that it was too dangerous to try for water at the present time. They must wait in the thickets down by the moonshine still until it was safe. His wives knew that he had always been right, and his wishes were their commands. They dutifully moved their anxious, thirsty children down to the old still and waited.

After breakfast the men gathered the tools they would need to uncover whatever was buried in the latrine and crawled again into the Schwarzwald. Slowly and carefully each place that had been marked was dug up; after an hour, a pile of shrapnel from exploded cannon balls sat on the edge of the latrine. Mike was digging at the south-ern end about two feet down when he called out, "Hey, John-Morgan, I got something, and I don't think it's another piece of cannon ball."

Everyone crowded around as Mike enlarged the hole.

Then he reached down and brushed away dirt from something that appeared creamy white. "Looks like an old piece of china," said Bubba. "They threw a lot of broken stuff down into the latrines."

"I think it's an old pitcher," echoed Mike as he continued to remove dirt from what he had found. After a few more seconds he suddenly shouted. "It's a skull! Holy shit, we've found a skull!"

Five heads gathered closely around the hole as Mike dug in excited determination. Sure enough, a human skull began to take shape in the ground. The ridge of the eye orbits became clear, and then the nasal cavity. As the excavation continued, the entire skull appeared, complete with a lower jaw grotesquely gaping open. It was resting face up; gold fillings dully shone in the mandibular molars. Further excavation revealed the remains of the cervical vertebrae, the scapula, and then the rest of the shoulder girdle.

"Good Lord," said John-Morgan, "I think we have a complete skeleton here."

"How old do you think it is?" asked Lloyd.

"I'm not really sure, but I don't think it's from the Civil War. It's too well preserved. Besides, look at those fillings. They're pretty extensive, not like the kind of work done back then. Most people just had their teeth pulled. And this is a latrine. Soldiers weren't buried in latrines, at least not in the Confederate Army."

In the cool density of the Schwarzwald, the five men sat on the edge of the pit and discussed their find. "I guess we have to tell the police," said Mike. "I mean they just have to be told. We got a dead person here, no matter how long ago he died."

"I agree with you, but he sure wasn't put here yesterday. If it is a he. There's no big rush. We can still finish digging him out and check the rest of the latrine for anything else. But I'll hate it if this makes the news. That means this little secret fort on our secret island ain't gonna be a secret anymore."

Mike looked around sadly and nodded. "I know, but we can't just pretend that he's not here. The guy was probably hunting on the island and came back here after something and had a heart attack. Nobody knew exactly where he had gone to hunt and they just gave up on looking for him."

"Well then," said Bubba, "we ought to find his shotgun or something. Besides, some of the stuff we dug off him was the buildup of dead leaves, but this guy was buried. He had dirt over him a foot-and-a-half deep. Dead men don't bury themselves."

"You're right about that," said Lloyd, "and nobody buries a body out here unless they don't want it found, especially in these thickets. I think this person was probably murdered and then carried out here and buried so he'd never be found."

Vinnie could not have been more excited had they found the pharaoh's tomb. His mind was in fifth gear as he wondered about what had happened to the person whose remains rested half-buried before him. "Who was this guy, and what happened to him?"

"Good question," replied John-Morgan. "I guess I better go back to camp and call the police on the cell phone. I forgot about the tide. If they're going to come out here, they've got to catch it when it's high. They'll need some advance notice."

"I'll come with you," said Lloyd. "I've got to check in at the church and make sure everything is OK." Bubba said he wanted to get his camera and take some pictures before the police dug up the place, so all three crawled away down the tunnel, leaving Mike and Vinnie alone in the Schwarzwald with the mysterious skeleton.

"I tell ya," said Vinnie, "I wish I'd have told them to bring me back a beer or something. I could use a drink right about now."

Mike smiled. "Hey Vinnie, you remember us talkin' last night about smoking those Thai sticks over in Nam?"

"I sure do. They blew my head off a couple of times.

Never smoked anything like that again in my whole life. Couldn't get anything like that in the states."

"Well, I don't have any Thai sticks," said a grinning Mike, "but I do have a couple of real nice numbers rolled up right here in my pocket. Care to join me?"

"Hell yeah, it's been a long time. Now I'll really get into digging out this guy!"

"Just don't get freaky on me." Mike lit one of the joints, took a long pull, and passed it to Vinnie. In a considerably more constricted voice he added, "This stuff is killer weed. Don't let it creep up on you."

Vinnie snickered. "This ain't my first rodeo. Everybody claims to have killer weed."

"OK. You'll see."

Sure enough, it was killer weed. After a few more hits the joint was finished. Mike and Vinnie sat on the edge of the grave and stared as if hypnotized at the skull, thinking the deep thoughts that only cannabis can induce. After a long silence Vinnie was finally able to speak.

"This is like the stuff we used to get when I was at Temple back in the seventies. You're right. Killer weed, man, killer weed!"

"Hey, I think I'd like some music. I always love music when I'm stoned. I'm going back to the camp and get my CD player. I've got this copy of Wagner's *Götterdämmerung* played by the Berlin Philharmonic. It'd be cool as hell to listen to that stuff while we dug up the rest of the skeleton, don't you think, Vinnie?"

"Yeah, that'd be far out. Bring me a beer while you're at it, OK?"

"Be right back," said Mike as he got on his knees and started to crawl down the tunnel.

THE INVISIBLE EMPIRE STRIKES BACK

IT WAS NOW ALMOST six hours after dawn and the Grand Dragon still had not been able to lead his subjects to the borrow pit for a drink of water. Even he was having trouble controlling the urge to move to the watering hole. His wives complained bitterly about their thirst, and his children started to move about restlessly and grunt. Afraid the noise would reveal their position, he decided to make his move.

The Grand Dragon had been down by the humans' campsite earlier in the morning, hiding in a stand of short palmettos, gathering information. He had seen only one of the humans, but the others had made noises in their tents much as his own subjects did when they slept. He had been heartened by this and quickly left to return to his subjects and tell them the news. After he left, it was impossible for him to know that the humans had awakened, eaten, and then invaded his fortress again.

If the humans were at their camp, thought the Grand Dragon, they would be able to see him and the members of his klavern when they moved to the borrow pit through the open space behind the old fort. And if the humans saw his subjects, they would make the thunder come and he would lose a wife, or perhaps even worse, a son. Because of this, he decided it would be much better to lead his subjects through the maze of tunnels in his thicket fortress. This would surely shield them from the eyes of the humans and provide them with safety as they moved to their watering hole.

The Grand Dragon, with all of his descendants in line behind him, proceeded down the tunnels of the Schwarzwald. He rippled his snout several times to sample the air, and checked for sound with his radar-net ears. The air was still full of the human's scent, but this had been there

yesterday. He could hear human sounds, but the dense
underbrush distorted the sound waves and he thought that
they were coming from the humans' campsite. The Grand
Dragon decided it was safe to move on, but he passed the
word back to move quietly.

The weed Vinnie had smoked had greatly enhanced his
powers of concentration. His total attention was focused
on the skeleton from which he was carefully removing
dirt. He was lying on his stomach, scooping soil from the
eye sockets with his Swiss Army knife. He had cleaned
out the left side and was working on the right about two
inches into the socket, when he uncovered a metal object
that appeared to be copper in the center of the skull.

After removing a little more dirt from the piece of
metal, Vinnie recognized what it was. There, buried in
what had housed the brain, was a bullet. He had to take
a couple of deep breaths. "The bullet," he said to himself,
that killed this person. Vinnie was sure of it, and it gave
him a most uncomfortable feeling.

The cannabis was working; the enclosed space, the
walls of sharp thorns and thick vines, the old deserted fort
on a remote and mysterious island, and most of all, the
skeleton in the grave before him, served simultaneously
to frighten and excite Vinnie in a way he had never known
before. He couldn't take his eyes off the bullet that was
staring back at him through the eye socket.

Vinnie's heart was racing as he pushed himself up off
his stomach. For a moment he had the frightening sensation that someone was watching him. He looked up, and
in the same second a vile, rank stench hit him and took
his breath away. Then he met the eyes of the Grand
Dragon.

He stood there, eyes boiling, jaws slavering, neck-
hackles rigid as needles; and when Vinnie reached for the
Beretta underneath his shoulder, the beast covered the distance between them in a kinetic blur and a roar of fury,
and although Vinnie was able to draw his pistol and re-

lease the safety, he didn't have time to aim the weapon. The wild boar hit him with a massive blow squarely in the chest, and Vinnie soared through the air, smashing against the far end of the latrine pit. He hadn't uttered a sound as he was hit, but he did pull the trigger on his pistol.

The explosion didn't phase the Grand Dragon as he drove home his attack. He made a terrible piercing sound as he slashed at the human with his tusks.

Losing consciousness quickly, Vinnie could only try to protect his face and scream. The instant Mike heard the shot, and then the nightmarish sound of the attacking boar, he raced down the tunnel toward the latrine. John-Morgan, Bubba, and Lloyd also heard the commotion, and they too began crawling toward the tunnel.

As Mike neared the latrine, he could clearly see the beast on top of Vinnie, straddling his chest and goring him in the upper body. The stench gagged him and burned his eyes, but he reached for his .44 magnum, cocked it, and then charged out of the tunnel. About three feet away from the struggle, he stopped and took aim at the boar's head, but did not fire. He could not get a clear shot; he was afraid he would hit Vinnie, or that the bullet would travel straight through the animal and then kill his friend. Two or three seconds stretched out to infinity for Mike; he had to act immediately or Vinnie would be chopped into bits. If he could not protect his face for even a moment, the creature could easily gouge out Vinnie's eyes.

The Smith and Wesson that Mike carried was one of the most powerful handguns in the world. It was also heavy, weighing almost five pounds when fully loaded. Mike now brought this weight down on the back of the Grand Dragon's head with all his might. The animal let out a curiously delicate squeal of pain and dropped to his knees momentarily, but then continued his savage attack on Vinnie.

Vinnie's situation was now dire. He lost all consciousness, and his arms fell away from his face. Mike and the

beast realized this in the same moment. With the same
instincts, both moved together—the boar to Vinnie's exposed face and eyes, Mike to the animal's back.

Mike Sullivan was not a particularly large man at six
feet and a hundred and ninety pounds, but he was quick
and determined in a fight. He grabbed the boar by the
neck and jerked it off the limp body of his friend, and
both fell to the ground. Mike was on the back of the
animal, one leg curled underneath, and the boar whipping
furiously from side to side with his massive head.

John-Morgan had covered the length of the tunnel with
impressive speed for a man on his knees. He paused with
his pistol drawn where the tunnel let into the latrine, but
he too could get no clear shot as Mike and the horrible
animal rolled together as if glued, Mike screaming garbled
curses and the boar bellowing primeval thunder. Mike
tried to point his pistol at the head of the boar several
times without success, but then, in a pure adrenalin surge
of survival blindness, he brought the muzzle of the pistol
to the ear of the Grand Dragon and fired.

A huge flash of white-orange flame burst from the end
of the forty-four. In daylight the flash appeared to be two
feet long. In darkness it would have sent out a flame six
feet or more. The thickets of the latrine jumped, sending
down a cascade of dead leaves; and the Grand Dragon
crumpled and fell motionless.

Bubba and Lloyd arrived only seconds later. John-
Morgan and Bubba rushed over to Vinnie, and Lloyd
made straight for Mike.

He lay on his back with the boar partially on top of
him. Mike coiled and writhed to roll the filthy animal off.
Lloyd pulled hard at the boar's hind legs and Mike flipped
loose. A trickle of blood ran behind the animal's right ear.
He was completely still, but he was breathing.

"Not hurt," Mike gasped, his eyes wild but lucid, a tic
twitching now at the corner of his mouth. He sat up, sway-
ing. "Not hurt."

"Good Lord, he's still alive," said a startled Lloyd as

he looked closely at the great hulk of the boar.

"Shoot the bastard!" yelled Bubba.

Lloyd reached for the revolver in Mike's right hand, but Mike jerked it away and shouted in a wild voice, "No, goddamn it, no! No more killing around here, not around me! No more goddamn killing, do you hear me? No killing of nothing. I can't stand it! I can't stand it anymore!"

Lloyd drew back in amazement. Michael Sullivan seemed a man possessed. Terror and rage surged through his voice, and desperation haunted his eyes. He was close to the edge of whatever it was he feared falling into—hanging on, but only barely.

"No more killing, ever," he cried as he furiously scrabbled out of the latrine and down the tunnel to the outside.

"We'll look after Vinnie," said John-Morgan. "You better see about Mike."

"Yeah," Lloyd stammered. "I'll go after him, right."

Vinnie began to regain consciousness as John-Morgan wiped away the blood and inspected his wounds. There were no facial injuries. On his right forearm he had a four-inch laceration about a quarter of an inch deep. A superficial vein in that area had been opened by the tusks, which was why there was so much bleeding. The left arm was ploughed with a two-inch gash of similar depth, and one maroon puncture wound appeared just below the elbow. But the heavy clothing Vinnie wore had protected him from more serious and deeper wounds. He had been lucky. Very lucky.

John-Morgan left him with Bubba and crawled over to the Grand Dragon. He closely examined the area behind the right ear and could find no bullet hole, only a furrow cut through the scalp of the boar by the close passage of the .44 slug. "He missed him," said John-Morgan. "The concussion of the muzzle blast must have knocked this bugga out."

"We better be getting out of here. He looks like he might be coming around."

"Lemme get a look at him first," said Vinnie, trembling

as he got up and pressed his T-shirt against his wounds. When he reached the Grand Dragon and looked down at his massive bulk, the murderous tusks, and the shiny path the bullet had cut across his head, all Vinnie could say was, "Holy shit! Ho-lee shee-it!"

GUILT AND PENANCE

EMERGING FROM the thicket, Lloyd caught sight of Mike making his way up the side of the old fort. He found him in the gun pit, sitting on the remains of the broken cannon, his face a wreck of despair. Without speaking, he eased down next to Mike.

"Are you here to save my soul, Father?" Mike snorted bitterly.

"Does it need saving?"

"Better question might be, Do I even have a soul?"

"Did you leave it in Vietnam?"

"If there are things such as souls, I left mine scattered over a couple of hundred square miles back there."

"There are such things as souls, Mike. Do you really doubt that you have one?"

"Look, Lloyd, you're a nice guy, but you don't have a clue about what the hell my life has been like. You don't know the things I've done. It's easier to ignore the possibility that when I die, I will be judged for my actions than to contemplate what will happen to me if there really is life after death. I don't bother God, so I don't want to be bothered, OK?"

"You think that what you did in Vietnam was so bad that God can't possibly forgive you?"

"God? What God? Where was He when I was put in a Huey and given a machine gun and taught to kill? Where was He when I grew to like it? Where was He when I finally loved it? I was just a fuckin' kid, but I became a killer."

Mike's voice began to rise, his face a splotchy red.

Tears darkened his eyes. "I shot up whole villages, gunned down people as they ran from their stinking little huts. I fuckin' loved it, and when I got back to the base, I'd get stoned out of my mind . . . then joke about it with my buddies. For kicks when I wasn't shooting up the countryside, I'd go into town, pay a few lousy bucks to screw twelve-year olds. When I was screwing them, I didn't look at them because I hated their nasty gook-ass faces. I hated all the gooks, theirs and ours."

"Have you ever talked about this to anybody before, Mike?" asked Lloyd.

"Shit no! Out of character. I'm a fuckin' war hero. Medal of Honor winner. Heroes don't do the shit I've done."

"The things you've done are part of war. They're terrible, but you were in a war and things are different in war. You can't be judged on the same standard as peace time. Combat is a kind of temporary insanity for those involved in it." Lloyd was calm but conscious of his priestly tone.

"Lloyd, God bless you man, but you don't know what the fuck you're talking about. They weren't all like me. They didn't all like what they were doing. You know that little medal I won for saving John-Morgan's ass? Well let me tell you something that nobody else knows, and then maybe you'll understand what's eating at me. The pilot of that chopper didn't want to go back in to get John-Morgan and his buddies. So I put a gun to the copilot's head and threatened to shoot him if he didn't. When the son of a bitch still refused, I shot the poor bastard in the leg and then put the pistol back to his head. I would have blown his brains out if the pilot hadn't taken the ship back to the village. Both of them got killed because of me. There is no forgiveness for that, and there is no God that would allow it."

At that point Mike started to sob. His left arm dangled at his side; the other arced across his eyes. His body shook as low and painful cries emptied him. Lloyd reached out, put his arm around his friend, and drew him close, speaking softly·in a strange motherly tone.

"I know it's been a long time since you thought about it, Mike. But do you remember the Gospel story about the cripple that Jesus cured when he was in Capernaum? It's the one where the crippled man was lowered through a hole in the roof on a stretcher because the crowds were pressing so hard to hear Jesus speak that they wouldn't part to let the stretcher pass."

Mike regained control, but he didn't sit up or acknowledge Lloyd. After a moment, Lloyd continued.

"When the stretcher was finally put before Jesus, the crippled man shouted, 'Jesus, Son of David, have pity on me. I have been like this since I was a child because of my sins and the sins of my ancestors. Have mercy on me and heal me.' Then Jesus touched the man and said, 'Arise, pick up your stretcher and walk, your sins are forgiven.' Do you remember that, Mike?"

Mike finally sat up, wiped his eyes, and said in a detached voice, "Yeah, I remember."

"Do you remember what happened next?"

"What's the point in all this, Lloyd?"

"Do you remember what happened next?"

"OK, he picked up his stretcher and walked. End of story."

"No, it's not the end of the story, nor is it the point of the story. After the man walked, the elders of the village reproached Jesus and asked him who he was that he could forgive sins. They said only God could forgive sins, and they called him a blasphemer. Then Jesus asked them— and this is the most important part of the story—which is easier, to say 'Pick up your stretcher and walk,' or 'Your sins are forgiven'?" Confidence steadied Lloyd's voice now.

Mike was beginning to show irritation. "Sorry Lloyd, I don't follow you."

"That's because you don't understand what Jesus was really saying. The man wasn't crippled because he had some terrible physical disease, he was crippled because of his guilt. He thought he was so bad that he deserved to be crippled, and his mind made it so. It was a psycho-somatic illness. Jesus recognized it for what it was and cured him by forgiving him."

"So what's all this got to do with me?"

Lloyd got up in exasperation and walked to the other side of the gun pit. Then he turned and faced Mike, threw his hands in the air, and shouted, "Dear God, these Irish-men have such thick skulls. Please help me with this one!"

Mike looked up at Lloyd in surprise. Lloyd quickly knelt at his feet and took Mike's hands in his.

"Don't you see, Michael Sullivan, this guilt that you have carried around inside of you for so long has crippled you? Let yourself be forgiven, find the faith that you once had, and free yourself! For the love of God, man, free yourself."

The look on Mike's face slowly started to change. Af-ter a long and thoughtful silence, he spoke. With the back of his left hand he rubbed his eyes like a sleepy child. "It's been a long time, but will you hear my confession, Father?"

"I think you've already been to confession, Mike. Just say a good Act of Contrition."

Thirty years or more had passed since he had last ut-tered the words of the confessional prayer, but Mike re-peated them from memory without hesitation as Lloyd quietly said the prayers of absolution and made the sign of the cross over Mike's head. When they finished and were sitting silently on the remains of the Breastplate of St. Patrick, Mike looked at Lloyd and asked, "What about my penance? There's always a penance after confession."

Lloyd smiled and thought for a moment. Then he said, "I think you've done enough penance to last you a life-time."

When Lloyd and Mike arrived back at camp, John-Morgan had just finished suturing the wounds on Vinnie's arms. Now he was bandaging them.

"Normally I would have done this in the ER, but I don't know how long it'll be before we get back to town, so I went ahead and closed the wounds. You'll need some antibiotics and a tetanus shot when we get back." With his cell phone, John-Morgan called the Chatham County police and told them about the skeleton. They could only come in on the high tide, so the detective in charge said that someone would be out the next day.

A breeze picked up, and everyone moved closer to the fire. Vinnie managed to hold a beer in his right hand despite the bandages. After a long pull from the bottle, he said, "What about that pig? What's gonna happen to him?"

"He's probably gone by now," said John-Morgan. "I stayed for a little while after you got out and watched him. When he started trying to get up, I left. He'll have a bad headache, but he'll be OK."

That night, around the campfire, the entire episode was relived again and again. Vinnie got a little drunk and thanked Mike several times for saving him from the Grand Dragon. Around eleven, he announced that he was ready for bed. John-Morgan and Bubba helped him into his sleeping bag and then crawled into theirs. By the flickering firelight, into the early hours of the next morning, Mike and Lloyd talked of killing and healing, living and dying, growing old and growing wise.

THE GRAVE

"DAMN!" SAID JOHN-MORGAN as he looked through his binoculars. "I don't believe this. Of all the people in the world to show up out here!"

Mike was standing next to him on the river bank and squinting at the police boat out in the distance, a hand shielding his eyes from the sun. "Who is it?"

"Son of a bitch!" John-Morgan kept the glasses to his eyes and followed the boat as it curved back and forth along the creek leading to the rear of Raccoon Island, but he did not respond.

"Who the hell is it?" Mike repeated, in a somewhat more impatient voice.

"I didn't know they were bringing a television crew. This really screws things up. We can kiss this place good-bye now, cause by tonight everybody in Chatham County will know about it."

Mike snatched the binoculars away from John-Morgan and peered anxiously at the distance. He fiddled with the focus for a second and then let out a dramatic sigh. "Damn," he muttered as he shook his head. "You were right. Of all the people to show up out here."

Vinnie, Bubba, and Lloyd had heard the sound of the boat's engine and walked down the end of the pier. "Right on time," said Bubba as the boat navigated the final turn in the creek and headed to the bank where they stood.

"Are we all packed and ready to leave when they finish?" asked John-Morgan.

"We can leave right now if you want to. We're all set," answered Bubba.

"Naw, I want to hang around here for this. Kind of see what else they find. We've got a good two hours before the tide is too low to get out of here. They ought to be able to get most of what they want by then."

The engines growled into reverse with a hearty throat as the props strained to slow it and idle up to where John-Morgan and his friends were standing. Captain Billy Strickland, chief of detectives for the Chatham County Police Department, stood on the bow. He tossed a line to Mike, who pulled the boat in close to the bank and tied it around a palmetto.

Standing in the back of the boat, dressed in tight blue jeans, wearing a western-style, wool-lined mauve suede jacket and expensive soft-kid, mail-order hiking boots, was the star reporter and television personality of WTOC-TV. She looked up at John-Morgan and said, "Well, aren't you even gonna say hello to an old friend?"

John-Morgan smiled, reached down and grasped her outstretched hand, and helped the reporter out of the boat. She slipped a little on the uneven bank. John-Morgan caught her and held on till she regained her footing. Then he said, "Hello, Charlotte. It's been a long time."

"Well I should say it has," said Charlotte sweetly. "It's been years since I've seen you." She kissed John-Morgan on the cheek, then twirled around and looked at Bubba. Charlotte let out a little sorority-girl squeal. "Why, Bubba Silverman, it's been a long time since I've seen you too!" She hugged him, pressing her breasts intentionally into his chest hard enough to prompt a wary, "You haven't changed a bit, Charlotte. Just as pretty as you were in high school."

"Oh my goodness, it's Mike Sullivan too!" Charlotte positively oozed as she hugged Mike in the same way. Then she looked over at Lloyd, and in a suddenly dignified manner put out her hand. "Father Bryan, I am so pleased to see you again. I'm sure you don't remember me, but I'm Charlotte Drayton. You were gracious enough to let me do a story on you and the wonderful work you've been doing in the poorer parts of town. It's been several years now, but I've never forgotten how moved I was by all the good you've done."

Save the bullshit for the airwaves, Lloyd thought, but he smiled and shook her hand. "I remember you very well, Miss Drayton, and I greatly appreciated the kind things you had to say about our efforts in the inner city. The publicity was a great help to us in reaching out to the kids of that area. Thanks again for all you did."

"Don't mention it, don't mention it all. The station is always ready to do what it can." Then Charlotte looked over at Vinnie, who was totally unprepared for her green-eyed beauty and heavy Southern charm. He was quickly overcome. Charlotte sensed this and moved in for the kill as she glanced back at her old beau. "And who is this handsome new friend of yours, John-Morgan? He looks like a movie star." Then she noticed the bandages and said, "Oh my goodness, darlin', what happened to your arms?"

A smitten Vinnie blurted out, "I got attacked by a wild hog, damn near killed me. Would have if Mike hadn't gotten him off me just in the nick of time."

"Oh my Lord." John-Morgan put his hands up as if to say "hold it for a second" and proceeded to introduce Charlotte to Vinnie.

John-Morgan had had enough, so in a jocular mockery of propriety he said, "Miss Drayton, allow me to present Dr. Vincent DiNapoli. Dr. DiNapoli, my old and dear friend, Miss Charlotte Drayton."

"My distinct pleasure, Dr. DiNapoli." In a teasing voice she added, "Tell me, suga', are you married?"

Everybody laughed, and when Vinnie replied that he was, Charlotte put on a very sad look. "Darn it, everybody on this island is. What's a single girl to do in a place with no eligible men?" The whole crowd laughed again and then began to move toward the campsite. Charlotte fell in next to John-Morgan and hooked her arm around his. "You've just got to tell me all about your children and your practice. I can't believe it's been so long. I must tell you I feel just dreadful about the way I treated you the last time we were together. You know, out there at Little Tybee?"

"It all worked out for the best, Charlotte. I'm doing just fine. Ann Marie and I live in my grandparents' old place out at Isle of Hope. We've got two boys and a girl."

"Oh, John-Morgan, I was just teasin'. I know all about you. I've kept up with you over the years. I'm a reporter, it's my business to know. You know I'd never forget you. We had some wonderful times together. I was such a fool."

Charlotte was looking up at him as she flirted, but he kept looking straight ahead. "I know all about you, too. I see you just about every night on the news. I'll swear you're just as pretty now as you were in 1965."

"That's sweet of you to say," cooed Charlotte as she

tightened her hold on his arm. "You always were the sweetest man I ever knew."

"Do me a favor, Charlotte. For old time's sake."

"Anything, if I can."

"I know you're here to do a story. Just don't let on where this place really is. If people figure out where we are, they'll tear this place apart hunting for things. I'll help you with your story if you don't tell anybody how to get here, OK?"

Relieved, though perhaps also a little disappointed that John-Morgan had not rebuked her for her intimacy, Charlotte smiled. "It's a deal." Without another word, and without touching him again, she turned and started walking toward the campsite. Her flattery and caresses gave him a passing weariness of guilt, a vague sense of letting go again. Innocence uncomfortably revisited.

Around the campfire, John-Morgan filled in Billy Strickland and the other two police officers on how they had found the skeleton. Charlotte had her cameraman tape the entire conversation. Then she taped John-Morgan as he showed Billy to the opening in the Schwarzwald where they had entered on their search for the latrine.

Although it had been thirty years, Charlotte had visited Raccoon Island before with John-Morgan. She remembered how dense and foreboding the Schwarzwald had been, and how the loud grunting sounds coming from the thickets had frightened her. That fear drew a chill over her now as Billy Strickland spoke.

"Well, Miss Drayton, we're about to go in. If you'll stay out of our way, and aren't scared to crawl in there, I don't see any reason why you can't get a little video of this here grave site."

Channel Eleven had always been good to Billy over the years, making sure that his picture appeared on the tube and that he was fully credited with the busts he was in on. He figured the good PR helped him move up in the department, so he watched out for WTOC just as it watched out for him. Besides, Miss Drayton was awfully good-looking. He was proud just to be around her. Billy didn't know of a girl in her twenties in the whole town of Savannah who could hold a candle to her, and hell, she was in her late forties. Fine woman, thought Billy as he patted the pistol in his shoulder holster and said aloud, "Any damn hawg comes at you in there, Miss Drayton, he'll have to deal with me and this here three-fifty-seven first." He was about to add, I took down a three-hundred-pound nigger once with this thing, but just in time he remembered about Lloyd and just finished by saying, "I'll take care of you, mam." Then he dropped to his knees and started to crawl into the thicket.

Only John-Morgan went in with police. There wasn't enough room for the other campers around the grave. The bright light from the TV camera lit up the latrine with a garish brilliance, but John-Morgan forced himself to watch as the police carefully unearthed the skeleton and placed it into a body bag uncomfortably like the ones he knew in Vietnam.

John-Morgan looked at his watch and told Captain Strickland that in about another thirty minutes the tide would be too low for them to leave. They still had to check through the dirt under the skeleton for more clues, and it would take a lot longer than half an hour to do that. Then Billy pushed his hat up on his head and wiped his brow. "Miss Drayton, you got all you need, honey?"

"Everything I need, Captain Strickland. I really appreciate your help, as always. This is gonna make a great story and you're the reason. I can't thank you enough."

"Well, I'm proud to be able to help you." Turning to John-Morgan, he added: "It don't look like we can finish up in time to catch the tide outta here. It's against police procedure to leave the scene unattended, but we ain't got no choice. I hadn't got a man to spare with the parade comin' up, and this is out in the middle of nowhere. Procedure'll have to take a back seat. We'll have to come back, Dr. Hartman. We don't need ya'll anymore though. If you boys don't go tellin' anybody about where this place is, and if Miss Drayton can hep us out too, I think everything will be all right 'til Monday. We can't get back out here 'til then 'cause of the parade. Every man we got is gonna be doin' parade duty over the weekend. We can't spare a soul 'til after it's over. Ya'll think you can keep quiet about this place 'til then?"

"I know *we* can," said John-Morgan immediately, and then looked at Charlotte. She smiled blankly and pleasantly in his direction.

"That's no problem with us either," said Charlotte, still focused on John-Morgan. "We don't plan on letting on exactly where this place is anyway. We don't want people digging up the fort. I understand it has historical significance and needs to be preserved."

"Well, that's just fine," said Billy as he gathered up his things and started for the tunnel. "I guess it's time to be gettin' outta this place anyway. It gives me the creeps."

As Charlotte leaned over to enter the tunnel, John-Morgan touched her. "Thanks," he said.

Charlotte patted his hand. "Any time, John-Morgan."

A FAREWELL TO THE ISLAND

THE DISCOVERY of the skeleton spoiled all the plans for fully excavating the latrine and finding the fabled Driscoll treasure. St. Patrick's Day was tomorrow, so the fortune hunters were obliged to get back to town for the festivities. They spoke eagerly of returning to the island soon, but they were all professionals with schedules and obligations, and they realized that an early return to search for gold was unlikely.

"Do you think that was a man we found?" asked Vinnie as he wiggled into the port-side captain's chair.

John-Morgan slipped the ignition key into its slot and tilted down the engines. "Pump the priming balls for me, Lloyd," he said, as the twin Mercuries settled into place on the transom.

"Yeah, by the shape of the pelvic outlet. He also looked like a laborer. He had a lot of bone formation at the origins and insertions of the muscles in his arms and legs."

Bubba had been listening to John-Morgan as he stacked the last cooler in the back of the boat and joined the conversation. "He was wearing work boots too. I saw the steel caps to the boots down at his toes. There wasn't any leather left, but the soles were rubber and I looked at the bottom of one. It said 'Goodyear,' plain as day."

John-Morgan hit the ignition and the two engines coughed a few times, then roared to life amid a cloud of blue smoke. As the engines warmed, everyone gazed back at the island for one last look. John-Morgan then put the engines in gear and crept his boat down the creek.

Bubba stood next to John-Morgan and Vinnie, watching the sonar show increasing depth as the boat moved further away from the island and deeper into the marshy expanse. "Captain Strickland told me they found some coins by the skeleton about where a pocket would be."

"Yeah," said John-Morgan, "a 1943 steel penny, a '46 liberty dime, a bus token for the Savannah Bus Company, and a 1950 nickel."

"What about the bullet?" asked Mike. "What kind did he think it was?"

"I talked with him about that, and he thinks it was a nine millimeter. Said it was too short for a thirty-eight special, and it had a full metal jacket. Only automatic pistols use full-metal-jacket stuff. He thinks the gun was probably foreign, because it was so long ago, and not many American pistols were nine-millimeter autos back then."

"Does Strickland have any theories about how he got killed?" asked Lloyd.

"We talked a little about that too, but he said any guess was as good as his. He did think it might be a professional hit. He said he was pretty sure the guy was killed somewhere else and taken to the island and buried."

John-Morgan guided the Grady White out into the open Ogeechee and advanced the throttles, causing the Mercuries to begin a well-tuned mechanical whine as they approached four thousand rpm's. The hull smoothly planed out over the water. The men watched as Ossabaw Island grew larger on the starboard horizon and the last cold fingers of a fading winter whipped around inside the boat. Their cheeks stung, and they were glad that St. Patrick's Day and spring were only a few hours (and days) away. But they were also nostalgic as they watched Raccoon Island and Battery Jasper fade into the distance.

Back on Raccoon Island, down by the borrow pit, the members of the Invisible Empire were finally able to quench their thirsts.

IX

SEAL OF THE CONFESSIONAL

And add the halfpence to the pence
And prayer to shivering prayer, until
You have dried the marrow from the bone

Bless me Father for I have sinned, I confess to Almighty God and you Father that I have sinned.

—OPENING PRAYER OF CONFESSION PRE-VATICAN II

CONSEQUENCES

THREE MONTHS BEFORE the discovery on the island, Abe Bryan's life had hit bottom. He could not quite understand how. Abe had become what he had always feared he would become; and although he bitterly rebuked his folly in assuming that he might escape this fate, he also knew that there was no use in reliving his thousand mistakes. No one could keep from getting old, he told himself, except by dying. Then he scowled and said he was a tiresome fool full of talk-show banalities.

Growing old wasn't what Abe dreaded, but rather growing old in this fashion. He was now what he had heard the white boys say about so many black men, what the crowd of white lawyers down at the old county courthouse on Wright Square called an "Old Nigger." When Abe was young, he had nothing but contempt for that band that shuffled around with those little smiles on their faces that all the "Old Niggers" got when they reached a certain age. It seemed as though time had beaten them into a posture that said: "I've had enough, I ain't got no more fight in me. Ya'll done made me behave." He could see it in their puppet-like gestures, in the way they wore their hair, and most of all in their nice neat white shirts and bow ties and suits that had been pressed so many times they shined. It was the way they followed their wives out of church on Sundays and drove their plain-looking Chevrolets up West Broad Street across the Talmadge Bridge into South Carolina, where they'd have dinner with a bunch of fat old churchgoing ladies who had outlived their husbands and now enjoyed watching other women's "Old Niggers." Abe used to imagine how these "tamed niggers" got grease spots on their Christmas ties and how they'd catch hell for it from their wives.

"Yep," he said, "I'm an Old Nigger now." But he wasn't a proud one.

Abednigo had learned over the years that a lot of those "Old Niggers" had pride, and that gave them perspective. The fried chicken they dropped in their laps didn't matter so much. For Abe, however, everything had changed. It hadn't come for him all at once, it just seemed to seep in on him. He knew that he could never win his wife back, but maybe he could gain a little respect from her. He didn't even dare to think about all the things he had thrown away when it came to his boy, but maybe he could have a little respect from him too.

"Maybe, just maybe they might even come to see me if I ever get so sick I got to go into the nursing home one day. Maybe they might even come to my funeral and cry a little. I ain't never been to a funeral where there wasn't no cryin'. Right now, I don't know of nobody who would cry over me at my funeral. That ain't no way for a man to leave this world."

Abe had lost almost all the money he had garnered over the years. When the moonshine business went bust because of legal whiskey, he had become a respectable property owner and lived off his rents. Over the years, however, he had been forced to sell off almost all of his buildings to pay his gambling debts. Now there was nothing left.

Abe used to have a lot of "moonshine cash" hidden away. Sometimes he'd take twenty or thirty thousand and go to Las Vegas for a week or so. He'd do some gambling, some whoring around with good-looking white girls, and catch a few shows, but mostly he would outfox the government. The IRS had started asking questions about his sources of income, but Bubba Thompson, who used to own all of the slot machines at Thunderbolt and Tybee, had taught him a good trick years ago that kept the IRS happy. Whether or not he had won in Vegas, he'd walk up to the window and declare winnings, pay the IRS, get the receipt, and head back to Savannah. That way he could always say that he got his money from gambling, and he had the tax receipts to prove it.

This ploy had worked for years, but eventually Abe began to lose more in Vegas than he took out there. The booze was also starting to fog up his head. He was well-known in some of the smaller games around Vegas, and the casinos would spot him ten or twenty thousand because they knew he was good for the money. Abe would wire his buddy at the Carver State Bank, who would cover the loss by sending him the cash. As soon as he returned to Savannah he would replace it with cash from his hiding place, and everything would be fine.

As the years went by, Abe's bankroll shrank precipitously. On his most recent trip to Vegas he lost heavily again, but this time the bank refused to cover the loss. Word on the street was that Abe was nearing the end of his stash. He had lost his edge; the booze and his age had finally caught up with him; and he was heavily in debt from gambling both in Savannah and out west. The worst thing was that everybody knew it.

When Abe couldn't cover his losses, a few boys from Vegas came back with him to Savannah. They weren't there to help celebrate Epiphany. They wanted their money, and they wanted it now, and it was clear that serious bodily harm would befall Abe if he couldn't come up with the cash. The words of his friend at the bank now returned to eat through his gut and soul: "I ain't coverin' you for shit no more. I damn near didn't get back what you got from me in December. Remember that? My ass almost got fired 'cause of you. I told you that was it, and I meant it. You turned into a worthless nigger."

Abe was able to hunt around and find a little money from some of the people who owed him. He also got a big chunk from the quick sale of his last piece of rental property, but he was still short—more than he could ever come up with as long as he lived. The guys from Vegas got on the phone with their bosses and were told to squeeze the rest, but Abe was sure he could find the money if they gave him a week or so. The big boys agreed, but their henchmen stayed around Savannah to act as a visible reminder to Abe that he wasn't in debt to a charity. He told them to enjoy the city: "It's a beautiful town, the oldest in Georgia." They didn't seem amused. Now Abednigo was desperate. There was only one way out.

For years Abe had thought about what he had seen Big Tony O'Boyle do on Raccoon Island. Turning him into the police had never crossed his mind. A man like Abednigo Bryan didn't operate like that. He thought that one day he might need to use what he knew about Tony O'Boyle. Now that time had come.

It was difficult getting an appointment to see Mr. O'Boyle right away, but with a little kowtowing and persuasion, Abe found himself sitting in Tony's lavish office the next morning. The secretary seated him across from a gloriously ornate cherry-wood desk, polished to a glowing-coal shine and covered with knick-knacks and mementos Tony had accumulated over the years. On the corner sat a large blueshell crab dipped in polyurethane and mounted on a wooden base. It had a rope around the sides with Tony's name on it spelled out in little shells. Abe guessed that this had been a gift from one of the marijuana-smuggling Thunderbolt shrimpers whom Tony had represented successfully during the 1970's. Though caught with four tons of Columbia red, he had gotten off real light. It was the talk of the town for months. Some people claimed that Tony had made hundreds of thousands of dollars off that drug money. Abe didn't doubt it one a bit, especially knowing what he did about Raccoon Island.

O'Boyle's office was on the third floor of the O'Boyle Building, situated in the corner overlooking a park from enormous windows that ran the entire height of the fourteen-foot room. Tony even had his own balcony. One could walk on to the balcony and touch the branches of one of the oak trees that surrounded the building. Abe shook his head and muttered to himself. "There's very few white people and no niggers at all that got a place this fine to work in. I wonder how Mr. O'Boyle's gonna feel like when he hears what I got to tell him?" Abe grinned a little but reminded himself that Tony O'Boyle was no pushover. Only thing about Mr. Tony is that he's old now, thought Abe. He ain't got the fight or the years left that he used to. This old man's just gonna want me to go away.

Abe was gazing at the various Savannah-scene paintings that colored the office walls when the door swung open and in walked Big Tony. He still had a quick step and was in great shape for a man of eighty-three. Tony wore a dark blue double-breasted suit with a snappy hand-tied bow tie. The latter were his sartorial trademark. For years he was just about the only man in the city who wore them, but now they were back in style. Tony had always predicted they would be. He used to have them ordered specially for him at the Men's Quality Shop when it was on Broughton Street. During the warm months, he would also wear a "skimmer," a crisp straw hat popular around the turn of the century. This, too, was one of his trademarks, and he relished the singularity it imparted.

As he walked around his desk he said a quick "Morning, Abednigo," without even looking at him. "What's this I hear that's so damn important you had to see me right away?" He said it with that authority and air that Abe had heard so many times over the years from white men, and what it really meant was, "Look here nigger, I'm an important man and this better be good." Abe almost smiled to himself, because this *was* going to be good!

After ostentatiously arranging some papers on his desk, Tony finally let his gaze fall upon Abe, who was dressed in a suit too large for him because of all the weight he had lost over the last few years—but it still didn't shine in the knees or the seat. Abe was aware of and cautious about such things. He blinked a few times from behind

his black horn-rimmed glasses with the thick cataract
lenses that made his eyes seem twice as big as they really
were.

Although Tony had known Abe all of his life, he
hadn't seen him in a long time. It struck him now how
old this old nigger had become. Then he remembered that
he and Abe were about the same age. He, too, had grown
old. With a sigh Tony softened a little, and he rephrased
his question in a more modest tone. "What can I help you
with, Abe?"

Abednigo leaned forward in his chair, elbows on his
knees and hands beneath his chin. "Well, Mr. Tony, it's
like this. I'm gonna come right to the point, suh. You
knows that I'm a gamblin' man, kinda use to be a high
roller in my time." Tony leaned back in his chair and
smiled. "Well, you see suh, I done got myself in a heap
a trouble with them bad boys out dere in dat Las Vegas
place. They even sent back two real mean fellas with me
this time to collect what I owes. I done paid down all but
$23,000 and I is tapped out. I cashed in the whole lot and
I is still short and I ain't got nowhere to turn. Them folks
is right here in Savannah, a waitin' on me to come up
with the rest or they is gonna hurt poor ol' Abe bad.
That's what they done said, suh. I is in need now and
that's a fact."

Tony's grin widened as he shook his head a little. His
blue bow tie with the red polka dots moved under his chin
as his head went from side to side. Then he leaned forward and asked: "So you want me to lend you $23,000?"
Again he was really saying, Yeah, in a million years!

Abednigo sat back in his chair, straightened up, and
looked squarely at Tony O'Boyle. The shuck-and-jive accent was gone this time, as was the step-n-fetchit attitude.
"No, Mr. O'Boyle, I don't want you to loan me $23,000.
I want you to give me $23,000. Really, you might say I
want you to sort of make a payment to me of $23,000 for
services rendered over the last forty years or so. You
might say it's kind of a tip for being a good nigger and

keeping my mouth shut about something I saw you do on Raccoon Island back in 1953. You do remember what you did on Raccoon Island in 1953, don't you, Mr. O'Boyle? The grave, the body of your little brother that you buried there? I was still cooking shine out there then. You didn't have a clue I was there. I saw you come up in your nice little mahogany boat with that real fine Evinrude on the back. I followed you back to the bushes, and when you had finished and gone, I dug up the body and moved it to another location. I even took a few things off it just to prove I was there and who I had dug up. That poor boy with that bullet hole in the back of his head. What a terrible thing! Why the next day when you and him turned up missing, I even said a little prayer for your safe return. And my goodness, how we all were amazed that you had managed to save yourself from that stormy and treacherous Ossabaw Sound. You must have been in the Boy Scouts to have survived the way you did for those two days, Mr. O'Boyle. The whole town was worried about you back then, even us colored folks."

The last thing that Abe thought he would feel for Tony O'Boyle was pity, but that was what he did feel in some strange way when he saw the man change before his very eyes. Abe was a little scared at first because he thought Tony was going to have a heart attack and die right then and there. Then Abe would never get the $23,000 he needed.

Tony gripped the arms of his chair and sat back slowly. His eyes fixed on something behind Abe's head and his own head tilted back a little. His mouth opened and his chest heaved; and first he turned white, then afterward gray.

Eventually the blood returned to Tony's face, and slowly he nodded his head. Then he said in a low, calm voice, still without looking at Abednigo, "Yeah, OK, no problem. I can give you the money now, but we've got to talk. I can watch out for you for a long time, if you're reasonable about it. I'll give you no cause to talk. You can carry this to your grave, can't you?"

With that, Tony fixed on Abe. His eyes looked like those of a little child whose mother had just died. For a moment Abe had a sense of shame and guilt at what he had done to the man, but then he remembered what Tony had done to his own brother. Which man should feel more shame? Abednigo wondered.

Without saying another word, Tony got up and went to a closet just off the office. He opened a cabinet to expose a safe. After several nervous tries, he got the combination right and opened the door. There was a stack of money on one of the shelves, and Tony picked up two bundles, one in each hand. He returned to the desk and sat the bundles down in front of Abe.

Another man might have been impressed with such a pile of cash or the fact that someone would keep so large an amount on hand. Not Abe. Back when times were good he had often kept that much around the house. It was in smaller bills too, so the piles were higher. In his secret hiding place outside the house, he kept a couple hundred thousand in cash. That was real money back then.

Tony counted out the money and then went scrounging around for something to put it in. In the bathroom he finally found a paper bag his wife had left after one of her famous Town and Country shopping trips. Without thinking, they both helped each other place the cash into the bag. Abe tucked it under his arm and started to leave without saying a word.

"Abednigo, I want you to know why I did it." Abe nodded, so Tony continued. "Do you remember all those killings that were taking place at about the same time, back in the early fifties? The ones where the bodies were all chopped up? They kept finding arms and legs all over town?"

"Yeah, I remember that."

"Well, do you remember the killer was never caught?"

"Yessah."

"The reason he was never caught was that it was my brother doing the killing. He was retarded, mentally ill. I just happened to find out about it before the police because I got suspicious and went though some of his things. I was horrified. I couldn't believe it. He was an animal. My brother. If it got out, it would have killed my parents, ruined my entire family. Al would have been sent to a mental hospital for the rest of his life and kept like an animal in a cage. I guess like the animal that he was. So I decided to do away with him myself and spare everyone a lot of tragedy and pain. I've carried this with me my entire life, and you're the only other person who knows."

"I'm the only person who ever will know, Mr. O'Boyle. I'm not planning on coming back to you for no more. I quit the fast life. All I want now is two things: for them boys from Vegas to leave me alone—and this here money will buy me that. The other is the love and respect of my boy. But never mind. Just in case, I've taken certain precautions against you doing anything to me so as to keep me quiet. If you knows what I'm gettin' at. Somethin' bad happens to me, then everybody's gonna know about Raccoon Island. I die peaceful in my sleep and the secret dies with me."

Abe's extraordinary calm stunned Tony a little. He stood there stupidly for a moment, then blurted out: "Oh no, nothing like that. I couldn't stand another death on my hands, no matter what. For God's sake, no. Just be careful with that money. I mean walking home with it. You might get hit over the head. It's bad on the streets now."

Abe smiled. "That's no problem, Mr. O'Boyle. Them Vegas boys is waitin' right out front in a car, and I'm gonna give this to them right away. Then I think I'm gonna go over to my son's church for noon Mass. You goes to Mass at the cathedral, don't you, Mr. O'Boyle? I'll bet you've even taken Communion from my boy. He's the pastor at that church."

With that, Abednigo turned and walked out of the fine office, closing the big mahogany door with its shiny brass door knob quietly behind him. "High roller in my time," he muttered to himself, chuckling inwardly. "*High* roller."

FATHER AND SON

As HE WALKED ALONG Gwinnett Street to Abercorn, Abe wondered how much harder life would seem if he didn't have the beauty of his city around him to ease the pain. Once he had resented all these wonderful homes because no black person was allowed to own a house in this neighborhood. Now, life had mellowed Abe. He was glad that someone, black or white, had taken the time and care to create such loveliness. He never ceased to be amazed at how time had changed him in so many ways.

As he turned the corner on to Abercorn and began walking up the street, the twin spires of the Cathedral of Saint John the Baptist came into view. Whenever Abe saw a Catholic church, he thought of his wife. For years he could never understand her devotion to that religion, the way her life seemed to revolve around its calendar of events and feast days. Back when she had converted, there was not even one black Catholic priest in the entire state of Georgia and only a handful of blacks who belonged to the Catholic church.

Abe never cared a thing for religion back then, but it used to make him angry that his wife would be part of a church that didn't even have a black preacher. He used to accuse her of what he called "suckin' up to the white boys," saying that she must have some kind of a "thing" about how everything white was better, even when it came to God.

At first Elaine would try to explain to him that it was the religion itself that attracted her, but after a while she just started ignoring him. She did make it clear to Abednigo that Lloyd was going to be raised as a Catholic and he had better keep his mouth shut about the church around her boy.

As he walked across Lafayette Square and approached the broad stone steps of the great white cathedral, Abe admitted that he had never been much of a father to his son. He remembered how in later years he had been glad that Elaine Mae had been so involved with her church because of the influence it had had on Lloyd, but now he tried to fight off those feelings of guilt as he entered the church and walked up the center aisle to the front pew. Abe had been there before, but it still took his breath away everytime he came back. Once, he had spent most of an afternoon just looking at the statues, the paintings, and the stained-glass windows. He never forgot how surprised he was to find a stained-glass window with a black saint on it, and a black man on one of the ceiling murals. Now his own son, a black man, was the pastor of the grandest church in the whole state of Georgia.

Abednigo eased himself into the first pew and waited for Mass to begin. He was looking intently at the window above the altar—the one that depicted the baptism of Christ by his cousin John—when the bell rang, and out walked his own son dressed in the rich robes of the priesthood, flanked by two white altar boys. There came, deep within him, a feeling that Abe had grown to love, to long for. He decided that it wasn't so much pride as the satisfaction of knowing that such a significant part of him had become someone special, something pure and good, despite the failings of an absent father. Abe finally decided that it was relief, perhaps, more than anything else.

The Reverend Bryan spotted his father immediately, but did not acknowledge him. He feared that he had come wanting something that would embarrass them both, that he would have to relive that type of pain once more. During the Mass, Lloyd prayed for the strength to endure what he felt lay ahead.

When the Mass was over and Lloyd was in the sacristy changing into his street clothes, Abe rose from his pew, climbed the sanctuary steps, and walked behind the massive main altar of white Italian marble. He quickly found his son, who had been half-waiting, half-wanting to leave as quickly as possible. They were alone, and stood facing each other silently for a few seconds.

"Hello, Daddy. It's been a while since I've seen you. How have you been?"

"I been fine, son, just fine. How's your mother? I haven't seen her in such a long time. You look fine, son. I was hoping that I'd get to hear you preach a sermon. Don't they do that in the Catholic church?"

"Momma's fine, Daddy. Yes, we preach sermons in the Catholic church, but not at the noon Mass. It's designed to be short so people can come during their lunch hour and then get back to work. What do you want, Daddy?"

The inquiry was a little terse, and it hurt Abe. But he understood. He understood so very much now. Abe dropped his head a little and took a deep breath.

"I use' ta want a lot, son. So damn much that it made me blind to the things that was really important. The things that count. And I wasted a lot of time, too, on trashy things and things that don't last. But I been thinkin', maybe I still got time enough to do somethin' right with my life. Somethin' that will set me straight with God."

Abe shifted his weight, looked at the floor and then back at Lloyd, and continued. "I don't know much about God, but I 'spect that He knows a lot about me. I ain't proud of what He knows either and I want to set it right. I'm ready to get religion, to get saved, like they say. I guess you could say I'm scared, being that dying ain't so far off for me now. But I heard this preacher say on TV one day that Jesus don't care what your reason is just so you is ready to change your life and be saved. If that's true, then I'm ready. I thought that since you is my son and all, that you'd help me to be saved, even though I ain't been much of a daddy to you no how. I don't want nothin' more from you than that, Lloyd, just to be a Cath-

olic like your mamma and to know Jesus like she do, and
be saved."

By the time Abednigo had finished, he was a pitiful
sight in the eyes of his son. There was no doubt about his
sincerity. Lloyd really didn't know quite what to say or
think, but he was touched as he never thought he could
be by his father.

"OK, Daddy. I'll arrange for you to have instructions
on becoming a Catholic. It's not easy and it's not an overnight thing. The Catholic church doesn't work the way
that TV preachers do. It takes time and study."

"I got nothing but time now, son. I 'spose it's near
'bout time I done studied something other than raisin'
hell. You make the arrangements and I'll be back to Mass
tomorrow and you can tell me then. Oh, and thanks for
doin' this. I know it don't make you too happy to be
around your old man and I understand. Well, guess I'll
be easin' out now, so bye, son. It's been good to see you
again."

With that, Abe turned, straightened his back, and
walked out of the cathedral with a feeling that, perhaps,
he had already been saved right then and there.

As for Lloyd, after his father was gone, he went out
into the sanctuary and then to the side altar on the right
devoted to the Virgin Mary. After lighting a candle, he
knelt at the altar and prayed and thought. Mostly he
thought. Later that day he enrolled his father in religious
instruction classes and then called his mother to tell her
the news.

CONFESSIONS

AFTER ABE LEFT, Tony cancelled the rest of his appoint-
ments and sequestered himself in his office to think. A little before noon he did the only thing he really could do—
he called his son and told him to come to the office. Big
Tony told Little Tony the entire story, from the murders

his Uncle Al had committed to the money he had just given Abe.

At first, Little Tony was shocked by the story and overcome by a feeling of helplessness. As he and his father talked, however, he began to regain composure and strength. They discussed many options, from having Abe killed to going to Raccoon Island and searching for Al's remains. In the end the two O'Boyles agreed that the only thing they could do was go along with Abe and hope for the best.

After they had discarded the idea of looking for Al's body, silence fell on the room for several minutes. Then Tony spoke.

"I just want you to know I think you did the right thing, Daddy. I know it must have been the hardest thing you ever had to do in your life, but you saved everybody an awful lot of pain and suffering, most of all Uncle Al."

Big Tony looked at his son for several seconds and finally replied. "That means a lot to me son. I just hope that what I did doesn't ruin your chances of being governor. If I can get you elected, you'll be the first Irish Catholic to ever hold that office. Come to think of it, you'll be the first person from Savannah to be governor since the royal governor, James Wright, back before the revolution. Nothing must go wrong. I've worked night and day on this for the last three years, and I think I've played all of my cards right. Everybody tells me the nomination is yours for the asking, and you're a shoo-in to be elected. That's why I'm so upset about what happened today. Even though it doesn't involve you, the fallout could ruin you in the state. When people heard the name O'Boyle, all they'd think about was what Al did to those people and then what I did to Al. It simply must not get out."

Tony shrugged his shoulders carelessly. "He'll keep his mouth shut. He has nothing to gain from talking."

"I hope you're right. I think the nigger will keep his part of the bargain. He claims to have gotten religion now, and you know how preoccupied they are with that stuff. The only thing that troubles me there is he'll probably be back in here next week wanting a contribution for his church. The darkies are great ones for that kind of thing."

Little Tony smiled. "Yeah, I know. I guess we'll just have to deal with that problem when it comes up." He stood. "I've got a speaking engagement at the Oglethorpe Club in thirty minutes. Some heavy hitters I think will come through for us at election time. I'd better be going."

Elaine Bryan had prayed so often that Abe would let God become a part of his life. She could not understand how a man with so many good qualities and such intelligence could not see the virtue in a relationship with Almighty God. Those had been her feelings in the early years, when she still thought that Abe could change. Then the most awful thing he had ever done to her happened, and her feelings for husband simply died.

Elaine had suspected, and then known, that Abe had other women during their marriage, but she had forced it out of her mind. She loved him so much that she convinced herself the other women weren't really Abe's fault. Abe was so handsome that women threw themselves at him, and he was a man; he would weaken from time to time and have a brief affair. Lots of men did things like that.

For a few years these excuses worked for Elaine—until her husband gave her that disease, that germ he had picked up from God only knew where. From that point onward Abednigo Bryan ceased to live within Elaine's heart and prayers. The discovery, the shame, the trip to the doctor in Atlanta so that no one in Savannah would know what had happened—these had been a horror Elaine could never forget.

The night she found out about her infection, Elaine sent Lloyd to his grandparents and confronted Abe about it. She neither cried nor cursed Abe; she simply told him, with an icy demeanor, that they were through and why.

He would no longer be a part of her life and a very little part of her son's.

Abednigo tried to bully her. He told Elaine that he was glad that they were through because she no longer attracted him the way she used to. He said all she cared about was Lloyd and the church, and he was glad he would be free to find someone who really appreciated him. He also said he'd be glad to give her a divorce and that he would amply care for her and his son.

With subdued fury Elaine told Abe that she didn't want a divorce because the Catholic church forbade it. She also said she didn't want any of his money and that she would get a job scrubbing floors if necessary before she would take a cent from a man like him. Finally she made it clear that if she ever thought he was being a bad influence on Lloyd, she would kill him with her own hands. Abe believed her, and because of that he had seen very little of his son over the years.

The hardness had remained throughout all this time, but when Lloyd told Elaine about his father's newly found faith, she could almost feel herself soften. She was surprised at her feelings, but even more awed by the power of her prayers and the way God worked on his own time and plan. Quietly Elaine kept track of Abe's progress as he received instructions in the Catholic faith.

Abe too was surprised by what he felt. In the beginning he had decided to take instructions merely to gain the respect of his son, but after a while it turned into something more. Abe was beginning to feel something inside himself that he had never felt before; he had discovered a thirst for knowledge about why he lived and where death would take him. He progressed well in his studies, and Lloyd was surprised at how forcefully Abe applied himself. Just before Valentine's Day, Abednigo was ready to join the Catholic church.

Because he had already been baptized when he was a child, it was not necessary to do so again. Abe's entry into the Catholic church would be complete after he had

received the Sacrament of Penance by going to his first
confession on a Saturday morning and then receiving the
Sacrament of the Holy Eucharist for the first time on the
following Sunday. Abe had asked his son to hear his confession, but Lloyd declined at first. Later he submitted
after lengthy pleadings by his father.

In the privacy of Lloyd's office at the cathedral rectory,
Abe got on his knees before his son, made the sign of the
cross, and started with the opening prayer of confession.

"Bless me, Father, for I have sinned. I confess to Almighty God and to you, Father, that I have sinned."

Lloyd was so tense he could not look at Abe. He was
seated next to a small table with a crucifix on it—eyes
closed, head bowed. Then Abe began his confession.

"I done a lot of things in my life. I lied, I stole, I
cheated, and I ran around on your momma."

At that point Lloyd held his hand up and told Abe that
he didn't have to be specific, just mention the general sins
he had committed and be truly sorry for them. He hoped
that this would spare him the agony of hearing all the
gory details of his father's life.

"Yeah, well I guess you pretty well know all them
things anyway," said Abe. "That ain't no secret, that's for
sure. Most of that's a long time ago too. But you see, I
got another stain on my conscience, a new spot on my
soul that I needs to wash out, that I gotta confess so's I
can have God's forgiveness."

Lloyd took a deep breath and motioned for his father
to continue. This time no details were spared. For half an
hour Lloyd was held in rapt attention as Abe, in intimate
detail, told him how and why he had extorted money from
Tony O'Boyle. He covered everything, from the day he
had seen Tony hide his brother's body on Raccoon Island
to the stacks of hundred dollar bills he had carried from
Tony's office months before and given to the boys from
Vegas. Lloyd hadn't expected to hear anything like this,
and when Abe finally finished talking, Lloyd slumped
back in his chair and said nothing.

He felt hollow within, but after a few seconds he raised his right hand and made the sign of the cross. "May our Lord Jesus Christ absolve you, and by His authority I absolve you, from every bond of excommunication and interdict to the extent of my power and your need. And finally, I absolve you from your sins, in the name of the Father and of the Son and of the Holy Spirit. Now, go forth and sin no more."

When Lloyd had finished, Abe quietly raised himself from his knees and left the rectory without saying another word. Lloyd sat alone in his office for a long time and watched the sun's shadow etch the floor, his desk, and then his eyes. The burden of the seal of the confessional had just taken on a new weight for Father Lloyd Bryan.

SECRET DEEDS

IT HAD BEEN ALMOST one hundred and seventy-five years since a group of Savannah's Irish immigrants had first celebrated St. Patrick's Feast Day by marching from Mass to the Knights of Columbus Hall for a Communion breakfast. From that humble beginning, and in the hyperbole of local reckoning, the second largest St. Patrick's Day Parade in the world now took place each March 17th in Savannah. That Southern celebration already eclipsed Chicago's; it had almost outdone New York's in 1996, the year of the Atlanta Olympics. Celtic jingoism decreed St. Patrick's Day in Savannah to be the springtime equivalent of the Macy's Thanksgiving Day Parade and the East Coast rival to the Rose Bowl Parade.

For Tony O'Boyle, Sr., this St. Patrick's Day was to be the Mount Olympus of his vigorous life. He was assured of his election as grand marshal of the parade. Little Tony would serve as his aide, and through this position the old man would formally present his son to the people of Georgia as a candidate for the office of governor. Tony had arranged for his son to deliver the toast to the state

of Georgia at the Hibernian Banquet, the traditional climax of St. Patrick's Day in Savannah. He had even made
certain that the secretary of defense, who was of Irish
descent and the featured speaker at the banquet, would
generously remember and richly praise his son's war record in Vietnam. National television coverage of the
speech was a given. Big Tony was a master of the political
game. He was playing on his home field on St. Patrick's
Day in Savannah. He had almost forgotten about Abe
Bryan and Raccoon Island. But it would not go away.

The thought that Abe might still talk troubled the
O'Boyles. So they had resolved to do something more to
assure his continued silence. Abe's threat of a fail-safe
scheme to protect himself had successfully thwarted any
prospects of having him killed, but Big Tony still felt he
had to do something more to assure Abe's silence. He
would call Abe in for a second, reassuring talk. He would
offer Abe more money, just as an insurance policy. The
meeting would take place in Tony's office, and Little
Tony would hide in the safe closet and listen to the conversation.

Little Tony paced back and forth on the pastel Aubusson
rug covering the heart-pine floor in front of his father's
desk. He had taken special care to look his best, as he
was addressing the League of Women Voters at lunch, so
he was impeccable in a dark-gray pinstriped double-
breasted Oleg Cassini suit, slightly padded in the shoulders. The tassels on his Florsheim loafers made a faint
flicking sound as he walked; and because he was a stickler
for sartorial details, he had debated sticking a handkerchief in his breast pocket. Tony decided that the League
of Women Voters were sophisticated enough to appreciate
that flair, but it was *not* coordinated with his tie: that
would have been gauche and too flashy. Instead he wore
a simple, fifteen-dollar, Irish-linen white handkerchief
peeping a mere half an inch above the pocket.

The one thing he always wore was his favorite cologne,

a crisp but subtle fragrance, finely masculine. He had discovered it a few years back at Saks Fifth Avenue. His wife told him to use only one splash, but Tony always used two. He wasn't hearing any complaints from the ladies. None at all.

When his father's secretary buzzed back and announced that Mr. Abednigo Bryan was in the outer office, Little Tony slipped into the closet and left the door open a crack so he could hear. Big Tony greeted Abe in a pleasant manner and got right down to business. He asked Abe if the "arrangements" they had agreed upon were still satisfactory and if there was "anything further you might be needing."

"No suh, Mr. Boyle, like I done said, I got all I needs from you. You got nothin' to worry 'bout from me. Ole Abe is a man of his word, suh, and that's fo sho."

"Well, to be honest, Abe, that's not what I was worried about. What has really troubled me was that if something bad happened to you and it wasn't our fault. I mean my fault. You know, you got that plan to protect yourself and I gotta be sure that it don't come back to bite me on the ass."

"You just gonna have to trust me on that, Mista Tony. I got a plan that'll keep you safe long as I'm safe. I ain't gonna tell you 'bout it though. That'd be stupid now, wouldn't you say, suh?"

In actuality, Abe had no plan at all. He was shrewd enough to know that merely bluffing would be enough to deter Tony from causing him any harm. It was hardly a gamble.

Tony leaned back in his chair for a moment and spread his meaty, mottled hands on his legs. He looked down at his Benedictine class ring, which he had worn for over six decades. Then he looked at Abe, and Abe could see the pain in his eyes. Abe almost felt sorry for Tony again, but he was wary—especially in this company.

"Well, I've just been sick about this whole thing. I've carried it with me for so many years." Tony stopped himself all at once. He had covered that ground before with this "nigra," and once was damn sure enough with a darky, so he abruptly stood. "Well, I think that about wraps up what I wanted to talk to you about. If you have any problems and get the itch to talk, talk to me first."

Abe rose from his seat at the same time, holding his hat in his hand. He said nothing for several seconds, trying to place the source of the smell that filled Tony O'Boyle's office. It had struck him when he first walked in, because it wasn't the usual aftershave that men use. This was different. Abe knew he had smelled it before.

Then it hit him. He had noticed that "perfume," as he called it, at Mass in the cathedral last Sunday. He had been standing right behind Tony O'Boyle, Jr., in the Communion line. The smell filled the office, as if Tony were there.

As he turned to leave, Abe cast his eyes to the closet in which Big Tony kept his safe. The door was ajar, just a mite. The toe of a black shoe with tassels peeped out. Somebody was hiding in the closet, listening to his conversation with Tony O'Boyle. For sure, it's Little Tony, Abe thought. When he got to the office door, he turned to Big Tony, nodded, and placed his hat back on his head. "No need to worry now, Mista Tony. Ole Abe don't go back on his word. Oh, by the way, how is Little Tony doin'? I ain't seen that young'n in a montha' Sundays?"

"Fine, Abe, just fine. I'll tell him you asked. You take care now, ya hear?" Abe left and Little Tony emerged.

"Well now, Daddy, I don't know whether to feel better or not. It's just a hell of a spot this old nigger has us in. I guess there's not a whole lot we can do about it, though. So far so good. Let's just pray he dies in his sleep. Well, I gotta get goin' down to the Pirates' House and that bunch of busybody old ladies. Shit, most of 'em are nothin' but a bunch of big-mouth Yankees from Skidaway Island."

As Big Tony sat back down in his chair, he grunted. "Just remember that those lovely ladies vote even if they do talk through their noses and come from New Damn Jersey or somewhere."

Tony walked around to his father and kissed him on the forehead, as was his custom. "Yes, sir. I'll see you later, Daddy. Damn that nigger. He still bothers me."

Just before Tony opened the door, his father called out. "And stop usin' that word *shit*. It's low class. You gonna' slip up one day and let it fly in front of a TV camera, and then your goose is cooked. Now go on and get to that meetin'."

"Yes, sir." The door shut quietly, leaving Big Tony staring up at the brass ceiling fan over his desk and wondering how in the name of holy hell all this would end.

Lloyd Bryan knew his place. Even though he was probably the most recognized person in Savannah, he still knew his place. If he hadn't been famous—and he admitted with humble honesty to his fame—he would never have been assigned to the cathedral. The bishop was something of a high-powered politician and showman himself, and Lloyd could not help feeling that he had used him to stimulate interest in the cathedral parish, which had been in steady decline for years. It could hardly support itself, and the upkeep of the building was staggering. The entire church was an absolute work of art, and works of art require constant care and maintenance.

The cathedral had gained celebrity status all over the country since Lloyd had been stationed there. All of the network morning shows had done segments about him and the cathedral, and now the cable stations were coming by to do travelogues on Savannah's cathedral and its priest. All Lloyd wanted was to be back at St. Benedict's parish in his old neighborhood, where he could watch over the people of his roots and maybe save a kid or two along the way. He wanted to go to the barber shop where his uncle worked, read *Sports Illustrated*, and talk with the boys who hung around the shop. He wanted to go to Eta's Confectionery and watch the old-timers play checkers under the shade of the live oaks and drink an ice-cold beer when the temperature hit ninety-six. But that was impossible, now, and maybe forever. But of course he would be obedient to the wishes of his bishop.

Now, however, the knowledge he carried about the secret deeds of Tony O'Boyle were an even bigger burden, because Tony would be the grand marshal of this year's St. Patrick's Day Parade. For almost a month Lloyd had wondered how he could face this man and smile and act as though all were right with him and his world. He could never tell anyone about what he had learned in the confessional from his father, and that was difficult enough. Unfortunately, even more was to come.

Since his conversion Abe had gone to noon Mass and Communion at the cathedral daily. It had become his routine. He never hung around after Mass, though, or tried to make conversation with his son, because he knew it made Lloyd uncomfortable. Therefore, when Abe showed up in the sacristy after Mass that Friday, Lloyd braced himself for the possibility of more distressing news.

"Son, I just come from Mr. O'Boyle's office and there's somethin' I think you should ought'a know. Mista Tony was scared I was gonna let on about what you 'n me talked about when I made my confession. Ya' see, the only one I ever told was you, and I know you can't tell nobody cause if you do, then you goin' to hell for that. Leastwise that's what they taught me when I took instructions to be a Catholic. Now, ain't that right, son?"

"Yes, sir, that's right, Daddy. It's called the seal of the confessional. I can never tell anyone, in any way, what has been revealed to me in a person's confession. It's the worst sin that a priest can commit. I guess I'd go to Hell for sure. Yes, sir."

"Well now, that's what I thought. But you see, there's one more thing that I done found out about that I want to tell you. I don't need to go to confession this time cause it ain't no sin. It's just somethin' I found out that's got me troubled cause this man might be a man in power one day, and I don't think that he got what it takes, down inside hiself, to be a man that the people truss."

Lloyd let out a breath and leaned against the drawers where the vestments were kept. Abe continued.

"I think that Tony O'Boyle, Jr., is in on this coverup thing with his old man. I think he know his daddy killed his own brother to save his ass, and I think he know his daddy done paid me money to keep quiet. Something like that is bad, son. It's bad if a man like that get to be the governor of this here state, and I know old man Boyle sure can make him that. You gotta think of something to stop that boy. He mean as his old man. Lawd, I gotta pray on this."

X

THE DRISCOLL
TREASURE

They weighed so lightly what they gave.

It's St. Patrick's Day in Savannah,
all the boys are on parade!
Sure the folks down here never miss a year,
may their valor never fade!

—Beginning lines from the song
"It's St. Patrick's Day in Savannah"
by A.J. Handiboe

FALSE CLUE

THE DISCOVERY of the skeletal remains on Raccoon Island was a sensation in the local news—and John-Morgan knew that his special and secret place would be no more. The newspaper and all three television stations sent reporters and camera crews to interview him. He had long been known as a kind of expert on local history, especially the Civil War period, but now he was getting calls from the networks asking for interviews. The situation was moving too fast, and John-Morgan didn't like it.

Finding human remains in an essentially unknown Civil War fort was a story with appeal in and of itself. Five professionals out on a camping trip, however, hunting for artifacts on an isolated island and finding a skeleton instead was too gothically seasoned to be just a story. It became an event. Add the presence of Father Lloyd Bryan—Notre Dame-Dallas Cowboy-priest—and the story went stratospheric. Media people were after Lloyd too, and he couldn't duck them.

Abe hadn't told him the actual island on which Al O'Boyle's body had been buried, but Lloyd knew instantly whose skeleton was in that old latrine the moment he saw it. Alas, he couldn't tell; he couldn't even hint in a tiny way that he knew something. It would break the seal of the confessional. He didn't know what to do, and the added burden of all the media attention, plus the worries about his father and the O'Boyles put him under damnable stress.

It was beginning to grow dark as Abe Bryan locked the door to his apartment on East Broad Street and started to walk to the cathedral. He didn't notice the two teenage boys coming up behind him. He didn't hear them either.

"Gimme what'cha got, old man!" One of the boys

grabbed Abe's arm with unusual strength and whirled him around like a top. The other pulled his neck with one hand and started to go through his vest pockets with the other.

"Let me go, you no-good, worthless black son of a bitch!" The boys just laughed as Abe screamed at them and then called for help. There was no one to hear his cries, or at least no one who dared to come out and help him.

Maybe the boys wouldn't have hurt Abe if he hadn't resisted with such fury. But when he, a veteran of many a street fight, kicked one of them between the legs, they went berserk and smashed Abe in the face. First they broke his glasses, then his nose. After that it was his jaw. Abe began to crumple, but he did get in a few good licks. He drew blood and saw it with satisfaction just as he lost consciousness and fell. When his skull hit the pavement, it fractured. Less than an hour later, Abe Bryan was dead.

"Jesus H. Christ!" gasped Big Tony over the phone when his son broke the news. "I guess this is the end. Whatever deal that old nigger had to protect him will probably kick in now. What the hell do we do?"

"I think we just sit tight, Daddy. It's all we can do. Say a prayer to St. Jude," Tony added sarcastically. He didn't believe in such nonsense, but right now he might give anything a whirl. "Let's just be cool and see what happens. Maybe this'll all blow over. It's obvious it was a real mugging. One thing's for sure—Abe Bryan isn't talking to anybody ever again. And that's good."

"Well, when that damn Hartman boy found the body out there, I almost died. Now this. You know I'm not a young man any more, son. This whole thing has really been a strain on me."

There was a pause, and then Little Tony asked about anything on the body or in the clothes that might lead to an identification. His father said he had removed the Miraculous Medal from around the neck, but that was all. He hadn't gone through his pockets or anything. He thought about it later, but could not bring himself to dig up the grave. He just left and hoped that nothing would happen. At the time, he said he was sure he had not been seen. The grave would never be found. On that he had obviously been wrong.

Lloyd was certain his father had been killed by someone paid by the O'Boyles, but he knew he couldn't prove it, and he knew he couldn't talk. He vowed to himself, however, that after the funeral he would think of something to expose those murderers.

The day before St. Patrick's Day, he finally devised a plan. It was really more of a ploy than a plan, but Lloyd was severely constrained in what he could do. He remembered what one of the old priests used to say when he was at Benedictine:"The guilty will flee when none pursueth." With that Lloyd hit upon the ideal subterfuge.

He would be seeing the O'Boyles at a reception that very night. Lloyd would "let slip" some bogus information in the presence of the two Tonys. That would almost certainly send them scurrying.

For two weeks before the St. Patrick's Day Parade, the grand marshal attends at least one planned event each night. Savannah has almost a dozen Irish organizations, and each has its own banquet somewhere around that time. Over the last several years, a group of wealthy and influential Irishmen had begun to gather at the home of Tony O'Boyle, Sr., for a black-tie cocktail party. Though it had started out informally at first, it had slowly become organized. Now it even had a name and an organized membership.

The Celtic Society consisted entirely of friends of Tony, but not all of them were Irish. They were, however, all Celts, and this included Scotsmen and Welshmen. It was a brilliant political move on Tony's part to foster the idea of the Celtic Society as a political base. Nobody had to show proof of ancestry; the board members took the applicant's word for it. A background check was unnecessary anyway, because Savannahians who traveled in such circles made it their business to know their ancestries. So did their associates.

The members of the society invited guests to the big bash, and invitations had become a coveted commodity in Savannah society. But it was strictly a stag affair, with the reputation of getting its participants politely and properly drunk. Because of this, the Celtic Society was renowned for throwing "a damn good party."

The bishop of Savannah was a member of the society, and this year he had decided to take Father Lloyd Bryan as his guest. Lloyd would not be the only black guest, however: doctors and politicians would also be in attendance, especially if they had decided to become Republicans—or if they could help get Little Tony elected governor regardless of affiliation. They would never become members of the Celtic Society, but they were welcome to drink as much expensive whiskey as they could hold. Civil rights was a wonderful thing.

The O'Boyle family had always lived "downtown," although not always in the same place. When it suited Tony Sr.'s political needs, he would brag about how he had grown up in the "Old Fort" area of Savannah: no "lace-curtain Irish" ways for him. Now, however, he rarely talked about the Old Fort. Tony would rather his present circle of friends assume that the O'Boyles had always lived in the exquisite mansion he owned across from the cathedral on Lafayette Square. Everyone had come to refer to it as the "O'Boyle Mansion"—but the old-timers knew, and Tony knew that they knew. When he was around *them*, therefore, he always made it a point to talk about their days in the Old Fort. Tony knew that Irishmen were a sensitive lot.

Guests started arriving a little after seven. They were greeted by a butler dressed in white tie and tails. Even the food and drinks were served by men in swallow-tails and white gloves. There were sterling silver serving trays for the finger foods and cut crystal Waterford tumblers for the whiskey. The finest linen and floral lace from Ireland covered the tables, and the food was varied and extraordinary. Lighting in the house was provided by candles, and the glow reflected off the huge Victorian mirrors in the formal parlor and set the silver and crystal sparkling. The overall effect was stunning.

Tony stood with his son in the long hall that led from the front door and greeted each guest personally. Over his right shoulder he wore the green and gold sash of the grand marshal of the St. Patrick's Day Parade. Tony, Jr., stood at his side, wearing a sash with "Marshal's Aide" embroidered across it. The party occupied the entire house and flowed into the walled garden in back. A large porch and balcony overlooked Abercorn Street. On it were three bars.

The weather in Savannah on and around St. Patrick's Day was usually perfect. Today was no exception. The azaleas were in full bloom, and the two hundred guests in Tony's house that night would neither sweat in oppressive heat nor be dampened by rain. It was truly a splendid party on a splendid night. If only the two Tonys could have relaxed and enjoyed themselves on this wonderful and joyous evening.

At the front door the receiving butler bowed to some incoming guests, turned to the O'Boyles in the receiving line, and announced in a deep, clear voice: "The governor of the state of Georgia and his party." The governor promptly shook hands with Tony and made promises to Little Tony of support. Throughout the evening that deep voice at the door would call out "the senior senator from Georgia and his party" or "the bishop of the diocese of Atlanta and his party." And so it went for the first hour as all manner of dignitaries and friends of the O'Boyles filed in to eat Tony's expensive food and drink his Jack Daniels and Wild Turkey, his Jameson and Bushmill, Glenlivet and Bombay gin. Nothing but the best for the O'Boyles.

Around eight o'clock the butler announced: "The bishop of the diocese of Savannah, The Most Reverend Francis Xavier Collins, and his aide de camp, the Reverend Lloyd Bryan." Lloyd and the bishop chatted politely with their hosts for a few minutes until Big Tony turned to the bishop and said: "Your Excellency, I'm dry as a bone. Won't you and Father Bryan join me and my son on the porch for a taste?" The bishop smiled and, with his arm around Big Tony, strolled through the parlor on to the porch. Lloyd and Little Tony fell in behind them, exchanging small talk as they walked. On the porch O'Boyle gave his condolences to Lloyd over the death of his father. Controlling himself with an effort, Lloyd politely thanked him.

The two younger men gazed for a while at the cathedral across the square. The centerpiece of Lafayette Square is a fountain, and tonight its dyed green water sprayed an emerald mist.

"So, Lloyd, thanks for coming. I see you at Mass but don't get much of a chance to talk with you. I'm one of those Catholics who like to split right after Communion."

"Thanks for having me. This is quite an affair. Don't worry about leaving church early, you're not alone, I assure you."

"I guess you're working as hard as you always have, Lloyd, and I know what happened to your father has to be real distressing. Other than that, though, what else is new?"

This was just the opportunity that Lloyd had hoped for; he could scarcely keep from smiling. "Pretty much same old same old. One thing was exciting—that skeleton we found out on Raccoon Island. I was one of the group. Did you hear about that on the news?"

"Oh, yeah, I sure did hear about that. John-Morgan is something else with all that Civil War stuff. Most people wonder if he even cares about medicine. Just his first love, I guess. You know how that is. Anyway, have the police made any progress in identifying the remains?" Tony was trying to be casual, but his tense eyes betrayed his interest.

Lloyd, enjoying this, took a very slow sip from his drink. "Well, I was at the police barracks yesterday—I'm the chaplain for the county police now—and I was told they think there's probably a lot of stuff in the grave that could identify the bones. They only took the skeleton that day because of the time, but they're going back on Sunday to look for more clues. They said there are always clues in situations like this. They wanted to go tomorrow, but it's St. Patrick's Day and they can't spare the manpower. So they're planning to go Sunday for sure and work all day if necessary. Detective Strickland thinks with a little more to go on, they can probably get a positive ID and maybe the year he was killed. Age and sex are easy to determine. So is race. That DNA stuff is wild. He said they could even figure out if the person is Irish or German or Italian from the DNA. That's just incredible to me." Lloyd took another placid sip.

Tony took a quick pull from his glass and hoped that Lloyd didn't see him turn pale. He tried hard not to seem upset or too interested, but inside he was dying a slow death. His old ulcer was already acting up, and this only made it worse. The whiskey didn't help either, but he needed it more than ever now.

"That's fascinating. I wonder who it is? I wonder if it's anybody we know of, or maybe our parents knew? Probably not, but it's interesting to think about."

You bastard, Lloyd said to himself, then he smiled. "I see the governor of Georgia coming this way with Senator Trosdal. You gotta go to work now so you can get elected. Good luck. I'll see you at Mass tomorrow. Eight-thirty sharp now, don't forget."

Tony laughed and shook Lloyd's hand. Then he turned and walked toward the governor. For a second or two Lloyd felt a little guilty about what he had done, but then he muttered, "That son of a bitch" and walked off to find John-Morgan.

* * *

Little Tony had a hard time getting through the rest of the party. At about ten-thirty he pulled his father aside. The two of them quickly slipped upstairs to Tony's old room.

"Now Daddy, you gotta be real straight with me and tell me what was left out there on Al's body. We're damn lucky they didn't dig through the rest of the grave the day they found it, but Lloyd Bryan just told me the police were going back out to the island on Sunday to check again for clues. You gotta think hard now. Did you leave anything on Uncle Al's body that could link you up with him?"

The old man sat down on Tony's old bed. He reached out his hand and touched the pillow where his son's head used to rest and thought of different and better days.

"I've thought about that many, many times. I'm really not sure, but I didn't go through his pockets before I buried him." Big Tony almost shuddered at the thought and looked down at the floor. "I think he may have had my old Army dog tag with him. I gave it to him after I came back from the war. He didn't wear it around his neck; he carried it on his key chain. I looked all over for the thing when I got back, but I couldn't find it anywhere. I almost went back and looked for it. God's knows I started out a dozen times, but I could never bring myself to go. I never even went out that way on the boat again." Big Tony again paused for a moment before looking up at his son. "Tony, it was terrible. You know that picture of Kennedy gettin' shot? The Zapruder film?" Puzzled, Little Tony shook his head. "Well, that film proves Kennedy was hit from the back just as the Warren commission said. You know how I know?" With his mouth half open in befuddlement, Little Tony ever so slightly shook his head back and forth. "The reason I know is cause that's just the way Al's head went when I shot him as he sat there fishing. Remember how Kevin Costner kept showing the Zapruder film in the movie *JFK*? Remember how he kept showing the sequence where Kennedy got hit in the head and he kept saying "back and to the left, back and to the left?"

That damn fool thought that proved Kennedy was hit from the right. Hell, he'd never seen somebody hit in the back of the head with a bullet. I have. Al moved back and to the left just like the President, and I did the shooting."

Big Tony stopped for a few seconds to wipe the tears from his eyes and then continued. "I simply couldn't bring myself to going back out to that island and dig him up and go over his body for that dog tag. I always said I might go to the electric chair one day for that, but I still couldn't do it. Now I guess my hunch was right."

Tony sat silently on the bed staring at the floor, so Little Tony had to take charge. Quietly but firmly he tried to reassure the old man.

"Not quite, not quite. Tomorrow I'm going out to that island and I'm going to go through that grave and find whatever is left. I'll take Steve's metal detector."

"But tomorrow's St. Patrick's Day. You're my son, my chief aide. You've got to ride in the parade with me or people will know that something's wrong. You can't go."

"I'll ride in the parade with you tomorrow, and I'll even sit in the reviewing stand for a while. Only I'll leave before it's over 'cause I'm gonna feel real bad tomorrow and I'll have to leave the parade early to rest 'cause I don't want to miss the Hibernian Banquet. Leaving then will be just fine, 'cause high tide isn't until one o'clock, I think, and I can't get in to the island too much before that. Actually, it works out just right. As a matter of fact, I'm not feeling too well now. I'm gonna leave and get the boat and everything ready to go tomorrow. I sure as hell won't have time in the morning. Make the excuses for me, Daddy, tell everybody I'm not feeling well."

Tony then went over and hugged the old man, kissed him good-bye, and told him not to worry. After his son left, Big Tony sat on the bed for a little longer than he should have, but at last he pulled himself together. He straightened his grand marshal's sash in the mirror behind the door to his son's old bedroom and started down the stairs to the party.

TOWARD RACCOON ISLAND

BEFORE THE PARADE starts, the center of action on St. Patrick's Day is the Cathedral of Saint John the Baptist. Regardless of their religion, all successful politicians and wanna-bes show up for the church services. A solemn High Mass begins at 8:30, when the grand marshal walks down the center aisle. The entire Mass is broadcast live over local TV and every old Irishmen who can't join in the festivities will be glued to the set from the start of the Mass to the finish of the parade. This is Savannah's biggest day, and every ethnic group takes a part. Everyone's Irish on St. Patrick's Day.

The Knights of Columbus honor guard began to form a line of twos on the cathedral steps, signaling that Big Tony and his aides were to prepare to enter. The Mass seemed extra long to both of the O'Boyles, but for different reasons. Little Tony was eager to get to the island and dispose of the evidence. Big Tony was thinking about all of the things he had done in his life and to his life, especially the murder of his brother.

The parade took three hours to wind its way down the streets and around the squares of the city until it reached the traditional finish in front of the Knights of Columbus at Bull and Liberty streets. There a reviewing stand had been erected, where Big Tony and other dignitaries would sit and watch the parade they had led.

Before long, Little Tony leaned over and whispered to his father. As he stood and exited the reviewing stand, he spoke and shook hands all the way down the line.

Tony had to control himself as he walked to his Bull Street office because he wanted to run the entire way. He picked up his car and drove as fast as he dared to his home at the end of Bluff Drive on Isle of Hope. Tony parked his car in the garage and quickly covered the hundred and fifty feet over the marsh to the dockhouse.

There he changed into his old Navy Seal cammos, the ones he had worn in Vietnam; and even now, in the midst of all this anxiety, Tony found satisfaction in the fact that they still fit after all those years. He kept himself in good shape—and a curious sense of pride assailed him, exactly as when he prepared for a mission "in country." "It's strange," Tony muttered, "but I'm getting excited. Damn, I'm almost beginning to enjoy this."

He reached into the old duffel bag and felt for the pistol he knew so well. It was there, waiting patiently—a loyal friend. As his hand fit around it, those old feelings truly began to return. A commando never forgets. This was a mission, and he was in form once again. He was "Lieutenant Lucifer, the Prince of Darkness," the terror of the Mekong Delta. Tony was in character now. He was complete, and nothing had really changed.

Tony loved the sound his Colt made as he racked back the slide, let it bite a round off the top of the magazine, and then drove it into the breach. To him the Colt was a magnificent machine; it never jammed, it always fired, and in all the times he had used it he had never, never missed. He stared at the pistol for a moment, then quickly holstered it and strapped it to his waist. The pistol felt as if it was always meant to be there.

Then he lowered his seventeen-foot Whaler into the water. The night before he had stocked it with his son's metal detector, a shovel, and his police scanner. As soon as he hit the ignition, the 130-horse Mercury roared to life. The boat was fast. On a calm day it could easily reach sixty-miles-an-hour.

Tony quickly checked the river and the adjoining docks for any activity. Not a soul was in sight as he eased the boat away from the dock. Without hesitation he pressed forward on the throttle, and in a few seconds Tony was screaming down the Skidaway River toward the back side of Raccoon Island. There was little wind, the river was calm, and he made excellent time with the tide. "Shit," he

crowed to the wind, "I'll have all the time I need to do
what has to be done and get out of there."

Tony had never dreamed that he would ever need or
want to know where the ridiculous John-Morgan had done
his silly Civil War diggings over the years, but now he
was glad he had found out. That in itself had been a stroke
of luck; quite by accident, a girl he was seeing on the sly
had shown him exactly where it was.

Although married, Tony had to have other "interests"
going. The women he preferred were into recreational sex
just like him; they were not the kind to fall in love and
become jealous of his wife. Charlotte Drayton made the
perfect girlfriend on the side.

She and Tony had a rendezvous the very night she got
back from Raccoon Island. Excited about the story, she
jabbered on to Tony and even played the unedited video
tape. This showed where the grave was located and exactly how to get there.

Now, as he thumped across the water to Raccoon Island, Tony replayed the entire incident. "That dumb broad
showed me where everything was. 'Oh, I won't tell, I
promise. Who the hell would I tell anyway? TV's got it,
why should I talk?' Stupid slut." Charlotte had made the
cardinal error of talking about how *cute and sweet* John-
Morgan was—"That dickless SOB! Screw him!" Tony
was growing angry just remembering the evening. Finally
they both got in a huff, and he left. No sex for Tony that
night—nothing, in fact, but that tape he once had thought
was just a lot of horseshit. "Hot damn!" he hooted, "how
quick things can change!"

As soon as Mass was over, Lloyd drove out to John-
Morgan's house, where he kept his own boat—one of the
few indulgences he allowed himself. Lloyd still enjoyed
being on the river. When he was a little boy, his father
had taught him how to fish, back before the time when
Abe stopped coming around: back when he had been a
happy child. Before all this mess that saddened and dis-

turbed him—Abe's death, the body at Raccoon Island, now his plan to lure Tony out to the island. This was a sorry mission now. Lloyd had to do it, but his sleazy manipulation of the O'Boyles bothered him. Not that they deserved better. *I* deserve better, he thought, but not them. The immoral, groping sophistry of vengeance blindsided him. So his plan moved on.

Ann Marie skipped the parade because her baby was sick with a sore throat. She was down at the mailbox when Lloyd pulled up in front of the dock, just across the narrow street from their house. She was pleased, but very surprised.

"Hi, Lloyd. Why aren't you down at the parade? I thought you and the others were gonna get together?"

"Tell you the truth, I didn't feel like doin' much. Not with all that's happened. You know, my father and all. I just thought I'd do a little fishin' and thinkin'. You know, just be alone a little. I'm not exactly set for crowds right now."

"I'm sorry, Lloyd, I should have known. I hope you feel better. And catch something, too. I'll be up at the house if you need anything. Bye."

Ann Marie smiled and returned to the house. Climbing the stairs, she looked back at Lloyd and noticed he didn't have his fishing tackle. No cooler, no tackle box, nothing. That's odd, she thought. Maybe he really just wants to be alone. But she watched from the veranda as Lloyd shot off from the dock at full speed, ignoring the no-wake zone. That was very strange, and not at all like Lloyd. He was always a stickler for rules. Then she remembered something else: Lloyd was supposed to be sitting at the parade with the bishop—command performance of sorts. All this was very mysterious, but Ann Marie paid it little mind.

John-Morgan had marched in perhaps thirty-five St. Patrick's Day parades. He still loved to do it. Today he would miss marching because a patient, the wife of a friend, was dying. He had coverage for the day, but he knew Dave O'Brien would be at his wife's bedside, just as frightened and concerned as the night before. What the hell, he thought, I made the Sinn Fein breakfast and caught the beginning of the parade. I'll just shoot over to Memorial and check on things. Dave's missing the parade too, because his wife is dying. I can't have somebody he doesn't know taking care of her now.

David O'Brien was glad to see John-Morgan walk through the door, even though the first words out of his mouth were: "What the hell are you doing here? Why aren't you downtown?" WTOC's coverage of the festivities was on. Doug Weathers' voice filled the room as John-Morgan leaned over the bed and listened to Ellen O'Brien's chest. She smiled weakly and scolded him for not being at the parade.

For an hour the trio talked of old times and watched the parade together. When he was ready to leave, John-Morgan said good-bye to Ellen O'Brien and patted her hand. He and his old friend walked out of the room and down the hall to the elevator.

"How much longer you think she has?"

"It looks like days now, David. Maybe less. It's spreading rapidly."

"You won't let her hurt, I mean, you know?"

"She won't hurt, David, I promise. She can have all she wants."

With that the elevator door opened and John-Morgan stepped in. David O'Brien managed a sad smile. "Happy St. Patrick's Day." The elevator door closed. Later that night Ellen Kelly O'Brien died peacefully.

The hospital trip so dampened John-Morgan's spirits that he didn't feel like going back to the parade as he had planned. He decided to drive back home and relax—not a bad idea, as the Hibernian Banquet was that evening. Besides, all the furor around the Raccoon Island discovery had worn him to a frazzle.

At Jue's 7-11 on DeRenne Avenue he stopped for gas.

Standing beside his car, gas pump nozzle in hand, he suddenly saw Tony O'Boyle's black Mercedes roadster speed by. Where's the fire? John-Morgan thought. It was very strange that Tony should not be at the parade—but then he remembered the rumor that Tony had been ill the night before. I'll bet he got sick on the reviewing stand and had to leave. Maybe he's driving so fast because he's got diarrhea. God, I hope so! Envisioning that possibility, John-Morgan smiled, replaced the gas cap, and headed for home.

He was surprised to see Lloyd's car parked out front. Ann Marie called out to him from the end of the dock.

"Hey, what are you doing home? Why aren't you down at the parade?"

"I just had enough. I went by the hospital and saw Ellen O'Brien. She doesn't have much time. I told David days, but it could be hours. She's got the look. I just didn't feel like going back downtown. I'm dead tired anyway, and I've got the Hibernian tonight. I thought I'd just come on home and rest. It's not as if I've never seen a St. Patrick's Day Parade before."

Ann Marie eased up to her husband and placed her arms around his waist. Head on his shoulder, she said quietly, "I'm glad you're home."

The sun was bright and warm, but the tropical heat that defines Savannah in the summertime had not arrived yet. A cool south-westerly breeze made standing out on the dock almost a sensual delight. John-Morgan let the sun warm him for a few moments and then said, "I see Lloyd had the same idea I did. It's a nice day to be out on the water."

Ann Marie looked up at John-Morgan and squinted in the sun. "You know, he told me he was going fishing, but he didn't have a pole or anything. No bait, no cooler. I watched him from the house and he just got in the boat and took off. Real fast, too. You know something else funny? Not too long ago, maybe thirty minutes or so, I was out here and I saw somebody shoot out from under the O'Boyle's dock house. In their boat, dressed in Army fatigues. It looked like Tony, but he's down at the parade. I thought he had to be because his daddy was the grand marshal and all."

John-Morgan stiffened and then leaned against the railing, looking intently down the river in the direction of Raccoon Island. He thought for a while and then asked, "Did Lloyd leave before O'Boyle?"

"Uh huh."

"Did they both head in the same direction?"

"Yeah, real fast too. Why, is something wrong?"

"I don't know." John-Morgan turned and started walking up to the house very quickly.

"Where are you going?" Ann Marie called out, but she received no answer. "John-Morgan, answer me. Where are you going?"

He turned back to his wife and tried his best to be calm, but John-Morgan knew that he could never hide the apprehension he felt. "I think I'm going for a boat ride too." With that he quickened his pace to a jog as he headed up to the house. Ann Marie was immediately on his heels, shouting for him to explain.

They talked as John-Morgan changed into old clothes. He tried to play down his fears. He even tried to convince himself that this was all a coincidence. So he told Ann Marie he just had a funny feeling.

"It is probably nothing. But Lloyd is out on the water by himself. I just want to check on him, just to make sure." All the while John-Morgan was really wondering about what Tony was doing on his boat—especially if he was supposed to be sick, above all on this special St. Patrick's Day; and why Lloyd was there, when he was supposed to be with the bishop—at a command performance, as he had said. Something was definitely not right.

He didn't tell Ann Marie about seeing Tony pass by him at the gas station. He wouldn't be able to handle her then. Instead he went over to his closet and got out his old leather bomber jacket.

Ann Marie didn't see him slip his pistol into the pocket, but his rambling explanations, excuses, and reasons did little to ease her fears. She followed him, urging him all the way down to the boat to be careful. Ann Marie stood on the dock as he started the *Graf Spee* and watched as he untied the lines. Then she jumped into the boat and kissed him good-bye. She had an even stranger feeling than John-Morgan; she pleaded with him to be careful. Before he pulled away from the dock, John-Morgan shouted over the roar of the engines: "If you don't hear from me in a couple of hours, give Bubba or Mike a call. Mike's got his cell phone with him. Tell 'em I headed out for the island. I thought something might be wrong." John-Morgan also ignored the no-wake zone.

Ann Marie watched her husband until he rounded the bend and faded from view. Then she turned sharply up the dock ramp, muttering to herself. "A couple of hours, my fanny. I'm going to call them right now."

LIEUTENANT LUCIFER

AN UNUSUALLY HIGH and beautiful spring tide swept the marsh from horizon to horizon, and only slim needle tips of new green grass were visible. The extra water increased the window of approach to Raccoon Island. Tony could have slipped in with relative ease even on a normal tide, but now there was nothing to hinder him as he glided up to the causeway.

O'Boyle was now functioning in his warrior mode: half man, half animal, and all Navy Seal. The tension of the moment had sharpened his senses to combat edge, and he grinned in recollection of his training. He could still bring it back after all this time.

He tied his boat and moved quickly through the underbrush to where the entrance should be. In an automatic reflex, his eyes searched from left to right, then down to the ground—looking for tripwires and booby traps, scanning the trees for movement. He sniffed the air for the scent of man, walking in a crouch to the side of the trail where he could quickly find cover. Nothing had changed in him. It had all come back so easily, so quickly, so completely. This mission was like a potion of rejuvenation.

When he got to the clearing, he spotted the old fort—which looked exactly as he had remembered it from years before. Then he followed the brush line about thirty feet to the left just as Charlotte's video camera had shown him, and found the entrance through the dense undergrowth. Tony took one last, long look, and then entered the crawl space to begin his journey into the heart of the "mysterious" Schwarzwald.

This is nothing, he thought. I used to go down into VC caves back in Nam just for shits. Tony didn't have to go into the caves; that's what the grunts were for. But he wanted to do it just to see who had the biggest balls. "Wasted a couple of slopeheads right down there in their own little rat nest, too," he had told some of his buddies one night at the Yacht Club. "They turned out to be women, but shit, who asked? What's more, who cared? They were VC and they would have killed me if I hadn't gotten them first."

"Wasted a couple of gook whores," was how he had explained it when he crawled out the cave. The grunts who had been waiting for him at the mouth of the cave were wide-eyed with awe at the crazy Seal. They proclaimed him a bona fide wild man and said he was nobody to fuck with—and Tony had loved every word of their evaluation. Later that night, drunk in their hooch, they all laughed as he told them how ugly the "gook whores" had been. He said he probably wouldn't have shot them if they had been decent enough to screw. The Marines he had been entertaining with his bravado howled in loud approval.

After about a hundred feet or so, Tony came upon the scooped-out grave. He turned on the metal detector and started sweeping the area, especially down in the grave itself. It wasn't long before he began to get hits. He resisted the temptation to start digging at the least little thing, but rather decided to get a feel for whatever was in the grave. After a few minutes, he had collected six individual strike areas of varying intensity and decided that it was now time to go to work. Tony took his shovel and began scraping away dirt from the area that seemed to indicate the largest piece of metal. After a minute or so he uncovered what looked like a piece of cannon ball. Tony cursed, threw it aside, and then he started on the next area.

Lloyd Bryan arrived at the island two hours before O'Boyle. He had taken the little stream cutoff from the main creek—a tight squeeze, to be sure, but it went right up to the island. Not many other people knew about it— maybe only John-Morgan, himself, and Lloyd's father, now dead. A crumbling oak, whose massive limbs twisted out over the creek and dipped into the marsh, clung to the bank right where the little creek came up to the island. A small boat could easily be hidden behind its mossy branches. Lloyd's was lying there now.

Patiently, in the throbbing silence, he waited for the sound of Tony's motor. Lloyd wasn't certain that Tony would come, but he thought there was an excellent chance. In any case he had to do something to flush the O'Boyles out—although in truth Lloyd was now puzzled about what he would do if he actually found Tony looking through the grave. But at least it was a start.

There was no surprise. Lloyd even smiled when he heard the sound of Tony's boat pulling up to the island. From his hiding place at the fort, he watched as the camouflaged commando crept up to the tunnel entrance and crawled in. For almost thirty minutes Lloyd sweated it out before he entered the tunnel.

By then O'Boyle had uncovered a few more fragments of metal shot and some coins—about a dollar and a half in quarters, nickels, and dimes, all bunched together in one spot. None of the coins were dated after the time his Uncle Al had disappeared. But there were still no dog tags. Tony moved the metal detector closer to the end of the grave and had another hard strike.

With the shovel he uncovered an old, rusted metal box which he immediately pried open. Tony gasped in astonishment.

"I'll be goddamned!"

The box was crammed with old gold coins and jewelry, and Tony knew instantly what he held in his hand. This was the Driscoll treasure. It had to be; it couldn't be anything else. He smiled wolfishly in his triumph, but Tony was still an O'Boyle. He didn't stop. He didn't gaze in wonder. He didn't even run his fingers luxuriously through all those coins and jewels. There was work to be done. There were dog tags to be found. So with the discipline—and the cunning—of an O'Boyle he set the box aside and returned to his digging.

A few minutes later the machine gave a long, loud beep. As Tony began to dig, Lloyd began to crawl. O'Boyle was oblivious to everything around him, except what might be at the end of his shovel.

Slowly and quietly Lloyd crept forward. He began to hear digging sounds mixed with Tony's heavy breathing. He could smell earth and the unmistakable scent of the marsh, along with the heady aroma of the new leaves that surrounded him. The black, mucky tunnel dirt felt cold on his hands and knees—and when Lloyd began to approach Tony, he felt even colder. He was not merely scared: he was frightened deep in his bones. He could hardly control his breathing, and pulses drummed in his throat and ears. This was a new feeling for him, and Lloyd stopped. He considered turning around and leaving the island, but something within pushed him on. A new awareness stilled his senses. He began to say Hail Marys to himself in bunches.

Lloyd now stopped to watch as he saw the form of

Tony O'Boyle through the scrub. The future governor had no idea that anyone was even on the island, let alone spying scarcely ten feet away.

On Raccoon Island nobody paid attention to the sound of boats in the river. They were there all the time. Very little sound reached the Schwarzwald's catacombs in any case. Thus neither Tony nor Lloyd paid any attention to John-Morgan's boat as it passed in front of Raccoon Island, entered the Florida Passage, and pulled next to Tony's seventeen-footer. They also heard nothing when John-Morgan entered the tunnel and began to crawl toward the grave.

At last Tony's shovel blade clinked suggestively on metal, and he began to dig with his hands. In a few seconds he held up an old chain with four keys and a military identification tag reading "O'Boyle, Anthony A." His father's blood type and serial number were also embossed on the little piece of metal. With a sigh of profound satisfaction, Tony began to cover his holes and scrape over his tracks. It was then that Lloyd decided to move into the clearing and confront him.

He eased himself forward until the tunnel started to open up into the latrine area, but Tony was so intent on what he had been doing that he didn't hear a sound until Lloyd spoke.

"Tony, we gotta talk. This isn't right."

O'Boyle, his back still to Lloyd, froze for almost ten seconds. He didn't turn, he didn't say a word, but in those ten seconds, the change was on him again. He had let it drop away while he was digging for the old dog tag. Now he was complete once more because he had been threatened.

In a movement so smooth, so seamless that Lloyd never really saw it start, Tony reached for his pistol and turned to face his adversary. At the end of the movement was an outstretched right hand; at the end of the hand was a pistol. The hammer was back, a finger was on the trigger, and the eyes were cold.

"How did you find out about this, priest," Tony rasped in the low, guttural sound of desperation.

"I can't tell you that. All I can say is that you can't pull this off. It isn't going to work, Tony. It's over. The police are going to find out about what happened here, and there is nothing you can do about it. So just stop now before you do something you will truly regret. Put the gun down and come on out with me. You haven't done anything wrong. Nobody is going to do anything to you. Stop now and nobody will ever know what happened here."

John-Morgan could hear talking as he crawled down the tunnel. He didn't know the situation, so he decided to be quiet and keep on moving. But then he saw Lloyd's back, and Tony's gun. It was pointed directly at Lloyd's head.

Oh Jesus Christ! said John-Morgan to himself in silence. A chill went down his back as he remembered that he hadn't chambered a round before he entered the tunnel. To do so now would make too much noise; Tony was bound to hear him. All he could do was clench his teeth and wait.

"Come on, Tony, let's put an end to this crazy stuff. You haven't done anything. You can't be held responsible for something you didn't do."

"Fuck you, you asshole priest! This is about my family. My whole goddamn family! You hear me? My life is right here in this goddamn hole, and I'm not letting anybody fuck with it or me. You've fucked up big this time, priest!"

He was again Lieutenant Lucifer, the Prince of Darkness, out of the past and into a black hole. It was as though some great serpentine spark had jumped across a transformer the way they did in old Frankenstein movies and reshaped him. Tony couldn't think past the immediate threat before him, and he was going to do what was necessary to protect himself. It would be deadly, and it would be swift.

Lloyd saw the transformation. He had seen it once before, on the face of a Vietnam vet just before the boy put the gun in his mouth. The boy had been demonically possessed. Tony was demonically possessed. But Tony hadn't pulled the trigger as decisively. That split second made all the difference.

Although his view was not as clear as Lloyd's, John-Morgan could see enough to know that Tony was going to shoot Lloyd—possibly in the next instant. If he didn't want to see his friend's head blown off, he needed to act and act now. He had to shoot Tony. There was no time to think it over.

John-Morgan quietly eased back his jacket and drew the big automatic and chambered a round, but Tony was fast—oh God, was Tony fast! John-Morgan didn't even have the pistol aimed before Tony had already turned and fired in his direction. There was a huge boom. Hot air and bits of leaves and small twigs flew in John-Morgan's direction as he heard the bullet rip by the side of his head.

SLAYING THE GRAND DRAGON

FROM A DIFFERENT DIRECTION, one other unseen observer had crept silently forward along another tunnel to the grave. He heard the people when they came up to his island. He watched each of them enter his forest.

Slowly, soundlessly, he sidled up to the old latrine. The people were so busy digging and talking that they had not heard him. They hadn't even smelled him, although they should have. He stood back in the bushes and watched the one with the gun aimed at the head of the darker one. Then the one with the gun suddenly moved, pointed it in another direction, and fired. This was wrong, and he had to pay.

Before the echo of the gunshot even came, the Grand

Dragon launched himself out of the tunnel and into the side of Tony O'Boyle. The great boar caught him under the armpit and buried his vicious tusks into Tony's chest. Then he whipped his head maniacally from side to side, tusks slashing through flesh, shattering ribs, lacerating blood vessels, and tearing out pieces of lung.

The boar stopped and backed off for a second. Then, with a tremendous bellow that reverberated throughout the island, the porcine Minotaur charged again. This time his head sank into Tony's stomach. The tusks razored belly and bowel. When he raised his head again and pulled, a luminescent string of intestine uncoiled from Tony's body.

Lloyd recoiled in horror, but was soon frantically looking for Tony's pistol. John-Morgan scrambled out of the tunnel before the Grand Dragon could gore his victim a third time, and still kneeling, he swung his pistol to within a foot of the great boar's head. He fired and fired till only a clicking was heard. All thirteen rounds of his Sig Sauer .45 went into the mammoth skull, and when the firing had finally stopped, the Great Grand Dragon of the Invisible Empire of Raccoon Island lay dead. His head rested in a pool of gore between Tony O'Boyle's legs.

The two looked at each other for a single, shocked moment; then, without a word, they pulled the boar off the body. Lloyd took Tony's head in his arms and John-Morgan began stuffing his shirt into Tony's gaping chest wound. "Nothing like a sucking chest wound to ruin your day," was all that Tony could manage as he looked up at Lloyd.

"Don't try to talk Tony, let John-Morgan help you."

Then the dying man said something that surprised Lloyd. "Bless me, Father, for I have sinned."

"Don't try to talk, Tony, OK."

"Bless me, Father, for I have sinned," came the voice once again, weak and pleading.

"I think he wants you to hear his confession, Lloyd," said John-Morgan as he feverishly tore apart the rest of his shirt and began stuffing it into the holes in Tony's gut. "You should while he's got time."

Lloyd was in a daze, but the words brought him out of his fog. "Yes, of course. How long has it been since your last confession?"

Tony was beginning to gurgle up blood, but could still speak. "Shit, must be thirty years. I did all kinds of things. I quit believing in God a long time ago, back at BC. Maybe I still don't believe. Maybe I'm just covering my ass right now. A good lawyer does that, ya know." Tony began to cough up dark clumps of clotted blood. Lloyd steadied him. Then Tony continued, "For these and all the other sins I can't remember, I am heartily sorry."

Blood foamed and rolled out of Tony's mouth in a steady stream. His pupils blackened, and his face turned gray, but somehow he kept his already sightless eyes fixed on those of Father Bryan. "Your Blessing, Father, your blessing."

"OK, take it easy." Lloyd raised his right hand over Tony's face and made the sign of the cross. Then he said the words of absolution. Tony's eyes seemed to follow Lloyd's hand. Then they closed. Two blood-soaked gasps followed, and Tony O'Boyle was dead.

John-Morgan and Lloyd sat for a while in silence. Finally Lloyd looked at John-Morgan and said: "Don't ask me how I knew to come out here. I can never tell you." He picked up the old key chain and handed it to his friend "He was after this."

John-Morgan gazed dumbly at the corroded old dog tags. "What does this mean. It's got the name of Tony's father on it?"

Lloyd looked down at Tony's face for a second, then back at John-Morgan and said, "The skeleton we found here was Tony's uncle. His father killed him over thirty years ago to hide the fact that Al O'Boyle was a serial killer. You know, the one who killed all those guys and then cut them up and threw the parts all over the city in paper bags? It happened back when we were boys."

John-Morgan nodded his head. He remembered.

"Tony came out here because he thought there was something that would tie his old man to this thing. He was right. Now this man's blood is on my hands and I don't know what I'm gonna do."

"Why the hell is it your fault?"

"Because I set him up. I lured him out here because I knew about the whole thing and I was afraid he and his father would get away with it. I was trying to play God and now a man is dead."

Within what they had named the Schwarzwald so many years ago, the two men sat on the side of the old grave. At their feet lay the bodies of two beasts—one guilty, one innocent. Lloyd was consumed by guilt over the pride that had driven him out to the island. He babbled on and on about how "Pride always goes before a fall," and how he had "fallen as far as any man could." He was "arrogant," "steeped in pride," "responsible for another man's death." John-Morgan tried to reason with him, but the tormented priest could not be moved.

"This is probably the end of my ministry," he said, "the only thing in my life that was ever really worthwhile. Now someone will need to hear my confession." As he gazed at Tony's wounds, Lloyd had another, wrenching thought. "What do we tell his wife? What do we tell his father? That I lured him out here because I knew that Big Tony murdered his own brother forty years ago?"

"I don't know, Lloyd," said John-Morgan as he shook his head in disbelief, "I just don't know."

Following her instincts, Ann Marie made half a dozen cellphone calls to locate Mike and Bubba. She finally tracked them down at the WTOC broadcast booth. She carefully explained to Mike why she was concerned about John-Morgan. "Something's crazy wrong, Mike. I know it is. Listen, ya'll take John-Morgan's old Whaler and go look for him, please." Her voice cracked. "I'll run it down to the marina and have it in the water by the time you get here." She was afraid.

"What's goin' on, Ann Marie? Where is John-Morgan, anyway?" asked Mike, a thread of terror coiled inside him.

"Ya'll come on," she said. "Hurry now."

When Mike and Bubba drove up, Ann Marie met them. She was pale. Her face seemed to have aged.

"I'm sure he went to Raccoon Island. I'd go too, but I can't leave the children, Brendan's sick. The boat's in the water. Plenty of gas in it. Hurry!"

THE DRISCOLL TREASURE

"JESUS, WHAT HAPPENED? What in hell *happened* here?" Mike could gasp out little more as he staggered into a sitting position on the side of the grave with Bubba. They gawked like drugged men, first at Tony's body and then at the great boar's. Crammed into the cave of vines and briars and slaughter, back and forth they looked. It was all the motion they could manage. Bits of bone and flesh were plastered stickily all over the brush on the other side of the grave—a harlequin abbatoir of man and beast where comprehension for the moment was stilled.

No more than two feet away to their right lay the huge carcass of the Grand Dragon of Raccoon Island with part of his head missing. A dark pool of coagulating blood deepened under his chest, down to his stomach, and even to the hind legs. The rank stench burned their eyes; the humid air seemed to stick in their lungs like a syrup of sand and gunsmoke. Bubba gagged.

To the left of the boar, lying half in the grave and half out, was the body of Tony O'Boyle. Although blood was everywhere, his face was as gray as a December moon. Pieces of John-Morgan's shirt hung out of the many holes in Tony's chest and stomach. A six-foot-long piece of intestine protruded from his gut and looped around the

ground between his legs. Crushed leaves and grass ad-
hered to the intestines where a greenish liquid oozed from
several tears in the bowel wall.

Over at the front of the grave sat John-Morgan and
Lloyd. Lloyd was almost catatonic. John-Morgan finally
looked up at the newcomers and said, "Give it a while.
Let Lloyd get control and we'll talk. We gotta think of
something or some innocent people are gonna really get
hurt."

Bubba and Mike nodded in unison, though they still
surveyed the scene in utter incredulity. Then Bubba's eye
caught something at the foot of the grave, a glitter from
a rusty metal container the size of a large cigar box.
Bubba picked it up. He and Mike began to finger through
it. The Driscoll treasure had finally been discovered.

Taking one of the gold coins out of the box, Bubba
rubbed slow circles on it between thumb and finger. He
carefully studied it, then another, then another, and soon
was tearing through coins in the box. A huge smile spread
over his face as he announced to no one in particular:
"This may be one of the biggest finds of rare coins in this
century." He looked seriously at Mike, who knew he had
been a coin collector all his life, and continued: "I've read
about these things, but nobody really believed they existed. A lot of people think they were never even minted.
Confederate coins are rare. They cost a fortune. But if
these are what I think they are, then they're the rarest of
the rare. They're the Dahlonega mint Cavaliers. The ones
most folks say were never even made. These could be
worth a million dollars or more."

There was silence in the old latrine; it was as if some
epiphany of a new trinity had enlightened them. Mike and
Bubba stared first at the bodies, then at the coin box, and
finally at each other. John-Morgan broke the silence. As
rapidly as possible he explained what had happened to
Tony and why. "So now we gotta do something. We gotta
have a plan."

"This is too much!" exclaimed Bubba. "This is the

most incredible day I've ever lived. What do you mean, 'do something'?"

"Lloyd thinks he's through as a priest, that everything he worked for so hard is over, and I'm afraid he may be right. Unfortunately, we can't help him. Tony was an SOB prick, but his wife isn't, and his children aren't. His old man is a double prick; but if Big Tony goes to trial over this—well, think about his wife—imagine the load she's had to deal with over the years. And look at his son down there. How do you think that's gonna make him feel? How much pain do you want to put on a man? How much pain do you think the innocent can stand? Isn't it enough that Tony's dead? Do we have to tell everybody why? It would only be vengeance. What good is it gonna do? If it gets out how Lloyd lured Tony out here, he certainly will be finished as a priest. Maybe being quiet could help him. Maybe—"

"Good God Almighty, John-Morgan," interrupted Bubba, "Tony's old man killed his brother and then buried him out here. He did it in fucking cold blood and then lived his life as if nothing happened. What the hell's wrong with you? We gotta tell what happened here and why it happened. That asshole can't get away with what he did. I don't care why he did it, who he did it to, how old he is, or how much pain it will cause. He killed his own brother, and he isn't God!"

"You *do* care who'll get hurt, Bubba. I've known you all my life, and I know you care. Just hear me out, OK?"

Bubba nodded and looked at the ground. Mike didn't say a word.

"Here's what we'll do, see how it sounds," said John-Morgan. "We'll say that Tony was out here looking for the coins because he knew about the Driscoll treasure, that somehow, through TV maybe, he found out where to look. Maybe somebody told him latrines were hiding places for valuables during the Civil War. Maybe he just knew it. And when he heard about us finding a body in a latrine, he couldn't resist coming out here and looking."

John-Morgan waited for a moment, looked directly at Bubba and Mike, and then continued. "And he found it. He found the Driscoll treasure. Unfortunately the Grand Dragon found *him*. He found him and he killed him too. That's no lie. We just don't mention the rest. We'll just let God handle that, the way Lloyd thinks he should have done from the beginning. We tell people we had the same hunch about the treasure but when we came out here to look today, Tony was already here—he had already found the coins. And as he was trying to leave the latrine, the Grand Dragon attacked him right in front of us—me and Lloyd—and I shot the bastard trying to save Tony. Shit, it's the truth! Let's not stir the pot anymore!"

John-Morgan stood, raised his right hand, and said, "My hand to God about this, I don't want to be a part of any more suffering. I've been hanging on by the skin of my teeth since Nam, and you damn well know it. Not many people do. But you do, Mike. Christ, do you want to see anybody hurt again for the rest of your life? Especially this kind of thing? Didn't Nam fuck your head over enough? Don't you want to just let it stay here?"

Mike nodded his head in agreement. "I've caused and seen enough pain in my life, and I sure as hell have suffered for it. If we can leave it here and not have anybody else hurt, I say fine. Old man O'Boyle will have all the punishment he needs when he finds out about Tony. What else are we gonna do to him? He probably doesn't even have five years left—and they'll be spent in agony. I say leave it right here."

Bubba was still unconvinced. "I don't know, John-Morgan, I just don't know. Legally we could be in a real world of shit. Do you know what could happen to us if the police found out about this? That's obstruction of justice. Hell, in a murder case! We could all go to jail for this. Think about the pain that will cause to *our* wives and kids. Think about that, OK?"

Lloyd moaned like a great, sad child. The tunnel swallowed the sound where it rose.

It was something to think about. Jail. Family. Look
what we will do in the name of family. What Tony did,
thought John-Morgan. "Now we're covering it up. Is that
what you mean Bubba? Like the O'Boyles?"

"Well, sort of, yeah. Don't you see it?"

John-Morgan walked over and sat next to Bubba. "Yes,
I see it alright. But let me tell you something . . . I'm not
old man O'Boyle's doctor, but Pat Foran is. I was with
Pat in X-ray last week when he was going over Big
Tony's films. He has cancer, advanced cancer of the pan-
creas. It's not an easy way out. Probably won't live to the
end of the year. He doesn't know it yet. Pat wanted to
wait until after the parade." Lloyd hissed a long sigh that
shrilled oddly as it faded. "None of the family knows
either. Allow me this sophistry. How can we conspire to
save a dead man from a murder charge? Lloyd, you OK?"
Lloyd nodded twice in slow motion. "By the time any of
this can come out, Mr. O'Boyle will be dead. How are
they gonna charge a dead man? Can we live with this, do
you think? I'm thinking of family too. Can't we find the
grace in ourselves to let all this be?" John-Morgan jerked
his arm around in a cramped crescent encompassing the
mess around them. "Can't we just leave it here? It's a
tomb. All of it. Can't we just leave it be?"

CASE CLOSED

THE STORY OF RACOON ISLAND and Battery Jasper became an even bigger story after Tony O'Boyle's death. It
was the perfect ending to a treasure-mystery-skeleton
story. *60 Minutes* even sent down Ed Bradley to do a
segment on the gold coins and the old fort. They loved
the part about how the ancestors of John-Morgan and
Lloyd had fought side by side at the fort during the Civil
War. It was irresistible: young master and slave, one loading the cannon and the other firing, dying in each other's
arms. Some civil rights leaders protested the content of

the story, claiming that it glorified—one more time—the
myth that slaves were treated well in the South. They
demanded that CBS offer a retraction. Instead the network
got its highest rating of the year with that particular show
and chose to ignore the protests.

In Savannah, *The Morning Gazette* called the entire
episode the "Story of the Year" in its New Year's Day
issue. The paper said that it would probably be the outstanding local story of the 1990's when the century ended.
It even bragged that the Olympics in Wassaw Sound
didn't have half the interest of the Raccoon Island story.

As for the skeleton, its identity was never determined.
The police said they had nothing to go on after so many
years and speculated that the body had been a moonshiner's, killed by one of his own kind in a turf war. Case
closed.

The state of Georgia naturally tried to lay claim to the
Driscoll treasure because the island was state land, but
when John-Morgan proved through family records dating
back to 1864 that the gold had belonged to his great-
grandfather, the old treasure was his entirely. It surprised
no one when he decided that each of his three friends was
entitled to a share. He vowed never to return to Raccoon
Island.

Sometimes, though, when the weather was nice, John-
Morgan and Ann Marie would take the *Graf Spee* out in
the afternoon for a cruise and have dinner on the boat as
they watched the bronze sun glide down over the marsh.

On other afternoons he would mosey over to his parents' house, where he and his father would sip a sour
mash or two, straight up, and lay back to discuss the Civil
War late into the night. When Mr. Hartman got sleepy,
John-Morgan would see him to bed, as his father had done
with him when he was a child. Before he left for the night,
he was always sure to hug his father and to tell him that
he loved him. It was, in the end, the life they both had
always wanted to live.

THE
SEVENTH
SCROLL

A Pharaoh's treasure lies hidden for 4,000 years. An ancient riddle tells where. Now a man and a woman will risk everything to find it—their fortune, their reputations . . . their lives.

7TH 5/01